THE CAST:
A dangerously unstable ex-CIA killer
An undercover "dragon"-turned-housewife
called out of retirement
A radical lawyer and jealous husband
A revolutionary leader who stubbornly
refuses to die
An invisible but ever-watchful agency

THE SETTING:
An island paradise that explodes in a crescendo
of mounting violence

THE RESULT:
A many-layered shocker of action and intrigue
by a master of modern suspense fiction

TURN LOOSE THE DRAGON

George Chesbro

BALLANTINE BOOKS • NEW YORK

Library of Congress Catalog Card Number: 81-22888

ISBN 0-345-29029-1

Manufactured in the United States of America

First Edition: August 1982

MIAMI, FLORIDA

Friday, October 19, 198—; 10:45 P.M.

Claude Moiret

The area was a twenty-square-block concrete clot of broken buildings and boulevards tangled in the heart of an otherwise healthy middle-class community. The ephemeral living tissue of the neighborhood, the spirit of its occupants, had died years before, victim of a social leprosy no politician or sociologist professed to understand; the blocks had been ignored and neglected, then finally abandoned to derelicts and wraithlike street people who entered their maze to play vicious night games and prey upon one another.

Had anyone been there to see him, the tall, elegantly dressed Frenchman would have appeared ludicrous and dangerously out of place in the ripped streets, easily mistaken for a soft, foolish tourist who had strayed too far from the protective aura of the resort hotels that glittered like a brilliant diamond cluster of light in the ring of darkness around Miami Beach one bridge, four miles and a sea of sad dreams away. A night player making such a misjudgment would not have lived to make another: Claude Moiret, high-ranking executive of the French Secret Service and controller of a private stable of free-lance assassins and general intelligence operatives, was prepared to kill anyone who approached him—an act he would carry out with characteristic, almost casual dispatch. Yet, such a confrontation would be a distraction, however slight, and Moiret did not want his attention drawn from the business at hand. He had taken pains not to be noticed; cloaked in the near-tactile, velvet warmth of the Miami night, he stood stiffly erect, his back inches from the disintegrating, powdery facade of a brick building, camouflaged by quivering, amoebic blots of moonlight that bled through the swaying

1

fronds of a palm tree rising in majestic defiance of the rotting garbage girdling its base in front of a ruined movie theater across the street.

Moiret's left hand rested casually on the bone handle of a spring-loaded stiletto in the pocket of his double-breasted suit jacket, while his right cupped the throbbing glow of the lighted Gauloise that traveled back and forth to his thin lips with metronomic regularity. When that cigarette was finished, he ground it out and immediately lit another. Aside from the movement of his arm Moiret was motionless, the expanding carpet of cigarette butts at his feet the only sign of his nervousness.

He passed the time trying to analyze the nexus of conversations and commitments and pinpoint where he had lost control of this operation. He finally realized the futility of such analysis, recognized that in fact he had never had control; his client had steered events from the beginning, making all the decisions and effectively manipulating him. Reversing the usual procedure, Rick Peters had apparently conceived the project, then made the initial low-level contacts before inviting Moiret to step in and play his accustomed role in negotiating a final, detailed agreement.

Moiret had always considered the American no more than a journeyman assassin with a polished but limited range of expertise, an evaluation that had slotted Peters in only the middle echelon of the Frenchman's group of professional killers and spies. Moiret belatedly realized that he had seriously underestimated the American; as a result, Peters had surprised him each step along the way. Now, the Frenchman thought, he might have to pay a high price for the inability to break into the decision-making process, and the bemused curiosity that had kept him involved long past the stage where his instincts had told him to drop out. He was exposed, but he suddenly found himself at the end of negotiations without knowledge of the identities of his high-echelon counterparts and still knowing only the barest details of his client's plan.

Moiret had not believed Peters capable of formulating a plan that could accomplish all he had said it would. Now the Frenchman was less certain. Moiret recognized that his ability to judge had been clouded by his growing conviction that the project struck deep personal overtones in the

American, considerations separate from the scheme's potentially catastrophic impact on the world and the huge amount of money involved. Moiret had no idea what those interests might be. In this matter, the Frenchman thought, Rick Peters was being driven to excellence by some dark psychic engine emitting an ominous, low hum that could be heard clearly if one listened long and hard enough.

Adding to Moiret's considerable distress was an acute awareness of the fact that the success of Peters' operation could mean that a third world war was less then a year away.

There was a sudden crescendo of sound, the raucous, stuttering bray of a car with a broken muffler. A few seconds later a taxi careened around the corner to Moiret's left and abruptly bucked to a halt with a high-pitched, wavering screech of worn brake linings. Dust swirled and eddied in the pale yellow cones tunneled out of the night by the taxi's headlights. Moiret immediately ground out his cigarette and watched as a man opened the door on the passenger's side and stepped out into the dust-moiled intersection.

In the eerie glow cast by the cab's interior light, Moiret could see that the man was dressed in his usual manner: French-cut jeans, cowboy boots to offset his slight stature, short-sleeved Oxford shirt beneath one of the sleeveless cashmere sweaters he habitually wore regardless of the weather.

The man paid the driver, then closed the door. The driver made a tight, squealing U-turn and the taxi skittered off like some metal insect toward the safe world of light and whole streets a few short blocks away.

"Here," Moiret said softly.

With a curt nod of his head, Rick Peters signaled that he'd heard, then glanced up and down the street. Apparently satisfied that they were unobserved, he strode quickly to the Frenchman. The hollow popping of his bootheels on the concrete seemed loud to the tense Moiret, like small-arms fire.

The two men shook hands perfunctorily, and Moiret, as always, marvelled at the forty-two-year-old man's youthful appearance. Peters had a gymnast's body, muscular and lean, with no trace of fat. His face, momentarily caught in a rippling band of moonlight, was that of a man perhaps ten or fifteen years younger. He had a full head of wavy blond hair; fair, freckled skin; large, innocence-filled eyes that in most light looked almost white, but were in fact a very pale blue.

"Are we set?" Tension made Peters' voice sound nasal and slightly metallic, as if he had a cold.

"I'm not sure."

The pale eyes suddenly glinted with anger, triggering a bizarre, fleeting metamorphosis of aging in the surrounding flesh. A tic fluttered momentarily in the hollow of Peters' right cheek as he clenched his jaw muscles. In those few seconds Moiret thought the other man looked almost as old as he actually was.

"If you're not sure, Claude, what am I doing here?" Peters' words were soft but clipped, his tone impatient. "On the phone you told me that the meet was set."

"It is. I'm just not sure you should go."

"Why the hell not?"

Moiret slowly raised his right arm, then waited for Peters to turn and look in the direction of his pointing finger—the movie theater across the street.

All of the glass in the theater's wide bank of doors had been shattered. The surrounding facade was a case study in social geology, a pitted surface covered with layer upon layer of flaking, peeling graffiti rendered in at least three languages, fragmented evidence of the ethnic tides that had washed through the area before the neighborhood had finally died.

"Because," Moiret said flatly, "that's where they want you to meet them."

Peters abruptly spun to one side, out of the moonlight. The sudden movement from light to dark had the curious effect of making the smaller man appear to blink out of sight, and Moiret felt tiny blisters of sweat dew his forehead and the backs of his hands. The Frenchman knew that Peters, like most members of his profession, was more than a little paranoid; furthermore, Peters was a man who seemed incapable of forgetting or forgiving any real or imagined slight. The American was clever, incredibly quick physically, and tended to make instant decisions. At the moment, Moiret thought, Peters was very suspicious, and rightfully so. The Frenchman knew what he might think if their positions were reversed. and his pulse quickened.

A disembodied voice very close to Moiret's right ear said, "Who are they?"

Moiret stood very still, his hands conspicuously held out a few inches from his sides. "I don't know, Rick. I'm sorry. I don't have names, and I haven't met them face to face."

"You know that this is a very big hit, Claude. The world's going to be a different place when I'm through. I'm thinking that maybe you've decided it's too big; maybe you got nervous." There was a prolonged silence, during which Moiret concentrated on the whining drone of insects and tried not to be afraid. Finally the voice came again. "Claude, are you trying to take me out?"

"No," Moiret said evenly, slowly exhaling. The danger had passed. "We've worked together for ten years; you know I can be trusted. I'd be dead right now if you really believed I might have set you up."

Peters reappeared in the banded moonlight. The tic was gone from his cheek, but the mask of youth that was his face was still askew, wrinkled with tension. "What organization are they with? Alpha Nine? Comando Muerto? Sierran Nationalist?"

"I don't think these people belong to any of those organizations."

"The people I first spoke with were from Alpha Nine."

"I know, but I've been through five negotiating sessions since you asked me to come in. The personnel kept changing, and the Alpha Nine people were phased out early. That was smart; everyone in the business knows who they are. At least it shows these people are serious. They've gone to a lot of trouble to make certain they can't be traced."

"Good for them," Peters said angrily. "What about me? Christ, what about you?" He clenched his teeth, shook his head in disgust. "Claude, you've got your own bureau; you're plugged into the CIA, the Mossad, KGB, and God knows how many other intelligence services. Now you're telling me you don't have any idea who's waiting for me over in that theater?"

"I'm sure they're not professionals," Moiret said tightly. "If they were, I'd have some kind of line on them by now; I'd recognize a voice, a style. My guess is that they're the

money-men who've been bankrolling the Sierran counter-
revolutionaries for the past twenty years. They're tired of
the bullshit and amateur bomb tossers they've been getting
for their money, so they've decided to take care of business
themselves. I think it's their first move into the actual
organization of a field operation, and they're being very
cagy. They called me only an hour ago to ask for this final
meet with you. I tried to stall them, but they said the deal
was off if you didn't show up. That's when I called you.
Two million dollars is a lot of money. You have to make
the decision."

"Don't get mealymouthed with me, Claude; I don't need
to be told that it's my decision. You're my representative.
You're supposed to take care of the details and look after
my interests. Having a meet in a place like that is a chickenshit idea to begin with, and now I find out I'm supposed
to go in there bare-assed, without knowing a damn thing
about the people waiting for me."

"But you don't have to go," Moiret said quietly. "Indeed,
I don't want you to go. My advice is to pass on this one."

"It's a little hard to pass on two million dollars, Claude.
I'm saying this is no way to do business. You blew it."

Moiret turned his face away to hide his own annoyance.
"I agree with you," he said without inflection. "They
forced it. If it weren't for the considerable amount of money
involved, I'd have broken off talks without even asking
you. But this has been your project from the beginning."
He looked at Peters, shrugged. "The money's only good
if you live to see it and spend it, Rick. I called you here,
but I suggest you direct me to go in your place and tell
them that the deal is off unless we can reschedule the meet
for someplace that's mutually acceptable. If they won't
agree, I'll make arrangements to give them back their deposit. We'll be out clean."

"They just might kill you."

"Then I'll have earned my commission, no?" Moiret replied evenly. The suggestion of a smile quickly faded. "It's
my responsibility."

Peters abruptly turned again and stared for some time
at the movie theater. His body was still, but his fingers
wriggled nervously. When he spoke, his voice was taut with
anticipation. "You say they did come up with the deposit?"

"Yes. Ten times the usual talk fee. I asked for a hundred thousand just to see how they'd react. They paid it when I let them see your dossier—which is another reason I didn't back away earlier. The only thing they wouldn't do was show or identify themselves. They always wore hoods."

"How many?"

"Three at the last meet."

Peters' fingers gradually ceased their movement as he continued to gaze at the ruined building across the street. "I'm going in," he said at last.

"*Pass*, Rick," Moiret said with a quiet urgency. "Even if the deal is on the level, I don't believe you can fulfill this contract. You may be able to get into San Sierra, but you can't hope to make your hit and get out alive."

"You're wrong, Claude," Peters replied matter-of-factly. "My plan will work."

"Why don't you tell me what you're going to do?"

"I will, but not now." Peters laughed sharply, without humor. "What are you worried about, Claude? You'll be a million dollars richer if I get killed. That's the up-front money, and I want you to take care of it for me, as usual."

"I was offering my help," Moiret replied tersely, barely controlling the anger that had been steadily building in him. "If I wanted more than my commission, I'd tell you to go. I'll admit I mishandled the negotiations, but I was dealing with your contacts in a situation which you'd created. Now let's handle this like the professionals we are. I say we cut it off here."

Peters slowly turned back to face the Frenchman. The American's boyish features were strangely blank, his gaze slightly out of focus, as if he were looking through, or somewhere beyond, Moiret. "It has to work," he said in a hollow voice. "I'll be getting rich at the same time that I finally tie up the one loose end in my life."

Moiret frowned. "*Merde*, Rick. What on earth are you talking about?"

Peters' pale eyes came back into focus. Naked cruelty flickered like heat lightning across his face and was gone. "I'll be in touch," he said. He turned, stepped off the curb and started across the street.

Rick Peters

He ducked his head and stepped carefully through a jagged necklace of glass shards that remained stuck in the brittle molding of the metal frame of one of the theater doors. Two small yellow bulbs, which Peters assumed were powered by battery or gasoline generator, dimly illuminated a cavernous lobby ankle-deep in paper refuse, empty liquor bottles, and the slippery rubber residue of hurried, furtive sex. Rats skittered in the paper depths as Peters waded through the lobby and passed under the lights through the door.

He immediately sensed the presence of a man behind him, but made no move to defend himself as a thick, sloppily tattooed forearm snaked over his right shoulder and tightened across his throat. There was the smell of Old Spice. The bore of what felt to be a cheap, small-caliber pistol was pressed against the base of his skull, and Peters instantly registered the fact that the man was almost certainly left-handed. With the pistol in place, the arm came away from his throat and a hand began to fumble clumsily over his body.

"I don't have a gun," Peters said easily. "There's a knife in a sheath inside my right boot, but I'd consider it a courtesy if you left it there. This is supposed to be a business meeting."

"Shut up, turkey." The voice was big, like the man, with a lugubrious, lilting Sierran accent soured by menace. "Take the boot off and give me the fucking knife."

Peters slowly and tentatively started to bend over. He lowered his head away from the gun while at the same time lightly pressing his buttocks into the man's right thigh in order to gauge position. He shifted his weight to his left foot and, when he was not ordered to stop, proceeded to remove his boot.

The man was not only untrained but monumentally stupid, Peters thought, with no instinct for danger. From his crouched position he could easily spin under the gun to his left and slice open the man's stomach, or even stab back up through his own legs into the man's groin or anus. However, at the moment he could not see what purpose would be served by killing the man. He slowly handed the knife back over his shoulder to the man, then pulled his boot on.

'Straight ahead," the voice commanded, and Peters was prodded hard between the shoulder blades with the gun. "Down to the front and up on the stage."

More of the dim yellow lights had been strung inside the theater, the line running down the center aisle and splitting to a T to light the lip of the stage. Peters walked ahead through more debris that had somehow drifted into strange patterns, like windswept snow, driven by no more than the pressure of time. He sensed the man close behind him, still in perfect position for him to whirl inside the gun hand and kill the man if he wanted to. Peters smiled thinly, thinking that anyone wanting to kill him would have hired a man considerably more skilled than the thug bringing up his rear. He would have been killed, probably machine-gunned, the moment he'd stepped into the theater lobby.

As he approached the front of the theater there was a loud metallic click offstage to his right, then a sharply rising hiss. Overhead, an arc spot briefly glowed orange before casting a tightly focused beam of golden light on a straight-backed metal folding chair that had been placed in a small, cleared area in the middle and at the front of the stage. Peters walked briskly up on the platform, but abruptly halted and stood still when he reached the chair. He heard the man behind him grunt with surprise and anger.

"Sit down, turkey!"

"First put the gun away," Peters replied calmly. "You know I'm not armed."

The man's response was to rap Peters on top of the skull with the barrel of his pistol. It was a sharp blow that caused the assassin's knees to buckle momentarily and his eyes to tear, but its most devastating effect was humiliation; Peters knew he would have to respond. He waited a few seconds for his vision to clear, then slowly turned.

He found himself looking up into the strikingly handsome face of a young man whom he judged to be no more than seventeen or eighteen. The boy's wavy hair was close-cropped, his skin the color of very light coffee. Large black eyes mirrored surprise and uncertainty at Peters' sudden if subtle act of defiance, and there was also the first, small glint of fear at what he saw in the shorter man's strange, pale eyes. He was a big boy, Peters thought, but nonetheless a boy. Worse, from Peters' point of view, the boy was obviously a civilian, a crude kiddy-thug swept up off the street and paid a few dollars to play heavy with a gun he'd probably never used in a situation he knew nothing about.

Peters did not like practicing his skills on civilians; it was unprofessional and too often led to unforeseen complications. But the boy had left him no choice; he knew he could not allow himself to be humiliated in the eyes of the men who had to be watching and evaluating him from somewhere in the theater. And he most definitely would not allow himself to be shamed in his own eyes.

"Sit down, you son-of-a-bitch, or your brains are going to be running out your nose." Despite his words, the boy's voice betrayed indecision. Peters watched the hand holding the gun begin to tremble slightly, dangerously.

Peters recognized the very real danger of the unreliable weapon firing accidentally and killing him; still, he did not move. He knew he had to make a quick judgment as to whether the boy was simply overplaying his part or was following specific directions. It occurred to Peters that he might have made a serious mistake in not taking out the young Sierran earlier; the boy could represent a test, and he might well be expected to display his skills by disarming or even killing the boy before he would be dealt with seriously.

He was measuring his angle of attack when his decision was made for him.

"Enough, Roselle!" The voice, deeply resonant, rich and commanding, came from somewhere above him and at the back of the theater. "Back away, but keep your gun on him."

The boy scowled and stepped back a few paces. Peters turned his back on the Sierran and sat down in the chair.

"I trust you're the 'Mr. Jones' we've been expecting," the deep voice continued laconically.

Peters squinted, fixing his gaze on the first row of the balcony far at the rear of the theater, but the hot arc spot, while not shining directly in his eyes, created a peripheral barrier of glow he could not see beyond. He nodded curtly, then leaned back and crossed his left ankle over his right knee. He wished to appear relaxed and off balance, but in fact he was keenly alert and prepared to spring out of the chair in any direction in less time than it would take the hulking Roselle to pull the trigger on his pistol.

"What's your real name?"

"I'm no more likely to give you my name than you are to give me yours," Peters answered quietly but firmly. His voice carried easily in the vast, empty theater.

"No? Roselle!"

The boy lumbered forward and eagerly poked the bore of the pistol into Peters' right ear.

Peters willed himself to remain motionless, without expression, while he slowly counted off twenty seconds. When he finally spoke, his voice retained its soft, even timbre. "You don't need my name: you have my face, which is more than you've given me."

"You've been given one hundred thousand dollars."

"And you have me here to see and talk to, which is what you paid for with your hundred thousand. You've seen my dossier; if you didn't think I was capable of delivering what I say I can, you should have kept the talk fee and I could have stayed home. I came here to discuss a business matter, but I won't talk while your man is trying to clean the wax out of my ear with a gun."

"You could be CIA!"

"*You* could be CIA!" Peters shouted back, calculating that it was time to display some emotion. "There comes a time when people in our circumstances simply have to trust each other! This set-up is chickenshit, and I'm beginning to think that you're chickenshit!"

There was almost a minute of near silence, broken only by a low, almost imperceptible rustling sound of men whispering far away in the darkness.

"You're not what we expected." It was a different voice, higher pitched, a tenor to the first man's bass.

"You should have gone uptown if you wanted to see a movie. Do you want to talk to an actor or do you want Salva killed?"

Peters heard a sudden, sharp intake of breath to his right, and he knew that it was a corpse holding a gun on him; if the unseen men in the balcony hadn't told their young employee what the meeting was about, it almost certainly meant they planned to kill the boy when he was no longer needed.

There was another whispered exchange, and then the man with the deep voice said, "Your dossier indicates that you have a predilection for explosives. Do you plan to blow up Manuel?"

"It's possible."

"We want to know your plan."

"No."

"We insist."

"How I fulfill the contract is my business."

"The two million dollars you ask us to pay for your services makes it our business!"

"No." Peters was sweating heavily from the heat of the arc spot, a warmth accentuated by the thin cold circle of the gun bore in his ear. But it was time to make a move. "Take it easy, Roselle," he said calmly. He slowly uncrossed his legs and stood up, ignoring the increased pressure of the gun barrel against his head.

"Shit!" Roselle barked. "You want to die, turkey?!"

The tenor shouted, "Don't shoot, Roselle!"

"It's a question of security," Peters said evenly, placing his hand on the boy's chest and casually pushing him away. "I know I'm not CIA, but any one of you up there could be; your gunbearer here could be CIA, or even DMI. One of you might have some second thoughts later; organizations are penetrated, perceptions change. This condition won't change: once I leave here, you can be absolutely certain that Manuel Salva is going to die. Assuming, of course, that we cut a deal."

"When?"

"Within six months." Peters hesitated, carefully considering how much he wished to reveal. Finally, he continued, "I'll say this: if you're in the right place at the right time, you'll know about it almost the moment it happens. In any case, you'll find out about it within minutes. That's when you call my representative and arrange to give him the second million."

"How do you know we'll pay?" the second man asked.

Peters shrugged. "I could have your names in a month.

I don't know who you are, but I know *what* you are. It's enough."

"What are we?" the deeper voice responded sharply.

"You're businessmen, a long time out of Angeles Blanca. You've done all right here with the money you made under Sabrito and brought out, but Manuel Salva still sticks in your craws even after all these years. He took away your whorehouses and casinos, he busted up your narcotics operations and white-slavery rings, and then he chased your asses out of the country. So much for patriotism and ideology. You've built up a good operational network here, but Miami can never be old Angeles Blanca. You're still looking to even things up. It's worth two million dollars to you to see Salva dead, and I don't think you want to be looking over your shoulders while you're enjoying your victory. Naturally, I'll hunt for you if you don't pay."

"We could find many men who would work for cheaper wages."

"You do what you want," Peters replied evenly, "but I know I don't have to remind you gentlemen that you'll get exactly what you pay for. I can get the job done, and I may be able to give you a bonus."

"Please explain," the tenor said warily.

"I'm betting that you still dream of one day returning to San Sierra, so I'll tell you this: my plan involves making the assassination look like a CIA operation. All hell is going to break loose in this country as well as in San Sierra when Salva dies, and you people just might be able to parlay the chaos into political gain. Considering what you stand to gain from my work, I'd argue that you're getting me cheap."

There was more whispering; this time the disjointed, ghostly mumbling had a tense, underlying hum of excitement. It was the bass who finally spoke.

"You say you can make it appear that Manuel has been assassinated by the CIA?"

Peters shook his head. He was anxious to conclude the deal, and he had been willing to scatter additional chum for the sharks he needed for financing, but he would reveal no more. "I won't try to lie to you. I can't guarantee that. It's a factor in my primary plan, but obviously I have to have a number of contingency plans. I'm contracting to kill Salva. You make of his death what you can."

"What?"

"That's enough!" Peters snapped, his voice taking on a hard edge of authority. "The meet's over. You'll contact my representative within twenty-four hours and make arrangements for the transfer of nine hundred thousand dollars, according to instructions he'll give you. If that happens, Salva will be dead within six months—at which time you'll repeat the procedure and transfer another million dollars. If my agent doesn't hear from you, the deal is off, permanently. Whatever you decide, you won't have a chance to change your minds."

Peters expected more whispering, but there was none. There was complete silence in the theater for almost two minutes, and then a third voice spoke.

"Very well, Mr. Jones, the bargain is struck. You understand, of course, that you cannot hope to escape with our initial payment. You have exactly six months from this date to carry out your end of the bargain. If Manuel is not dead within that time, you will be hunted down and summarily executed. *That* contract won't cost us anywhere near two million dollars, I assure you."

"I understand perfectly."

"Roselle, you may go. Leave the gun on the stage."

The young Sierran glared at Peters for a few moments, but finally put the gun down before turning and walking off into the darkness.

"Good luck, Mr. Jones."

Peters nodded and casually rose from the chair; instead of descending from the stage and going back up the center aisle, he walked slowly, unchallenged, into the wings. Once hidden in darkness, he moved very quickly. He removed his boots and picked them up in his left hand, then ran swiftly and silently along the rear lip of the stage, making his way by the shafts of smoky yellow light that knifed through rips in the rotting backdrop curtain. He came to the end of the stage and leaped down to the pitted concrete floor, landing lightly on the balls of his feet barely a body's length from the startled Roselle. The Sierran had just lit a cigarette and was about to step through a backstage exit. The burly young man spun around and almost tripped over his own feet. Like an actor who had forgotten his lines, he allowed his face to slip into a loose mask of confused emotions. Peters wondered idly if the boy had been thinking of the conspiracy of which he had just learned, or perhaps of a woman he was on his way to meet. It made no difference to the assassin.

"You forgot to return my knife, Roselle," Peters said easily.

The boy swallowed hard and cleared his throat before finally finding his voice. "Get the fuck away from me, turkey. I'll give you your knife; I'll stick it straight up your ass."

"No, I don't think so. You got a little too excited, sonny. You should't have hit me with the gun. Now I have to hurt you in order to even things up."

The boy started to reach for his back pocket, but Peters had already leaped into the air. He rolled into a half-turn as his body reached an apogee at the level of the boy's head, then lashed out with a perfectly aimed side kick that caught the Sierran on the side of the neck, just below the jaw. Both men fell to the floor at the same time, Roselle in a splayed heap and Peters on the four points of his hands and feet, perfectly balanced.

Peters felt for a pulse and was relieved to find that the boy was only unconscious. He was convinced that Roselle would soon be dead anyway, and he did not wish to perform any service, no matter how small, for his employers without pay. His business with Roselle was a personal matter.

Peters retrieved his knife from the boy's pocket, then straddled the massive chest and slowly, precisely, began to slice off the right ear.

POMONA, NEW YORK

Thursday, January 3; 4:00 P.M.

Alexandra Finway

It had begun to snow heavily. There was no wind, and the thick flakes tumbled down through the still, cold air like chips of weightless white marble, accumulating rapidly, muffling sound and light in the densely wooded residential section of Rockland County where the tall, statuesque woman ran. It was the nadir of an oppressive afternoon, with mothers and their children seeking comfort indoors and workers not yet on their way home. The only sound on the narrow, winding road was the rhythmic squeak of the woman's running shoes on the fallen snow, punctuated by her heavy breathing.

The firm, full contours of Alexandra Finway's body were evident even under the loose folds of her gray warm-up suit, and she ran with the powerful, steady, and confident lope of an experienced runner and trained athlete. She had strong yet sensual features, accented by high cheekbones now blanched ivory by the force of her passage through the freezing air. Her dark brown eyes were focused intently on the roadway at her feet as she tried to concentrate on the strange, almost mystical pleasure of the sensory messages transmitted to her by her extended body. Her long gray-streaked black hair, held back from her face by a crimson terrycloth band that was now stained with sweat despite the frigid air, bobbed in a rippled wave back and forth across her shoulders in counterpoint to the rhythmic sway of her body.

Alexandra grimaced with effort as she accelerated into the final leg of her daily six-mile run, racing against the rapidly approaching darkness and the now-familiar feelings of bitterness and frustration that had begun to rise in

16

her, snapping at her heart like some great black mastiff rushing from a hidden driveway of the soul.

Tears came without warning, erupting suddenly through an unsuspected fault in the normally well-tended intellectual membrane surrounding her emotions. Sobbing uncontrollably, Alexandra stumbled off the road into a thick copse of bare trees and sat down on a log. She leaned back against a tree trunk and, still sobbing, raised her face to the sky. The heavy snowflakes melted in her tears, producing a cold, stinging sensation everywhere but on the tiny, star-shaped areas of scar tissue beneath each eye—milky crosses that plastic surgery had been unable to erase and that Alexandra no longer even bothered trying to hide with makeup.

Her weeping subsided, then finally stopped altogether. She took a deep, shuddering breath that hurt her lungs and made her cough, then shook herself. Tears and sweat were freezing on her face and body, chilling her and threatening hypothermia. She could get very sick, Alexandra thought; she could catch pneumonia, which would solve nothing and would probably be nothing more than a childish, self-destructive attempt to punish John for . . . for whatever he was doing. And for not talking to her about it.

"Damn you, John," Alexandra whispered, suppressing another sob that stirred uncomfortably in her chest. "Why won't you at least tell me? Can't you give me that?"

Shivering, she finally rose and walked stiffly back out of the woods to the road. She was very cold. The snow that had spilled over the tops of her sneakers was melting, chilling her feet. She quickly performed a series of limbering exercises to loosen her muscles, then jogged the rest of the way home.

The telephone began to ring as Alexandra entered the house. An attractive, raven-haired teenager stepped out of a small den off the living room, smiled and waved when she saw her mother.

"I'll get it, Kara," Alexandra said to her fourteen-year-old daughter. "Where's Michael?"

"Kristen took him sledding on the hill down the street."

"Would you get me a big towel, sweetheart?"

"Sure, Mom," the girl said, turning and starting to walk

away. "I'll bring you some aspirin, too. You look like you need it."

Alexandra picked up the telephone receiver. "Hello?" she said, her voice warped by a shudder.

There was a brief pause, then a man said softly, "Alexandra?"

Alexandra's mouth suddenly felt parched. Her stomach muscles fluttered and contracted painfully, making her feel nauseous. "Who is this?" she asked in a strangled voice, knowing. It had been many years since she had heard that voice, yet Alexandra still found it deeply hypnotic, like the hooded, swaying head of a cobra. It was a voice that was instantly recognizable, a poisonous sound striking at her across a barrier of space and time.

"C'mon, baby. A lot of things may have changed in fifteen years, but my voice isn't one of them: you know who it is. Are you free to talk?"

Alexandra felt light-headed, and it seemed to her that the scars beneath her eyes had begun to burn. Afraid she was going to faint, she leaned forward slightly and braced herself on the phone stand while she concentrated on breathing deeply and regularly. The vertigo passed.

"Alexandra?" The voice had risen slightly.

"Hey, Mom? You okay?"

Alexandra turned to find her daughter standing behind her. Concern showed clearly in the girl's dark eyes. "I'm all right, Kara," Alexandra said, muffling the mouthpiece against her shoulder as she took the large, thick beach towel held out by the girl. "Thanks for getting me the towel."

The girl shook her head and clucked her tongue disapprovingly. "Mom, you're going to catch pneumonia. You'd better get off the phone and out of those clothes. I'll fill the tub with hot water."

"Thank you, sweetheart. I'll be right there."

"Alexandra?" Peters' voice was slightly louder now, more insistent.

Alexandra waited until she heard the sound of water running in the bathroom, then spoke in a low, harsh voice. "My God, Rick, how did you find me?"

"Our former employer provided me with your address and phone number."

Alexandra felt a quivering in her thighs and a cold in her stomach that had nothing to do with the temperature outside. She gripped the receiver tightly, breathed; "What are you talking about?"

"I thought I heard you talking to someone. Is there anyone around you who can hear us?"

"If there were, I'd hang up. What do you want, Rick?"

"I know this is a shock, but I couldn't very well show up on your doorstep, could I? We have to talk. I can't begin to tell you how important it is."

It seemed to Alexandra that time was collapsing in on itself, threatening to suck her away into a black hole of memory, an amoral universe of tricks where she had once almost been destroyed. She closed her eyes and fought to control the sea of conflicting emotions, powerful tides of terror and fascination, surging across her mindscape and squeezing her glands. However, her voice was steady when she finally spoke. "I'm listening."

"Not on the phone, Alexandra," Peters said, a slightly reproving edge to his voice. "It's much too sensitive. Some special people we know are looking for a valuable pair of matched dragons."

"God, Rick. Is this a joke? Are you—"

"Listen to me: you know this isn't a joke. All I need to do is speak to you in person, and then I'll have done what I said I would. But it has to be soon. Give me a safe place where we can meet tomorrow."

"Just a minute," Alexandra said, willing herself to maintain a steady tone. "Let me think."

She clapped her hand over the mouthpiece and squeezed hard, as if through sheer physical effort she could somehow erase the call and crush the agonizing memories, the terrible excitement, it had stirred. She tried to imagine herself maintaining her composure and containing her apprehension until the next day, and she knew her control would not last through the night; she had been too long out of training. She had three children and a husband to protect from her past. Whatever evil Rick Peters was trying to conjure back into her life would have to be exorcised at once.

She removed her hand from the mouthpiece, said, "Now."

"Now?" For just a moment Peters' voice had betrayed confusion, but it was gone when he continued speaking. "In case you haven't noticed, there's damn near a blizzard outside."

"If we're going to meet at all, it has to be right now. Where are you?"

"Only a couple of miles away. At a Holiday Inn in Nanuet, near the entrance to the Thruway."

"I know where it is. I'll come to you."

"No good," Peters said quickly. "Too close to your home, too much chance of us being seen together."

"Do you have a car?"

"Yes, but I don't know if I—"

"You can get to the Palisades Parkway off the Thruway. Ask at the desk for directions. Drive south on the parkway until you come to the Alpine Lookout parking area. That's where I'll meet you. I'll be there in about half an hour."

"Hey, Alexandra, I don't know if I can get out of the goddam parking lot."

"Well, you're going to have to. If you don't show up, don't bother to call again."

Alexandra put the receiver down hard and pulled herself up very straight as she took measured breaths and tried to focus her wildly milling thoughts. The realization slowly came to her that she had stopped trembling. She no longer felt cold, although melting snow dripping from her socks and sneakers had puddled around her feet. What she did feel was an all too familiar aura of sick euphoria that she'd believed had died in her a long time before. That shimmering internal glow could not be ignored, she thought; it had to be guarded against carefully, forced as quickly as possible back into whatever dark place in her psyche from which it had leaked, and then sealed off.

She had learned, almost too late, that demons rode the dragons.

She strode quickly into her bedroom and changed into dry socks and boots. When she came out she took her mink coat, the warmest garment she owned, from the closet and slipped it over her shoulders.

A moment later Alexandra's daughter appeared at the door to the bathroom, just down the hall. Kara Finway stared in confusion at the sight of her mother wearing a

mink coat over her running suit. "Mom, the bath's ready.
What are you doing with your coat on?"

"I have to go out for a few minutes," Alexandra said
tensely. "Will you and Kristen give Michael a snack and
some hot chocolate when he comes in? Dinner may be a
little late."

Kara frowned. "I can start dinner, Mom, but it's snowing
like crazy out there. What should I tell Dad if he—"

But Alexandra was already out the door, hurrying
through the drifting snow to where her car was parked in
the driveway. She brushed snow off the car's windows, got
in, started the engine, and pushed lightly on the accelerator
until the treads of the snow tires caught and bit. The car
slewed out of the driveway, exploding through a yard-high
ridge of plowed snow into the street.

The storm was gradually diminishing, making driving
surprisingly easy on streets that had been recently cleared
and were empty of traffic. Traffic coming from New York
City was piling up in the northbound lanes of the Palisades
Parkway, but Alexandra had the southbound lanes virtually to herself. Within twenty minutes she had made the
necessary U-turn and was proceeding slowly and carefully
into the unplowed parking lot at Alpine Lookout.

A lone, snow-blanketed car, which Alexandra assumed
belonged to Peters, was already in the lot. She stopped her
car a few yards from the other car, turned off the engine.
She hesitated a few seconds, then opened the door and
stepped out. She did not approach the first car; instead,
she walked forward to stand in front of a stone retaining
wall erected at the edge of a cliff. She pulled up the collar
of her coat and squinted against the snow, peering through
the milky air at the barely perceptible, ice-clogged band of
the Hudson River below her and the ghostly, shifting images
of New York City rising from its far bank.

She heard a car door open and close. Crunching footsteps
approached and stopped just behind her. She rapidly in-
ventoried her emotions in an effort to make her face appear reasonably composed, then forced herself to turn
around.

Alexandra was startled to find that Rick Peters looked
almost the same as she remembered. They were the same
age, yet Peters showed almost no signs of aging. His eyes

were so light that, seen through the swirling snow, they appeared to lack irises, like bullet holes that passed through his head. He was hatless, and his straw-blond hair whipped lazily in the rising wind. He wore cowboy boots and a light, worn leather jacket that he had not bothered to close. Beneath the jacket he wore a brown-striped Oxford shirt and a brown cashmere sweater that Alexandra knew would be sleeveless. Despite his light clothing he seemed perfectly comfortable, like a feral brother to the storm.

Alexandra was acutely conscious of the continued tightness in her thighs and the sudden, rapid beating of her heart.

"Hello, baby," Peters said evenly.

"Hello, Rick."

Peters inclined his head slightly to one side and stared at Alexandra for a few moments. "I'd forgotten how nice your hair looks loose," he said at last. "After the rape happened the first year, I don't think I ever saw you without that big ivory barrette in your hair—not out of bed, at least."

Not trusting herself to speak, Alexandra remained silent.

Peters lifted his face to the sky and slowly extended his arms out to his sides, palms up. "Beautiful, isn't it?" he continued in the same easy, conversational tone. "People like you and me are the only ones who can appreciate just how ephemeral it all is. There are a lot of crazies around who'd really like nothing better than to blow the whole world away, despite all their idealistic political bullshit. You know, the shooters and the bombers are a lot more sophisticated now than they were when we worked together."

"Rick, I didn't come out here to reminisce," Alexandra repiled shortly, grateful that her voice didn't crack. "Get to the point."

"The least you should have done was to say good-bye to me," Peters said with surprising force and feeling as he dropped his arms to his sides. "I loved you, Alexandra." He paused, smiled wryly. "I do believe I still love you."

"No you don't," Alexandra responded quickly, "and you didn't." She didn't add that one of the reasons she had not told Rick Peters she was dropping out of his life was because of her fear that he would kill the man she loved.

"Yes," Peters insisted. "And you loved me. You fooled yourself into thinking you were in love with John because

you were burning out. You were looking for an escape
hatch, and John was it."

He was half right, Alexandra thought, but for reasons
he could never understand. "Lust isn't love, Rick. What
you and I shared was a common sickness. John helped me
get well."

"Did you ever tell him about the dragons?"

"Of course not. Do you think I'd be standing out here
in a snowstorm talking to you if John knew?"

"Why haven't you told him? It's been fifteen years."

"For one thing, the existence of the dragons was classified information. I assume it still is."

Peters arched his eyebrows. "Is that the real reason?"

"It's a reason."

"But not the only one?"

"It's none of your business, Rick."

"True." He paused, staring at her, then slowly smiled.
"And so you will remain a woman of mystery to me as
well as to your husband."

"No mystery, Rick," Alexandra said sharply, anger rising in her at the man's continued and casual familiarity.
"It's just that John might find it difficult to forgive and
continue living with a wife who spied on him and his
colleagues for close to a year, and spied on his 'side' for
four years before that. You may vaguely recall that our
side killed his sister."

"*I* killed his sister," Peters replied emphatically, ignoring the sarcasm in Alexandra's voice, "and I wouldn't give
a damn if you told him. Your husband's sweet baby sister
was merrily toiling away in a Weatherman bomb factory,
blithely making plans to blow up people she didn't know.
All I did was rig the bombs to go off a little early. It's too
bad she happened to be in the building when they exploded, but she wasn't any hotshot radical lawyer; she was
a chickenshit terrorist who got exactly what she deserved."

The words, cold as the wind, hit her like a fist, almost
driving her backwards. She knew there was truth in what
Peters said, but she had not fully realized until this January moment, more than a decade and a half removed from
the event, how much she had changed, how much John's
quiet but passionate words and ideas had reshaped her
view of reality. She saw certain things now in different

colors, heard words like "betrayal" and "patriotism" in a different key. It was not a feeling she wished to share with Rick Peters, and she waited until she was certain that her tone could reasonably match his.

"John might take it a bit more personally," Alexandra said without emotion. "Especially in view of the fact that I was your partner. Now: you may be cold-blooded, Rick, but I'm just cold. Does all this light chitchat about the past mean that you're here to blackmail me?"

"You're still a mean one when you want to be, Alexandra," Peters said softly. His thin smile did not touch his eyes, which were piercing and expressionless, taking in everything and giving back nothing in return. "If you were still wearing a barrette, I might have lost an eye, huh?"

"That's the second time you've brought up that subject. Do it again and I walk."

"Then I'd better say what I came to say," Peters replied evenly. "Shall we sit in my car?"

Alexandra brushed past Peters and waded through the snow toward his car. Peters caught up and opened the door for her, then trotted around to the other side and slid in behind the wheel. He started the engine and turned on the heater before opening the window an inch and lighting a cigarette.

"Speaking of crazies," Peters continued casually, blowing a thin stream of smoke out into the freezing air, "somebody's thinking seriously of trying to assassinate Salva."

"So what?" Alexandra snapped. Her anxiety over meeting Rick Peters had been supplanted by a seething anger with herself for her nervous impatience and for leaving her children alone in the well of such a lonely, dark afternoon. "People have been trying to kill Salva since the day he was old enough to say nasty things about Sabrito. The CIA couldn't even make his hair fall out. Salva will die of either old age or lung cancer."

"Don't make book on it. This time it looks as if the assassin may damn well pull it off. And the citizens of this country will have an opportunity to see it all live in prime time, in glorious color, on their television sets. Do I have your attention?"

Alexandra shifted in her seat so that she was facing Peters. Her fear of seeing him had been erased, but the unfocused, electric excitement generated by his presence remained, making her feel flushed and nervous. "You have my attention," she said, still very conscious of her fast heartbeat.

"You probably know there have been regularly scheduled tourist flights to San Sierra for a couple of years. The group leaving the nineteenth of this month has had something special added to its itinerary; anyone who wants them can get tickets to the San Sierra–USA boxing matches that are scheduled to take place the night of Friday, the twenty-fifth. The Sierrans are staging the bouts in Tamara Castle—that's a little scenic touch owing to the fact that ABC has permission to televise the matches live, complete with the Goodyear blimp. It's the sort of Commie sports spectacular that Salva loves to cook up and wouldn't miss for a billion tons of sugar cane. He's certain to be in Tamara Castle that night, and that's where and when he's going to be assassinated."

"By whom?"

"Unknown. It's probably an Alpha Nine man, but all the Company knows for certain—or all they've told me—is that at least one of the people leaving with that tour group on the nineteenth is an assassin. God knows who told them. Actually, it's quite clever. With his macho personality, Salva has to be the most vulnerable head of state in the world. Hell, it's a miracle he hasn't been blasted off some pitcher's mound before this. All the killer has to do on this gig is keep on truckin' through the week, then knock off Salva at the boxing matches. The assassin will almost certainly be killed himself, but that doesn't seem to make any difference."

"A kamikaze."

"Yeah. It has to be, and it's next to impossible to stop those bastards. Who else would plan to knock off Salva in front of so much company, right under the nose of DMI, on 'Wide World of Sports'? One of the Top Ten hits in history play-by-played by Howard Cosell. Sounds like an outtake from *Bananas*, huh?"

Alexandra nodded thoughtfully. She felt her face burning, but did not know whether the fire had been kindled from fever or fascination. "Any idea how it will be done?"

Peters shook his head. "No. I think we can assume he

won't try to take a weapon through customs. There'd be a very high risk of being caught, and opportunities like this just don't come around that often. Arrangements have probably been made for a weapon pickup in San Sierra."

"Rick, what does all of this have to do with me?"

Peters' eyebrows arched slightly. "Our old friends want us—you and me—to stop him."

Alexandra stared hard at Peters for a few moments. The air in the car suddenly seemed crystalline, too thin; the effort of breathing made her chest ache. She had been so absorbed in what Peters was telling her that it took a few seconds for her to grasp the import of his last words. When she did, she felt something like cold moss touch her between the shoulder blades.

"The Company wants *us* to stop him? I don't understand, Rick; let's back up a minute. Are you still working for the CIA?"

"Are you kidding? I became an ex-dragon about two months after you took off. I have my own real estate agency in Florida. I got a call from a controller yesterday morning. It wasn't our old C, but he had all the code words right."

"What happened to our old C?"

"He died nine years ago; that much I was able to check. Each team of dragons had its own code; since you haven't even mentioned the dragons to John, I'm satisfied this C is the genuine article. Besides, what he had to say is so off the wall that it has to be the truth. You know I've always had a good nose for bullshit."

"Why didn't he call me?"

"Oh, he was planning to. I figured he didn't understand the situation with John, so I told him I'd deliver the message personally. *Voilà.*"

Peters removed a slip of paper from the pocket of his jacket and handed it to Alexandra; it was a telephone number writtten in the private code only she and Peters had used and understood. Despite the passage of more than a decade, Alexandra instantly recognized all of the symbols.

"That's the number where you can reach the C," Peters continued. "I assume you'll want to confirm the tasking request. You have forty-eight hours to make your decision. I'll wait at the motel in case you want me to pass it on, or you can tell the C yourself. I know you have a lot of things to weigh, not the least of which is coming up with a convincing excuse to disappear for a week."

"What happens if I decide not to go?"

Peters shrugged. He flicked his cigarette out the window and immediately lit another. "Nothing—at least not as far as you're concerned. I suppose I'd be willing to try a solo, but I imagine the Company would prefer to get me another partner, if they used me at all. You know how they like experienced teams."

Alexandra laughed in disbelief. "Another partner? For God's sake, Rick, why do they want us for something as important as this to begin with? 'Off the wall' doesn't describe it; it's insane. We haven't been in the field for fifteen years, and we were never regular CIA agents. I'm surprised anyone at Langley even remembers us, much less believes we're the people to stop an attempted assassination. Why on earth would we even be considered for this assignment? They've been testing hallucinogens on themselves."

Peters didn't smile. "They're dead serious, Alexandra. They want us precisely *because* we were never regular CIA. First, they've got what's left of the Hughes-Ryan Act to contend with. Things are finally going their way again, and they don't want to get caught in a fuck-up; there's just no time to touch base with the required Congressional committees.

"Second, what you used to read in the newspapers about the CIA is apparently true. Watergate, bacteria testing in the New York subways, and all the other disclosures really wiped out the Company's covert-actions capability. Things have been picking up in the past couple of years, but they still don't have the kind of black capability they once had. The few good operatives they managed to hang onto would probably be spotted by DMI the minute they stepped off the airplane at Angeles Blanca, if they weren't picked off earlier in the visa process. Just about everybody Langley has that's any good is blown, and the rest are green. We're different; the dragons were always kept on the fringe of the organization, and we were deep-insulated. Only a handful of people knew of the dragons' existence. The Sierrans probably still think of you and me as culture heroes, red-eye radicals from the Sixties—that's if they remember us at all. We're trained for this kind of operation. School's been out for a long time, to be sure, but you don't forget the kinds of things we learned."

"To be sure," Alexandra said distantly.

"In a crunch, our track record and reputations in the revolutionary underground could bail us out."

Alexandra looked away from Peters' steady gaze, again shifted in her seat and rested her burning forehead against the car's icy window. "Are you married, Rick?"

Peters stared at her for some time before finally answering. "No, I'm not married," he said with a bittersweet wryness.

"Well, you know I am. I have three children. The Company must know that. They could have gone after another team; you and I weren't the only dragons."

"Right; but there's no question about our being the best. They want and need the best for this job. We're supposed to identify the assassin and any backup, try to determine what organization tasked him, then do whatever killing may be required before the boxing matches."

Alexandra shuddered and drew her coat more tightly around her. Rick Peters had never been one to hide behind euphemisms, she thought, and the word "killing" seemed to echo inside the car, floating in the thin air with an eerie, tangible life of its own. She had almost forgotten that she had killed, more than once. She wondered if she could ever kill again, even to save her own life. Different colors, a different key.

But the same terrible excitement.

"Why do they want to go to the trouble?" Alexandra asked, the dry, dull tone of her voice belying her churning emotions. "Why does the Company suddenly want to protect Salva after they've been trying to get him for more than twenty years? It seems to me they'd figure that somebody with ball bearings for brains was trying to do them a favor."

"Different set of circumstances. Believe it or not, it seems the foxy bastard is just about ready to kiss and make up with the United States. According to the C, Salva and the Secretary of State have been carrying on negotiations for almost four and a half months. Apparently, Salva's ego isn't being sufficiently stroked by the Russians or his un-aligned nations anymore, and he thinks the Russians are getting to be a pain in the ass. He just doesn't trust them any longer; in fact, he's convinced they're already training some stooge in Moscow to take over when he goes, which makes him a very nervous dictator. I think Afghanistan and Poland shook him up, and he's looking to San Sierra's future. Whatever else the bastard may be, I guess you have to grant that he's a patriot. The C says that Salva's now convinced that San Sierra's best interests lie in a politi-cal realignment with the United States." He paused and laughed loudly. "The irony of it is that the big Sierran ex-odus is what started the negotiations. Talk about a diplo-matic coup! The Russians will go crazy!"

Peters dragged deeply on his cigarette, then began to drum the fingers of his other hand on the steering wheel. "That's as much as I've been told," he continued. His voice became quieter, more reflective. "I think there's more, but I don't know what it is. The Company knows that a lot of shit is going to hit the international fan if Salva is assassinated; there's just no way the United States would be able to convince the rest of the world that the CIA didn't do it. Alpha Nine would like that, of course; they've never forgiven the Company for not backing them at Beach of Fire.

"If the Russians are sufficiently pissed, they might use Salva's assassination as an excuse to start throwing their weight around in Western Europe. With the atmosphere in this country being what it is, the White House might decide it can't afford to take any more crap from anybody. I buy the reasons the C gave me for the government wanting to protect Salva, but I also think the Company is seriously concerned about the possibility of the assassination setting off a global war."

"I can see that," Alexandra said thoughtfully. "Which brings us to the obvious question: why doesn't some genius at the Company or State simply pick up a telephone and give Salva a ring? Warn him."

"Good question," Peters said, returning Alexandra's in-tense gaze. "As a mater of fact, that's the first thing I asked the C. The answer is that State doesn't know anything about this assassination plot. The official version from the C is that the CIA, as usual, doesn't trust State not to botch it somehow. The Company doesn't trust Salva any more than they think Salva trusts the United States, and they think State is being hopelessly naive. Their position is that Salva hasn't asked us to dance yet, and they've put together a scenario where Salva nabs the assassin we hand him and puts him away for insurance; Salva can always have the guy worked on, then present him to the world as a CIA agent who was sent to kill him. I think it scans. A stunt like that isn't beyond him, you know."

"You said it was the 'official version.' You don't think that's the whole story?"

Peters laughed drily. "Nothing our friends try to lay on you is ever the whole story. You know that. I think the C told me the truth, as far as it goes. I think we're also witnessing the old wheels-within-wheels syndrome. If the Company, by itself, can abort this assassination and break up the organization that paid for it, it puts more pressure on Salva to come over, and—the real point—it completely reverses the agency's fortunes. No more shit from Congress. The good old CIA that we knew and loved is back in business, with two Company men in everybody's attic."

"You're saying that you think the Company is willing to risk a major confrontation between Russia and the United States just so they can score some bonus points with Congress?"

"Are you kidding me? Of course they're willing." Peters grinned broadly. When Alexandra didn't respond, he turned serious once again. "And who's to say they're not right? After all, if Congress hadn't gutted them in the first place, we aging dragons wouldn't be sitting out here in the snow, would we?"

Alexandra absently ran her hand over the padded vinyl on the dashboard. "You're definitely going?"

"Yes, if they want me. Like I said, if you pass, they may cancel me out and look for another team of dragons who've worked together."

"Why do you want to do it, Rick?"

Peters laughed self-consciously, then fell silent. Alexandra felt herself compelled to turn and gaze into the pale, intense eyes.

"Because I care," Peters said quietly.

"About what?"

"This country."

"Bullshit," Alexandra said harshly. "What you really cared about was the game, the same as me. We were players, Rick, and that was all that mattered."

"It amazes me that you can say that now," Peters replied evenly. "It's absolutely true, and *I* knew it all the time. *You* were the one who thought that the name of that game was patriotism. You've changed, Alexandra, and so have I. If the Company says it needs me in San Sierra, then I'm ready to go; but now it's because I do care. I get all the excitement I need selling real estate. You do what you want. I'm to deliver a Company message, not to plead their case."

It was true that she had changed, Alexandra thought. Her love for, and life with, John had turned her inside out. She still felt the old excitement, but the difference was that John had taught her, too, to truly care.

Alexandra studied Peters' face. His mouth was set in a firm line, but his eyes, as always, revealed nothing. "The departure date is only two and a half weeks away. How can we get visas in time?"

"The C said that's been taken care of. Clever, thoughtful folk that they are, the Company applied for visas in our names before they bothered asking us how we felt about it. They probably ordered up a batch for a number of ex-dragons, and they'll cancel out all but the two they use. In any case, they'll be bona fide visas, nothing at all phony about them. Yours will also list your maiden name, Scott, just in case we have to cash in some Sierran I.O.U.s."

Peters smiled warmly as he reached across to the seat and rested his hand lightly on Alexandra's shoulder. "What about it?" he continued quietly. "It's freezing here, which makes it a good time of year to go to San Sierra. Shall the meanest set of dragons go to war again?"

Alexandra slowly and deliberately reached up and removed Peters' hand from her shoulder. "I'll get back to you within forty-eight hours," she said coldly, then stepped out of the car into the storm.

John Finway

Naked, John Finway studied his reflection in one of the full-length mirrors in the locker room of the New York Athletic Club. He started to turn away, but then felt compelled to look again. He took a step forward and peered closer, as if to see if he looked as much a stranger to himself as he felt.

His body was in good shape, John thought. He played squash and swam a half mile three days a week, and jogged on weekends. The result was a flat stomach, good wind, and excellent muscle tone.

His thick hair, like his eyes, was iron-gray except for an inch-wide band of silver running in a zigzag pattern from just above his left temple to the top of his skull—the curious legacy of a Chicago policeman's club that had landed on his head at the Democratic convention of 1968.

He had a rather distinctive face, John thought sardonically; not handsome, but probably interesting. It was a face that had accompanied the lead stories on hundreds of news telecasts during the 1960s, a face that was still recognized by millions of Americans who reacted with either hatred or respect depending upon the political combat zones through which they had marched during the decade in which the two great battlegrounds had been the rice paddies of Southeast Asia and America's streets.

His nose, mashed twenty years before by a construction worker's fist, was bent slightly askew. He recalled that Alexandra had always claimed that the crooked nose lent him "character"; he wondered what she would think now.

John knew that his face represented many things to different people, but he now feared that it had simply become the face of a fool. He thought of his hard body as a facade, an unreliable vessel of muscle sheets and bone struts barely containing a storm that had twisted his heart, corroded his will, and rendered his intellect useless. In the eye of that storm lived lies, he thought; the lies were voracious little beasts, piranhas of the soul requiring constant care and feeding and which, he'd learned, still turned and gnawed at their keeper the moment attention wandered.

There was little he could do about the storm, John

thought as he started to dress, but he knew that the lies had to be cast out, soon, before he was eaten away.

Forewarned by the emergency weather reports, John and his law partners had closed their New York offices at the first sign of snow. As a result, despite his stop at the athletic club, he'd had a head start on the snow-snarled crush of traffic and had made reasonably good time on the Palisades Parkway. He arrived home at 6:15, reacting with surprise and some alarm when he saw that Alexandra's car was not in the driveway. He managed to drive his own car into the garage, shut off the lights and engine, and walked into a house redolent with the aroma of linguini and clam sauce.

"Hey, watch out!" John cried in mock alarm as his son ran into his arms to be lifted and swung around.

His daughters, wearing matching flowered aprons, came out of the kitchen and hurried across the living room to kiss him.

"Happiness is two beautiful, gifted daughters who cook like French chefs," John continued, masking his concern with a barking laugh that was an odd, sonic mark of his personality heard only by his family and a few close friends. "Where's your mother?"

"We don't know, Dad," Kara Finway answered, worry evident in her tone. "She left the house about an hour and a half ago."

John heard the door open and close behind him. Michael pulled out of John's arms and ran around him to Alexandra.

"Hi, Mom," Kristen said, obviously relieved to see her mother arrive home safely.

John turned and was startled to see his wife wearing her mink coat over a running suit that was stained with dark blotches of dried sweat. He was even more disturbed by the expression on her face. Alexandra's features were stiff and contorted, as if she were trapped somewhere between a scream and a sob. It was a tortured look John had often seen on Alexandra's face, but that had been many years in the past, after he had first met her in the holding pen of a Washington jail.

John was certain he knew the reason for the expression; he had hoped—eventually, somehow—to at least partially undo his past deceit, but now he was sure that it was too late. His stomach hurt.

"We were worried, darling," John said quietly. His smile felt unnatural and forced as he searched Alexandra's face in vain for some indication of what she knew and what lay in wait for him that evening.

"There was no need to be," Alexandra replied evenly.

"Where'd you go?" John had tried to make the question seem casual, but he knew that it sounded like the first exploratory probe in the interrogation of a reluctant witness.

"It's not important, John," Alexandra replied abruptly. "We'll talk about it later."

John felt uncomfortable and awkward as he stood to one side and watched his wife hug and kiss their son. Then she straightened up and kissed him with cold, dry lips that John was certain were sore from more than the wind and snow outside. Finally, Alexandra put her arms around her daughters' waists and walked with them into the kitchen. John gripped Michael's small, outstretched hand and followed, still sick with the certainty that he knew what had upset his wife.

"Thanks for making dinner," Alexandra continued, hugging Kara and Kristen. "It's no secret that your father prefers your cooking to mine, but you were still doing my job. I'm sorry I abandoned you like that."

"Hey, Mom," Kristen said brightly, "no problem. You know we like to cook and look after Michael."

"Would you like me to make you a drink?" John asked quietly as he helped Alexandra remove her coat. His neck and jaw muscles ached with tension.

For a moment, Alexandra's features seemed to soften. Her brown eyes gleamed with their usual vitality as she grinned and again kissed John. "God, yes! One double vodka martini, three olives, a couple of ice cubes, and easy on the vermouth."

"The usual order, times two. I think I can handle that."

"Girls, do I have time for a quick shower?"

"Go ahead," Kristen answered. "We'll keep everything hot."

"I don't want you to wait," Alexandra called over her shoulder as she hurried out of the kitchen. "You guys start. I'll join you."

John slowly mixed Alexandra's drink, then carried it to the steamy bathroom and left it on the shelf across the tile floor from the hissing shower. Then he went into the dining room to join his children for a dinner that was being expertly served by the girls, complete with candles and a decanter of John's favorite white wine. The children were in a good mood, looking forward to a day off from the schools, which they were confident would be closed because of the storm.

John made an effort to join in the talk and laughter, feigning a happiness and appetite he did not feel. He relaxed somewhat when Alexandra, dressed in a warm terrycloth jumpsuit and with her hair wrapped in a bright red towel, joined them at the table. For a few minutes Alexandra appeared animated and cheerful, but John once again became anxious when he sensed her gradually drifting away from them, asking for simple questions to be repeated, growing increasingly distracted.

It was too late, he thought. He had waited at least one day too many to share and attempt to explain his shame and agony. His lies had inflicted wounds from which neither he nor his wife would recover quickly, if ever.

The girls wanted to clean up, but John and Alexandra insisted they go read or watch television. Kara volunteered to read a story to her brother and prepare him for bed. The children left the room, and John and Alexandra began clearing the table.

"The girls are so mature that it's easy to forget they're only fourteen," John said when he and Alexandra were alone in the kitchen. He knew he was simply trying to make conversation, hoping to postpone what he was certain must come, but he could not stand the pain of silence. "Do you think it's possible we give them too much responsibility?"

"No," Alexandra replied distantly. "They are mature, and very gifted. We don't give them anything they can't handle, and they do enjoy helping. There's no natural law that says Kara and Kristen have to act like simpering, brainless adolescents."

"You seem distracted," John said carefully.

"Do I?" Alexandra answered with what seemed to John feigned lightness. "I'm sorry, darling. I don't mean to."

"Is something bothering you?"

"No."

"Kara told me someone called just before you left the house. Did the phone call upset you?"

"I'm not upset," Alexandra said, bending over to stack the dishes that John handed her into the dishwasher. "As a matter of fact, the call was from the plumber. He wanted to apologize for not showing up last week when he was supposed to."

John studied his wife's back as she rearranged the dishes in the washer. He could feel a demand for truth inexorably building inside him. He suddenly realized that he was glad Alexandra finally knew, and even more ashamed that he hadn't been the one to tell her. "You looked like something was bothering you when you came in the house," he said at last.

"Not really. I didn't realize how bad the roads were, and I thought I'd run out to the deli and get something special for dessert. I got stuck halfway to the shopping center. A couple of men pushed me out, and I came home."

John tentatively placed his hand in the small of Alexandra's back and began to gently massage the muscles; he took the hand away when he realized it was shaking. "You must have known how bad the roads were; you'd been out running on them fifteen minutes before you left." He paused, swallowed drily. "Are you sure the phone call didn't have something to do with me?"

Alexandra's reply was sharp and terse, punctuated by the rattle of dishes. "John, the call had absolutely nothing to do with you."

John swallowed again. He had a sudden, desperate craving for a glass of ice water, but he knew that the few steps to the refrigerator would be nothing more than one more small, futile postponement. "You know, don't you?"

Alexandra turned her head. Her gaze darted up to her husband's face. "Know what, John?"

John quickly looked away and blinked back tears. "I'm in trouble, baby," he said, his voice cracking. He cleared his throat, continued, "I'm falling apart."

Alexandra slowly pushed the dishwasher rack into the machine, closed the door, and straightened up. "Oh, that I know," she said with an air of weary resignation. "Let's see; I think I noticed the first little chunk of you fall off about a year ago. Is that about right?"

John nodded. He rubbed his eyes clumsily with his knuckles, then blew his nose. "Christ, it's insane," he finally managed to say. "You remember that crazy little Nazi in the Bronx I was asked to defend?"

"I remember," Alexandra replied gently, as though touched by her husband's pain. "You defended that creep when nobody else would. I was proud of you; three unlisted phone numbers later, I'm still proud of you."

John's quick burst of laughter was tortured and self-mocking. "Well, clever old John Finway managed to get himself emotionally involved with the twenty-two-year-old wife of said Nazi. Christ, I almost wish he weren't so stupid; if he found out about it, he'd shove a hand grenade up my ass and solve all our problems."

Alexandra abruptly turned her face away. She remained still and silent for a long time, and John had the eerie sensation that he could almost hear tumblers clicking inside her, walls shifting and doors closing, sealing off and containing all the terrible rage she must feel; and with the rage seemed to go all that was so remarkably warm and feeling in her. What was left was a psychic surface like cold, burnished steel.

John had seen the peculiar and striking metamorphosis before, in the months between their first meeting and their marriage, but not since. At the time he had been impressed and intrigued by Alexandra's remarkable ability to distance herself from the most outrageous pressures, almost as if she had been trained to do so. His reaction now was quite different; this was the second time that evening that Alexandra's look had reminded him of the past, and it frightened him.

"Please don't drift away from me, Alexandra," John continued softly. "Scream at me, hit me, but please don't drift. I need to talk."

"What the hell did you think you were doing?" Alexandra said in a voice husky with hurt and anger. "What *are* you doing? This isn't like you."

"Good night, Daddy."

John breathed deeply, then turned and picked up his son. He held the boy tightly, closing his eyes and pressing his face hard into Michael's flannel pajamas. When he opened his eyes he found himself staring over Michael's shoulder into the startled face of Kara. The girl quickly dropped her gaze, obviously embarrassed by the sight of her father's red-rimmed eyes. John put Michael down and Kara quickly led the boy away.

"Jesus," John said. "I wish Kara hadn't seen that."

There was a long silence during which John stared vacantly at the floor, slowly shaking his head like a wounded animal, struck dumb by the terrible force of the conflict inside him.

"John," Alexandra said quietly, turning back to face him, "I can see that you're hurting. If it will help to talk about it, go ahead, I'm listening."

"I'm just goddamn ashamed of the way I've handled this, baby," John murmured. "Or haven't handled it. I don't know what to do."

John groaned softly as he felt a steel fist of self-contempt strike him in the chest at the same time as insidious desire for the woman, Selma, rippled through his groin like warm oil. "I feel like I've been hit by a truck," he said at last.

The fleeting smile that rippled across Alexandra's rigid features was tight and bitter. "Welcome to the scene of the accident."

John pressed his hands to his temples and tried desperately to focus his thoughts on the conflicting emotions raging inside him, groping blindly in a black vortex of primitive feeling for simple words that would describe the geography of the volcanic, heaving internal land to which he had been exiled.

"It was an accident, Alexandra," he said at last, puzzled by his inability to find any other words for what had happened to him. "That's the only way I can explain it. Her name's Selma, and she's just about what you'd expect the wife of a Nazi creep to be; she doesn't know much about anything."

"Oh, ho! Now I understand perfectly. This was a poor, misguided, ignorant waif for the noble and wise John Finway to take on as a protégée-mistress and introduce to his bright, shining world of intellect, brotherhood, and rationality. Watch out, darling, I think your ego is running out your ears, along with your brains."

"There was a tremendous physical attraction," John murmured, stung by Alexandra's sarcasm but preferring the heat of that to the cold, strange absence that was the alternative. He knew that what she said was true, and what startled him anew was an awareness of the gulf between truth and feeling, how little one had to do with the other. His lust was a brainless slug-thing that paid no attention, understood nothing. "I suppose I was being a wise-ass. I thought I could steal a little extramarital sexual excitement off the shelf and not have to pay for it. I didn't see how a few lunches, a few walks, could hurt." He laughed again, a quick, sad sound. "After all, her husband was in the slammer awaiting trial for getting drunk, dressing up in his Nazi togs and burning down a synagogue. I mean, you had to feel sorry for this woman, right?"

Alexandra didn't smile. "It's your deceit that's tearing you apart, John. We had a contract, written and unwritten; it's called a marriage. You've broken it. You've been living a lie for a year, and it's not the kind of work you have a stomach for. Some people, yes, but not you."

"I know that. I discovered it."

"It sounds to me like this poor, innocent woman made a shrewd decision to chuck her imbecile husband and try to latch onto a rich and famous lawyer. Doesn't it occur to you that she's been stroking your ego just as hard as she's been stroking everything else of yours?"

John flushed. "Of course it occurs to me," he said, dropping his gaze. "It's occurred to me from day one. What I'm saying—and it's hard for me to admit this, but it's the truth—is that it just doesn't make any difference what I know. I can't get her out of my mind, no matter what I do. I feel incredibly stupid and childish, Alexandra, but I'm obsessed with the goddam woman, and it's driving me crazy."

"Why didn't you tell me before, John? We've always been honest with each other. Always. Didn't you think I'd know there was something bothering you? The deceit is what I have trouble understanding and forgiving."

"I wanted to talk to you about it. I was afraid. I told myself that it was better to be less honest and more kind."

"How charmingly condescending of you," Alexandra said through clenched teeth. The flesh over her chin, cheek-bones, and forehead was blanched white by unreleased fury and tension.

"I know," John said softly. "I can't stand dishonesty."

He took a glass and a bottle of Scotch from a kitchen cabinet, poured himself a stiff drink. He sipped at it, then set the glass down on the table and stared into the depths of the amber liquid. "I never believed in the relationship, Alexandra," he continued woodenly. "Not for a second. One reason I didn't tell you was because I didn't want to risk losing my wife and children and home for a relationship I couldn't believe in. I kept waiting for the urge to pass; it didn't. It just kept on growing."

"Until it swallowed you up."

"All right, yes," John said, slowly nodding. "I've tried to break it off a half-dozen times in the past year. One time I went for three months without seeing or talking to her. It didn't work. The pressure just kept building up until I couldn't think of anything else. I'd start feeling cheated and angry. I know it sounds banal, but I felt as if I weren't being true to myself. I couldn't—"

John suddenly felt alone, as if Alexandra had left the kitchen. He glanced up and found his wife staring vacantly out the window. Her face was once again set in the con-torted, anxious mask that had disturbed John earlier in the evening.

"Alexandra?"

Alexandra turned to him and shook her head slightly. She blinked, and her eyes slowly came into focus on his face. "I'm sorry, John," she said distantly. "I was thinking of something else."

"You were thinking of something *else?*"

Alexandra's lids narrowed, and her eyes suddenly glinted like pieces of polished brown marble. "I apologize if I haven't been paying sufficient attention to your confession, John. Frankly, it's an old story and it's getting boring. I'd be interested in what you plan to do now. Have you cooked up an ending yet?"

John stared back at her. The terrible space and cold were back, not to be displaced again. Suddenly Alexandra seemed a stranger to him. That she should be hurt and angry was totally, agonizingly, understandable to him, but there was a dimension to her present coldness and distance that tolled a small, muffled warning bell deep inside him. But then, he thought wryly, he had not exactly brought her good news.

"I told you I feel like I've been run over by a truck," he said. His voice had grown steadier, and he had the not unpleasant sensation that he was floating up out of the cold fog of some deep valley, soaring from dark to light. He realized that what he felt was relief. For better or worse, he was finally on his way to the end of this confrontation; a measure of his torment was being drawn from him by the coarse but pure poultice of truth. In one way or another, he thought, his conflict would be resolved soon. "I know I've hurt you terribly, first by my betrayal and then by keeping it from you, but I've hurt myself too. I'm not being facetious when I say I feel like I'm having an emotional root-canal job. By tearing you, I've torn myself. I have to get myself straight, and I know that I have to go away in order to do that."

"You don't have to leave if you think of leaving your home as some kind of self-inflicted punishment," Alexandra said softly. She was again staring out the frosted kitchen window. "At least you've told me about it. Maybe now you can work it out here."

"I can't, Alexandra. Talking to you makes me feel better, but it won't resolve the conflicts I feel. I have to go away."

"When will you leave?"

"Tonight. Now that it's out in the open, I want to leave as soon as possible. They've plowed the roads. I'll find a motel."

"Is she waiting for you?"

"No," John replied quickly, an edge to his voice. "I'm not running away, Alexandra, not to another woman and not from responsibility. I have to find some way to free my mind of all the crap that's been building up in it for the past year; I have to find a way of working this out. I know it's petty, self-serving, and absolutely useless to say I'm sorry, but I am. I hate the person I've become, and I have to find a way of living inside my own skin. I hope you'll believe me when I tell you this stranger still loves you, very much."

Alexandra turned from the window and stared at him strangely. "Oh, I believe you, John," she said at last. "I know you love me. I'm sorry for both of us that you got yourself into this mess."

John could not meet her gaze. The remote look in her eyes and the hollow tone of her voice made him feel even more uneasy. "I'll figure out something to tell Michael and the girls," he murmured, turning his attention back to the glass of liquor on the kitchen table.

"Don't tell the girls 'something,' John. Tell them the truth. We'll both be sorry if you don't. But wait until tomorrow to talk to them; at least let them get a good night's sleep. I'll think about how we should explain it to Michael."

John felt that he should say something else, but there were no words left inside him. The turbulent sea of feeling that had wracked him was finally gone, boiled down to a leaden residue of silence that had settled painfully in the pit of his stomach. He kept his head bowed as Alexandra walked past him, then sensed her pause at the kitchen door.

"Good luck, John," Alexandra said simply. And then she was gone.

John picked up the glass in front of him and drained it.

Friday, January 4; 6:30 A.M.

Alexandra

The effect of the previous day's two emotional firestorms had been to leave Alexandra temporarily suspended in a strange, quiet place between them, supported for the moment in a kind of protective spiritual hammock comprised of pride and ingrained self-control. She might already have lost John to another woman, Alexandra thought, or she could lose him to the dark secrets of her past if she accepted the challenge presented to her by a man who had risen like thick, fetid mist from the bog of a nightmare time she had almost forgotten. Betrayal had been balanced by betrayal—almost; her betrayal of John was still hidden. In a way the two rending events had cancelled each other out, leaving Alexandra feeling physically numb and emotionally anesthetized. .

She perceived a certain irony in the fact that it was her harsh psychological conditioning and training as a dragon —a legacy of her betrayal of John—that enabled her to think in a reasonably clear manner, to compress the facts of the situation into a small, hermetic place in her mind which she could enter and explore with relative calm, sheltered from the tempest of feeling that screamed through the rest of her. Using this painfully acquired technique, she had been able to sleep through the night, even after she had heard the front door close behind John with a kind of resolute finality.

She awoke at five, feeling resigned but curiously refreshed, prepared to analyze her situation. In this state of mind she lay staring at the dark ceiling, waiting for dawn, thinking. By six-thirty she had decided on the preliminary steps she would take to resolve the only conflict over which she had any control. To work was to escape.

She rose, dressed in slacks and a sweater, and had a steaming breakfast of pancakes and sausages ready for her children when they came downstairs. School had been cancelled, and the girls immediately began planning for a "cross-country" skiing expedition to their friends' homes around the snow-covered neighborhood.

Alexandra allowed the children to assume that their father had left for work early. She waited until the girls were gone and Michael curled like a cat in front of the fireplace in the living room with a book before she went to the telephone in John's study.

The rich wood, the books, and the littered desk momentarily penetrated her emotional shield and brought tears to her eyes. However, despite her pain, Alexandra was resigned to the fact that there was nothing she could do about the situation with John. She knew her husband to be a brilliant, complex, and passionate man who, like most such individuals, suffered more than his share of private demons. For as long as she'd known him, John had suffered other people's pain and indignities as his own, and, in his gentle way, taught her to do the same. In the 1960s, his keen sense of justice had, like a great righteous wind, swept him into countless demonstrations for civil rights and against the war in Southeast Asia, and then into courtrooms across the nation where he'd used his prodigious legal and oratorical skills to defend himself and his fellow radicals against the charges that were constantly being pressed by Federal, state, and local governments. He had won the vast majority of his cases with relentless efficiency, in the process frequently providing the intellectual foundations for new interpretations of Constitutional law.

Alexandra recalled that the death of his sister in the Weatherman bomb factory explosion rigged by Rick Peters had only strengthened John's resolve to fight within the framework of the laws he had done so much to help define. With the end of the Vietnam war, he had turned his full attention to the continuing legal battles for the rights of minorities.

But America had been changing, and Alexandra remembered her husband's almost childish bewilderment upon discovering in the 1970s that much of the nation had fallen into step behind him, however reluctantly. Virtually by default; John had become a part of the legal establishment, a wealthy and widely respected man.

Perhaps, Alexandra thought, it was precisely this acceptance that had undone the heart and mind of a natural rebel. With social activism mushrooming, co-opted by courts and other activist lawyers whose collective consciousness he had helped to raise, John had suddenly appeared spent and without direction. Alexandra suspected that John, feeling trapped in middle age with his fiercest battles won and behind him, had unconsciously turned his attention to capturing the heart and mind of a young woman who had been guileless enough to marry a ridiculous and pathetic Nazi sympathizer.

John had finally been ambushed by his demons, Alexandra thought. It was a condition about which she knew a great deal; she certainly knew enough to understand that John would have to find his own way out of the strange, haunted places of his mind back to her, his family, and his peace of mind. She knew that she could not fight this battle of the heart for him, could not even help.

However, the dilemma Rick Peters had created for her was an entirely different situation, and it was to this problem that Alexandra addressed herself as she picked up the telephone receiver and dialed the number Rick Peters had given her.

The phone was picked up in the middle of the fifth ring, as required by procedure, and Alexandra had a brief but pointed conversation with the man at the other end of the line. The voice had a slight French accent, but Alexandra was not concerned about that; many of the posts in both the Operations and Human Intelligence sections of the CIA were manned, of necessity, by foreign-born Americans speaking many languages. What was important was the fact that the man followed the intricate telephone-contact procedures precisely. He quickly confirmed Peters' story, then subtly but distinctly pressed the point that, in the CIA's carefully reasoned view, she and Rick Peters were the best choice to undertake the San Sierra task. It became obvious to Alexandra that the controller wanted her to commit at once, but she told him in a firm voice that she needed more time to consider her position and that she would give her decision to him or to Rick Peters within the forty-eight-hour period she had originally been given.

Next she called La Guardia Airport in New York City, and then a neighbor who was also a close friend.

These calls completed, Alexandra dressed Michael in his snowsuit and drove three miles through freshly plowed streets to a pay phone in a deserted shopping center. Leaving Michael busy with a coloring book in the car parked a few feet away from the booth, Alexandra dropped a dime in the slot and called a Washington, D.C., number collect. The man who answered immediately accepted the call.

"Hi, Dad."

"Alexandra!" The voice was mellow, supported by an undercurrent of good-natured laughter. "I didn't expect to hear from you so soon after the holidays. What an unexpected pleasure. Happy New Year again!"

"And to you, Dad. Is Mom around?"

"No. She went for a walk. You know how she likes fresh snow. Did you want to talk to her?"

"I need to talk to you, Dad. I wanted to make sure Mom wasn't around."

There was a short pause at the other end of the line. When Alexandra's father spoke again, his easy, bantering tone was gone. "Is something wrong, Alexandra?"

"I don't know. Something has come up—from the past. Are we on a clean line?"

"No reason to suspect otherwise, but it doesn't hurt to be careful."

"I need your help, but I can't tell you why. It wouldn't be good for either of us."

"I understand perfectly," Robert Scott replied evenly. His tone had shifted to that of one professional talking to another. "I won't ask you any questions. Just tell me what you want me to do."

"Do you still have contacts at the firm?"

"Yes, but now everything is strictly on a social level. I'm not plugged in any longer."

"That doesn't make any difference. Do you think you could carry a message for me? It would have to be delivered to someone at a very high level, an administrator whose loyalty and discretion you have absolute confidence in. I don't have much time, so it has to be someone who can get results in a matter of hours. Can you do that?"

"I can try, Alexandra. I have someone in mind."

"Do you want to get a piece of paper?"

"No. I'll remember what you say."

"Okay. I'd like you to do this: Ask your contact if the firm really wants the dragons turned loose. Tell him I've been asked to do something very unusual. I've been out of action for a long time, and it occurs to me that people with certain information could run a game on me, for whatever reason. Tell your man I said that the dragon task they're proposing is just too important for me to consider accepting without a second confirmation from a high official that you know personally and who's willing to identify himself to me. If they won't give me that, I pass. Have you got it, Dad?"

"Yes."

"I checked with the airport and the planes should be flying out by eleven. I'm taking the one o'clock shuttle to Washington. I want your friend to come with you to meet me at the airport. I'll bring Michael with me. If you can get Mom out of the way, I was hoping we could use your home as a safehouse while you play grandfather with Michael."

"I guess I can send your mother someplace," Alexandra's father said thoughtfully, concern evident under the flat, businesslike terseness of his tone. "What about the girls?"

"They're skiing around the neighborhood right now, and I have a friend coming over later just to keep an eye on things. I told my friend you were sick and that I had to make a quick trip to check on you."

"What about John? He's rather fond of me. He might insist on coming along."

"John's . . . away. He won't know."

"Alexandra?"

"Yes, Dad?"

"I know this must sound like a rather odd statement coming from the man who recruited you, but what you did and what you were is a long time in the past. You're over forty. What about your physical condition?"

"I'm in good shape."

Robert Scott was silent for a few moments. Finally, he

said, "I don't know what this is all about, Alexandra, and I'm not asking, but you have a family now that needs you. Maybe you've done enough."

"I'm not making any quick decisions, Dad. It will be a big help if you can deliver that message. If no one shows up, the decision will have been made for me."

"I'll do my best, Alexandra. I love you, sweetheart."

"I love you, Dad," Alexandra said, and hung up.

LANGLEY, VIRGINIA; CIA HEADQUARTERS

Saturday, January 5; 3:45 A.M.

Harry Beeler

Harry Beeler paused in the corridor just outside the office of the CIA's Director of Operations and studied his reflection in a panel of veined, polished marble. Although he was a reasonably attractive man, Harry's motive for staring at himself was practical rather than narcissistic; it was an aid to the form of mild self-hypnosis that he used to help him slip "in role."

Harry smiled wryly as he speculated on what the Director of Operations might think, or do with him, if he knew that his top expert in "psychological disguise" had to manipulate his own mind simply in order to walk into the Director's relatively small, spartanly furnished office.

The contents of the thin leather attaché case he carried were so bizzare and potentially damaging politically that he had chained the case to his wrist, even though he had not been ordered to do so. The originals of the documents were at that moment being re-interred in the agency's files by the four insulated teams of researchers he had coordinated, and Harry was certain that the copies he carried would be shredded immediately after the meeting.

It meant he was going to be tasked, Harry thought, and he didn't like it. He never liked it.

Harry knew that, at thirty-six, he was one of four or five top agents in an already elite corps of twenty-five covert operations specialists who had been carefully "buried" during the great CIA purges of the past decade; he also knew that he was fast burning out. He badly wanted to move up the career ladder into Administration, perhaps in Satellite or Human Intelligence, before he flamed out.

He knew what the problem was: fear. Harry was not

ashamed of his anxious, amorphous dread; indeed, he thought of himself as a courageous man. There was a distinction in his mind between true courage, which was a product of reflection, and the impulsive acts born of love of danger or an urge to self-destruction. He did not believe that authentic courage could be forged or wielded wisely without the catalyst of fear. He had proved his valor and effectiveness many times over in the field, but the fear of death, of pain or maiming, or long, lonely imprisonment in an alien land was always there, and Harry was tired of having to deal with it.

Harry decided on his "character," one of a half-dozen subtle variations on the role he had played for the past two years when dealing with the Director of Operations. Satisfied with the feel of this "person" in his mind, he stepped forward and rapped twice, firmly, on the door.

"Come in, Beeler." The deep, commanding voice carried clearly through the thick oak door.

Harry opened the door and stepped into the office. He was confident that his character's face was impassive as he walked across the hardwood floor to stand in front of the burnished steel desk that had been custom built for Harley Shue, the gnomish, secretive, and occasionally savage Director of Operations. There were three straight-backed steel chairs set equidistant from one another in a semicircle around the front of the desk, behind which sat the slight, vaguely sinister figure of Shue.

The chair on Harry's left was occupied by Vincent Scapelli, a sixty-two-year-old Company veteran whom Harry knew well, liked, and respected. Scapelli appeared haggard and hollow-eyed.

The middle chair was empty, and the CIA Director, Geoffrey M. Whistle, sat in the third chair. Whistle, a retired Army general and a political appointee, was infamous among the agency's professionals for his outrageously photogenic good looks and overall incompetence. Although Whistle had held his position for three and a half years, it was the first time Harry had met him, or even seen him in person.

In keeping with the occasionally stiff manner of the character he was playing, Harry acknowledged each man's presence with a respectful but curt nod of his head.

"Beeler, you know Mr. Scapelli," Harley Shue said in the grating bass voice that Harry always found so striking in a man of Shue's diminutive size. "This, of course, is the Director."

"Please to meet you, sir," Harry said to Geoffrey Whistle. He listened to the subtle, shifting cues inside himself and discovered that his character would have an urge to say something that would be hopelessly inappropriate, perhaps vaguely insubordinate, in a wry tone of voice. "I hope we're not keeping you up."

Harley Shue wore heavy, horn-rimmed glasses, and as his head snapped an inch or two to his right a warning flash of light was reflected from the thick lenses directly into Harry's eyes. Harry had seen the trick many times, and it never failed to impress him.

The CIA Director chuckled. "Harry, I've heard a great deal about you. People say you're a really top man."

"Thank you, sir."

Shue tapped the steel surface of his desk once with a thin index finger. His fingernail on the metal produced a sharp click—a sonic command. Harry unlocked the handcuffs on his right wrist and laid the attaché case on the desk before his superior.

"Tell us what you've discovered about Mrs. Finway, Beeler," Shue said easily, resting his hands on the attaché case. "Judging from the chain around your wrist, I assume the agency has indeed had some highly sensitive dealings with her."

Harry glanced at the hands folded over the case and knew that he was being tested. He was ready; it so happened that the character he was playing had an excellent memory. "That's correct, sir."

"Then kindly proceed. Be succinct, yet as comprehensive as possible. The Director has just joined us, and he hasn't been briefed at all."

"Alexandra Finway is forty-two years old," Harry began in the flat, disinterested tone of voice he'd found was preferred by the Director of Operations. "As Alexandra Scott, she was recruited by the agency out of UCLA in nineteen sixty-two. Her father is Robert Scott, a former executive in Humint, now retired. It was Scott who recommended his daughter, who at the time was studying for a graduate degree in sports biophysics. She was a member of women's All-America teams in volleyball, basketball, and track. She won silver and bronze medals in track at the nineteen-sixty Olympics.

"At the time of her recruitment the agency had perceived a serious gap in its intelligence-gathering function. Widespread campus unrest was just beginning, and the CIA had hard information that a number of the student groups were receiving money and direction from various subversive groups, both foreign and domestic. The KGB, in particular, was rumored to be infiltrating the organizations. Of course, it's the mandate of the FBI to perform domestic counter-intelligence operations of the sort called for, but it was the agency's belief that Director Hoover was long gone over the hill, obsessed with discrediting the civil rights movement and destroying Martin Luther King. Regardless of whether or not Director Hoover had gone a little nutty, he certainly wasn't delivering the goods the CIA felt it needed to do its job."

"You know how to deliver a report properly, Beeler," Shue said drily. "Do so, please, and let's try to stay away from unnecessary personal characterizations."

"Yes, sir," Harry replied evenly. "The CIA's response to the situation was to form a covert domestic-penetration group code-named 'the dragons.' The dragons were comprised of two-man teams of student types who were carefully trained and equipped as field operatives but were clearly told from the outset that they could never be given official CIA status. Theirs was a one-time, continuing assignment of indeterminate duration that could not in any way be construed as a career step. The existence of the dragons was known to only a handful of top-echelon officials within the agency. Neither the President nor the National Security Council were ever informed of the operation."

Harry paused and glanced quickly at both Whistle and Scapelli; Scapelli looked interested, Whistle confused and slightly anxious. "Certain memos in the files seem to indicate that the dragons' deep-insulation was due more to fear of Director Hoover than sensitivity to the inherent illegality of the dragons' function," Harry continued, turning his attention back to Shue.

The warning lights flashed in Shue's thick glasses. "Keep on track, Beeler."

"Each dragon team was deep-insulated, not only from the agency but from other teams. They always received instructions from, and reported to, a single controller outside regular agency channels. It's probably not much of an exaggeration to say that a dragon in Baltimore was more isolated than a regular operative working out of Moscow. The dragons were tasked to penetrate and collect information on radical campus groups—the leaders, foreign financing and control, if any. The dragons were paid, of course, but it was assumed that their primary motive for cooperation was essentially patriotic. This was the basis on which they were recruited.

"Alexandra Scott's partner was a man by the name of Rick Peters, also recruited out of UCLA. Scott and Peters proved out as one of the most daring and effective of all the dragon teams. They penetrated the Weathermen at an early stage, and this led to connections with dozens of other radical groups. They were responsible for uncovering a number of foreign links, including money pipelines from Russia, China, Cuba, and San Sierra.

"Scott was attacked and raped by a Weatherman leader soon after she and Peters had penetrated the group. After that experience she took to wearing a large ivory barrette in her hair. She bought the barrettes in a crafts shop in New York's Greenwich Village. Each clip had a heavy steel needle clasp, and she became very proficient in the use of the barrettes as defensive weapons. She could stick the needle into a man's eye, belly, groin, anus—any soft tissue. There's no report from her controller of Scott ever being attacked again, although she apparently left a number of one-eyed, sore-assed, or dead men in her wake. She—"

"We get the picture, Beeler," Shue said impatiently. "Go on."

"I was about to say that Scott and Peters acquired a kind of legendary status among the very people they were spying on in the radical underground. They were never blown." Harry paused and smiled slightly as he stared directly at Shue. "The woman's a tough cookie, sir."

"She's a strong and courageous woman, Mr. Beeler," Vincent Scapelli said with undisguised feeling. "A very fine woman. I know her father personally, and I know of Alexandra. She's a bit more than a 'tough cookie.' "

"Yes, sir," Harry replied evenly. "I meant no disrespect. In nineteen sixty-five she was indicted for conspiracy in connection with an explosion in one of the radicals' bomb factories. Incidentally, John Finway's sister was killed in that explosion, and the controller suspected that it was rigged by Rick Peters. In any case, Finway led the team of lawyers that defended the group—successfully, I might add, with only light jail sentences for the leaders. At her controller's suggestion, Scott developed a relationship with Finway, and she reported on his activities for about six months or so after the trial. Then they got married—not at her controller's suggestion—and Scott immediately resigned from the dragons. Presumably, she settled into the role of housewife. We have no record of her current whereabouts, but her husband's a noted attorney and it shouldn't be difficult to find an address. There's no way of knowing if Mrs. Finway ever shared classified information about the dragons with her husband."

"It's doubtful," Geoffrey Whistle interjected thoughtfully. "With that bastard's political predilections, he'd have been crawling all over our backs long before this if he'd had that kind of information."

"What about Peters, Beeler?" Shue asked tersely.

"Peters' story is essentially the same as Alexandra Finway's. Both are the same age, and both come from families with long traditions of government service. Peters is an expert in electronics and explosives, especially plastique. Peters stayed with the dragons until the program was dissolved, at which time he requested permission to become a regular agent. He was turned down and cut loose. He probably would have been rejected even if it weren't for the unique circumstances of his work as a dragon; the last reports from his controller indicate that Peters was showing signs of mental instability. As a dragon he was reliable, cool, and highly effective, but he was unpredictable if he considered his personal honor threatened."

"Would you describe him as paranoid, Mr. Beeler?" Vincent Scapelli asked.

"I'm not a psychiatrist, sir," Harry said, "and the controller doesn't use that word in his report. From what I've read, I'd describe him as a very mean and dangerous man. At least he was when he worked as a dragon. He's a man who probably wouldn't hesitate to kill over an insult."

The Director of Operations tapped his fingers on his desk and seemed about to speak. Harry waited expectantly, but Harley Shue had apparently had second thoughts about whatever he had been going to say, and he remained silent. Harry resumed his report.

"Peters expressed a lot of bitterness about being turned down for regular employment, and the agency was afraid he might start telling dragon stories to unauthorized personnel. He was yellow-flagged for two years after the dragons were disbanded, but as far as we could tell, he never broke confidence. The flag was dropped, and he doesn't show up in the files after nineteen seventy-three."

"Well, he's shown up now," Vincent Scapelli said in a strained voice.

Harry looked inquiringly at the older man. "Sir?"

"Sit down, Beeler," Shue commanded.

Harry moved around the empty chair and sat down. The steel surface was hard and uncomfortable. He folded his arms across his chest, but kept both feet flat on the floor.

"Beeler," Shue continued, "you've done an excellent job in a very short period of time. How do you assess the chances of one of your researchers putting together all of this information?"

"There's always that risk, sir. They're all very bright and, naturally, each person knows different bits and pieces of what I've just reported. I tried to minimize the risk by keeping the teams physically separated and working in discrete time frames."

"Good. Would you like some coffee? Something to eat?"

Shue was being positively munificent, Harry thought. He was being stroked, which no doubt meant that his task was going to be a major one. Very dangerous. He said, "No. Thank you, sir."

"Very well." Shue removed his glasses and wiped the lenses carefully with a linen handkerchief. "Vincent," he continued when he finished, "would you brief Beeler and the Director, please?"

"I spent three hours with Alexandra Finway yesterday afternoon," Vincent Scapelli said, moving to the edge of his chair. In contrast to Harley Shue's studied pace, Scapelli's delivery was quick and tense, his voice breathy. "She'd been approached the day before by Peters; Peters told her that the agency wanted the two of them to go to San Sierra with some group of tourists in order to stop an attempted assassination of Salva. Thank God she was enough of a professional to ask us for a second confirmation."

"But there are no more dragons, are there?" Whistle asked. His voice was anxious and uncertain. He glanced nervously at his Director of Operations, obviously requesting his own confirmation. "Peters hasn't been tasked by us, has he, Harley?"

Harley Shue swiveled in his chair and smiled benignly at the CIA Director. "No, sir. I can give you absolute assurance that the dragons were disbanded many years ago, and that Rick Peters has not been tasked by us."

Harry decided that his character would begin to take a more active role in the proceedings. "Even if the dragons were still operational," he said, "Peters' story wouldn't be plausible. Why would dragons be used to protect Salva?"

"Mr. Peters had a rather interesting tale to tell Mrs. Finway," Shue said drily. "Vincent?"

Harry turned to the aging administrator and watched the man tug nervously at his shirt cuffs as he spoke.

"Peters told Alexandra that Salva had been conducting secret negotiations with State that could lead to San Sierra coming over to our side."

"Jesus Christ," Geoffrey Whistle breathed, leaning forward.

Vincent Scapelli looked inquiringly at the head of the agency, and Whistle gestured for him to continue.

"Naturally, a realignment of San Sierra with the United States would cause the Soviet Union considerable distress," Scapelli resumed in a thin, dry voice. "At the same time, it would re-establish the integrity of our hemispheric sphere of influence. In such circumstances, Salva would be infinitely more valuable to us alive than dead. Almost as important, if Salva were killed, the Third World nations—indeed, the rest of the world—could never be convinced that the CIA was not responsible. It seems Peters was very convincing. You see the problem, of course."

Harry nodded. "Interesting fantasy. Did Mrs. Finway think to ask why the agency would want to task two people who were never regular operatives to begin with and who haven't worked for years?"

"She did," Scapelli said, nervously licking his lips. "Peters told her that we didn't have anybody else. According to Peters, they were the best choice because of their past reputations as revolutionaries; there would be no chance of the Sierrans turning down their request for visas."

"When did Peters say that this assassination was supposed to take place?"

"Friday night, January twenty-fifth, at the Sierran-USA boxing matches that are scheduled to take place in Angeles Blanca on that date."

"The assassin?"

"He told her the identity of the assassin was unknown, but that we'd determined he'd be in the tourist group leaving for San Sierra the week of the boxing matches. Peters claimed that we wanted him and Alexandra to go with the group and identify and kill the assassin before he could kill Salva."

Harry was already fairly certain where he was going, and for a moment his fear almost ate through the protective membrane that was the character he was playing. The character did not worry about Sierran prisons or firing squads; Harry did. If he were to go to San Sierra, he thought, he wanted to know the precise nature of the wind that was blowing him there.

"Actually, it does sound like a good foundation for an assassination plot," Harry's character said evenly. "But Peters' story is a fantasy. He's obviously trying to run a game on Alexandra Finway. May I ask what our specific concern might be?"

"Half of the fantasy just happens to be true," the Director of Operations said drily, staring at Harry through his thick lenses. For the first time his deep, reedy voice showed signs of tension and emotion. "Mr. Peters seems to be a remarkably prescient story teller."

"Manuel Salva *is* thinking of lining up with the West," Whistle said tightly. The Director shifted uncomfortably in his chair, crossing and uncrossing his legs. "This fact is known only to the President, a very few people at State, myself, Director Shue, and now you two gentlemen. It's absolutely incredible that this Rick Peters should be talking about something that's top secret." He paused, shook his head. "The man knows things he shouldn't," he added unnecessarily.

Harry felt a muscle on the inside of his left thigh begin to twitch. He realized with some surprise that at the moment the real Harry Beeler was more intrigued than afraid. "Maybe Peters doesn't really know anything," he offered. "As Director Shue said, only half of Peters' fantasy is true, and Peters doesn't even realize it."

Scapelli cleared his throat and nodded in tentative agreement. "That's quite possible. Peters seems to have a number of details wrong. For example, Salva's more afraid of economic collapse than he is of the Russians, as Peters claimed. The Russians are pumping millions of rubles a day into San Sierra, and the economy's still sinking. Salva knows we're the only country that can keep San Sierra afloat over the long haul. Also, he's having to deal with the rising expectations of his people."

"I'm not sure I understand," Whistle said apologetically.

"It's possible that the whole thing is made up as far as Peters is concerned," Harry said, leaning forward slightly and looking at Scapelli. "The man's banged a very big bell he didn't even know was there."

"But what's he up to?" Geoffrey Whistle asked distantly, his voice betraying his confusion and concern.

Harry glanced quickly at Harley Shue. Their eyes met, and for the briefest moment there was an intimate, veiled communication between them, a shared contempt for their mutual superior. The contact was broken as Shue turned his head a fraction of an inch and flashed light in Harry's eyes.

"Peters must be planning to kill Mr. Salva himself," Shue said matter-of-factly.

"*Jesus!*" Whistle said. He half rose from his chair, then sat back down again hard, scraping the chair legs on the wood floor. "Jesus. What does he want with the Finway woman?"

"She's his cat's paw," Harry said, glancing back and forth between Shue and Scapelli. They were three professionals war-gaming now and enjoying it. "For some reason, she seems to be an essential part of his plan."

"Why Alexandra?" Scapelli asked in a hoarse voice.

Harry thought about it for a few moments, then said, "Who else with even a peripheral connection to American Intelligence is he going to run that story by? Let's suppose for the sake of argument that Peters has figured out a way to use her, and only her. What use could that be? Their past connection to the CIA, however tentative, could be the answer. Maybe Peters has figured out a way to publicly link Alexandra Finway to the agency after the fact. Maybe he has documents, proof of the dragons' existence. Peters cancels out Salva and manages to pin the assassination on us. He uses the woman to accomplish something he told the woman they were supposed to stop someone else from doing. Cute—and vicious. It would fit into Peters' profile."

"Shit," Whistle mumbled. He glanced at his watch. "I'd better call the President right away."

"Perhaps we should wait a few minutes on that, sir," the Director of Operations said, his tone disarmingly soft and solicitous. "We wouldn't want to unduly alarm the President until we're reasonably sure of our facts and assumptions, and the difference between them. If Peters does intend to use the Finway woman in an assassination, it seems to mean that he's not going to be a kamikaze. He's planning to get out of San Sierra alive. That leaves us with the question of just how Mr. Peters intends to assassinate Salva—*if* he intends to assassinate Salva. The bouts are scheduled to be staged in Tamara Castle, and that's pretty tight quarters for an assassin who intends to walk away from the mess. I'm sure the President will want our clear thoughts and recommendations on this matter. We may want to discuss it a bit further before you make a formal presentation of what we know."

Somewhat confused, Harry considered Shue's questionable argument, turning it over in his mind and probing what he considered to be its myriad soft spots. He glanced up and found Shue looking at him, his eyebrows arched slightly, expectantly. And Harry understood. He was, he thought, about to become a party to the manipulation of the

CIA Director, and he suppressed a smile as he shifted in his chair.

"Peters may not be the actual assassin," Harry said. "He could easily be the point man for somebody else. It's possible that Peters' responsibility is simply to maneuver Finway into position for a frame while a second man does the actual killing. Also, we have to bear in mind that Peters, as far as *he* was concerned, was lying to Finway. We can't know for certain that Tamara Castle is really the intended killing ground, or even that the actual assassin will be part of the tour group." He paused, glanced at Shue, and caught the almost imperceptible nod of approval. "It would certainly be interesting to find out who hired Peters."

"That's it," Whistle said, slapping his hands against air where armrests would normally be and springing out of his chair. "The President has to be told. This thing is just too dangerous. I'm going to advise that State inform Salva of this Rick Peters business. We can let State and the Sierrans take it from there."

Harry watched with intense interest and growing tension as Harley Shue continued to tap his fingers on the top of the steel desk. The Director of Operations waited until the CIA Director was halfway out the door before uttering the words that Harry had been certain were inevitable.

"I still think you might want to give this some further thought before you act, sir," Shue said evenly, not even looking at the departing Director.

"Why is that, Harley?" Whistle asked impatiently.

The Director of Operations slowly rose from his chair, then leaned heavily on his desk with both hands. It was a masterful performance, Harry thought. The slight man's bowed head and halting delivery gave the impression that he was only now sorting out his thoughts. Harry knew that was most certainly not the case.

"I think Beeler has a good point, and it has to be considered," Harley Shue said quietly. "Beeler suggested to us the possibility that Peters actually knows nothing whatsoever about the talks between Salva and State. To borrow Beeler's metaphor, not only was Peters ignorant of the 'bell' he banged, but he still hasn't heard the sound."

Shue paused for a few seconds while he rubbed the

bridge of his nose. "However," he continued at last, "we cannot be sure that such is the case. That's why, in my opinion, we must be very careful how we proceed from this point. What concerns me is the distinct possibility that Peters did know exactly what he was talking about. There could be a leak at State."

Whistle fumbled for the edge of the door, gripped it. "At *State*? My God, man, you're talking about the Secretary himself and a few top aides."

"Pardon me, sir," Shue said evenly, "but I must point out that we know no more about what goes on in the top echelons of State than they know about what goes on here. I think we have to consider the possibility that someone at State is working against this country's interests; we could be talking about a Soviet agent who's managed to penetrate our top policy-making councils. But we don't know. I'm sure you'll agree that it's premature to offer these kinds of mere suppositions to the President. We need more information."

Shue paused, obviously inviting a reply. The ashen-faced CIA Director simply stared at the smaller man, and Shue continued. "Besides, informing Salva would only postpone the inevitable. Whoever's after Salva now will go after him again, at a different time and in a different place. We know about this plot; we may not be so fortunate the next time."

Harry cleared his throat. "Sir, there's also a good possibility that Salva could try to screw us."

Whistle looked at Harry, slowly blinked. "What?"

"Peters told Alexandra Finway the same thing," Vincent Scapelli said in a hollow voice. "My God, a lot of what we're saying is almost a verbatim copy of what Peters told the woman. It's almost as though he's written a script for us to follow."

Except that it would come as quite a surprise to Peters for him to find out there really were other players, Harry mused, but kept the thought to himself. "Peters knows the business," Harry said, sensing that Shue wanted him to assume the lead for a while. "The plausibility of the details—what we would think, how we might react—in his scenario is probably what made Alexandra Finway take him seriously in the first place. Be that as it may, Salva will almost certainly try to use the information we give him against us if he decides not to come over after all. Above all else, Salva's a pragmatic man. At the very least, this information will give him a better bargaining position to get whatever he's asking from us. If we stop Peters here, we tip our hand and the organization that hired him just finds someone else; if we leave it up to San Sierra's DMI to snatch them, Peters can be counted on to try and bargain his way out with the information he has on the dragons. Either way, sir, Salva will have us by the short hairs."

"State should have to bear some of the responsibility for deciding how to proceed," Whistle said petulantly as he closed the door and walked slowly back to his chair. "And the President, of course."

"Excuse me, sir," Shue said quietly. "I'm afraid the President might well say it is *our* responsibility to at least make a strong recommendation for a course of action. In that vein, there's something else Peters told Alexandra Finway that you might think especially prescient: he told her that the CIA was tasking them in this manner, secretly, in order to prove to the President and Congress that the agency needs an even stronger covert-operations capability than is currently authorized. Frankly, I like his reasoning. Handling this matter ourselves is not only the best way to stop the assassination, sir, but it is also an opportunity for us to hoist our own colors. Without knowing it, Peters may have afforded you a rare opportunity to lay the necessary groundwork for rebuilding the CIA in the way I know you want it done."

Harry glanced quickly at Vincent Scapelli. The man looked ill. His eyes were dull, and the flesh around his mouth had a greenish pallor.

"What do you suggest we do, Harley?" Whistle asked carefully, staring at the floor.

Harley Shue's response was immediate and forceful. "I recommend that we have Vincent give Alexandra Finway the second confirmation she requires. She'll be led to understand that everything is exactly as Peters said it was. We'll send Beeler along to keep an eye on things."

Scapelli looked even more stricken. "Can't we tell her?"

Shue hummed softly, a sign of extreme disapproval. "Vincent, we have no way of vetting the present level of her skills. If Peters even begins to suspect her of playing a double role, he'll kill her immediately. It's safer for her if she doesn't know."

"And Alexandra Finway becomes our cat's paw," Scapelli said in a cracked voice.

"She's willing to go if we confirm the task, Vincent," Shue said in a commanding voice as he looked directly at Scapelli. "She's a patriot who, as in the past, is willing to perform a valuable service for her country at considerable personal risk. We'll simply be giving her that opportunity, in a different manner than she thinks. It's the only way to root out the conspiracy and destroy it." Shue paused, then abruptly turned to look at Geoffrey Whistle. "Sir? The decision is yours."

The CIA Director's response was to rise and walk quickly from the room. It meant, Harry thought, that Whistle had never been at the meeting. Harley Shue had pulled it off: he'd been given tacit approval to mount an illegal covert operation that could mean the rebirth of a virtually autonomous, all-powerful Central Intelligence Agency—or its final disintegration.

It could also bring on war with Russia, Harry thought, although he was not sure Geoffrey Whistle had seen that permutation. Harley Shue certainly had.

"I take exception, Harley," Vincent Scapelli said forcefully.

Shue abruptly sat down. "Yes, Vincent; it's noted. Give Mrs. Finway her second confirmation. Naturally, she's not to mention anything about your meeting to Peters. Put a sharp point on that."

"Yes, sir." Vincent Scapelli replied in the firm, even tone of a professional who would obey an order from his superior. However, his gait was unsteady as he rose from his chair and walked slowly out of the office.

Harley Shue waited until the door had closed behind the other man, then reached into a drawer and took out a large, black cigar that Harry thought looked suspiciously Cuban. Shue cut off the end with a pocket knife, lit it. It was a gesture of relaxed informality that Harry had never before seen the man display.

"This spy business can be interesting, eh, Beeler? It's not all satellite photographs and computer readouts."

"Not much room for error on this one, sir," the real Harry Beeler said. "If this operation doesn't shake out right, it could conceivably mean war."

If the Director of Operations recognized a caution, a warning from a subordinate, in Harry's voice, he gave no indication of it.

"Find out what's going on, Beeler. Find out who's behind Peters if you can, and stop him. Protect Alexandra Finway if you're able, but that's not your primary task. Understand?"

Harry nodded. "What about documents?"

"We don't have the time to get you quality goods, so I guess we'll have to see if we can't substitute you for somebody already booked on the tour. We'll put our best men on the documents, but you know they're not going to hold up if there's any kind of secondary check. Bear that in mind. Sorry we don't have time to do better by you."

"It can't be helped, sir," Harry said he as headed toward the door.

"Beeler?"

Harry paused at the door, turned. "Sir?"

"What part do you have in mind?"

"Well, sir, since it's a tourist group, I thought Asshole might be appropriate."

Shue considered Harry's reply for a few seconds, then nodded approvingly. "Asshole seems right." He started to wave his cigar in dismissal, then added, "You've been looking a little peaked lately, Beeler, but I have to send you on this one. You're the best man I've got. I'll hate to lose you, but you've got your Administration post after this one. So don't fuck up."

POMONA, NEW YORK

Wednesday, January 16; 9:45 A.M.

Alexandra

Alexandra started when she heard the front doorbell ring. She set aside her reading glasses and took off her shoes. Staying clear of the windows, she glided silently in her stocking feet through the kitchen to the front of the house. At the entrance she stood against the doorframe, gripped the molding and stretched her body across the door to slide open the peephole and look through it. She was startled to see John standing outside. Her husband was holding a single red rose and a large stuffed bear, tokens of love that to Alexandra suddenly appeared as threatening as sticks of dynamite.

Alexandra frowned and breathed deeply in an effort to compose herself. She had to wait until she stopped trembling, she thought, then realized that she could wait all morning without decreasing the turmoil that John's presence caused her. She set her mouth in a firm line, straightened her shoulders, and opened the door.

"Good morning, Mrs. Finway," John said quietly.

"Good morning, John." She sounded too cold and mechanical, Alexandra thought, but staying at a distance was the only way she could be sure of keeping herself under control.

John's gray eyes seemed unusually large and liquid, clearly mirroring his feelings; Alexandra watched with growing discomfort as rippling shadows of hurt, regret, and supplication passed in rapid succession across their moist surface.

"May I come in, Alexandra?"

"Of course you may come in," Alexandra said, trying earnestly but in vain to put some warmth into her tone.

It was as if, having locked her emotional thermostat at the level necessary for blocking out her personal turmoil and carrying out the Sierran task she had accepted, she could not quickly change it back, even for John, without risking ruinous breakage. It had always been that way with her. No matter what happened now with John, she was committed to a task that could affect a great many issues. She moved aside. "This is your home."

John stepped into the house and closed the door behind him. Alexandra felt her heart begin to hammer inside her chest as John looked down at the floor, sighed deeply, then glanced up into her eyes. Alexandra's response was to stiffen the muscles in her face even more.

"These are for you," John said uneasily, offering the rose and stuffed bear.

Alexandra started to reach for the items, then reacted with a stab of alarm when she realized that she was still holding a pamphlet on Tamara Castle in her hand. She deliberately set the pamphlet face down on a nearby table, then took John's gifts and placed them on top of it. "Thank you," she said evenly.

John shoved his hands into the pockets of his overcoat and hunched his shoulders. He sighed again, then raised his eyes and stared at a section of wall just above Alexandra's head. "How are the kids?"

"You know; you talk to them regularly."

"Yes. We talk, but we don't talk. I think you understand what I mean. The kids and I don't communicate very well any longer."

"Kara and Kristen are very sophisticated for their age, John. They put up a good front, but they're unhappy. What can I say? Naturally, they miss you. They think it's banal that we're apart; they say everyone does that when they have problems. Michael doesn't really understand yet. He thinks you and I are playing some kind of game."

Alexandra forced herself to remain still as John's eyes searched her face.

"Are you all right, Alexandra?"

"Yes."

"You look very strange."

"How do you expect me to look, John?"

John continued to study his wife's face for long moments, then finally looked away. "Thank you for saying this is still my home, but the fact is that I forfeited my home when I walked out of it the way I did. I forfeited a lot of things. About the only thing I can say is that I was an idiot who didn't know what else to do about what I was feeling. I won't ask you to forgive me now; I know it's going to take a long time for the hurt I've caused to heal. What I am asking for is permission to come back and try to make it up to you."

"I never asked you to leave in the first place, and you don't need my permission to come back. What about your girl friend?"

"She was never my 'girl friend,' Alexandra."

"No? Is 'mistress' a better word?"

She shouldn't have said that, Alexandra thought. Under the circumstances, the words were too hard. But they had come of their own accord out of an angry core within the cold place that was her heart. She was almost certain that she would not have accepted the Sierran task if it had not been for John's betrayal, and her reaction was ambivalent. Now she wanted to go to San Sierra, wanted to play the great game of life and death again, and she profoundly mistrusted the drive even as it hammered at her. And she would have to spend the week with a man who had always had a sexual hold, as strong as it was unexplained in her mind, over her.

She was, Alexandra thought, enraged at John for his role in nudging her over a soft, ambiguous edge of frustration and desire into waters that she knew from experience were dark and bottomless. It was the very sea he had once unknowingly helped her escape from when she had been drowning.

"Selma was my problem—a wound I couldn't find a way to close," John replied after a long pause. "She's not a problem, or wound, any longer, and I'm not confused anymore. Something happened to my head almost the same day that I walked out of here. I found I didn't want her anymore; I wanted you. All I felt about that relationship was shame. The pull of my love for you and the kids and everything that we've built together was just so strong that it finally wiped out everything else. I always knew it would, but I had to make the move I did before things fell into place.

"I wanted to turn around and come back right then, sweetheart, but I didn't. The reason I didn't was because I knew that I'd torn things between us; what I'd done was shattering. Things had been broken inside me, just as I'd broken things inside you. I'd left for a reason, and I wanted to make certain that the problem was absolutely resolved before I asked to come back. I saw a great deal of Selma, Alexandra. I didn't want to, but I did. I saw her because I wanted to make sure that I'd never be haunted by her again. Three days ago I told her it was over for good. I've waited these three days just to make sure I knew it was over. It is. I want your permission to come home, Alexandra. I want the chance to find my way back into your heart. Please forgive a fool. I love you so very, very much."

And I love you, John, but you can't come home now. I'm not home myself: I'm far away in a place you don't and can't know of. You don't know the woman you're talking to. I must stay this person a little longer, my darling. Just a few more days, and then we can both come home again.

"Alexandra?"

"Would you like to take off your coat and have a cup of coffee?"

Alexandra struggled to keep her gaze steady as John stared at her.

"That's all, huh?" John said at last.

Don't give up, darling. Please don't give up. There is something I must do and it makes me act this way. After next week you'll find me again, be able to touch me.

"I'm not sure what you expect me to say, John." She'd tried to make her voice sound reasonable, even gentle, but she knew she still sounded cold. "When you told me about that woman and then left, it was a bit of a shock to me. I guess it's going to take me some time to recover."

Only a few days, sweetheart. Give them to me.

"I can understand that," John said tightly. "Let me stay and try to help you forgive me."

"There's nothing to be forgiven. You told me you had a problem. You finally shared it with me, and then you went about trying to solve it. I don't know what else I could have asked of you. The point is that I need some time now to get my bearings."

"You don't love me?"

Leave, John! Become angry and walk out. Come back a week from Sunday and ask me then if I love you! Ask me then if I forgive you!

"I didn't say that."

"What are you saying?"

"I told you: I need more time to think. You tell me you've solved the problem of the woman, but I remember you saying that you'd broken it off before and still couldn't forget her."

"This time it's dif—"

"I've already made plans to go away, John. I think we should wait until I come back before we talk about where our relationship is going."

Alexandra's pulse quickened and she stiffened as John pointed to the pamphlet she had placed on the table.

"You're going to San Sierra?"

"Yes," Alexandra replied flatly. She would have preferred that John not know where she was going, but she realized that he would have found out anyway, from her parents. Her parents would be staying with the children, and she had already told them where she was going, if not why, and given them her itinerary. Her mother and father were in their seventies; in case of emergency, she wanted to be certain they could reach her.

"Up the revolution," John said wryly. "When are you leaving?"

"Saturday. I'll be back a week from Sunday. We can talk then." She saw anger flare in her husband's eyes, and for a moment she thought he was going to leave. He didn't. The anger abruptly melted to a moist film of disappointment, and Alexandra had to avert her own eyes. "I'm sorry, John," she continued softly. "I need the space; you'll give it to me if you really want things to be the way they were. I don't want to see you until I come back. If you want to move back in, you're welcome, but then I'll move out."

Forgive me, darling! There are so many parts I must play! It's the only way I can do this thing!

John shrugged resignedly. "You do what you want, Alexandra. Who's staying with the children?"

"My parents are flying in."

"Then they know I left?"

"Of course. I didn't know I was expected to keep it a secret."

Once again, John stared into her eyes for a long time. "I don't want you to go, Alexandra," he said at last in a strained voice. "You look very strange. I'm worried about you. Let's both spend the week together here. We'll talk everything out."

Oh God, John, please just go away!

"No, John," she said firmly. "I've told you I need time and space. Please give them to me."

John turned, but paused with his hand on the doorknob. "Let me stay with the kids while you're away," he said quietly. "I'll take the week off from work. I owe it to them; I have a lot to make up for."

"All right. I'll call my folks."

"May I drive you to the airport?"

"No," Alexandra said curtly, her tone and words cutting her heart. "And I don't want you to pick me up. I'll see you here in the house a week from Sunday, but not before. That's very important to me. By then I'll have my feelings in order. If you're going to stay with the kids, I'd appreciate it if you'd pick them up from school on Friday and keep them with you overnight. I'll be out of the house early Saturday morning."

John bowed his head in a brief nod of resignation. "I'll pick up the kids on Friday." He opened the door, then stiffened. "I've been a terrible fool, Alexandra," he continued quietly. "I've had a fever, but now it's gone. I love you very much. I think the life we create together will always be better than anything we can create apart. I hope you'll give that a lot of thought while you're away."

Alexandra did not reply. Finally John left, closing the door behind him.

Alexandra leaned against the door and tried desperately to get in touch with some part of herself which she knew and liked. She could not. John had been so vulnerable, she thought, and yet there had been nothing she could do or say to ease his pain. She wanted to cry to release her tension, but she could not do that either. It worried her. She remembered well how, in the past, tension and pressure and deceit and danger had twisted her into another person, almost destroying her.

She quickly reminded herself of the fact that the previous process of personality disintegration had taken years. In less than two weeks this last task would be finished and she would be free to be herself again, a person she could live with and respect, the woman her husband's love had once rescued and nurtured.

She was dealing now with days, she thought, not years. It was a very short time, and she could not understand why she should be experiencing so much anxiety.

John would be waiting for her when she got back, she thought. Hoped. He had to be.

NEW YORK CITY;
JOHN F. KENNEDY AIRPORT

Saturday, January 19; 10:45 A.M.

Peters

Rick Peters allowed himself the luxury of a broad grin of triumph when he saw Alexandra hurrying toward him across the vast rotunda beneath the arcing, wing-shaped ceiling of the Trans World Airlines terminal.

The dangerous phase was yet to come, he thought, and it would require very precise timing and not a little luck. However, he felt that he now had considerable control over events. As far as he was concerned, the most difficult phase was over.

She was dressed perfectly, Peters thought. His erect penis throbbed painfully, and he knew he was close to having an orgasm.

"You made it," Peters said as Alexandra ran up the steps at the rear of the rotunda and embraced him.

Alexandra kissed him hard on the mouth, then moved back slightly. "Did you doubt that I'd be here?" she asked quietly. "You knew I'd accepted the task."

"Your eyes, sweetheart," Peters said in a low voice, smiling for the benefit of anyone who might be watching them. "The rest of your act is great, but your eyes are going to give us away. They're like ice. Loosen up; warm up. We've got a long way to go."

Alexandra nodded, smiled. "You're right." The hard glint in her eyes softened somewhat. "Better?"

"Much better. Your working outfit brings back warm memories. I like it. Who knows? You might even start feeling good about this assignment."

Alexandra put her hand on the back of Peters' neck,

brought her head forward and nuzzled his ear. "Rick," she whispered tensely, "you can't imagine how difficult this is for me. I'll do the best job I know how. I'm prepared to do whatever's necessary to get the job done and get us safely out of San Sierra, but you have to help me."

Peters placed his right hand in the small of Alexandra's back, bracing her, then thrust his hips forward so that she could feel his desire.

"Oh, I'll help you, sweetheart. You keep blowing on that ear and we'll have to look for a phone booth."

"*No*, Rick!" Alexandra whispered harshly. She did not make any abrupt move away from him, but instead dug a tapered fingernail into the soft flesh behind his right ear and held it there. "You'll help me by remembering that we're professionals working together on a tough job. That's all there is between us. We'll never see each other again when this week is over. Help me by respecting the fact that I'm a wife and mother. Act, Rick, but don't feel anything toward me, and know that I'm not feeling anything for you. That's how you can help me."

Peters pushed Alexandra away gently but firmly. The pain behind his ear ceased. Alexandra was half a head taller than he was, and he stared hard up into the woman's dark brown eyes. He wanted to reach out and touch the star-shaped scars beneath those eyes, but he was not sure that she would tolerate such a gesture, even under the scrutiny of the dozens of pairs of eyes that were on her at any given moment, appreciating her sensuality and beauty.

"You may need more than that from me before we're done," he said in the same low voice. "We have seven days and some death ahead of us. It could be a very long time."

Alexandra shook her head. Her smile was still fastened firmly in place, but her eyes had again grown distant and cold. "No, Rick; it could never be that long."

"I don't believe you don't feel anything for me. You're wired."

"Believe it, Rick. Any electricity you feel is coming from you."

Peters shrugged. "What excuse did you give John for taking off for a week?"

"What difference does it make? Let's talk business. How long have you been here?"

"About an hour," he lied. "I wanted to get an early look at some of our fellow passengers."

Alexandra gave a brief nod of her head. "I meant to be here earlier. I got tied up in traffic after the bridge."

"If you'd been here earlier we'd have both wasted our time. Too many people waiting for too many different flights. Also, this place is too open. Whoever took this contract has to be a top pro; he knows as much as we do, and he's not going to give himself away in some airline terminal."

"What's that for?" Alexandra asked, nodding in the direction of the large portable radio Peters carried in his left hand. Once again she pressed close to him and whispered in his ear. "Knowing you, Rick, it's probably a bomb."

Peters laughed easily, noting Alexandra's effort to suppress her hostility. They would, after all, be spending a lot of time together. At the same time he was sure he recognized ambiguity in her voice, and that pleased him. "You got it," he said softly, smiling at the same time as his gaze darted around them to make certain there was no one within earshot. "If we don't make the target by Friday night, we'll just arrange to blow up everyone." He paused, continued seriously, "A little extra precaution. Any Commie hotel, if it's not bugged, probably has walls made of toilet paper. We'll play this whenever we have to talk business."

"Always the pro," Alexandra said appreciatively. "God, do I ever feel rusty."

"You'd never know to watch you." Peters glanced at the large display board below them in the main rotunda, to their right. "We're boarding," he continued, taking Alexandra's arm and turning toward the secured corridor leading to the boarding area.

Peters felt Alexandra stiffen. "Rick," she said tightly, "we've got enough trouble without there being any unnecessary tension between us. You'll remember what I said?"

Peters smiled reassuringly. "I'll remember, Mrs. Finway. You can't blame a guy for a little wishful thinking. Come on, let's go to work."

John

The pamphlet had told him all he needed to know.

Obtaining a visa had not been a problem. John had the necessary contacts and more I.O.U.s from various leftist organizations than he could use in a lifetime. He had gone to the Sierran Mission to the United Nations in New York City armed with letters of reference, but they hadn't been needed; the Sierrans at the Mission were familiar with his reputation and had been happy to accommodate him. The slip of paper that would have taken an average American a minimum of four weeks to obtain had been in John's possession within a half hour. After a call to his sister in the Bronx, John's surprise for Alexandra had been made ready.

It had been so easy, he thought. Surprise. All he had done was rip the bottom out of his life.

That wasn't true, he thought, rage elevating his blood pressure to a point where tiny explosions of light formed rainbow amoebas that quivered, vanished, and then reappeared in his field of vision. It was Alexandra who had done the tearing: all during the time she had affected hurt at his relationship with another woman, she had to have been thinking of her own deceit with a man John had come to loathe after meeting him fifteen years before. Rick Peters was a man he hated.

In retrospect, John realized that he'd viewed his suffering over a woman as being vaguely noble, his guilt and pain a kind of moral alchemist's gold glinting in the dark murk of the lie he had lived for a year. He had indeed been a fool, he thought, but not in the sense that he had described himself to Alexandra. His ego had made him appear as a kind of tortured prince in his own eyes, while in fact he had been court jester and cuckold all along. For how long? he wondered. Months? Years? It occurred to him that his wife and Peters might never have ceased being lovers.

It was some time before he realized that the roses he'd bought had slipped from his fingers and lay strewn across the floor behind the large Seiko display case where he was standing. As he bent over to pick up the flowers, his hat, which he always wore in public when he wanted to protect his privacy and not be recognized, slipped off his head.

He quickly put it back on, then pressed his wrap-around sunglasses snug to the bridge of his nose. John hesitated, straightened up. He absently gathered the flowers into a pile with the toe of his shoe, then slowly and deliberately crushed them under his feet as he went back to staring through the plate glass of the display case.

Twenty-five yards away, framed in John's vision by cameras, watches, and calculators, Alexandra stood at the top of the rotunda steps, pressing against Rick Peters' body as she kissed his mouth. She was dressed in tight brown leather slacks and jacket, and her hair was drawn back from her face, held in place by a huge ivory barrette. John experienced a piercing sense of déjà vu. He had seen the hair style, the barrette, before, but not in fifteen years, not since the days just before they were married.

Alexandra was wearing the hair style and leather outfit to please Peters, John thought, feeling sick with humiliation, rage, and desire. Alexandra had never looked more beautiful and desirable to him than at that moment, cradled easily in the arms of another man.

John badly wanted to hit Peters. He started to step out from behind the display case, but then stopped and ducked back. He couldn't do that, John thought. He was simply too well known; any emotional outburst or cathartic violence he indulged in here would be paid for by Michael and his daughters in the soiled currency of public humiliation. The story of John Finway confronting his adulterous wife and her lover at JFK Airport would be reported in every newspaper in the country.

He dropped his boarding pass on top of the crushed flowers, turned, and started to walk toward the nearest exit. Then the rage and need to hit returned, mixing volatilely with his humiliation and desire to paralyze his muscles. Vaguely, as if in an ether dream, he heard a woman's amplified, metallic voice announce that the flight to San Sierra was boarding. When John turned back, he saw that Alexandra and Peters were gone.

The prospect of returning home and waiting while Peters and Alexandra were off for a week in San Sierra walking arm-in-arm, laughing, making love, burned the lining of his mind with a corrosive, acid heat.

He had been a fighter all his life, John thought, and a

winner for most of it. What Alexandra had done and was doing was despicable, but what he had done was also despicable. His lust for and relationship with another man's wife had stripped him of his moral armor, and he had no right to judge Alexandra's sin as greater than his own. In the clouded land where he and Alexandra now lived, there were no innocent bystanders. Self-pity and outrage were wasted emotions; winning his wife back for himself and their children was all that mattered. He wanted to fight now, but he was immobilized by indecision, by not knowing where to fight, or how. However, no matter what he was going to do, he knew he could not wait a week to do it. If he did, he would not be the same man when Alexandra and Peters returned. Being forced to wait would gut him, and he could not let that happen.

He desperately needed time to think, but he knew he simply did not have it. Once the plane was gone, there would be nothing to do but wait and burn while his soul evaporated within him.

Still without knowing exactly what he was going to do, John spun around, picked up his boarding pass from the smear of ruined flowers and ran up the marble steps toward the security checkpoint at the neck of the corridor leading to the boarding gates. He carried no hand luggage, and in a few seconds he was through the metal detector and sprinting down the corridor.

A few moments later he became aware of someone running beside him.

Harry

"Jesus H. Christ," Harry murmured softly to himself when he saw the man's hat fall off to reveal a head of iron-gray hair marked by a distinctive silver streak. "What the hell is he doing here?"

Harry had arrived at the airport two hours ahead of time on the off chance that Peters, if he had an accomplice, might arrive early to meet with him. Harry had used his Asshole character to cover his early arrival, first complaining loudly to airport officials about misinformation concerning the time of departure for his flight, and then attempting to regale anyone who would listen with pictures of the snakes, turtles, and various other reptiles he claimed to keep in his apartment.

Despite Harry's frenetic activity, no one carrying a dun-colored boarding pass from the Sierra tour desk had escaped his attention. Manuel Salva was an immensely important and difficult target, and Harry knew there were dozens of ways in which a man or woman, under pressure, nervous and unaware of surveillance, could blow a cover. However, as members of the San Sierra tour group filed through the terminal, Harry had noticed nothing unusual to arouse his suspicion. With half an hour left before the scheduled time of departure, he had assumed a passive role, hiding behind a newspaper near one of the entrances to the terminal, watching and waiting.

Peters had arrived barely five minutes before Alexandra Finway, and Harry had been about to precede them to the boarding gate when a solidly built man with a dun-colored boarding pass, wearing a gray hat and wrap-around sunglasses and carrying a bunch of roses, walked past him. The man glanced around the rotunda, then stopped dead in his tracks.

Harry had frowned as he'd watched the man abruptly turn to his left and dart behind a large display case. Harry knew that even the most inept assassin would never behave in such an obviously suspicious manner, yet he had been intrigued because he was certain that the man's reaction had been triggered by the sight of Rick Peters and Alexandra Finway performing their own bit of business at the top of the steps at the far end of the rotunda.

Then the man's hat had slipped off as he'd reached down to retrieve the flowers that had fallen from his hand, and Harry had immediately begun trying to plot the complex new permutations in the situation brought on by the unexpected appearance of Alexandra Finway's husband in the TWA terminal. It was obvious to Harry that Peters and the woman were unaware of Finway's presence, and Finway appeared totally oblivious to everything but the fact that his wife was about to fly off to San Sierra for a week with another man.

"Surprise, surprise," Harry whispered wryly, and he grunted with annoyance.

The CIA agent glanced up at the display board overhead as the light beside his flight number began to flash, signaling boarding. He stayed where he was, watching the lawyer, then smiled grimly and nodded with approval as Finway turned and headed for an exit.

Harry's smile disappeared when the man stopped in the middle of the floor, apparently undecided as to what to do. "Go *home*, Finway," Harry mumbled, peering intently over the top of his newspaper. "Do us all a favor and go home."

He saw Peters and Alexandra Finway turn and disappear from sight as they moved with other members of the tour group toward the boarding gate. But John Finway remained motionless in the center of the rotunda, seemingly oblivious to the fact that the others had moved away to board a plane that was only minutes from takeoff.

Harry was painfully aware of the passing time. Yet, without knowing exactly why, he stayed where he was. His superior had made it very clear to him that protecting Alexandra Finway was low on his list of priorities. John Finway was not on the list at all, and Harry could not help but speculate wryly on what Administration post the Director of Operations would bestow on him if he reported back that, sorry, he wouldn't be able to prevent Manuel Salva's assassination after all because he'd missed the plane to San Sierra. Paper Clip Inspector. Horseshit Analyst in the Bio-Warfare labs.

Still Harry waited, his gaze fixed on the tense, still figure a few yards away from him.

Harry knew that a man like Rick Peters could kill quickly and silently, in a number of ways. He thought it possible that Peters, if he spotted Alexandra Finway's husband before she did, would kill Finway somewhere in the terminal, given even a slight opportunity such as Finway deciding to visit a men's room. The appearance of Finway in the tour group would, Harry thought, almost certainly unravel Peters' plans, whatever they might be. Having read Peters' dossier, it was even conceivable to Harry that an enraged Peters wouldn't even bother with subtleties; seeing his operation blown, he might perfunctorily kill Finway out of spite and run.

Harry cursed under his breath as Finway suddenly turned back, picked up his boarding pass, and ran toward the security checkpoint. Deciding that he had nothing to lose and wanting to prevent a needless killing if he could, Harry discarded a large chunk of his Asshole character along with his reptile pictures and ran after the lawyer.

Harry went through the metal-detecting device a few seconds behind Finway, then easily caught up with and trotted beside him. By then, Harry had slipped into the role of Giggler.

"I don't know why I can never get to airports on time," Harry panted, feigning breathlessness. "Running after things is the story of my life."

John Finway glanced at him blankly, then looked away without speaking. As they emerged from the tunnel into a large, open space by the boarding gate, Harry could see that they had run for nothing; the bulk of the group was bunched together, waiting to be funneled into the plane past a single official who was inspecting boarding passes. The black and silver crown of Alexandra Finway's hair could be seen near the narrow entrance to the boarding ramp on the far side of the crowd of thirty-five or forty people who were pressing forward in an attempt to get their choice of the charter flight's unreserved seats.

Finway abruptly stopped running and turned his back to the group. Harry ran on a few more paces, then stopped, turned, and casually walked back toward the other man.

"Hurry up and wait, hurry up and wait," Harry said, shaking his tow head in disgust. "That's the story of my life."

Harry noted without surprise that Finway now seemed glad to have him nearby. Harry subtly drew himself up to his full height and folded his arms across his chest as the other man moved a few steps closer, using Harry's body to shield himself from the sightlines of the other passengers.

Harry stood still as the other man furtively glanced over Harry's shoulder, then pulled his hat low over his forehead and bowed his head slightly.

"Uh, you fly a lot?" Finway asked tentatively.

"Every chance I get," Harry replied, pitching his voice considerably higher than normal. "I like to travel." His laugh was high-pitched, almost a giggle, as he settled firmly into his slightly altered psychic suit. "I'm a travel agent, so I get to take a lot of busman's holidays. You meet a lot

of nice, interesting people when you travel." Harry laughed
again as he stuck out his hand. "My name's David Swarzwalder."

"John Finway," the lawyer replied, absently shaking
Harry's hand and glancing furtively over Harry's shoulder
as the last of the passengers boarded. His smile was decidedly forced. "Enjoy your trip, David."

Harry moved aside as Finway, obviously anxious to
avoid a fey, clinging giggler, stepped around him and
walked quickly toward the brown-jacketed official who was
waiting impatiently at the head of the boarding ramp. By
now Harry had made a firm decision to try to attach himself to the radical lawyer for two reasons, only one of
which he knew would be looked upon with favor by his
superior.

His first reason was practical: Harry reasoned that, regardless of what happened between Finway, his wife, and
Peters, a relationship with Finway could afford him closer
physical proximity to the two principal targets of his surveillance. He was well aware that there were many variations of the confrontation which was certain to come that
might not suit his purposes, but he felt that the potential
edge he might gain was worth the risk. But he had to move
at once; while attaching himself to John Finway was an
option that could always be discarded later, it had to be
pursued immediately.

He knew that Harley Shue would certainly consider his
second motive irrelevant and potentially distracting, and
thus an unnecessary risk. Harry didn't care. No stranger to
violent death and an expert killer himself, Harry simply
did not like to see innocent people get caught in the line
of fire, and there was no doubt in his mind that Peters
would feel it necessary to kill Finway once the boyish,
blond-haired assassin became aware of the lawyer's presence. At the least, Harry intended to make that task as
difficult as possible. Consequently, Harry was close behind
John Finway as the other man walked through the cater-
pillar tunnel to the plane's entrance.

Harry waited as Finway paused at the door and looked
cautiously around the corner into the plane's interior.
Apparently satisfied with what he saw, the lawyer moved
quickly to one of the few remaining seats on the plane, just

behind one of the faded purple curtains now drawn back and bunched, normally used to separate sections of the Boeing 727, Harry slipped into the seat beside him.

"We made it, John," Harry said, flashing a broad, supercilious grin. He knew that he was going to have to modify the Giggler if he hoped to stay close to Finway, but it was difficult for him to keep shifting and remolding his characters in such short spurts of time.

The other man looked at Harry as though he were seeing him for the first time. As recognition came, so did displeasure. "Excuse me?"

Harry swallowed, took his voice down a tone. "Flying's exciting, huh? I always say the flight's half the fun of any trip."

"Yeah." Finway abruptly removed his sunglasses. He took a magazine from a cloth pouch beside his seat, opened it, and shifted his body so that the magazine was between himself and Harry.

Harry remained silent throughout taxi and lift-off. He waited fifteen minutes after the plane was airborne and cruising, then removed his seatbelt, rose, and walked toward the front of the plane.

He noted Peters' and Alexandra Finway's presence in seats near the front of the plane, just in front of the curtain used on regular flights to partition off the First Class section. At the moment the man and woman were both involved in an animated conversation with the passengers around them. Harry had a brief conversation with the Sierran representative on board, then returned to the rear section of the plane.

"Excuse me, John," Harry said in a low, confidential tone as he settled back into his seat. "May I talk to you for a minute?"

For a few moments Harry was not sure Finway had heard him. Then the magazine came down. At first the other man's eyes appeared glazed and unseeing; they took on a hostile glint as they came into focus on Harry's face.

"Are you talking to me, Mr.—?"

Harry cleared his throat. "David, John; David Swarzwalder. Look, this is kind of embarrassing and I hope you won't take offense. I noticed you're traveling alone. I'm traveling alone myself, and I thought we might share a room. I checked, and the woman from Sierratour will make the arrangements if you say it's okay."

"No," the lawyer said tersely, putting his sunglasses back on and raising the magazine. "Sorry. I prefer to be by myself."

Harry waited fifteen seconds, then spoke again. "John," he said, lowering his voice still further and keeping his tone just short of a plea. "I don't mean to press you, but we could both save a nice piece of change if we shared a room. I was told they'd refund the premiums we're paying for single rooms. To tell you the truth, I can really use the money. I don't make a big salary to begin with, and I couldn't get my usual agency discount for a trip to San Sierra."

Finway's reply was sharp and cold, muffled by the magazine he held in front of his face. "Why don't you ask some other single?"

"I checked; you and I are the only people traveling alone. Please, John. I promise I won't get in your way. I can really use the sixty-three bucks. I'd like to use some of it to buy presents for my sister's kids."

Harry waited tensely. Finally the lawyer sighed with exasperation and lowered his magazine. His mouth was set in a firm, tight line. "Look, Swarzwalder," Finway said, his voice humming with annoyance, "I don't want to be rude, but I've got things on my mind and things I have to do. It's nothing personal against you, but I do have to be alone. Sorry."

"Okay, John," Harry said, offering a hand which the other man reluctantly took. "I understand. I guess it was stupid of me to ask. No hard feelings."

Finway's response was to pull his hat brim back down low on his forehead, then turn away and lay his head on the headrest. In a few minutes he appeared to be asleep.

Harry took a deep breath, slowly exhaled it. He'd thrown the only ball in his bag, a floating fat one, and Finway had stuffed it down his throat. The lawyer was on his own. He put the seat back, lit a cigarette, and signaled the stewardess for a drink. It would be a double.

ANGELES BLANCA;
AQUA AZUL AIRPORT

4:10 P.M.

Alexandra

"My God, it's hot," Alexandra said, removing her coat as a Sierratour guide ushered them across the macadam toward the first of three gleaming, Russian-built buses that had pulled up alongside the airplane.

Peters nodded. "Yeah, but it beats that deep freeze we left behind."

"How do you read the people we talked to on the plane?"

Peters shrugged. "We've had verbal contact with eight people, visual contact with about twelve more. I read all the talkers as articulate, offbeat, liberal, intelligent."

"Agreed," Alexandra said. "Also, they all seemed pretty well traveled, if not well heeled. I suppose a trip to San Sierra isn't going to attract your average run-of-the-mill tourist."

"No. This could go right down to the wire on Friday night."

"Let's hope not. Look, maybe we should fall back and get on one of the other buses. We've already eyeballed the people heading for this one."

"We can do that if you want, but I think it might look strange; too conspicuous a move for too little gain. Hell, we're only going to the terminal."

"You're right." Alexandra sighed and shook her head. "Fifty-eight people is a lot to check out."

"Fifty-nine," Peters replied matter-of-factly. "I overheard a couple of the flight attendants talking about a man being added to the flight list at the last minute."

Alexandra stopped walking and pulled Peters aside to

allow others to board the bus. "Now, that's unusual. Did you get a name?"

The man shook his head. "Unfortunately, no. But it shouldn't be difficult to find out—unless it's some DMI agent who had to come home in a hurry. We'll see what we can find out at the reception tonight."

"On the other hand, anybody who could manage to get on this flight at the last minute is probably our least likely suspect."

"Still, it's a place to start," Peters said, shifting his radio to his left hand and using his right to help Alexandra up the steps into the bus.

There were seats near the front, a few rows behind the driver. Alexandra slid into a seat next to a window, leaned her head back, and stared absently at a large tackboard above the windshield festooned with hundreds of small pins emplazoned with Communist slogans. Manuel Salva gazed heroically toward the back of the bus from miniature, garishly colored posters that reminded Alexandra of the pressboard cards found in packs of bubble gum.

She was confident now that she would be all right. In fact, she was pleasantly surprised to find that she actually felt good—if not totally relaxed, at least confident. The tension of the past year had drained her more than she'd realized. It was unfortunate that she'd been forced to reject John at the last moment, but it had been unavoidable. The important thing was that John would be waiting for her at their home when she returned; everything was going to work out. She now realized that she was happy to be away, working at what she had always done best. She was certain there would be no repeat of her other problem; she would not be in the field long enough to arouse those demons.

Alexandra had not forgotten that the success of their task would almost certainly be capped by death. Their target was an assassin, a "hard player." Fair game. His life would have to be taken if the lives of others were to be saved and the interests of the United States protected. Still, Alexandra thought, Rick Peters would have to be the one to take care of that detail. Regardless of the circumstances, she did not think that she could kill, not again. And certainly not in cold blood.

The thought of a kill suddenly cast a shadow on her peace, an ominous, dark bridge to the memories of her past that chilled her. The dragon she saw there, what she had been, terrified her: the treachery and betrayal; the coldness; the lies. The terrible, enslaving bond of pain with Rick Peters.

Alexandra closed her eyes and shook her head slightly to chase the fear. This was different, she thought; the task was straightforward and of critical importance. There were no honest men to betray, only a professional killer. Reassured by that thought, she opened her eyes and felt the bulk of her misgivings leave her, melted away by the Sierran sun. She was glad she was needed, proud that she had been chosen.

A squat, broad-faced man with a ruddy complexion, dressed in an ill-fitting tan uniform, climbed up the bus stairwell, then stood in the aisle with his hands resting on the vinyl backs of the seats on either side of him. He was followed by two attractive women, a blonde and a brunette, dressed in the same type of uniform. The women stood just behind the man, smiling at the passengers over the man's shoulders.

"Welcome to San Sierra," the man said. "I am Raul." His smile was tentative, his muddy-brown eyes clearly mirroring hostility and suspicion as he nodded in the direction of the blonde, then the brunette. "I would like to introduce Constantina and Maria. We will be your guides throughout your stay in our country."

The women's smiles grew brighter as they rapidly made eye contact with all the passengers on the bus. Their manner was warm and eager, in marked contrast to Raul's.

"Why, it's Mr. Sierran Sunshine," Peters whispered.

Alexandra suppressed a smile. "DMI?"

"Who knows? Maybe he's just constipated. If the Sierrans do seed agents into these groups, you'd think they'd choose people smooth as glass. Maybe one or both of the women."

The man called Raul glanced quickly at Alexandra and Peters, obviously annoyed by their whispering. Alexandra flashed a broad, coquettish smile. Raul reddened slightly, then smiled back.

"We are very happy to have you here, and we think you

will be very impressed with all that our small, poor country has accomplished since nineteen fifty-six." Raul paused. His mouth was set in a grim, defiant line, as if he expected a challenge. When none came, he went on in a less combative tone.

"We have planned your trip so as to show you some of the many different faces of our beautiful country. After going through Immigration and Customs, we will board cruise buses and drive on to the Hotel Carazúl, which is about two hours away, near the town of Patanzas. Tonight we will have a lovely dinner, a *tipico* fish banquet, that we are sure you will enjoy.

"We will remain at the Carazúl until Tuesday morning, at which time we will go on to the Hotel Sierras Negras." Raul paused and thrust his chest out proudly. "Sierras Negras is a mountain resort which was just completed a few years ago. It is near the mountain range where my father and uncle fought with Manuel in the glorious revolution."

"Chickenshit," Peters whispered without moving his lips.

"On Wednesday, those of you who are interested may take a side excursion to the very old city of Peleoro," Raul continued. "We recommend that you all go; we think you will find it very fascinating.

"On Thursday morning we will board the buses for the last time and drive back here to Angeles Blanca, where you will stay until you leave us. Some of you may be interested in attending the boxing matches between our two countries on Friday evening. The bouts will take place on the grounds of Tamara Castle, which in itself is worth the trip even if you are not interested in boxing. If you wish to go, we will see that you receive free tickets. In San Sierra, we do not charge for admission to sporting events. We believe that sport belongs to the people, and tickets for events are given away to the workers.

"Again, we welcome you. We hope to get to know each one of you much better before the end of this journey of friendship. Are there any questions?"

There were none. There was scattered applause, and a woman in the rear of the bus shouted a revolutionary slogan. All three guides smiled appreciatively. Raul waved both hands in salute, then followed the two women off the bus.

There was a delay of a few minutes while the guides delivered the same message to the people on the other buses. Then the black-haired woman named Maria got back on the bus and they were driven slowly to the terminal building three hundred yards away.

"If we find the weapon, we find the assassin," Alexandra said quietly as she and Peters climbed off the bus and moved out from the edge of the crowd gathering at the entrance to the terminal building. "We'll recognize things a Customs agent wouldn't—assuming Customs opens the right bag in the first place."

Peters nodded. "Let's concentrate on physical contact at Carazúl, then try to do a room search at Sierras Negras. There'll probably be a lot of people going to Peleoro."

"Well, at least we can be reasonably certain that our man didn't bring a gun on board at JFK. The metal detectors would have got him." Alexandra paused, then continued tightly, "Of course there are weapons, and then there are weapons."

"I'll say," Peters said wryly, casting a quick glance at the barrette Alexandra wore in her hair. "He could have plastique, or even a disassembled one-use plastic gun. The state of the art has probably risen considerably since we worked, and the nice folks we hung around with were pretty crude to begin with."

"I don't think we should dismiss the possibility that he could be planning to pick up a conventional weapon here. We'll just have to—"

Alexandra cut her words off in midsentence as she sensed that someone had come up behind her and was standing close by. She turned, and had to slap a hand across her mouth to stifle a scream.

John

He would wait no longer.

A sour emotional brew of tension, humiliation, and blind rage had exhausted him, leaving behind dregs of bitterness and a cooler, more sustained anger. He was even more determined to win back his wife, but first the boils of resentment resting in his heart and stomach had to be lanced. It was time, he thought, for the other side to experience a little consternation and shame. He was no longer interested in violent confrontation; it would be enough for Alexandra and Peters to discover that he was with them, to realize that he knew and that he would be watching them. He would let them react and make of it what they wished. He had a week to maneuver, to make his "case" with Alexandra, and his opening shot would be the shock testimony of his presence.

He bolted from his seat as the bus on which he was riding braked to a stop. However, he had been sitting near the rear and there was nothing he could do but wait and chafe with impatience as the passengers in front of him filed off slowly.

When he finally reached the macadam he removed his coat, walked away from his group, and surveyed the passengers who had exited from the other buses. He immediately spotted his wife and Peters; they were standing off by themselves, the lower halves of their bodies blurred by a shimmering heat wave radiating from the macadam, holding hands and gazing into each other's eyes as they shared a whispered conversation.

As when he had first seen Alexandra with Rick Peters in the TWA terminal, John was almost overwhelmed with desire for his wife. Numbed by the beguiling familiarity of marriage, he had forgotten how much he loved her; but now the nerveless crust built up over years had been brutally ripped from his raw emotions, leaving him throbbing with a pain that would not cease.

He whipped off his hat and sunglasses and stalked forward, angling around to his right so that he would come up behind the man and woman. Alexandra and Peters were so absorbed in their conversation that John was able to approach and stop so close to Alexandra that he was almost touching her before she became aware of his presence. She wheeled, looked into his face, and her eyes went wide with shock. Her hand flew to her mouth and she made a small, strangled sound in her throat.

"It's one beautiful day, isn't it, folks?" John said with soft but stinging mockery. Now Peters also spun around, and John feigned surprise. "Why, if it isn't good old Rick Peters! Rick, I haven't seen you in God knows how long. How the hell are—"

Then he could no longer speak. Something stiff and blunt had been rammed into his solar plexus, just below his sternum. The terrible pressure lasted only a fraction of a second before being released, but the effect was devastating; John felt literally paralyzed, unable to breathe, speak, or move. He opened his mouth in a futile attempt to suck air into his lungs, then jammed his hands into his stomach and began to topple forward.

He felt Peters grab him under the left arm and haul him to his feet. "Don't panic," he heard Peters whisper urgently to Alexandra. "Let's get him on the bus."

With Alexandra supporting him under the right arm, John felt himself being dragged over the hot macadam toward the open maw of one of the shining, empty buses parked a few yards away. He was gasping like a landed fish now, but was still unable to coax any air into his lungs. His chest and the veins in his temples felt ready to explode. Writhing in agony, he rolled his eyes toward Alexandra. But his wife would not look at him. Her face showed the strain from the effort of dragging him, and her eyes gleamed with the kind of fear and confusion John had once seen in the eyes of the first and last animal he had ever shot, almost thirty years before; it was a look of human anguish, but nonetheless was not really human.

It was absurd, John thought, but it occurred to him that his wife and Rick Peters were going to kill him.

"This man's fainted," Peters announced in a loud voice to the people around them. "He needs to lie down out of the sun. We have medical experience; we'll take care of him. Please just give us some room and leave us alone."

John tried to resist as they dragged him to the entrance to the bus, but without air he was close to losing consciousness. Alexandra and Peters lifted him up the steps without apparent effort, dragged him down the aisle, and dumped him onto a seat in the middle section of the bus.

Peters knelt down in the narrow leg space beside the seat and began to rhythmically massage John's chest with his right hand, helping him to breathe. When John looked down, he could see that the index and middle fingers of

Peters' left hand were poised, stiff as a knife blade, inches from his stomach. John closed his eyes and focused all his attention on the prodigious task of sucking air into his lungs.

"He'll be all right," John heard Alexandra, in the doorway, call in a slightly quavering voice to the other passengers. "Just give us a few more minutes alone with him."

John heard the hinges of the doors squeak as Alexandra forced them shut manually. He opened his eyes, and a moment later Alexandra's face, bone-white and almost unrecognizable to him, moved into his slightly blurred field of vision, just behind Peters. She learned over him to loosen his tie and unbutton his shirt collar.

"You have to be absolutely still and listen, Finway," Peters said. His voice was pitched very low, but the tone was hard and unmistakably commanding. "If I think you're going to try and shout, I'm going to shove my fingers into your gut again. Can you breathe all right now?"

John nodded, and Peters stopped massaging his chest. John considered crying out, but when he glanced down again he could see that Peters' fingers were still in position to strike him. He fixed his gaze on Alexandra and tried to work up hate in his eyes, but he couldn't; he knew that his eyes reflected exactly what he felt: more pain than outrage, and a terrible confusion.

"This situation isn't what you think it is, Finway," Peters continued in the same controlled, hard voice. "It's a hell of a lot worse than you think it is. Right now you've got your wife's freedom—and mine—in your hands. If you say just one wrong word now or in the coming week—if you even *act* the wrong way—your wife and I are going to stay on this island for a very long time." He inclined his head toward Alexandra, snapped, "Tell him! Make it quick!"

Alexandra started to speak, but gagged on the words. "I . . . I can't, Rick," she choked. "I'm afraid I'm going to be sick."

"Then I'll tell him," Peters said in a clipped voice, staring hard at John. "But he gets the whole story if I tell him. Nothing left out. We haven't got time to chickenshit around. Do you still want me to do the talking?"

"Yes," Alexandra replied in a rasping whisper.

Harry

"Go get 'em, tiger," Harry mumbled to himself as John Finway swept down the aisle past him. Harry stood to let the woman next to him out and watched with faint amusement as Finway waited impatiently at the door, then rushed out into the bright Sierran sunshine.

Harry was not concerned about Finway being killed out on the macadam; Peters had no escape route, and there was nothing in the blond assassin's dossier to indicate that he was suicidal. Consequently, Harry was content to slide over on his seat and watch through the window. The proverbial shit, he thought, was about to hit Peters.

What he saw impressed him—or, rather, what he did not see. Finway had barely spoken a sentence to the man and woman before he was disabled with what Harry knew had to be a finger jab to the large nerve cluster of the solar plexus; however, Peters had executed the move with such blinding speed that Harry had not caught it.

Now Harry quickly got off the bus. He paused, narrowed his eyes, and nodded in professional appreciation as he watched the man and woman drag the hurt, semiconscious lawyer across the macadam and up into the temporary sanctuary of the lead bus. A few moments later Alexandra Finway spoke briefly to the people who had followed them, then pushed the doors shut.

"Is that poor bastard going to get an earful," Harry murmured wryly as he walked toward the swelling throng that was gathering, chattering excitedly, around the door of the bus.

He took up a position at the edge of the crowd, a few feet away from the door, and waited. He could just see the top of Alexandra Finway's head through the window, and he knew that Peters would have the woman's husband down on a seat while he quickly told him the same story he had told the woman. Peters would have no choice, Harry thought; their freedom, conceivably even their lives, would be in John Finway's hands for a week.

Or it could be over much sooner than that, Harry thought as the dwarfish Raul brushed past him and, with quick, nervous shoves and shouts, began clearing his way through the crowd toward the closed door. A soldier carrying a Kalashnikov assault rifle was trotting across the macadam from the direction of the terminal building.

Harry knew he had to make a quick decision. He had no way of knowing what kind of progress Peters and Alexandra Finway were making with the woman's husband; if Raul and the soldier burst in before Finway became sufficiently convinced of the need for him to remain silent, Peters and the woman could be out of commission, possibly for years, unless Salva bought their story that they'd been trying to prevent his assassination. Harry did not think Salva would be so obliging.

If Finway raised enough suspicions, Harry thought, Peters and his unwitting accomplice would be taken out by the Sierrans and would no longer be his concern. His job would be half done, and all he would have left to worry about was the possible existence of a second assassin who might be along to back up Peters. But that was going to be a difficult problem. Peters, at least, was a known quantity and an easy target for surveillance. Without Peters to track, Harry was keenly aware that he could spend the entire week looking for a person who might not exist, and then blow the assignment if the person was there and he missed him. Another consideration was the fact that Peters was the best, perhaps the only, source for finding out what organization had booked the assassination in the first place.

Finally, Harry thought, he had been tasked to protect Alexandra Finway, if possible. He decided it was possible.

Harry quickly pushed past the people in front of him and gripped the squat Sierran's wrist just as the man was about to force open the door. "Excuse me, Raul. I think the man just had a little fainting spell. Maybe you should leave them alone. The blond guy and the woman act like they know what they're doing."

Raul looked down at his wrist as if it were the hand on it that had spoken. When Harry released his grip, the red-faced man looked up and blinked rapidly. "They can't stay in there alone," Raul said, his voice shrill with anxiety and annoyance.

Harry giggled. "Why not? You think they're having an orgy?"

"It's not regular! They must come out!"

Raul turned around to speak to the soldier, who had just come up. Harry moaned loudly, let his jaw fall slack, and rolled his eyes back up into his head. He gave Raul time to turn back, then went into a Saint Vitus dance of flapping, disjointed movements. Suddenly his right arm jerked up, the hard knuckles catching Raul under the chin. Raul grunted with pain and surprise and leaped backward, colliding with the soldier. Both men went sprawling on the ground. Harry stiffened and fell back, slamming against the door and slowly sliding down the metal surface to end in a slumped sitting position on the macadam. There was stunned silence.

If they weren't finished inside, Harry thought, they had damn well better get finished. He twitched the muscles in his arms and legs, slowly counted to ten, then opened his eyes. "God," he moaned, clutching his head. He slowly looked up at the staring faces surrounding him. "Oh . . . I'm sorry," he said thickly. "Too much heat and excitement always gives me these spells. It's the story of my life."

The angry Raul and the soldier got to their feet. Raul stepped forward and glared balefully at the sheepish-looking Harry. "What's the matter with you!?" Raul bellowed, his voice quivering with outrage.

"I . . . I'm afraid I fainted."

"You had a fit! You hit me!"

Harry shook his head in confusion. "I . . . did?"

"Yes, you did!"

"Oh, Lord, I'm so ashamed," Harry whined, lowering his gaze and shaking his head woefully. "I'm so sorry. Just give my head a couple of minutes to clear. I'll be all right."

Raul gestured in frustration, then lifted his eyes to the heavens as if, forgetting himself, he were seeking Divine guidance. "Why is everyone getting sick? We can't even get out of the airport!"

Harry groaned, then slowly worked his way onto his hands and knees and made gagging sounds. There was the sound of feet hurriedly shuffling back.

"Are you all right, sir?"

Harry looked up to find the dark-haired Maria bending down over him. Her large, limpid eyes were filled with sympathy and concern. Constantina had arrived with a suitcase-size first aid kit and a thermos of water.

Harry drank a few sips of water, but shook his head when Constantina started to open the first aid kit. "All right," he mumbled. "Just needed the water . . . some air."

He waited until Constantina rose to push the people back, then sank down on one elbow and twisted around so that he could see the bus behind him. Peters was standing in the stairwell behind the door, watching the proceedings with mild curiosity reflected in his almost colorless eyes.

"I feel much better now," Harry said, allowing the pretty brunette to help him to his feet. "I'm really sorry, ma'am. You're very kind."

"It's perfectly all right, sir," Maria said soothingly. "The only important thing is that you're all right. If you'll permit it, I'll help you through Immigration and Customs."

Harry murmured his thanks. People began moving away, and Peters pushed the bus door open. His gaze flickered quickly, appraisingly, over Harry before he spoke to Raul and the two women guides.

"The guy inside the bus is all right now. He just had a fainting spell."

"I'll look at him," Constantina said, hefting the first aid kit.

"I think he'd just as soon not attract any more attention, Constantina," Peters said evenly. "He's embarrassed, and he knows you all have a lot of other things to do. My friend's had some nursing training. She'll stay with him for a few minutes, and then they'll be right along."

Constantina nodded, then turned away. Peters once again looked at Harry. Harry smiled shyly, then bowed his head as though speechless with embarrassment. He glanced up in time to see Peters walking quickly through the crowd, heading for the terminal building.

"All right, everybody!" Constantina called in a voice that was authoritative yet at the same time bright and ingratiating. "Everyone's all right now. Please! Let's all go back to the Immigration officer. We're running a bit behind schedule, and I imagine some of you would like to have a swim before dinner when we get to Carazúl."

The crowd obediently turned and began shuffling toward the terminal building, with Raul and Constantina gently but firmly shepherding them along. Harry allowed himself to be guided by Maria's hand on his elbow, leaving John and Alexandra Finway alone on the bus.

Alexandra

Alexandra swallowed repeatedly, but she could not work up any moisture in a mouth that was blistered and swollen from her gnawing at the soft tissue. John simply lay still, his left arm hanging limply over the edge of the seat, staring up at her. His gray eyes shone with a fever-glow of accusation and his mouth was frozen in a savage, sardonic smile. Those eyes were melting her insides, Alexandra thought. She felt small and getting smaller, as if the hard outer shell that remained were imploding; she was collapsing in on herself like a dark star, blinking out.

She had lost him, Alexandra thought, and she could not even afford to cry.

"Mrs. Alexandra Finway, Superspy," John said at last. "I love it."

Alexandra swallowed again. Her throat burned with thirst and the muscles at the back of her neck ached from tension, but she finally managed to speak. "Please, John," she said softly. "We have to get off and go with the others."

"Oh, hell, I'll get off. But I fainted, remember? I need some time to get my poor befuddled wits together. Oh, and I almost forgot. I thought you might be interested in hearing about our children. Remember Kara, Kristen, and Michael, Mrs. Superspy?"

"Please don't torture me, John," Alexandra said in a hollow voice. She imagined she could actually feel John's scorn pressing against her body like some fierce, invisible wind generated in his broken feelings and funneled through his piercing eyes; the scouring wind was threatening to blow her away. "Of course I want to know about them, but I assume you wouldn't be here if they weren't safe with someone."

"Well, that just shows what a poor judge of character you really are. The fact of the matter is that I ate them. I felt like having a snack before leaving the house and there wasn't a damn thing in the refrigerator."

"John, please don't act like this. We're all in dan—"

"I'm going to rip that little bastard's head off his shoulders when this fucking week is over," John said through clenched teeth, hatred momentarily twisting his features. He slammed his fist into the back of the seat in front of him, then abruptly sat up.

Alexandra forced herself to wait until the initial surge of fury had passed and John's gaze had come back to her face. "Please don't even think about that, darling," she said quietly, making no effort to hide her fear. "Stay away from Rick. Don't even talk to him. Not now, and not when the week is over. If you push him, he'll just kill you without giving it a second thought. He's very dangerous. You don't really know him at all."

"Ha! I don't know *him?*"

"Darling, all that we have to do is get through this week."

John punched the seat again and glared at her. "Is that all we have to do, *darling?* My God, you talk about lies! You've been living a lie since the very goddam day we met!"

"Not so loud, John. Please. You know there's much more at stake here than just our three lives."

"The hell there is," John shot back. But he lowered his voice. "Not as far as I'm concerned. Frankly, I don't give a small shit about Salva, Russia, or the State Department, and I especially don't give a shit about the fucking CIA. I mean, what are they thinking of, putting a forty-two-year-old mother of three children into a situation like this? This is the biggest bullshit operation I've ever heard of. They should've just picked up the telephone and called the son-of-a-bitch. Let Salva protect his own ass."

"It was considered, John. Rick told you that. He also explained why the decision was made not to do that."

"You spied on me." Now John's anger had grown cold and distant. "And you spied on my friends. That's precisely the kind of arrogant government horseshit a few good people were struggling against in the Sixties, and it turns out my goddam bride-to-be was doing a snoop number on me!"

Alexandra realized that she was almost panting. It was

hard to breathe, as though John's anger were burning up all the oxygen in the bus. "I was doing my job. Not everyone in the counterculture acted as responsibly as you. There were outlaws. You know that."

"You mean outlaws like Karen?"

Alexandra dropped her eyes and put a trembling hand to her forehead. "Yes," she managed to say. "Like your sister. I'm sorry, but it has to be said. She was a bomber, and you know damn well her people weren't planning on blowing up the Pentagon. They didn't care who they hurt. Also, that handsome mad bomber she was sleeping with just happened to be a KGB agent."

John stared at her, his lids narrowed and his breathing shallow. "Bullshit," he said at last. "How the hell do you know that?"

"John, I was a good agent," Alexandra said quietly, struggling to regain her composure. "It was my job to find out things like that. I killed him. I had to; he was going to kill me." She paused as a new emotion that Alexandra could not immediately identify swept across her husband's face. She was sorry she had mentioned the killing, but it was too late to take the words back. "I'm sorry if what I said about Karen hurts you, but it's the truth."

"A lot of things I'm learning hurt me, Alexandra. But what hurts most is to find out that you informed on me."

"I stopped when I realized I was in love with you, and I quit the dragons when we were married."

"But you never told me, Alexandra!" John cried out, his voice suddenly distorted with anguish.

Alexandra felt tears welling in her eyes and she struggled to hold them back. "Oh, John, can't you understand that I was afraid of losing you?"

John heaved a great, shuddering sigh. He sucked in a deep breath, put a hand on his stomach, and slowly exhaled. His anger seemed spent. He slowly rose to his feet, squeezed past her in the aisle, then paused in the stairwell and looked back. "If you want my opinion," he said in a low, hard voice, "this is the typical sort of quarter-assed operation our glorious CIA is justly famous for. Ever hear of Chile? Iran? The Bay of Pigs? How about San Sierra's Beach of Fire? Well, those fiascoes all seem like master-schemes compared to this baby; it had to be thought up by the same people who brought you Watergate. This operation isn't even quarter-assed, it's patently insane. Your three children are the only people you owe spit to, and they're not going to be too happy if their mother gets her ass shot off or ends up growing old in a Sierran prison. You might want to give that some thought."

"John—"

"You don't have to worry about me bothering the two of you, sweetheart. I won't talk to you; I don't even know your names. And I won't blow the whistle on your screwball plan, if you're still crazy enough to want to go through with it. All I want right now is to get through this week and go back . . . someplace."

"I love you, John," Alexandra said in a choked voice. "You still don't know everything. I need you. Please help *me* get through this week. I have to know that you love and trust me, and that our family will be together and whole when this is over."

But she knew he had not heard her. John had already stepped off the bus and was walking at a furious pace toward the terminal building where Raul was waiting, impatiently tapping his foot.

HOTEL CARAZÚL

Sunday, January 20; 6:20 A.M.

Peters

Peters had been awake, thinking, for more than two hours when the first ray of burnished tropical light pierced a crack in the Venetian blinds and fell across his face. He had been aware all the time of Alexandra standing silent and motionless by the window, but he had remained still, analyzing, unwilling to risk having stray emotions show on his face until he could be sure of how he was going to proceed and could then dismiss the problem from his mind.

One mystery that had caused him considerable anxiety had been cleared up. Peters had been very much concerned when he'd first learned of the last-minute addition to the flight's passenger list and it had taken a good deal of concentration to maintain a calm facade, not only when he'd first learned of the addition, but also when he'd relayed the information to Alexandra. His initial suspicion and fear had been that one of the faceless Sierrans he'd met within the Miami movie theater had been arrested, or had been a CIA agent all along. That would have meant that someone on the tour was a CIA agent watching every move he and Alexandra made, biding his time, waiting for an opportunity to kill them both. However, after the initial shock and danger of the confrontation with John Finway had passed, Peters had experienced a feeling of immense relief at finding the lawyer with them. Finway had to be the extra man, and Peters was no longer worried about being tracked.

He was still riding lucky.

His plan involving Alexandra had never been foolproof, he thought; there had always been factors over which he had no control, and he'd accepted that risk. He had intentionally waited until only a short time before departure to approach Alexandra as a way of putting additional pressure on the woman and preventing her from analyzing his story too deeply; he considered the idea of Manuel Salva wanting to switch sides after more than twenty years of faithfully serving the Communist cause rather preposterous.

He had no control over what Alexandra told her husband, Peters thought, and her discussion with him had obviously included the fact that she was going to San Sierra. Finway, for whatever reason, had decided at the last moment to come along and "surprise" her. Peters assumed the other man had used his contacts with the political left to quickly obtain a visa. It explained the added name on the passenger list.

There was no CIA agent.

But there was still John Finway, and he was going to have to be killed. Moreover, Peters thought, the lawyer would have to be taken out in a manner that would appear unquestionably to be an accident. He knew that, in addition to the obvious danger of being caught, killing Finway carried subtler risks: her husband's death could break Alexandra, the finely calibrated tool that was now essential to his plan. At the very least, Alexandra would be deeply shaken for the rest of the trip, and he could not tell whether or not that would be to his advantage. He did not like unknown factors.

Nevertheless, the fact was that every minute Finway remained alive in San Sierra represented a clear and unacceptable peril. If the lawyer didn't simply change his mind about cooperating and betray them directly, he might do it indirectly, possibly raising suspicions by his behavior. Peters knew that if the Sierrans, for whatever reason, did a thorough check and found out that Finway was actually Alexandra's husband, questions would be raised, to say the least. With the questions would come complications. His plan would almost certainly have to be abandoned.

He would kill Finway at the first opportunity.

Satisfied with his decision, Peters groaned and stirred as though just awakening. He sat up on the edge of the bed, stretched and yawned. "Good morning," he said thickly to the woman standing by the window.

Alexandra's response was to abruptly snap open the blinds, flooding the room with sunlight. She was dressed in a powder-blue robe and matching slippers, and Peters could tell by the firm uplift of her full breasts and the line around her hips that she was wearing only a bra and panties beneath the robe. He was naked but made no move to cover himself, even when he began to grow hard.

"Good morning," Alexandra said coldly, turning back to the window.

"You don't want to look at me?"

"I've seen you with a hard-on before, Rick. It doesn't bother me one way or another. Frankly, I don't feel like looking at it before breakfast."

"What about after breakfast?" Peters felt himself beginning to throb, and he debated whether he should try hurting her. He was not sure how she would react after so many years, and he decided against it—at least for the time being.

Alexandra had definitely changed. She had softened, matured. Ripened. If anything, she was now more beautiful than he remembered, and he loved the gentler reincarnation even more than the rougher version. That made it even more essential that this business be finished, and the account closed.

When she did not respond, he added quietly, "It used to bother you a lot."

"That was a long time ago, Rick," Alexandra responded dully. "We lived in another world, in another galaxy."

"Maybe our home planet isn't as far away as you think it is," Peters said, reaching over to the nightstand and turning on his large portable radio in order to mask their conversation. The sound of mellow rock from a Miami station drifted through the room. He pulled the sheet up across his lap and lit a cigarette. "That's the lumpiest goddam pillow I've ever slept on. Do you suppose they stuff the things with marbles?"

Alexandra turned from the window and stared oddly at Peters for some time before she answered. "I hadn't noticed," she said at last. Her tone was not so much hostile now as it was distant and preoccupied.

"Have you slept?" Peters asked, knowing the answer.

Alexandra's bed, shoved against the opposite wall, was still crisply turned back, as it had been the night before.

"Don't worry about it, Rick!" Alexandra snapped, her voice bristling with anger. "I don't need a nursemaid! I haven't forgotten why we're here, and I know how to take care of myself. My marriage may have fallen apart, but I haven't. You can still count on me, all right?"

"I never doubted it," Peters said evenly. "I'm sorry about what happened with John."

Alexandra tossed her head back in annoyance. "Why are you sorry? You didn't invite him along."

"I invited you along."

"I came along."

"Do you think John will hold up?"

"I know he'll hold up. He's just as tough-minded and strong-willed as we are."

"Good," Peters replied matter-of-factly. "Now, why don't you come to bed with me?"

"My God, Rick," Alexandra said, her eyes flashing and her voice rising with exasperation. "What the hell's the matter with you? Don't you listen?"

"There's nothing the matter with me, Alexandra," Peters said evenly, "but there is something the matter with you. I can fix it; you know I can. Together, we can make it better for both of us."

Alexandra glared at him for a few seconds, then stormed into the bathroom and slammed the door shut behind her. Peters rose, went to the door, and put his mouth close to the wood.

"You and I are very special people, Alexandra," he continued in the same flat tone. "We have very special needs. You understood that once, and you used to have the guts to satisfy those needs. We both enjoyed the physical pain we shared because it pushed away all the worse pain and pressure. The pain heightened our pleasure; it helped us forget all the shit coming down on us. Right now, you and I are the only two people on the face of the earth who can save Salva's life. That puts us apart from everyone else. The pressure of our work always kept us apart from other people. We knew how to provide each other with pleasure and relaxation, and we need that now."

He almost fell into the small bathroom when the door

suddenly opened. Alexandra was composed now, her tone once again distant and cold.

"What's the matter, Rick?" Alexandra asked scornfully as she brushed past him. "Do you want to cut me again?"

"I never meant to hurt you like that," Peters said in a clipped voice. "I just went out of my head. How many ways can I say I'm sorry?"

"You don't have to say it at all," Alexandra replied archly. "I went out of my head too. It's what I meant when I said that all we ever shared was mental illness. In a way, the cutting helped me; it made me realize the price I was paying for the work I was doing. That was when I knew that if I didn't get out I was going to change permanently into something I didn't want to be."

"Then marrying John *was* an escape."

"No. If John had come into my life earlier, I wouldn't have scars under my eyes." She paused, sighed wearily. "So no more attempts to seduce me, painful or otherwise. Okay, Rick?"

"I don't agree that we were sick, Alexandra," Peters said in a low voice. "I loved you. But your message is received. Just let me know if you change your mind."

He watched the enticing movement of Alexandra's hips as she walked back to the window. She stood there for a long time, staring down at the narrow strip of lawn in front of the hotel, the highway, a large stand of barren sand pines, and the blue-green sea beyond. Peters frowned when she began to absently trace her finger up and down the pane of glass.

"Still worried about John?"

"Yes and no," Alexandra replied. She paused, sighed. "There's nothing more we can do about the situation with John, but he said something that struck me. You talk about this being an incredibly important task, which it certainly is. John called it a quarter-assed operation. Well, maybe it's that, too; maybe it was quarter-assed for the Company to send us. A great deal is hanging on our success or failure, Rick, but we weren't even vetted, politically or physically. How could the CIA know what we would be like after all these years?"

"They know," Peters said carefully. "They had to have checked us out before they contacted us. They were satisfied. The CIA doesn't think it's a quarter-assed operation; they think our being here is their best option."

"I know," Alexandra said distantly. "Langley gave me a second confirmation."

A bubble of shock and fear as hard and hot as a bullet instantaneously formed and burst in Peters' belly like a grenade, exploding upward and squeezing his heart. There was a banging inside his chest and head, and he realized with alarm that his heart had begun to beat arhythmically. He managed to sit down on the edge of the bed just before he fell.

As Alexandra started to turn toward him, Peters desperately reached down into his mind, touched something solid and hid behind it. He stiffened his body, supporting himself by bracing his hands on either side of him. He searched frantically for something—anything—to say.

"Really?" His lips and the muscles in his face felt hard as concrete. "The C won't like that. I'll bet Langley didn't like it."

"I wasn't worried about how the C or Langley felt. I—Rick, what's the matter?"

"I don't know . . . dizzy."

Without giving himself any more time to think about it, Peters abruptly stood up. He experienced a few seconds of dizziness, but his legs supported him as he walked quickly into the bathroom. He leaned on the wash basin, opened the tap, and splashed cold water on his face. He heard Alexandra come up behind him and stop in the doorway.

"Hey, you okay?"

His pulse was still racing, Peters thought, but at least he was in control again. If only he hadn't given himself away a few seconds before. "Yeah," he mumbled. "I don't know what the hell happened. All of a sudden I just got dizzy."

He waited, forcing himself to breathe regularly, closing his eyes and listening in the terrible silence for Alexandra's next words, fearing suspicion, accusation—rejection. Without Alexandra's continuing trust and cooperation, the operation could not be carried out.

"I couldn't accept this task without a second confirmation from someone near the top of the agency itself."

Peters opened his eyes, smiled. It was all right. He concentrated on speaking slowly, calmly. "You didn't trust me or the C?"

"No offense, Rick, but I haven't seen you in years. The C was always just a voice. The man at the other end of that telephone line could have said anything you told him to say. I had to make absolutely certain that things were the way you said they were."

Peters splashed more cold water on his face, then turned off the tap and dried himself on the rough towel hanging on a brass rack next to the basin. He waited a few seconds to make sure that the muscles in his face felt right, then turned to face Alexandra.

"I understand perfectly," he said, pleased that his voice sounded casual and steady. Five minutes before he had feared he was going to pass out. "I'd have demanded the same thing. That's what makes us top professionals; it's why we're here."

"I wasn't supposed to tell you—procedures, you know—but I figure we've got enough problems without there being any tricks between us. It's really not that important, anyway. Call my little confession a peace offering."

Peters went back into the bedroom. He took shorts, socks and sneakers from his suitcase, sat down on a chair and began to put them on. Alexandra was still under his control, but a new and imminent danger had been introduced. His heart was pounding; his muscles were knotted, and the mainspring of his emotions was wound tight, locked. He was able to keep the physical reaction contained, insulated from his voice, eyes, and face, for the moment. He desperately needed to relax, to think. He needed mental and physical release quickly, and he'd learned that the best way for him to achieve that was through intense physical exercise.

"Accepted," he said at last as he finished lacing up his sneakers. He turned his head in Alexandra's direction and winked. "Confidentially, I did exactly the same thing. If I hadn't received a second confirmation, I'd never have come to you."

Alexandra laughed thinly. "Wheels within wheels. Hey, do you think it's a good idea to run right after you almost fainted?"

"I need a sweat." Peters stood and smiled at the woman.

"I was hoping for some more stimulating form of exercise, but I guess I'll have to settle for what I can get."

Alexandra reached out and turned off the radio. "Have a good run," she said absently.

"See you later," Peters replied, stepping out into the corridor and closing the door behind him.

Trembling with tension and fury, Peters did not bother to loosen his muscles with stretching exercises, as he usually did before running. The room was on the fourth floor and he bounded down the stairway, taking the steps two and three at a time. He forced himself to walk through the lobby, but once again broke into an abandoned sprint the moment he was outside. With his lips pulled back from his teeth in a grimace of rage and frustration, he sprinted across the highway and through the stand of sand pines, angrily slapping the rough bark of the trees with his hands. He emerged from the trees, veered right, and ran hard along the deserted beach until the sheer weight of physical exhaustion had squeezed the fear and tension from his system.

With sweat running in glistening rivulets down his sleek, hard body, his mind began to shift into a state of relative calm. Panting, he geared his pace down to a slow, shuffling jog and began trying to analyze what he knew or could guess.

The Company had tasked Alexandra for an operation that didn't exist; the woman had become a weapon turned against him.

It meant that the CIA knew what he was planning to do, and they were using an unsuspecting Alexandra, spending her to buy time. Now they were . . . what? Toying with him? No, he thought, that wasn't it. The Company would undoubtedly be overjoyed if he killed Salva. But they couldn't know why he wanted Alexandra, and that had made them nervous. They would have guessed the thrust of his plan, but not the details. He reasoned that they would try to stop him, but first they'd want to determine if he had a backup man with him on the tour, and then they'd try to find out what organization had hired him.

Obviously, he reflected, Langley was in no hurry. As far as the Company was concerned, he was a walking dead man they could tip over any time they pleased. Someone in the tour group was an agent tasked to watch him. The man would eventually move to capture him, then apply torture to force him to supply information before he was killed.

Chilled by that thought, Peters abruptly stopped and looked around him. The sea was to his left. On his right the beach sloped sharply upward, the sand flowing around the gaping black maws of abandoned bunkers that had been erected the length of the beach at seventy-five-yard intervals in the immediate aftermath of the Beach of Fire invasion. Satisfied that he was alone, Peters resumed his slow jogging.

Who? Peters wondered. Unknown, and unknowable—at least for the moment. He would just have to accept the fact that he was going to be under constant surveillance and not allow himself to be unduly distracted by the knowledge.

Another thought, a bizarre possibility, occurred to him. He was sure that it was Finway's name that had been added to the flight list at the last moment; it could mean that Finway was the agent.

Christ! he thought, smiling tensely in the face of the fear that had started to rise in him. What a neat trick it would be if Finway were, and always had been, a Company spook; what a neat trick that would be on a guilt-ridden Alexandra Finway, a dragon who'd informed on and then married one of her own anonymous dragonmasters without ever learning the truth. Wheels within wheels, all turning at different speeds in opposite directions.

He would not discount the possibility, but he doubted that Finway was the agent. There were a number of techniques for planting agents in an apparently closed group, even on very short notice. The CIA could have picked a real name from the passenger list available through various regulatory agencies and then taken the actual person off the tour; the pull could have been accomplished through persuasion, or by less gentlemanly means. The CIA would be baby-sitting the man while their agent took his place on the tour. It would mean a hastily doctored phony passport, Peters thought, which could be to his advantage. The agent's false document represented a potential weakness, a source of anxiety to the man.

Rage suddenly, unexpectedly, flared in him again. Christ, how he hated them! He picked up a broken shell and flung it far out over the shimmering surface of the water, clenching and unclenching his fists as he glared at the undulating ripples. He wouldn't be doing this, he thought, if the Company had been fair with him. He had always done his best job for them; he had been the best of the dragons, doing the CIA's bidding for years, at constant risk to his life.

He knew Alexandra had come to despise the work, while he had increasingly grown to love it, to—yes, he admitted to himself—*need* it. He'd come to understand that he would never be able to do anything else, never be able to adjust to life as a "civilian." The CIA should have understood that, he thought. They should have taken him in when the dragons were no longer needed. He would have made as good an agent as he'd been a dragon. But they were fools. Instead of giving him work, they had expected him to simply walk away. They had rejected him, and that rejection had been an unforgivable act of contempt.

Now, after all the years of seething humiliation and bitterness, he finally had the opportunity to get back at them. He had found a way to literally ruin the CIA while at the same time balancing things out with the only woman he had ever loved and who had also rejected him. They wouldn't—couldn't—stop him.

That, he thought, was the neatest trick of all.

The advantage had shifted back to him; he still had an edge. Thanks to Alexandra's "peace offering," he'd learned that there was, there had to be, a CIA operative after him, and the agent wasn't aware that he knew. He would have to be extra cautious and alert in order to avoid being trapped alone, but the all-important weapon of secret knowledge remained his.

Perhaps the most crucial advantage of all, Peters thought, was the fact that his hunter did not know how he planned to carry out the assassination. He would still do it, and he would still manage to escape. The CIA agent would be left with nothing but bloody chunks of Manuel Salva and Alexandra Finway.

The presence of the Company agent changed nothing.

Peters turned around and started to run back along the

shoreline. He loped easily for almost a half mile with his head down, mesmerized by the clear water exploding beneath his pounding feet. When he glanced up, he stopped so fast that he almost stumbled and fell.

John Finway was walking slowly toward him.

If Finway were the hunter, Peters thought, this was the trap. Although they were not a great distance from the hotel and the beach would surely be crowded later in the day, Peters could think of no reason why Finway, of all people, should be here at such an early hour. Not unless the lawyer had been following him. The other man was dressed in slacks and a baggy windbreaker, and could easily be armed. There was no place to run, even if he wanted to; he was hemmed in to his right by the sea and to his left by the embankment, which was too steep to climb quickly. He could not outrun a bullet.

The fact that Finway was walking so slowly, head down and hands jammed into the pockets of his windbreaker, could be a ruse to put him off guard, Peters thought. It wouldn't work. He slowly backed up the beach to a place where the sand was dry and reasonably firm. He stood with his right foot planted slightly behind his left, his muscles tensed. He knew that Finway would have to take him alive if he hoped to extract any information. Peters was confident that there were few men who could best him in hand-to-hand combat, and he intended to make the other man pay a heavy price if he intended to use a sap or other crippling device.

Then Finway looked up, and Peters' thinking instantly changed. The startled look on the other man's face was genuine, Peters thought; no one was that good an actor. Astonishment turned to anger in the lawyer's face, and Peters was absolutely certain that Finway was not the hunter. He was exactly what he appeared to be: a troubled man who, unable to sleep, was walking the beach.

Peters eased out of his fighting stance and waited, arms hanging loose but ready at his sides, as Finway stalked angrily up the beach and stopped a few paces away from him.

"I told Alexandra I wouldn't talk to you," the lawyer said huskily, the cords in his neck distended and writhing, "but

I can't let a precious moment like this go by. I just want you to know that *you're* the dumb son-of-a-bitch I'm going to hold responsible if anything happens to my wife. I'm going to cut off your balls if she gets hurt."

He would kill Finway now, Peters thought calmly, almost dazed by his good fortune. Finding the man alone on a deserted beach was more than he could have possibly hoped for, and he knew he would never get a better opportunity. It would be easy to make it look like a drowning accident; Alexandra might even consider her husband's death a suicide. However, Peters knew that he had to be careful how he handled the killing. There were sharks in the water, but there was no guarantee that they would get at the body. It would be necessary that Finway have water in his lungs and no marks on his body if the "accidental drowning" were to look genuine; Finway would have to be unconscious but alive when he went into the water.

Peters considered the finger jab the best blow for disabling a man, but his quarry had already experienced that and could be expected to be on guard against it. He decided he would try to get the other man to move on him, and then counterpunch.

"Your wife's a big girl, Finway, in more ways than one. She doesn't need your permission to do anything." He paused and smiled suggestively. "And I do mean anything."

Peters' heartbeat quickened as the lawyer moved up to him and pressed a trembling index finger against his chest. "Don't try to play dirty teenage word games with me, you little prick. If you were getting laid, you wouldn't feel the need to flap your mouth. Make damn sure you understand what I'm saying: you and the fucking CIA had absolutely no right to approach Alexandra and disrupt our lives after all these years. If she gets a *cold* while she's here, I go to the Sierrans and tell them everything I know. I may even make up a few details, just to make sure they shoot your fucking heart out. And I go to the newspapers when I get back. I may not be able to prove shit, but you can bet your ass I'll stimulate one hell of a lot of investigative reporting. Then again, maybe I'll just get a shotgun and blow you away, you motherfucker. Isn't that what you people do? Don't you just murder people you don't like?"

Peters waited, savoring the moment. He could see that

Finway was on guard, his stomach muscles tensed; he decided he would strike with the butt of his palm over Finway's heart at the same time as he lifted his knee into the other man's groin.

Peters shifted his weight to his left leg and was about to bring his right knee up when he heard the gargling shout in the distance. Finway spun around, and they could both see a man struggling in the water perhaps a hundred yards down the shore and twenty-five yards out to sea. The man's arms flailed the water, and his head kept bobbing up and down like a charred, fleshy cork. He shouted again, a desperate, bubbling plea for help.

"Jesus Christ," Finway said, his tone a curious blend of alarm, amusement, and disgust. And then he was sprinting down the beach toward the man, kicking off his shoes as he ran.

Peters remained where he was, watching, cursing softly under his breath. Finway reached the place where the man had left his clothes on the beach. The lawyer stripped off his jacket, shirt, and slacks, dove cleanly into the water, and swam out toward the man with quick, powerful strokes.

Peters grunted, then started walking down the beach, picking up Finway's shoes along the way. By the time he reached the twin piles of clothes, Finway had pulled the naked man, coughing and spitting water, onto the sand. Finway started to give the man artificial respiration, but the man shook his head and pushed the lawyer away.

"You okay?" Finway asked as he straightened up.

The swimmer coughed some more, but finally managed to speak. "Yeah, thanks to you," he said weakly. He tried to stand, but didn't make it. He slumped back down to the sand, then grabbed his shirt and clutched it to his genitals. "Boy, I thought I was a goner out there."

"It was a good thing we happened to be around," Peters said evenly. "You shouldn't swim alone." He found he was growing suspicious. The way the man was holding himself—knees up to cover his nakedness, wrists held limply —made him appear effeminate and comically frail. Peters was not sure that was the case; it was almost as if the man were somehow creating an illusion with his body, like a mime. Looking beyond the weak pose, Peters saw hard muscles. There were scars, one of which on the right shoulder looked like the kind of puckered crater a bullet wound might leave. It was the same man, Peters thought, who had fainted outside the bus at the airport; and he hadn't been in the water a few minutes before when Finway had come walking down the beach.

Peters immediately put the swimmer at the top of his list of suspects.

The man giggled inanely. He struggled to his feet, still holding his shirt over his genitals. "You're telling me! I'm an early riser. I was walking, and all of a sudden I just had an urge to take a swim. Like they do in the movies, you know? Well, what the hell. Screwing up is the story of my life." He extended his free hand toward Peters. "I'm David Swarzwalder," he said, grinning broadly. "I already know John, here. What's your name?"

"Rick Peters. Nice to meet you." He nodded in the direction of Finway, who had picked up his clothes, stepped around them, and was continuing up the beach in his shorts. "He could just as well dry out here. Not a very friendly guy, is he?"

"Hey, I'm not about to knock the guy who saved my life. Besides, John's an okay guy. Something's bothering him; he told me."

Peters ignored the silly, ingratiating smile on the other man's face and looked past what could be a mask into his eyes. If the man were an agent, Peters thought, he was very good—the best at psychological projection he'd ever seen. The man's deep blue eyes revealed nothing but a kind of boyish, overeager desire to be friendly. But then, he thought, Langley would send nothing but the very best. He wondered how well the man fought, and he knew he needed more time to study him.

"You look like you could use a drink, David. Why don't you come back to the hotel with me? We'll see who we have to bribe to get the bar open for breakfast."

"Thanks, Rick, but I'm not much of a drinker. I'm still a little shaky. I think I'll just wait here until I dry out."

"Then I'll finish my run. See you around."

The man nodded, then sighed and sat down hard on the sand. Peters started off at a slow lope, but gradually increased his speed as he widened the distance between himself and the other two men. By the time he reached the sand pines near the hotel, he was sprinting.

David Swarzwalder could be acting as Finway's watchdog, Peters thought. That contingency narrowed his options considerably. He had just lost the kind of opportunity he was too professional to think would ever arise again. He knew he would have to take advantage of the next opportunity, however small or tenuous. And such an opening was now presenting itself: both Finway and Swarzwalder were out, giving him an opportunity to search Finway's room and look for a personal item of the lawyer's that could be booby-trapped.

As before, he walked at a casual pace through the lobby of the hotel, nodding to a few early risers in the tour group who were heading for the breakfast room. When he reached the stairway, he bounded up the steps to his room. He estimated that he had perhaps a half hour before one or both men returned to their rooms. But that was assuming David Swarzwalder, bumbling, gurgling drowner, didn't suddenly metamorphose into a spy and killer.

He would allow himself fifteen minutes, Peters thought; five to determine if Finway's belongings included anything that could be rigged, and ten to prepare the booby trap if they did.

He quietly eased open the door of his own room and was relieved to find that Alexandra was gone. He called the desk, identified himself with the name of a passenger he had talked to on the plane, and got the number of John Finway's room on the second floor. He quickly slipped into slacks and a shirt, picked up his radio, and went out.

He cursed when he found that the Russian-made lock on Finway's door would not yield to his skill with a plastic credit card. Glancing around to make sure that the corridor was empty, he quickly knelt down and snapped open the back of the radio. Inside the hard plastic case was everything he would need for the assassination, a highly specialized tool chest and electronics kit built so ingeniously into the guts of the radio that none but the most canny of experts who knew what to look for would see anything more than the labyrinth of wires and transistors of an ordinary, if powerful and complex, multiband radio. He selected a long, thin piece of metal and immediately succeeded in picking the lock.

He found what he needed almost at once, in the bathroom. It was an electric shaver fitted with the necessary voltage adaptor, resting on top of a leather toilet kit that bore the lawyer's initials.

Peters set the radio on the floor, again opened the back, and took out what he required. Within six minutes he had made the necessary adjustments to the shaver. He replaced the appliance, making certain that the metal body, adaptor, and cord were in precisely the same position he had found them. He opened the door a crack, waited until two couples had disappeared into the elevator, and then stepped out into the hallway. He was satisfied that the problem posed by John Finway was solved.

John

It took twenty minutes of brisk walking before John felt the pressure of the anger inside him begin to subside. By then his shorts were dry and he was sweating copiously under the hot, fast-rising sun. He stripped off his shorts and dropped them into a pile on the white sand with the rest of his clothes, then plunged into the calm, clear aqua blue of the sea.

The chill of the water slammed against his body and squeezed him, causing him to shudder violently as he swam a few strokes underwater. However, after recovering from the initial shock, John found that the cold was not an altogether unpleasant sensation; the chill seemed to temporarily wash away his chagrin, resentment, and anger along with the oily sweat on his body. He surfaced twenty yards from shore, rolled over on his back, and floated, lazily kicking his legs, until his body adjusted to the temperature of the water. Then he narrowed his eyelids and squinted up in the direction of the sun through a spiderweb of misty, concentric rainbows.

His outrage at Peters and the CIA smouldered unabated, but the ire directed toward Alexandra had been largely dissipated in the glow of the realization that she was still his. She loved *him*, John thought, and that was probably the only thing that mattered; considering how he'd felt less than twenty-four hours before, he now felt virtually reborn. He had not been betrayed. He could live with the fact that she had spied and informed on him in the past. She had, he realized, been doing what she thought was right, at considerable risk to her life, and she had stopped when they'd fallen in love.

He needed no instruction in understanding the desire, however ill-advised, to keep something secret for fear of losing someone you loved.

It troubled him that Alexandra and Peters were sharing the same room, but he dismissed the anxiety as being adolescent; the living arrangement was obviously necessary for them to preserve their cover as lovers, and he knew he couldn't very well expect Alexandra to move in with him for the week just because he was jealous. He had begun this journey assuming he was cuckolded when he was not, and he considered it silly to worry about such an eventuality now.

His sole concern, John thought, had to be for getting his wife safely back to the United States. He was not insensitive to the problems Alexandra and Peters had outlined to him, and he had decided that he would cooperate with them for as long as he could and hope that they would succeed in what they had come to do. But there was a point he would not go beyond. He would not sacrifice his wife and the mother of his children for Manuel Salva, the CIA, or the image of the United States government.

He would go to the Sierrans at the first sign of risk to Alexandra. Regardless of the political uses to which the Sierrans might want to put the two captive dragons, they still had debts to him. He would call in all of them and take his wife home with him.

The Sierrans could have Peters if they wanted him, John thought with a grim smile. Fuck Peters.

He emerged from the water and stood quietly, eyes closed, in the hot sun for a few minutes until he was dry. Then he dressed and headed back to the hotel.

It was nine-thirty when he arrived at his room. He had a half hour before the breakfast room closed, he thought, and he would hurry. He had not eaten since just before leaving for the airport the previous morning, and he found he was suddenly ravenously hungry.

He laid out clean clothes before stripping to the waist and going into the bathroom. He ran a hand over his face, picked up his electric shaver and plugged it in. The tiny device that had bridged the two stripped, short-circuited wires inside the shaver head instantly fused into the wires, sending the amplified current arcing from the metal shaver to John's hand.

The deadly, spitting current made a circuit of John's skull, then coursed down through his collarbone and neck muscles into his heart, seizing the great pumping muscle and killing him.

Harry

Harry waited a few minutes until he was dry, dressed, then climbed up the far embankment and sat down on a rock just inside a line of trees where he could not be seen but where he had a clear view of the expanse of beach in front of him. He lit a cigarette and smoked slowly, thinking.

Although he did not intend to dwell on it, Harry knew he had probably made a mistake, perhaps a serious one, in risking his cover to save John Finway's life. The fact of the matter was that he had simply reacted instinctively, allowing the real Harry an important vote; the real Harry had decided to save a courageous woman's husband and the father of her three children. The real Harry liked happy endings.

He was definitely ready for Administration, Harry thought. He assumed it would be far easier to war-game and move pieces than it was to be a piece yourself, no matter how many parts you played.

As things turned out, Harry mused wryly, he might as well have been sharing a room with Finway. The small rooms assigned to singles were in a block, and Harry's room was next to the lawyer's. The walls were thin, and by placing his bed against the wall, he'd been able to monitor Finway's restless stirrings throughout the night. When he heard the other man go out around four, Harry had quickly dressed and gone after him. If Peters had a secret partner, Harry had reasoned, it was likely that the responsibility for killing John Finway had now fallen to the man. It was reasonable to assume that Finway would have difficulty sleeping, and Harry knew that a killer could be outside somewhere in the night, waiting for just such an opportunity.

Harry hoped it was true; if there was a man waiting for Finway, Harry would have him. He knew how to quickly extract information from a man. That done, he thought, it would simply be a matter of killing Peters, telling the Finways the truth, then getting out of San Sierra by one of three secret routes before the Sierrans got really serious about checking documents, something they were sure to do after two deaths among the tour group.

He'd trailed Finway as the man had wandered restlessly, aimlessly, all over the hotel grounds, and then finally headed down to the beach as the sun had begun to rise. Because of Finway's circuitous route, Harry had missed Peters when the blond-haired man had first run up the beach. Still, Harry had seen the assassin long before Finway. For a fleeting moment Harry speculated on what Peters was doing on the beach so early in the morning, but then dismissed the question as unimportant in the face of what was about to happen. To Harry's sharp, trained eye, Peters' reaction—the subtle shift of his body weight and the position of his hands—carried the clear message that John Finway was a dead man.

But then, Harry had thought with a grim smile of satisfaction, so was Peters. Peters might have Finway, but he had Peters. In a very short time he would be on his way home to Harley Shue's acerbic congratulations and his promised Administration post.

The only problem was that John Finway would be dead.

That's why he was always afraid, Harry had thought. The arithmetic of his business never worked out. Figures lied, columns never balanced. One day, if he didn't get out of the field, he was going to end up a missing digit that was simply ignored. The blind accountants at the CIA would just keep right on adding and subtracting.

The next moment he'd been sprinting across the sand.

Shue would chain him to a post in the HEW mailroom

if the Director of Operations knew what he'd just done, Harry thought as he ground out his fifth cigarette in the gritty, black soil at his feet. The hell with Shue.

He waited at his position until John Finway walked past on the beach below, then got up. Keeping at a safe distance, he followed the lawyer back to the hotel. He went to the desk to buy a pack of cigarettes and stayed a few minutes to banter with the desk clerk. They exchanged puzzled glances when the lobby lights dimmed, but the power came back on almost immediately. Harry turned and walked across the lobby to the elevator.

When the elevator doors sighed open on the second floor, Harry found himself looking down a windowless corridor that was without lights. The power was still out on this floor, and a number of people were out in the hallway alternately cursing Communists, looking inquiringly at one another, and entreating the dead light fixtures. Harry ran to Finway's room. He was prepared to jimmy the lock if need be, but the knob turned. He let himself in and slammed the door shut behind him.

The air in the room was thick with the acrid smell of burnt hair and plastic. John Finway lay in a hot pool of sunlight on the floor of the bathroom. Harry ran across the room, knelt down beside the lawyer's body, and felt for a pulse. There was none. However, Harry noticed that, despite the ghostly, waxen pallor of Finway's flesh, the man's body was still warm and the joints flexible.

Harry clenched his right hand into a fist and brought it down hard in the center of the other man's chest. He slowly counted to three, then punched the chest again. Keeping his right fist poised over the chest, Harry used his left hand to open Finway's mouth and bring the dry, coated tongue up from the back of the throat. He hit the chest a lighter blow, then bent forward and blew a quick, strong puff of air into the other man's lungs. Without losing his three-count rhythm, Harry felt for a pulse.

Nothing.

Harry hit the chest again, then resumed mouth-to-mouth resuscitation. There was a flutter in the pulse under John Finway's jaw.

"Come *on*, Finway," Harry whispered as he waited a three-count, then blew another puff of air into the still lungs. *"Breathe,* damn you! Don't let that fucker tag you out!"

The lights in the room flickered and came back on; the air conditioner resumed its soft, resonant hum. Harry started to lean over again when Finway suddenly moaned and coughed; his body convulsed twice before he abruptly rolled over and gagged. Harry gripped the man's forehead and upper abdomen from behind, gently, rhythmically pressing and releasing, helping him breathe until the first, tentative spasms of his lungs had evened out. Then Harry quickly wet some towels to cool the man.

"Don't try to sit up!" Harry snapped as Finway struggled to get on his hands and knees. "Just stay right where you are!"

Harry ripped the blanket off the bed in the next room, then came back into the bathroom to find the other man swaying unsteadily on his feet, bracing himself with both hands against the ceramic wash basin.

"What the hell happened?" Finway mumbled thickly.

"Nothing serious," Harry said, wrapping the blanket around the lawyer, picking him up, and carrying him to the bed. "You just died."

The charcoal-gray eyes closed for a few moments. The eyelids fluttered, then slowly opened again. "Who're you?"

"David Swarzwalder. We met at JFK. Who're you?"

There was a prolonged silence broken only by the metallic drone of the air conditioner and the hoarse breathing of the man on the bed. Finally the answer came: "John Finway."

"Good. Now let's hear you recite the alphabet."

Finway's eyes closed again. "Why?" he asked dreamily.

"The average brain tends to get upset when its host dies," Harry replied laconically, watching the other man closely. "I thought it might be interesting to find out how many IQ points you've lost, if any."

The other man lay still for a long time, then slowly sat up on the edge of the bed. "I know the alphabet," he said distantly, "but I feel as though there are other things I can't remember. There are gaps." His laugh was short and sharp, without humor. "I just can't think of what they are."

"That's to be expected," Harry said, keeping his eyes on the other man's face. What Finway did or did not remember, or when certain memories came back to him, would make a crucial difference to a lot of people, Harry thought. He and Peters shared one interest in common: they didn't want the Sierrans to have the slightest notion that anything was wrong. It was why he had not yet called for help; he had to try to evaluate just how much memory loss John Finway had sustained and then decide what to do about it. "A severe electric shock will leave you with some amnesia. With luck, it will only be temporary. It could last a few minutes, days, maybe a few weeks."

"What gave me the shock?"

Harry went into the bathroom and pulled the plug of the electric shaver from the wall. He quickly inspected the blackened, exposed wires and torn insulation, shook his head. He was certain Peters had stripped the insulation and crossed the wires, and he was fairly sure the man had used some kind of miniature transducer to amplify the current, but there was no way to prove it. Peters had done a thoroughly professional job, Harry thought, but it could provide a clue as to the type of weaponry Peters intended to use against Salva; he would know what to look for when he searched Peters' belongings.

He went back into the other room and handed the shaver to Finway. "That did it."

The lawyer turned the blackened shaver head in his hands, then dropped it on the bed. He looked at Harry and smiled thinly. "I think I'll switch to a straight razor."

Harry didn't smile. Finway was not a player, he thought; he wanted the man home and out of danger. "Judging from the way you're talking and moving around, I'd say you don't have any brain damage. But I'm not a doctor. We'll have to have someone look at you."

"Brain damage?"

"I told you: you were dead when I found you." Harry added a slight emphasis to the word "dead" and looked for the fear he hoped to see in the other man's eyes. There wasn't any.

"I feel like somebody's been using my head for a basketball. I thought I was supposed to see glowing figures and feel good. I didn't see anything."

"If you'll pardon an atrocious pun, I suggest you may have made the wrong connections in your previous life—

the one you were enjoying just before you plugged in the shaver."

"I want to thank you for saving my life, David," Finway said. He lifted his hands in a kind of supplicating gesture, then dropped them back to his sides. "Damn; talk about not knowing what to say. I guess I owe you a drink. Make that a case."

"Accepted. And I understand." Harry walked across the room to the telephone, but did not pick up the receiver. "You're going to need a lot of rest, John. You'll have to go home. Do you remember where you live?"

Harry waited while the other man thought about it. "I'm a lawyer," Finway said slowly. "I have a wife, three children. I live in . . . New York State. Pomona." He paused, glanced inquiringly around him, then looked at Harry. "Where the hell is this place?"

Harry continued to study the other man's face. "Think about it, John. Try to fill in those gaps."

The lawyer rose and walked unsteadily to the window. He stood there for almost five minutes, staring out. "San Sierra," Finway said at last. There was another pause lasting close to a minute, then he suddenly stiffened. "My wife!"

Finway remembered, Harry thought. Now he picked up the telephone receiver and dialed the main desk. "What about your wife?" he asked casually.

The other man turned slowly from the window. His face was now even more drawn, his eyes haunted, as if he had merely segued from one nightmare into another even worse. "I was about to say that my wife must miss me," Finway said absently. He blinked several times, then looked sharply at Harry. "I remember you too, David. I do and I don't. Something about you seems different."

Harry spoke a few words to the desk clerk, explaining what had happened, then hung up. He tried to wriggle back into the skin of his character, but he couldn't remember exactly who it was he had been playing. He decided to let it pass, to be the real Harry for a few more minutes.

"She won't have to miss you much longer," Harry said slowly and deliberately. "They're sending someone up to take you to a hospital, it's faster than waiting for a doctor to come here. I'm sure he's going to suggest you go back. You'll be home in time for dinner."

"I can't go home," Finway said, absently shaking his head.

"You have to. You were almost killed."

Harry kept his face blank as the other man stared at him oddly. "I have business here," Finway said at last in a strained voice. "I just can't go home yet."

Harry cursed silently to himself. He knew that whoever was coming up would arrive in moments, and he made a decision. He picked up the ruined shaver head from the bed, turned it over in his hands. "Odd how this insulation just frayed away." He reached down inside himself and brought up a nervous laugh. Company was coming, and it was time to slip back into character. "You have any enemies, John?"

Shadows moved in the other man's eyes, and he frowned. "What are you talking about?"

There was an urgent knock at the door. Harry opened it, to find Raul and Maria standing in the corridor.

"What's the matter?!" Raul asked quickly. His voice was even higher pitched than usual, and there was a clear implication in his tone that he would be personally offended if either of the men in the room had a complaint.

Harry tossed the razor to Raul. Startled, the squat, ruddy-faced man juggled the appliance in his hand but managed to hang onto it.

"My friend just had a close shave with that thing," Harry said, tittering and smiling ingratiatingly at the glowering Sierran. "Electric shock. It knocked him right out. I figured you people might want to have him checked out by a doctor."

"Electric shock?" Raul's thick, dark eyebrows shot up. "Are you saying there is something wrong with the wiring in the hotel?"

Maria spoke sharply to Raul in Spanish, then walked rapidly across the room and gripped Finway's right arm with both her hands. Finway started to protest, but by then Raul had followed the woman's lead, taking the lawyer's other arm and helping to usher him toward the door.

"John!" the real Harry said loudly. He waited until the lawyer looked back over his shoulder, then fixed Finway's eyes with his own. "San Sierra isn't all it's cut out to be," he continued deliberately. "Things here aren't what some people say they are. Let them send you home."

Raul started to protest, but the raven-haired Maria cut him off with a sharp word and an angry shake of her head. The Sierrans led Finway out of the room and down the corridor. Harry stood for a few moments staring thoughtfully out into the rectangle of orange-carpeted, empty hallway, then walked across the room and closed the door.

Tuesday, January 22; 1:15 A.M.

Alexandra

Having dressed in a slanting shaft of moonlight, Alexandra finished putting up her hair, combing out one thick strand in the center, positioning the heavy barrette, snapping the strong steel needle home into its clasp. She heard Peters stir in the bed across the room, and she wondered how long he had been awake.

"Where are you going?" Peters' voice was sharp, alert.

"For a walk. I need some air."

There was a sharp click and the radio came on, filling the room with soft music.

"Don't be stupid, Alexandra. You don't know who could be walking around out there. Why call attention to yourself?"

"I can't sleep. I need to let off some steam."

"Worried about John?"

"Of course I'm worried about John!" She took a deep breath, lowered her voice. "My husband was almost killed yesterday."

"He's all right now."

"How do you know?! I tried to get some information from Raul today, but he just looked right through me and started to talk about how Sierran doctors are the best."

"Never ask Raul anything. He's a bureaucratic asshole who thinks anything that goes wrong is part of a conspiracy directed against him. There were rumors flying around after people saw John being taken away in an ambulance, so Constantina made an announcement in the afternoon. You were out running. John's perfectly all right. He was brought back before dinner. You didn't see him?"

"No. What did Constantina say happened?"

Peters' voice was a shrug in the darkness. "She said he'd had an accident with his electric razor. Shock."

"I wonder," Alexandra said distantly.

"You wonder what?"

A dark, jagged thought—that her ruthless dragon partner, in an attempt to assure the successful completion of their task, had somehow been responsible—had jabbed at the quick of her mind when she had first heard of John's accident. Now it came again, but she pushed it away. Under the circumstances, she felt that she had no choice but to trust Rick Peters; to allow such a poisonous suspicion to grow would almost certainly destroy the delicate relationship they had to maintain and project in order to accomplish their task.

"John's famous for championing Leftist causes," Alexandra said at last, voicing an alternate suspicion. "Whoever's out to assassinate Salva could have decided to kill John out of spite, for 'old times' sake.' If so, he may try again."

Peters made a grunting sound of disapproval. "No way, Alexandra. You're not thinking clearly. The man hired to kill Salva is no meatball. We'd have picked up on an amateur like that before the plane left Kennedy; he'd have been sweating blood. Uh-uh. Our man leaves his politics home when he goes to work. He doesn't give a damn about anything but killing Salva. Why would he risk everything to kill a civilian who had nothing to do with it?"

Alexandra closed her eyes and sighed. "You're right, of course. God, I wish John would go home."

"So do I. Unfortunately, it doesn't look like he's going to."

Alexandra heard a soft rustling sound as Peters sat up on the edge of the bed. When she looked across the room the man appeared as a dark, amorphous shape vaguely silhouetted against the grayish blur of the sheets.

"I'm going out, Rick."

"Christ, Alexandra," Peters said huskily, a new urgency in his voice. "You're not going to try and see John, are you? You have no right to risk jeopardizing our position. You can't balance the success of this mission against your anxieties about John. I told you he's all right physically, and you told me he'd hold up mentally. He knows goddam well you could end up in a Sierran prison if he makes a mistake."

"Don't tell me the obvious, Rick," Alexandra said coldly, "and don't try to tell me my job or responsibilities. Of course I'm not going to try to see John, but I am going out. Go to sleep. I'll see you in the morning."

God, John, how I need you now.

Alexandra closed the door behind her and moved silently but quickly down the corridor to the elevator. It had taken all of her willpower to speak calmly to Rick Peters; she felt as if her center of gravity had dropped away and she were in danger of flying apart. As much as she loathed the fact, she realized that she had been tempted to join her former dragon partner in bed, to seek relief from the terrible pressure and anxiety in his arms and in the delicious pain, the exquisite torment, he would weave so expertly into the tapestry of their lovemaking.

She felt herself being inexorably drawn to Rick Peters. As in the past.

The dark, nightmare needs of her past had taken years to grow and fester, she thought. She had finally recognized their destructiveness and managed to vanquish them. She had never imagined that in a mere three days the pressures surrounding this task would brutally tear away the psychic scar tissue over those needs and leave her feeling panicked and empty, throbbing and in need.

John's love had been her lifebuoy once before, she thought as she got out of the elevator on the second floor. Now he would have to be again, in a way he could never be allowed to understand.

She waited by the elevator almost five minutes, looking and listening, but there was no sound, no indication that anyone had followed or was watching her. She walked down the corridor and paused outside John's room. She knew that her partner had been right. She was taking an unconscionable risk, but she felt she had no choice. She had less than a week left to remain in San Sierra, but the rest of her life to live. Her need was a gaping wound. She needed John to help her by stabilizing her emotions; she needed him to hold her and make love to her and hold her close again, if only for an hour or two; she needed to know that he loved her and had forgiven her past, as she had forgiven his. She needed him in her. Then she would be able to finish the assignment.

Insane, she thought, closing her eyes and clenching her teeth. Her thinking was an indication of just how bad her nerves were, and she was filled with shame when she thought how close she had come to doing something that would be incredibly stupid.

She started to walk away, then stopped when she was gripped by a new fear. She had excellent hearing, and even a sleeping man usually made some sound, however slight— a grunt, a snore, an arm flopping on the sheets. From John's room she had heard, sensed, only complete and ominous silence.

There were so many ways to kill a man, Alexandra thought. In his sleep. If someone *had* tried to kill John before, failed once, decided to try again ...

She removed a metal straight pin from her hair, slipped it into the lock and deftly manipulated it until she heard a soft click. Alexandra turned the knob, carefully pushed open the door, and slipped into the moonlit room. She glanced around and frowned at the sight of the rumpled, empty bed.

Peters

Peters slammed his fist into the lumpy bedding and swore violently as the door closed behind Alexandra.

It was Alexandra who was breaking down, he thought, not her husband. Her deteriorating mental condition was placing the plan of a lifetime in jeopardy; if the Sierran authorities ever came to suspect that there was a secret relationship between Alexandra and Finway and that it had been kept from them, there would be questions that would be impossible to answer.

But there was a bit of good news, Peters thought. As far as he had been able to determine before he'd approached her, Alexandra had always jealously guarded her privacy during the years of her marriage to an international celebrity. Still: there could have been news photos taken of them together; someone on the tour could have seen such a photo, remember ...

He rose and took a steaming-hot shower to relax his muscles. Then he toweled off, donned a loose terrycloth robe, and went back into the bedroom. He stood staring out the window at the shimmering chiaroscuro of moonlight on the black sea in the distance.

He did not understand how John Finway could have survived the "accident" he had rigged, but it was an indisputable fact that he had. The man would continue to be an ever-present danger, Peters thought, and he did not know when he would get another chance at Finway, if ever.

He could not control Finway, Peters thought with a thin, cold smile, but he could damn well control Alexandra. Alexandra had to be calmed down and brought back into the sharp, narrow focus that he needed, and he was sure he knew how to do that. He could feel her wavering, ready to slip into his orbit. It was time for the first big push.

He ordered a container of ice from what passed for room service in the Hotel Carazúl—a sleepy-eyed worker who had obviously been ordered out of bed—and then waited in the darkness, sitting on the edge of the bed and growing increasingly excited at the thought of what was to come. Forty-five minutes later he heard the door open and close behind him. Alexandra came around the bed and stood in front of him.

"What are you doing still awake? There's no sense in both of us losing sleep."

Alexandra's voice was tough, cold and distant, but Peters' eyes were accustomed to the dim light and he could see that the woman's eyes were red and swollen from crying. He looked up at her and smiled, opened his mouth as if to speak, then abruptly reached out with his right hand and locked his fingers around her left wrist. He sprang to his feet and in one fluid movement stepped around behind her, twisting her arm up behind her back. Then he shoved her hard between the shoulder blades, slamming her face down on the bed. Alexandra groped with her right hand for the barrette in her hair, but Peters was already astride her back, twisting her left arm even harder and slapping his free hand sharply against the soft flesh under Alexandra's flailing right arm.

"Rick!"

"Shut up, you bitch," Peters said through clenched

teeth. He slapped her right hand away from her hair once again, then pushed hard on the back of her neck, forcing her face into the bedding. "You want it as much as I do! You want it so bad you just about glow in the dark."

Still controlling Alexandra with his grip on her wrist, Peters grabbed her blouse at the collar and split it down the back with one quick snap of his wrist. He did the same with her bra strap, breaking the metal clasp and exposing the bare flesh of her back. Then he reached across her body with his free hand to the nightstand where he had placed the plastic bag filled with ice. He grabbed a handful of the melting ice and slapped it hard into the small of Alexandra's back.

Alexandra groaned and writhed under him, but Peters was satisfied that her voice was sufficiently muffled by the bedding. He continued to rub the ice against her skin for a few more seconds, then quickly switched hands on her wrist and climbed off her back to the left side of the bed. He bent over and put his mouth to the freezing flesh. Groping under Alexandra's body for her heavy breasts, he began to kiss, suck, and run his tongue over the reddish-white area along the lower part of her spine.

"Rick! Goddamn you, you stupid prick, let me up! Stop it!"

Even with Alexandra's mouth pressed against the bedding, Peters was certain he heard ambiguity in her voice— a clear, thrumming counterpoint of pleasure and desire shimmering beneath the anger. Maintaining the pressure on Alexandra's twisted arm, he slipped the fingers of his free hand beneath the waistbands of her skirt and panties and ripped the garments away. The muscles in her firm buttocks rippled with exertion, and the flesh glistened with sweat. Peters rubbed more ice over Alexandra's buttocks, then put his mouth on the soft tissue, sucking and nibbling her skin with his teeth.

"Relax, sweetheart," he murmured, biting her once, hard. "Enjoy it."

"Yes . . . *yes.*"

Peters forced Alexandra's thighs apart with his knee. He slipped his right hand between her legs, closed his eyes, and moaned softly with pleasure when he felt the thick, wet mat of her pubic hair, her moist labia. He withdrew his hand, loosed the belt of his robe and started to maneuver into a position where he could mount her from behind without losing his grip on her arm.

"Not that way, Rick," Alexandra whispered hoarsely. "You know I don't enjoy it that way."

Now Peters hesitated, trembling with excitement as he pressed his testicles and stiff penis into the cleft between Alexandra's buttocks. He remembered well how abandoned Alexandra could be when aroused, and he wanted that response.

He also remembered what some men who had tried to hurt her had looked like after she had finished working on them with the weapon she carried in her hair.

"*Please*, Rick," Alexandra moaned, thrashing even harder as she struggled to turn over. "Let me get on my back. I want to feel you in me! Put it in!"

Peters moved back off the bed and stood up on the floor. He circled Alexandra's right wrist with his right hand and gripped hard, ready to twist. Then he eased the pressure on her left arm, allowing Alexandra to twist around without his losing control of her. He immediately switched hands as she rolled over, grabbing both wrists when she was on her back and pulling her arms down to her sides. She positioned herself in front of him, spreading her legs and opening herself to him. Peters groaned in ecstasy and started to ease himself toward her warm, slick center. As soon as the tip of his penis touched her Alexandra began bucking wildly, kicking her legs into the air, heaving and panting.

"Goddamn it, hold still!" Peters gasped.

"Let me go, Rick. Oh, God . . . *God!* I have to *move!* You know I have to move! I'm coming . . . coming!"

Peters felt the muscles in his stomach and groin begin to quiver and he knew that he was about to ejaculate. Beyond thought, aching for the sensation of Alexandra thrusting herself up and against him, he released her arms. He placed his hands on the bed on either side of her and leaned forward, closing his eyes and cocking his hips for the deep thrust that would inject the mystery of her womb with his semen. A second later he gagged and froze, every muscle in his body knotted in anticipation of death.

Something needle-sharp was pressed delicately but firmly

against his closed eyelid at a point between the eyeball and bone socket.

"Get off me, you horse's ass," Alexandra said in a cracked voice thick with disgust and scorn.

"Ah . . . ah." Peters swallowed, and tasted vomit in the back of his throat. His eyelids fluttered, but he managed to keep them closed. The sharp, needle pressure on his right eyelid remained steady. "You were ready," he whispered.

"I was thinking about my husband, you stupid bastard," Alexandra said in a voice that was at once quavering and cold. "Since you're not him, I got bored and decided to pass." She sucked in a deep breath, then made a guttural animal sound and hissed her next words at him. "Get away from me, Rick! If you're not off this bed in one second, I drive this needle right through your eye into your pea brain. I really don't think you want to die for a cheap fuck."

Peters jerked his head and hips back, hesitated, then abruptly pushed off the bed and stood up. His entire body trembled. With the pressure of the needle gone, he had a sudden, vivid fantasy vision of the steel needle popping through his eyeball and entering his brain at the exact moment of ejaculation. He shuddered uncontrollably, closed his eyes, and spurted semen onto the sheet. Then, spent and trembling, he leaned against the foot of the bed and watched as Alexandra swung her legs onto the floor and stood up. She glanced at the stained sheet, then at him. The contempt in her eyes burned him.

"Better clean up here, Rick. You try sleeping in that bed, you're liable to slide out and break your neck."

Peters wanted to kill Alexandra then, and for a moment he lost control. He darted toward her, then croaked and diverted his forward motion upward and stood on his toes as Alexandra's hand flashed forward and he felt the tip of the barrette's needle pierce the flesh of his stomach. He stretched even farther up on his toes, sucked in his belly and stretched his arms wide. Long seconds passed before he slowly glanced down.

Alexandra, with the broad ivory medallion of the barrette clasped firmly in her palm, had stopped her thrust with the tip of the needle stuck a fraction of an inch into the skin of Peters' belly, just short of the striated muscle in the stomach wall.

"It would be kind of silly for you to kill me just because you can't sleep with me, Rick," Alexandra said. Her tone was dry and ironic, but her eyes shone with rage. "If you're that horny, go find a whore. I'm sure the Communists must have left some old fleabag lying around somewhere for emergency cases like yours. Or masturbate. Just be absolutely certain of this: I will kill you if you ever touch me again, and to hell with God, Country, and Manuél Salva. Do you understand me? I want to hear you say yes."

The puncture wound in Peters' belly was starting to burn as tiny rivulets of blood flowed in dual symmetrical streams, an inch apart, into his groin. He remained arched on his toes with his stomach sucked in, but he managed a thin smile. "I don't see why you have to be so melodramatic," he said wryly. "A little sex never hurt anybody."

"*You* hurt."

"You used to like it."

"No more. One of your problems, Rick, is that you don't listen." Alexandra pulled the tip of the needle out of Peters' stomach. "Get down off your toes; you're going to get a cramp. I'm going to bed."

Flushed with rage and humiliation, Peters went into the bathroom where he washed the tiny puncture wound, then daubed it with antiseptic. When he came back into the bedroom, he was astonished to find Alexandra under the covers of her bed, asleep as if nothing had happened.

He was not sure of the meaning behind Alexandra's ability to immediately fall asleep after his attack on her. Sheer neurasthenia, or easy and forgiving familiarity? Or was it contempt, the ultimate insult? In a way, the fact that Alexandra could now *sleep* disturbed him far more than anything else the woman might have said or done—which could be her point.

But then this attitude—the implacable toughness of her, the words and the quickness and the emotional control—were characteristics of the Alexandra he had known, the Alexandra that could be drawn back to him. She had to be made lean; the fat of gentleness, reflection, and warmth that had blossomed in her had to be pared away, or compressed and rammed back deep into her where it wouldn't interfere.

He decided he had made the right move.

"You complicated, hypocritical bitch," Peters whispered, his anger and stopped-up lust not mitigated by the respect he always felt toward Alexandra. "Whatever the hell's going on inside your head, at least I drain the tension out of you."

He slipped the semen-stained sheet off his own bed and climbed in under the rough woolen blanket. He closed his eyes and calmed himself with the thought that all insults would soon be repaid in full, with enormous interest.

John

He would have to sleep soon or risk collapse, John thought as he put his head back and closed his eyes. A few minutes later the bus started up, pulled onto the highway in front of the hotel and headed southeast toward the mountains and the Hotel Sierras Negras.

He calculated that he'd had a total of perhaps six or seven hours of fitful, exhausted sleep out of the past seventy-two. His inability to accept his situation and compose himself was not only self-destructive, he thought, but useless. *He* was useless here, and he suspected that realization was bothering him only slightly less than the circumstances of Alexandra's physical peril. He badly wanted to sleep, but each time he was about to slip under the surface of consciousness he would be shouted awake by the enormity of what Alexandra and Peters had told him. He wished there were something he could actively do to help Alexandra, but he knew there wasn't; San Sierra was not a courtroom, and it was certainly not the United States. He was odd man out in a game he was in no way equipped to play. This was Alexandra's game. The problem was that the penalty for a single miscalculation could be her death or imprisonment, and John knew he was only in the way.

Like a child, he had kept vaguely hoping all through the first day that he was caught in a particularly vivid dream, but, of course, he'd known all along that the situation was all too real. He had to sleep if he were to maintain a grip on himself. Now he was afraid that he was beginning to hallucinate; sometimes when he had walked during the night he had imagined he was being followed, but he had never seen anyone.

He opened his eyes, turned his head, and stared out the side window. Only two or three miles inland, the landscape had already begun to change and ripen. Away from the turquoise sea and white sands of the coast, the dominant colors of San Sierra were shades of green accented by the vertical brown stripes of the trunks of palm trees. Houses appeared every few kilometers, set off a few dozen yards from the edge of the highway. The dwellings were really nothing more than thatched-roof shacks, John thought, but they invariably appeared well constructed, clean, and pertly tidy, with lines of gaily colored wash waving in the warm, dry breezes like medieval banners. In the distance the Sierras Negras range rumbled lazily across the horizon, its ancient, tired humps etched sharply against a cloudless, luminescent sky that was a perfect robin's egg blue.

San Sierra was an incredibly beautiful country, John thought. One day he would like to return and enjoy it, with an unfettered Alexandra and their children.

He couldn't think of Alexandra, sitting in the lead bus with Peters, without reflecting on the assassination plot she and Peters had been asked to prevent. The thought always brought him up short, like a nightstick poked in his mind's belly, chilling him with the realization that one of his fellow passengers was a paid killer who, in three more days, could change this island country—and perhaps the world—forever.

John sighed and straightened up in his seat; sleep still would not come. There was ample room in the last bus, and he was sitting in the rear, away from the others. He could see David Swarzwalder sitting ten rows ahead of him, long legs stretched out into the aisle, talking to a group of people that included Raul. Swarzwalder appeared to catch his movement out of the corner of his eye, for the big man suddenly looked back and waved cheerily, inviting him to join them. John smiled wryly and shook his head.

He owed his life to Swarzwalder, John thought, and he'd intended to make an effort to be more pleasant to the strange man. However, after a halting attempt at conversation just before they'd boarded the bus, John had become distracted. He'd drifted away from Swarzwalder and the others and had sat in the rear, hoping to sleep.

John again closed his eyes and studied the gentle explosions of light on the back of his eyelids. Someone on the tour would be dead within three days if Alexandra and Peters accomplished what they were supposed to, he thought. That was assuming the assassin didn't kill the dragons first. Still, whatever happened, there was absolutely nothing he could do but stand by helplessly and watch; he could do nothing but wait for the *thing* to be over. It was a situation he was just going to have to accept. . . .

"Mr. Finway?"

"Huh?" John had just started to doze. He slowly opened his eyes to find Raul standing in the aisle beside him. It was only fitting that Raul should be the one to disturb him just as he was finally about to fall asleep, John thought. There were three guides, two of them beautiful, pleasant women, and then there was Raul; Raul was the reason the third bus was half empty and the other two so crowded. "Good morning, Raul."

The small, round man smiled tentatively, but it didn't seem to fit well on his face. It was obvious to John that smiling didn't agree with the other man.

"Are you comfortable, Mr. Finway?"

"I was."

"May I sit down?"

"Why not?" John replied, somewhat reluctantly sliding over on the seat. "They tell me it's almost a free country."

Raul frowned. "What do you mean?"

John sighed wearily as he impatiently motioned for the other man to sit down. "Never mind, Raul. My sense of humor's a little warped to begin with, and I'm feeling just a bit grumpy this morning. Come on and join me."

The Sierran eased himself onto the seat. There was a hint of embarrassment in his smile as he made a quick, curiously birdlike gesture at the landscape passing by outside the window. "Beautiful, isn't it?"

"Yes," John replied, studying the man's face. He was certain that the Sierran had not come back to give him a private tour lecture, and he wondered what was on the man's mind.

Raul's muddy eyes shifted away from John's, but the tone of his voice remained enthusiastic, if slightly forced. "Every section of the country shares equally in our good fortune. Before Manuel and the revolution, all of the wealth and skilled people remained in Angeles Blanca; there were no doctors anywhere but in Angeles Blanca; men had to send their wives and daughters to whore in Angeles Blanca so that their families would not starve. There were the rich in Angeles Blanca, and the rest of us were very, very poor. Now we are—"

"A lot better off, but at an economic dead end," John interrupted. "Excuse me, Raul, but I don't need the standard political speech. There's very little you can tell me about San Sierra under Sabrito that I don't already know or can't imagine. I'm ashamed of the fact that the United States supported Sabrito and every other dictator in Latin America, and I'm ashamed of the continuing boycott. Is that what you want to hear? I'm a great admirer of Manuel, and I'm also an admirer of the Sierran revolution—up to a point."

Raul tried and failed to erase the petulant scowl from his face. "I don't understand what you mean by 'up to a point.' Any revolution must continue if it is to survive. You are either for the revolution, or you are against it."

"No, Raul. The trouble with most revolutionaries is that they get addicted to the excitement and the power. They don't know when to stop because, most of the time, they don't know when they've won. Manuel was certainly right to throw out the bad guys, but it was a mistake to align San Sierra with Russia. Instead of massive aid from the United States, you got a blockade, and the Sierran people end up playing cannon fodder for Russian interests in Africa."

"We support the revolution—"

"No. Sierrans may support the revolution, but there are no revolutionaries in the Politburo. Russia is no more revolutionary than the United States. They're blood brothers, Raul, two sides of the same coin as far as their 'revolutionary' interests are concerned. Their chief interest is in maintaining order in their respective spheres of influence and in

trying to broaden those spheres. You can talk all you want
to about the ongoing revolution, and you can correctly
point out that the Sierrans are better off now than they
were under Sabrito. It doesn't change the fact that they
would be still better off if Manuel had lined San Sierra up
with the United States. America would have given a lot,
you know. The problem was Manuel; he was afraid that
the United States would pressure him to eventually hold
elections and give up some of his power. Manuel didn't like
that; he preferred to remain a dictator."

Raul shook his head angrily. A few of the other passengers were glancing back at them, and Raul lowered his
voice. "I don't understand you at all. I thought you were a
revolutionary. We have instructions to give you special
attention because you have always fought for our causes.
I understood that you supported San Sierra now."

"I do support San Sierra—when you get it right. San
Sierra's been making a lot of mistakes in the past few
years. I recognize bad guys when I see them, Raul. I don't
like them; I don't like what they do to people. I fight them
in any way I can, and it takes freedom to fight. Understand
this: I wouldn't last a week here or in the Soviet Union.
You can't fight the bad guys when they have all the power."

"You are saying that Manuel is a 'bad guy'?"

"I'm saying that it's long past the time when a great
warrior and hero should have retired. If anything happened
to Manuel now, this country would fall apart. Then you'd
see a lot of your glorious Russian revolutionaries up close,
because they'd be rolling right through your countryside in
their tanks, just like in Afghanistan."

Raul's face had grown brick red. "You think the United
States is better?"

John shrugged and smiled thinly. "In the United States
you have a better chance of getting rid of the bastards before they get rid of you. If they don't want to retire, we
throw them out." John suddenly reached across the seat
and placed his hand on Raul's shoulder. The man shied,
but John maintained contact. "Look, my friend," John continued, "I don't want to argue with you. I'm here as a
guest in your beautiful country. I didn't come here to
criticize San Sierra or debate your politics. I want to learn.

I'd like to see the country and get to know you and other Sierrans as friends. Okay?"

Raul, obviously uncomfortable, looked away and cleared his throat noisily. "There is something I would like to talk to you about."

John took his hand from Raul's shoulder, again leaned his head back and stared straight ahead of him. "What is it, Raul?"

"You don't look happy."

"I'm happy, Raul," John replied, choking off harsh laughter. "I appreciate your concern, but it's not needed. I don't want any special consideration."

Raul shook his head stubbornly. "You don't look happy," he repeated, an edge of bitterness creeping into his voice. "You haven't looked happy since you arrived here. Perhaps we do not live up to your expectations? After all, you could have gone to Bermuda."

John waited until he was sure that his rising impatience was under control before he answered. "I like San Sierra, Raul," he said softly. "I'm very happy. I can absolutely assure you that I'll remember this trip for as long as I live."

"Are you being sarcastic?"

John laughed sharply. "I've never been more sincere in my life."

"If you are happy, then why don't you show it, Mr. Finway? You always have what you Americans call a 'long face.' You stay off by yourself. Look." He gestured around the bus, as if the empty seats were John's responsibility and evidence of his duplicity. "Your long face makes people nervous. They do not want to be around you." He paused, dropped his gaze. "Then there was your accident."

John laughed again. "Jesus, Raul, are you afraid I tried to kill myself because I'm so unhappy?"

Raul laid his stubby hands in his lap and studied his palms. "Let me try to make myself clear, Mr. Finway. Have I done something to displease you or make you angry?"

"No, Raul," John said shortly. He was becoming angry. "You are without doubt one of the most gracious, brilliant tour guides I've ever encountered."

Now Raul looked at him. If the Sierran detected sarcasm or irony in his voice, John thought, his eyes gave no indication of it. He was glad; he did not want to offend the Sierran, only get rid of him.

"When a person looks unhappy and keeps off by himself, it can reflect on us," Raul said quietly. "It is our job to make people comfortable and happy. An unhappy face makes other people unhappy. With a famous person like you, it's even more important for tour guides to do a good job. If you were to complain, or return to the United States and write a bad article about San Sierra, it would be very bad for Constantina, Maria, and myself."

Except that Raul's "problem" had probably never even occurred to Constantina and Maria, John thought. It was Raul who was worried, and John was suddenly convinced that people on other tours had complained about Raul. John found he felt sorry for the squat, ugly bureaucrat who was trying so hard to hang on to his job.

"Listen to me, Raul," John said with genuine warmth. "I'm not going to make any complaints because I don't have any complaints. This is my happy face you've been seeing. Believe me, I *really* look mean when I'm disturbed about something." He paused and waited until Raul sheepishly met his gaze. "Now, I really don't want you to worry about me anymore, Raul," John continued seriously, emphasizing each word. "You're a tour guide, not my babysitter. From what I can see, everyone's having an absolutely marvelous time. Nobody but you gives a damn about me. If I want to be by myself, that's my privilege. Do I make myself clear?"

For just a moment John could see the full extent of the other man's anxiety, resentment, and hostility reflected in his face. Then the muddy eyes turned away.

"Your attitude has a bad effect on the other passengers," Raul insisted. Then he abruptly stood up and walked stiffly back down the aisle.

John stared at the departing man's back, thinking it over and regretting the conversation that had just taken place. Some spy he would make, he thought; he wasn't even involved in any plot or counterplot, and all he had managed to do was attract the hostile scrutiny of a Sierratour guide who was especially dangerous precisely because of his paranoia and insecurity.

John found that the thinly veiled confrontation with Raul

had left him even more impressed with the professionalism of Alexandra and Peters. When he thought back to the incident at the airport and realized how close he had come to exposing the dragons, it made his stomach muscles contract painfully.

The conversation had served to underline his uselessness, John thought. In his present situation, he was not only useless but represented a potential threat to Alexandra. He'd had a chance to leave, and he had not been able to do it. What he would do, he decided, was take steps to at least neutralize himself as a source of attention.

He stretched lazily, rose, and walked toward the center of the bus. Both Raul and Swarzwalder looked at him and smiled approvingly.

HOTEL SIERRAS NEGRAS

Wednesday, January 23; 10:30 A.M.

Peters

Peters stood at the stone railing of the hotel's second-floor balcony lounge. There were four other people on the large balcony with him: two men were playing a hotly contested game of table tennis, and a young French-speaking couple sat in the hot morning sun, completely absorbed, as far as Peters could tell, in a game of Scrabble.

Peters, standing with his back to the others, had positioned his body in such a way as to make it appear that he was gazing at the lake below and the mountains beyond. In fact, he was glancing sideways and focusing all of his attention on the two buses that were loading at the front of the hotel, below him and to his left, for the day trip to Peleoro. He was using his trained memory to make a mental note of the passengers' faces, linking them with names when he knew them.

Everything was going smoothly, he thought. Since arriving at Sierras Negras late Tuesday afternoon, he and Alexandra had broadened their contact with the other members of the group. They had taken turns walking the corridors of the four wings their group had been assigned, trying to match names and faces to room numbers, which had been listed on a mimeographed sheet given to each passenger. The result of their efforts had been a chart, crude and incomplete, but a starting point for the room search that was to come.

Peters was keenly aware that the search entailed a considerable degree of risk; no matter what precautions they took, there was always the chance they might be observed, or even caught in a room. Nevertheless, he considered the exercise absolutely necessary for two reasons. Since a room search was the next logical step in the hunt for the assassin Alexandra believed to exist, he knew there would have to be a search, or Alexandra's suspicions might be aroused.

But the search had become much more than a charade staged for Alexandra's benefit, Peters thought, as had his surveillance of the men and women boarding the buses. Somebody on the tour was most certainly hunting him; if possible, Peters wanted to take the man out before the tour reached Angeles Blanca. He considered it very likely that the CIA agent assigned to watch him had stayed behind and intended to search his luggage. Peters hoped that was the case. He had taken precautions, and anyone attempting to open his suitcase or radio would be killed almost immediately. Disposing of the body would, of course, pose some problems, but he was confident he could solve them. The important thing was that the agent on his trail would be gone, and he would be left with a clear field.

The bus doors closed and the buses pulled away. Peters turned and feigned interest in the table tennis game for a few minutes, then went back to the room where Alexandra was waiting for him. The rough room chart they had prepared was laid out on the bed.

"How many went?" Alexandra asked tensely as Peters entered the room.

Peters hesitated a few moments before answering. Her air of detached professionalism was at least in part a facade, he decided. Alexandra was bothered by his presence in precisely the way he wanted her to be. "Forty-two," he said at last.

"Did John go?"

"No."

"Damn," Alexandra said with quiet intensity.

"He looks like hell. I don't think he's been sleeping."

"He's worried about me," Alexandra replied distantly, looking up at the ceiling.

"Sure he is. But I wonder if he realizes how he stands out. He looks like some avenging angel, and he's making that fucking Raul nervous as hell."

Alexandra sighed as she uncapped a green felt-tip pen and wrote the number forty-two at the top of the chart. "All right," she said in a tight voice, "give me the names.

Maybe we'll find what we're looking for this morning. If so, we'll arrange a little reception for our man or men when the buses return. Our job will be finished and we can coast through the rest of this trip."

"Sounds good to me," Peters said casually, deciding it was best, for the moment, to match Alexandra's business-like manner. He moved to the side of the bed and took the pen from Alexandra's trembling hand. "Let me do it; it'll be faster. I don't know the names of all the people who went, but I think I can match up a lot of them."

Alexandra lay back on the bed, closed her eyes, and put her fist to her forehead as Peters began marking the rooms he knew to correspond with the people he had seen boarding the buses.

"Sorry about the other night," Peters said quietly, watching Alexandra carefully out of the corner of his eye.

"Yeah. Me too."

"Well, I deserved what I got. You're still unbelievable with a needle. You should see the neat little hole you put in my belly."

"Something for you to remember me by." Alexandra rubbed her eyes, sat up. "God, I hope we find something, Rick. I just want to take care of business so I can tell John it's over."

"Yep." *He'll know when it's over, sweetheart.*

"Who knows?" Alexandra said dreamily. "If we find who we're looking for and make a clean disposal, maybe I'll break training. I may just arrange a very private assignation with a certain well-known lawyer."

Peters lifted the pen from the paper and looked at her. "Don't get too loose yet, Alexandra. We've got at least one man, maybe two, to kill. We have to make his death look like an accident, and then we have to get home. Even with a lot of luck, it's going to take a bit of doing."

"I know," Alexandra said tightly. "Just daydreaming."

He brushed Alexandra's legs gently with the back of his hand. "Hey, it's okay. If we make our target today, the least you're entitled to is one assignation with your husband. I do envy him a lot, you know."

Alexandra looked at Peters. "Finished?"

"Uh-huh."

"Okay," Alexandra said, getting off the bed and smoothing down her skirt. Once again her voice was cold, emotionless. "Let's go to work."

John

John stood just behind the glass doors of the hotel lobby and watched the people boarding the buses. Swarzwalder, who had buttonholed him in the breakfast room and tried right up to the last moment to get him to come along, paused in the stairwell of the bus and motioned to him once again. John shook his head. He tried to smile, but his face felt as if it had been set in plaster.

Despite his earlier resolve to be more friendly and mix with the others, he had simply not been able to do it; and he had certainly not been prepared to spend a day in Peleoro watching his wife and Peters perform their act—walking arm in arm, pecking at each other, and in general behaving like lovesick teenagers. For him to try and act affable and carefree in that situation would, he knew, have resulted in a worse performance than the one he was giving now. He'd decided that he would simply have to wait out the week the best way he could and hope that Raul and the others would accept his explanation that he was naturally moody.

Swarzwalder had been the last person to board. John watched as the door sighed shut behind the big man and the buses pulled away.

Now he felt a new concern: Alexandra and Peters had not boarded the buses, and John could not understand why. All the feelings of anxiety, rage, and humiliation that had lacerated him at the beginning of the trip began to resurface. Recognizing and fearing the symptoms, hoping to burn them away with physical activity, he hurried out of the lobby and started off at a brisk pace toward the mountain lake a half mile away.

After all, he thought, they were supposed to be hunting an assassin who was not only unaware of their presence, but who was supposedly marking time until Friday night.

Where the hell are they?

There were, at most, a dozen people who had elected

to stay behind, and John knew that each individual had won the disapproving attention of Raul. John was convinced that an assassin would go to great lengths to escape such attention; the object of the dragons' search had to be going to Peleoro with the majority of the tour group. Alexandra and Peters should have been on one of the buses.

Unless something had happened between them.

He tried to dampen his jealousy, shift his thoughts to something else, but he could not. The pair had been lovers for at least two years before he'd met them, John reflected as he reached the lake and began walking around its shore. Old passions could easily have been reignited, especially under the intense pressure they had to be feeling.

They might be taking a day off, John thought with a grim smile. Even spies needed a little diversion from time to time. They could be in each other's arms at that very moment.

Stop it, you dumb son-of-a-bitch! If they are, so what? Ride with it!

He was around the lake in twenty minutes, but the fast walk did nothing to stem the bitterness and resentment growing inside him like tumors on his soul.

They should have gone on the trip! If they're supposed to be tracking a killer, that's what they should be doing! Not fucking!

He hated his thoughts, hated the shape of the person his jealousy and lack of sleep were twisting him into, but there didn't seem to be anything he could do to staunch the flow of psychic poison into his system. The pressure of his jealousy, magnified by his feelings of impotence, was becoming unbearable, and he knew he was in trouble. Tortured by vivid images of Alexandra and Peters making love, he did not think he could stand it for another hour, much less the rest of the week.

He had to *know* if they were making love, John thought. That would be enough. He knew he would loathe himself if he did catch them. However, physically and emotionally exhausted, he could no longer stand the uncertainty.

He made a quick circuit of the hotel's wooded, sloping grounds in the faint hope that Alexandra and Peters might be at the pool, or walking. They were not.

Despising himself, moving as if in a daze, John walked woodenly into the cool, dimly lit lobby, which was empty except for a tall, handsome desk clerk who was sitting on a high-backed stool, reading a paperback book. John nodded curtly to the man, then took an English-language magazine from a rack and sat down in an overstuffed leather easy chair a few feet from the desk. He opened the magazine and pretended to read, blinking away a persistent haze that turned out to be a fine curtain of tears.

Don't do this. Forget it. Nothing about this trip has anything to do with reality. If you're cracking, dummy, imagine what Alexandra's feeling. Let it go.

But he couldn't.

Five minutes later the clerk put down his book, came out from behind the desk, and headed for the lavatory at the opposite end of the lobby. Feeling like a hideous marionette helplessly tangled and strangling in its own strings, John rose and stretched over the desk to the key rack. He took the spare key to the room he knew Alexandra and Peters to be sharing, then went across the lobby to the elevator. He walked very quickly, as if trying to escape from something evil and disgusting that he knew was himself.

He rode up to the next floor, stepped out of the elevator and walked softly down the corridor to Alexandra's and Peters' room, where he stopped and listened at the door. Once he thought he heard a shuffling sound, but then there was silence.

They should at least be talking and moving around if they're up. If they're not out of bed at this hour, they're screwing! Goddamn them!

Moving very slowly and carefully so as to make no sound, John eased the key into the lock and turned it. Sucking in a deep breath and holding it in an effort to control his shaking hands, he turned the knob as far as it would go, then abruptly pushed open the door and stepped into the room.

What he saw caused his jaw to drop open and his breath to explode from his lungs. The muscles in his body contracted spasmodically with such sudden force that he staggered backward until he came up hard against the wall.

He had seen David Swarzwalder get on the bus, John

thought. And he had watched as the buses pulled away. Yet here was Swarzwalder in Alexandra's room, standing over one of Peters' suitcases and holding what appeared to be Alexandra's ivory barrette in his left hand.

Swarzwalder had spun around at the sound of the door opening, and now the two men stood a few feet apart staring at each other in a silent, frozen tableau.

He'd seen Swarzwalder change once before, John thought, but the man standing in front of him now was completely different from any previous incarnation. This man had the same deep blue eyes and longish, straw-colored hair as the giggling David Swarzwalder with whom John was familiar, but all similarity ended there. This man held himself differently; his face was twisted into a fierce grimace of anger and determination. There was death in the gleaming blue eyes.

John had never met a man who actually frightened him. Until now.

The moment of stunned silence was suddenly broken as Swarzwalder, in what seemed to John a single, incredibly swift motion, dropped the barrette beside the suitcase, leaped across the room to slam the door shut, then swung the side of his rigid hand toward John's throat.

Harry

"Oh, damn," Harry said, suddenly rising from his seat and clutching at his stomach as the bus reached the end of the steep, winding hotel driveway and rolled onto the narrow highway.

Heads turned in Harry's direction as he staggered up the aisle toward Maria and Constantina, who now stood and looked at him anxiously.

"Mr. Swarzwalder!" Maria said, gripping one of Harry's arms while Constantina supported him under the other. "What's the matter?"

"I'm sorry," Harry said, shaking his head and wincing as if in pain. He dropped his eyes. "I'm afraid my health isn't all it could be, as you've noticed. Now it's my ulcer. It always acts up just when I'm about to do something I've really looked forward to. I can't handle excitement. It's the story of my life."

Maria frowned and Constantina cooed sympathetically.

"Oh, dear," Maria said. "Isn't there something we can do? Maybe you'd like to lie down on the back seat for a few minutes?"

Harry moaned softly. "That won't do any good," he said forlornly. "I don't get attacks often, but when I do they're corkers; they last all day." He took a deep breath, as if testing, grimaced, and shook his head. "I'm sorry. I have to go back. Would you stop the bus, please?"

Constantina spoke to the driver in Spanish, and the man pulled the bus over to the side of the road. The driver spoke into a microphone on the dashboard and the lead bus pulled over and stopped a hundred feet ahead of them. A few seconds later the ruddy, grim visage of Raul appeared in the rear window of the first bus, popping up in the frame of tinted glass like the specter of a vengeful leprechaun.

"We're very sorry you're ill, Mr. Swarzwalder," Maria said, glancing anxiously back along the narrow highway. "We'll take you back if you have to return, of course."

"Oh no, no," Harry said quickly, patting his stomach as if to reassure the woman. He had scouted the area and chosen his spot carefully. "It'll be a lot of trouble to turn the bus around, and it's only a five-minute walk back to the hotel. I'll be all right."

"We can't just leave you here, Mr. Swarzwalder," Constantina said. Her tone was sincere, but her eyes betrayed her preference for Harry's suggestion. "You're ill."

Harry appealed to the two women in a conspiratorial whisper. "Please. I've had these attacks before, and I know how to deal with them. I don't want to inconvenience anybody; I have trouble making friends, and I don't like people to be angry with me." He stepped down into the stairwell and looked appealingly at the driver. "I'll be fine, honestly. Please just let me get off."

Constantina and Maria looked at each other, and Maria spoke to the driver. The driver pushed a chrome lever and the bus door sighed open. Harry stepped out.

"We'll miss you, Mr. Swarzwalder!" Maria called out. "Be careful walking back!"

"Will do!" Harry shouted, waving and stepping to the side of the road as the bus pulled away. "Enjoy your day!"

As soon as the bus was out of sight, Harry took his hands away from his stomach and stepped into the woods at the side of the highway. He leaned against a tree and slowly smoked a cigarette. He finished it, field-stripped the butt, then lit another.

He was sure that Peters would be forced to go through certain motions in order to keep Alexandra Finway convinced they were searching for an assassin. With half the week gone, a room search, however spotty and incomplete, seemed a logical step, and Harry had reasoned that the best time for the man and woman to conduct such a search would be while the bulk of the group was on the day trip to Peleoro.

Harry took a few minutes to check his "school-pack": what appeared to be a variety of pens and mechanical pencils clipped to a plastic shield inside his shirt pocket was in fact an array of entry-and-search tools. Satisfied that everything was in order, he checked his watch and lit yet another cigarette. As far as Harry was concerned, the fact that Peters and Alexandra were not on the buses confirmed his suspicion that they had planned something and were on the move inside the hotel. However, he knew he would have to be certain they would be out of their room for a reasonable length of time before he tried to take care of his own business.

He waited a half hour, then cut through the trees toward the hotel.

A narrow, wooded ridge extended almost to the hotel's south side, and this was the route Harry took. At the end of the ridge he paused just inside the line of trees and stared up at the hotel's facade of polished, gleaming windows. After five minutes he caught a glimpse of Alexandra Finway on the second floor. Harry watched as she stood at a window for a few minutes, then walked slowly to the opposite end of the corridor and paused there.

They'd begun, Harry thought. Peters was searching rooms while the woman served as a lookout. Harry noted with satisfaction that the man and woman were working in the hotel's A wing, while their own room was in the B wing. There was a second tour group of East Germans at the hotel, but with typical German cooperation, enthusiasm, and efficiency, the entire group had left for Peleoro an hour and a half earlier. Harry knew there was little chance of his being observed if he took normal precautions.

Satisfied that he had ample time and space in which to operate, Harry waited until the woman's back was turned, then darted across a short expanse of open ground to a fire exit locked from the inside. He used a flexible steel pick from his schoolpack to unlock the door, hurried down a corridor to the B wing, and bounded up a flight of stairs to the second floor.

He paused in the deserted corridor outside Peters' and Alexandra Finway's room, glanced at the lights above the elevator to make certain no one was coming up or down, then took a jeweler's glass from his pocket. Using his left forearm to brace himself against the door, Harry put his face close to the wood and inspected the entire surface of the door jamb through the loupe, looking for a single hair or trace of talcum powder that, if broken or smudged, would betray the fact that someone had entered the room. However, there was no sign of any tripping device, and Harry used his pick to enter the room.

Peters' attack on John Finway had given Harry an idea of what equipment to look for, and he immediately went to the large portable radio set on a nightstand next to the bed nearest the door. He leaned over and examined the exterior surface of the radio, but did not touch it.

Peters was a professional, Harry thought, and a good one. Such men normally took certain precautions, no matter how secure they might feel. Surprised and made suspicious by the lack of some kind of a warning device on the door, he again used his loupe to examine the back of the radio before touching it. The inspection saved his life, for he quickly found three tiny needles that had been spring-loaded into specially made pockets in the plastic bordering the snap-off access plate. On the tip of each needle was a dull brown stain that could have been cyanide but that Harry suspected was a liquid form of one of the new binary nerve gases, probably Sarin, which required only a drop on the flesh to immobilize virtually instantaneously and kill within seconds.

He tore off a strip of rough, grayish toilet paper from

a roll in the bathroom, then went back into the bedroom and carefully removed the needles, setting them on the tissue so as to be able to find them easily when he was finished. Then he opened the back of the radio. He moved the wires aside with the tip of the lockpick, then used a small pencil flashlight from his pack to look inside. He immediately recognized that the radio served as a kind of all-purpose electronics tool box, with dozens of components housed in black plastic pockets that had been glued between and around the regular circuit boards to make them appear part of the radio itself. Harry knew he would not be able to determine the function of all the components, even if he had the time to remove and examine them, but he did not have to. It was enough for him to recognize that a small, short-range transmitter had been welded next to the standard receiver component.

Harry snapped the access plate back onto the radio, replaced the poisoned needles in their spring cases, then carefully put the radio back in the position he had found it.

Harry considered the possibility that Peters used the transmitter to relay messages to an accomplice, but rejected the idea. If Peters did have to communicate with anyone, Harry thought, it would be easier, and probably safer, to use coded messages, or even simple hand and body signals. Besides, Harry had come to believe that Peters was working alone.

To Harry it meant that the transmitter would be used to detonate explosives, most likely plastique. It remained for him to find the plastic explosives, he thought, and, if he were really lucky, unearth some clue to the organization that had given Peters his contract. He doubted that he would be that fortunate, but was unconcerned; his primary responsibility was to abort the assassination. Once that was assured, he would have some breathing room and could turn his attention to the problem of putting Peters and his employers out of the assassination business. It had occurred to him that it might be enough simply to make Peters permanently disappear; a vanished assassin would certainly keep the people on the other end looking over their shoulders for some time.

He had already begun to suspect what form the plastic

explosives would take; the shape he had in mind would explain the curious game Peters had been running on Alexandra Finway. Even so, a cold shudder passed through him when he found what he was looking for.

Harry was not fooled by the smooth, ivory feel of the object. When he held it up to the light and examined the edges through his loupe, he confirmed the fact that the surface was in fact a thin plastic shell made of very hard plastic. The plastique had been molded, weighted, hardened, and stained to match the barrette Alexandra Finway wore in her hair. Pressure at its base caused the steel hasp holding the needle in place to move back, exposing a small cavity designed to accept a miniature transistorized receiver that would trigger the explosives when activated by a specific radio signal.

The amount of plastique was not sufficient to kill anyone beyond a range of a few yards, Harry thought, which would mean a reservoir of the liquid nerve gas inside. The shell would be variegated on the inside surface, and at the moment of explosion thousands of tiny, deadly slivers would whistle through the arena, bringing death to anyone they touched. All Peters would need was a single instant when there was a reasonable range of perhaps twenty or thirty yards and a clear sightline between Manuel Salva and the back of Alexandra Finway's head . . .

Rick Peters was a real prince, Harry thought as he stared at the deadly barrette and felt a wave of revulsion sweep through him. Salva would be gone, all right, along with Alexandra Finway's head and perhaps a hundred other people. Peters, standing a safe distance away, would escape in the ensuing confusion, probably by way of a high-speed boat that would be waiting for him in the harbor.

The man was a psychopath, Harry thought, and he was going to take real pleasure in killing him. It was a good last job to round out his field career before slipping into an Administration post.

The sound of the door opening behind him struck Harry's senses with the impact of a gunshot. He spun, ready to attack, then froze when he saw John Finway. Harry could not understand what Finway was doing in the room, but he knew that any hope he'd harbored that his last field task would go smoothly, without the kind of kinks that could torment even the toughest operative in his old age, was gone forever.

In the second or two that the men stood and stared at each other, Harry's mind raced, frantically searching for alternatives to the terrible action that he knew he should—must—take. He could try to explain the truth to Finway, he thought, but he knew there was no reason why Finway should believe him. He could show Finway the barrette that was plastique, but Finway might well conclude that he was in the room trying to plant it himself.

In any case, Harry concluded, it was fantasy for him to believe that Finway would accept anything he had to say without first checking with his wife, who would certainly discuss the matter with Peters. Exposed, Peters would kill the Finways and disappear. Salva's death would be postponed, but Finway and his wife would be dead. And he himself would be blown, Harry thought. Harley Shue wouldn't like that.

There was no reasonable alternative. He was simply going to have to do his job and kill Finway.

Harry was across the room in three quick strides. He slammed the door shut, then reversed his body motion and aimed at Finway's throat with a blow that, had it landed, would have crushed the other man's larynx and snapped his neck, killing him almost instantly.

But the lawyer had good reflexes, and Finway recovered from his initial shock in time to duck away and raise his left arm. Harry's hand glanced off the other man's forearm. However, Harry could see that the blow had partially paralyzed the man's arm; Finway's body was hopelessly turned, and he was defenseless. Harry spun clockwise to gain momentum and slammed the side of his fist into the other man's chest, over his heart. Finway fell backwards to the floor and Harry was instantly on top of him, straddling his chest with his knees. He raised his fist, the knuckle of his middle finger extended to deliver a killing blow to the esophagus of the man who lay prone and stunned beneath him.

Seconds passed, and Harry realized with growing astonishment that he simply wasn't going to do it.

It occurred to him that much of the fear that had constantly plagued him over the years had always been fear of a situation like this: being forced out of terrible necessity to kill a civilian he liked, a man like Finway, who would look into his eyes at the moment of death and never have any idea why Harry was killing him.

But now that fear was gone. He didn't want to kill John Finway, Harry thought, and he just wasn't going to do it. He would try an unreasonable alternative; he was going to have to be very, very persuasive.

Finway's gaze flicked to something over Harry's left shoulder. Harry saw the eye movement and plunged backward a second too late. The leather strap slipped over his neck and began to tighten. Harry clawed at the strap and twisted to the side, trying to anticipate and neutralize the sharp, neck-snapping tug he knew would come at any moment.

Peters

Peters waited thirty seconds with his ear pressed to the wood panel. When he heard no warning fit of coughing, he stepped out into the corridor, quickly closing the door behind him. Alexandra was leaning on the protective railing in front of the floor-to-ceiling window. Peters tugged at the front of his beige sleeveless sweater, walked over and stood next to her.

"Well?" Alexandra said anxiously.

"Nothing."

"So much for the Katzmans," Alexandra said resignedly, referring to an attractive, middle-aged Jewish couple. "I thought we might be on to something there; there's such a thing as being too nice."

"They're clean, unless they plan to beat Salva to death with five cans of Campbell's Chicken Soup."

"Maybe the cans are dummies," Alexandra said seriously. "They could be bombs."

Peters smiled thinly as he shook his head. "It's chicken soup. Besides, did you ever meet an assassin with a sense of humor?"

"Most of the killers I ran into were low-grade types. Let's hit the writer next. We know he's in Peleoro."

"All right, but I don't think we're going to turn up anything there either. He is a writer; I've seen his stuff. Writers sit on their asses all day thinking up plots, but they don't carry them out. Besides, he comes on as too much of a weirdo. His act's too abrasive to be a good cover."

Peters watched Alexandra out of the corner of his eyes, saw her frown with uncertainty. She was reacting the way he wanted her to, he thought. He wanted her paying attention to him, while at the same time always remaining slightly off balance psychologically.

"I don't agree with your logic," Alexandra said tightly. "Who says an abrasive weirdo can't be an assassin? You sound like you're getting discouraged, Rick. It's not like you. We've only done seven rooms. You stand lookout, and I'll take the next seven."

"Okay," Peters replied wearily, leaning his elbows on the railing. "You're right; I could use a break. Go ahead."

He waited until Alexandra had slipped into the writer's room, then glanced at his watch and saw that they had been out slightly more than an hour. It was more than enough time, Peters thought, for the man hunting him to try to search his room, if he were going to, and Peters was intensely curious as to whether his poisoned needles had found a mark. He knew it would take Alexandra at least ten minutes to search the writer's room, and he needed only three minutes at most to check their own room. If there had been a searcher there, he would now be a corpse that would have to be disposed of. If so, Peters knew that he would have to tidy the room and decide how to handle Alexandra. The first step was to determine if the trap had been sprung.

He walked quickly to the end of the corridor, hurried across a marble-tiled foyer to the B wing. When he was fifteen feet from his room he heard the unmistakable sounds of struggle coming through the door. Puzzled and alarmed, Peters whipped his belt with its razor-sharp buckle from his belt loops. He peeled off the grooved leather strip that shielded the sharp steel edges, then gripped the weapon by its tongue end. He slipped the key into the lock and let himself into his room.

Taking in the bizarre scene at a glance, Peters immediately rejected the multitude of questions that were unanswerable and focused all of his attention on the only thing that mattered: the giggler, the same man he had seen by the bus and on the beach, was the hunter. The CIA operative was about to kill Finway—which was fine with Peters as long as he could get his own timing right.

Peters could see that the men, in the heat of their struggle, had not heard him enter. He pushed the door closed and pressed back against the wall out of their sightlines, waiting anxiously for the giggler's fist to drive into Finway's throat or across the bridge of his nose. When seconds passed and it did not happen, Peters knew he could wait no longer.

He had entered the room prepared to wield his buckle-blade despite the ineradicable carnage that could have resulted. Now he was relieved to see that he would not have to; Swarzwalder's back was to him, and Peters saw that he could easily garrote the man. Gripping the length of leather at the tongue and behind the buckle, he quickly stepped forward and up behind the kneeling man. He dropped the belt loop over the head of the man who called himself David Swarzwalder and started to drive his knee into the man's right kidney.

Peters was extremely quick, but he wasn't prepared for the unexpected speed of the bigger man. Swarzwalder exploded backward, and Peters moved his head aside just in time to avoid being butted. As it was, Swarzwalder managed to twist his body halfway around and ram an elbow into Peters' ribs. Peters grunted with pain, but he managed to maintain his grip on the ends of the belt. He sprang off the floor with his left foot, once again getting behind Swarzwalder and pulling as hard as he could on the belt.

Swarzwalder suddenly thrust his arms out to his sides and again leaped up and back, carrying Peters into the air with him. Peters knew he had two choices: hold on to the belt and risk breaking back or ribs when the man's body fell on him, or loosen his grip and try to get out of the way. He tried to compromise, twisting in the air and attempting to control the other man's body with the belt so that they would both land on their sides. But with his body in the air he had no leverage, and the belt slipped loose. Peters tried desperately to slip the loop back into position and tighten it, but he was too late.

Swarzwalder was free.

Now Peters knew he had no choice but to go for any kill, no matter how messy. He backed off, gripped the belt tightly by its tongue, and began to swing it in an arc over his head as he crouched and inched forward, looking for an opening.

The CIA agent was incredibly strong, Peters thought, but not superhuman. The man staggered and clutched at his throat as he got to his feet, obviously hurt.

But Swarzwalder made no move to run or to defend himself. Instead, Peters was astonished to see the big man turn toward Finway, who had managed to get to his feet but seemed frozen with indecision, white-faced and stunned. The big man made gagging sounds, at the same time jabbing a finger in the direction of the open suitcase. Peters looked at the bed and was startled to see that the plastique barrette lay exposed to view on the bedspread, next to the suitcase.

Peters swiped at Swarzwalder with the belt buckle, then lunged sideways. He grabbed the barrette, shoved it into the case, and slammed the top down.

As Peters moved to the suitcase, the CIA agent came to life. Whatever was broken in his throat did not prevent him from suddenly ducking under the whistling arc of the belt buckle and striking upward with an explosive side kick aimed at Peters' jaw. Off balance and out of position due to the necessity of moving for the barrette, Peters was only partially able to avoid the blow. It caught him solidly on the chest; Peters' head snapped forward and he sailed backward, landing hard on the floor.

He was going to lose it, Peters thought; after all the preparations, he was going to fail and die. The woman he had planned to destroy had inadvertently destroyed him. He opened his mouth to scream a last curse of defiance before the killing blow he knew would come and against which he could not defend.

Suddenly the radio blared. Swarzwalder, poised above Peters, half turned in time to see Alexandra come hurtling across the room at him. Her forehead drove into Swarzwalder's chest at the same time as she drove the rigid needle of her barrette into his back, over his right kidney. Swarzwalder cried out in agony, clawed at his back, then crumpled to the floor beside the bed.

"John! Don't!"

"Enough, Goddamnit! You're killing him!"

Warned by Alexandra's shout, Peters, who had scrambled to his feet and started after the fallen agent, sidestepped the lawyer's rush. When Finway tried to shove him away, he brought his knee up into the man's stomach, then knocked him unconscious with a rabbit punch to the back of the neck.

Now Peters once again looped his belt around Swarzwalder's neck. The big man clawed at the leather, but his strength was gone. Peters put a foot in the small of the man's back and yanked on the ends of the belt. The man's neck cracked with a loud pop. His body convulsed crazily, like some drunken puppet, then slumped to the floor and was still.

Peters looked up to find Alexandra kneeling over her husband. She listened to his chest, felt his pulse, then glanced up at Peters.

"Is he all right?"

Alexandra nodded, smiled. "Just unconscious. Thanks for not ... really hurting him."

Peters nodded in return. In fact he would have liked to kill Finway, but it was not the time or place; one corpse was more than enough to handle, and Alexandra would certainly have crumbled. He found he was giddy with the realization that he was still alive. He took a deep breath, finally managed to say, "Better turn off the radio."

"Wait a second," Alexandra said. "The desk has to call. With the racket you guys were making, they must have heard you in Miami."

As if on cue, the telephone rang.

"You look a little worn out, Rick," Alexandra continued wryly as she got to her feet. "I'll handle it."

Alexandra went to the telephone and picked up the receiver. She shouted a few words, and only then turned off the radio. She apologized profusely to the man on the other end of the line, slurring her words slightly as if she were drunk. Peters watched admiringly as she finished the conversation by exchanging a few pleasantries and telling the desk clerk how much she and her friend were enjoying their stay in San Sierra.

She was the best, Peters thought. She had always been

the best, and she'd hardly lost a step over the years; he considered it only fitting that she should be his instrument for one of the most significant assassinations in history.

Alexandra hung up the receiver, looked at him and shrugged. "All set," she said tightly. "We've received a polite request to hold things down."

"Bless you, child," Peters said. "I must say, you made a timely entrance."

Alexandra frowned. "Where did you go, Rick? I came out, saw that you weren't there, and got worried. Then I heard all this crashing around. Thank God the place is deserted."

Peters jerked a thumb in the direction of Swarzwalder's body. "I saw him come out of a room that wasn't his. I ducked back, followed him, and saw him let himself into our room."

"But why should he do that, Rick?"

"I don't know. A very careful assassin, I suppose. We were searching rooms; he was searching rooms."

"Strange he should go to our room."

"Yeah," Peters replied evenly. "Strange. I guess we were next on his list. Then again, maybe the Company sprang a leak."

"Stupid," Alexandra said after a thoughtful pause. "He should have left well enough alone. I was beginning to think we'd never find him."

Peters said nothing, but he continued to study the woman. Flushed with excitement, she seemed to have crossed over some invisible boundary and almost to have forgotten her unconscious husband. Peters had not. Finway was just starting to come around, and Peters watched him carefully. He knew he was not out of trouble yet. The plastique he planned to switch with Alexandra's barrette had been found by Swarzwalder, and it had been lying on the bed, exposed to view. Peters had no way of knowing what had happened before he'd entered the room, but he was fairly certain he would know as soon as he saw Finway's face whether or not the lawyer had seen the barrette and, if he had, whether he had any idea what it was.

Finway groaned, stirred. He rubbed the back of his neck, then slowly got to his feet. Obviously shaken, he looked back and forth between Alexandra and Peters, then glanced at Swarzwalder's still, twisted body. Finway grimaced, then quickly looked away.

He didn't know, Peters thought, and bowed his head to hide the exultation he was afraid might show on his face. If Finway had seen the fake barrette, he hadn't made the connection, at least not yet.

"Well!" Alexandra exclaimed. Her voice was high-pitched, quavering on the edge of hysteria, and her movements were jerky and hyperactive, like a badly handled marionette. She threw her arms around her husband's neck and kissed him hard on the mouth. "My husband, the hero! This time you almost blew it, darling, but I forgive you. Imagine finding you in my room! I like that!"

Peters watched Finway turn his head slightly. The lawyer gripped his wife's arms, then gently but firmly pushed her away.

"What the hell's the matter with you, Alexandra?" Finway asked softly. "A man's been killed."

Alexandra's laugh was harsh and ironic, so jagged that even Peters looked at her with surprise. "Yes, John, I noticed. A man *has* been killed—despite your interference. I'm sorry if his death offends your delicate sensibilities, darling, but that big guy just happens to be the kindly gentleman who was trying to kill Rick and who would have killed you and me, not to mention the bearded fellow who runs this island. The man whose life you wanted to save was the joker we came here to get."

"Take it easy, Alexandra," Finway said slowly. "You're higher than a kite."

"Bullshit! *Bullshit*, John! You don't know what you're talking about! The man was a killer!"

John Finway stared hard at his wife for a few moments, then turned his back to the man and woman and walked to the window. "David Swarzwalder was the man who saved my life," he said quietly.

"All right," Alexandra said coldly, after a long pause. She was still obviously very angry, but seemed more in control of herself. "I hope it's not necessary to say that I'm damn glad he did. He happened to be in the right place at the right time, and he did you a favor. He was feeling magnanimous."

"He was in a no-risk situation," Peters said carefully to the other man's back. "When he saved you he became a hero, and hero is the best cover there is."

"It doesn't change the reality of the situation," Alexandra snapped impatiently. "Think, John!"

There was a prolonged silence. Finally the lawyer turned from the window. "You didn't have to kill him," he said to Alexandra. He looked at Peters, continued, "He was finished."

Peters arched his eyebrows. "Was he?"

"You could have handed him over to the Sierrans."

"Could we? You think maybe they'd declare a national holiday in our honor? Do you want to go home with your wife, Finway, or would you like to hang around in San Sierra for the next forty years trying to explain our situation to the DMI and the Sierran courts?"

There was another long silence, then Finway said tersely, "I'm sorry."

"It's all right," Peters said easily. He put his belt back on, then strode over to the other man and extended his hand. He had seen anger and something approaching disgust in Alexandra's eyes, and it occurred to him that Finway had lost his wife in the past fifteen minutes. Now, Peters thought, Alexandra might come to him of her own accord, and that would make everything perfect. "This isn't exactly your line of work."

Finway's grip was firm, but Peters noticed with satisfaction that the other man would not meet his gaze. "That's no excuse," the lawyer said tightly. "Swarzwalder was trying to kill you. I had no right to do what I did."

Peters shrugged. "It doesn't make any difference. It's over now."

"It's over!" Alexandra shouted, throwing her head back and laughing. "Over! We've done it!"

"Well, not quite," Peters said cautiously, noting with interest and some concern the accelerating trill of hysteria in the woman's tone and manner. She might be his now, he thought, but she was still far away, very high. He was going to have to reel her in. "We have to play it out to the end, just in case our friend Swarzwalder has someone else along with him on the trip."

Alexandra nodded thoughtfully. She stared at the floor for a few seconds, then abruptly looked up at her husband. Long moments passed, and suddenly she frowned and blinked rapidly. "John, what were *you* doing here?"

Peters waited, keeping his own face impassive as he watched the other man's features reflect a series of emotions: shame, wounded pride, and embarrassment vied for supremacy in John Finway's gray eyes. Finway stiffened, bowed his head and thrust his hands into his pockets.

"John?"

Finway's head slowly came up. Now agony was clearly reflected in his features. His mouth was a thin, tense line. However, he managed to meet his wife's gaze, and his voice was steady when he spoke. "I came here to see if you and Rick were sleeping together."

"Oh," Alexandra said in a small voice suddenly deflated of its resonant madness. She flushed, then quickly turned her head away.

"Swarzwalder was here when I came in," the lawyer continued in the same flat tone. "I caught him going through Rick's luggage. He came after me, and that's when Rick came in." He paused, directed his steady, tortured gaze at Peters, and drew himself up even straighter. "You saved my life. I thank you, and I want you to know that I'm very much ashamed of the way I behaved."

"Hey, forget it," Peters said, smiling broadly. "I'll know who to call if I ever need a lawyer. Right now we've got something else to worry about; we've got a body to get rid of."

Peters narrowed his eyes when he saw Alexandra turn her back on her husband. He was certain the gesture was symbolic as well as physical, a rejection, and the warmth in her eyes when she looked at him seemed to confirm it.

Alexandra turned the radio back on and adjusted it to a low volume. "What about the lake?" she asked softly, walking back to the center of the room. "We can weight the body."

Peters thought about it, shook his head. "That's the first place they're going to look when this guy turns up missing. We can't afford an autopsy. If they drag the lake and bring up a weighted body with marks on the throat and a little hole in the back, we're all going to be held up here some time. There'd be a background check, and we especially can't afford that. Besides, the desk clerk would be sure to remember the noise up here. We'd be in trouble."

"What then, Rick?"

"He needs a steep fall, something that will bust him up. He could have gone hiking."

"Well, we've got mountains."

Again, Peters shook his head. "The mountains are too far away, and we don't know the roads around here. We have to steal a car or a truck somewhere, and we could be gone too long; the party's over if we get caught out there. If there is a backup man, he'll have a clear shot at Salva on Friday night."

John Finway cleared his throat. Peters glanced at the man, but Alexandra did not turn.

"I went for a walk around the lake earlier," the lawyer said in a strained voice. "There's a steep cliff at the opposite end of the lake that you can't see from the hotel. There's a path leading up to the top. I suppose a man could fall off there and kill himself."

Peters nodded. "The lake's close enough, but we can't carry him down there. Too much open ground. Is there any kind of a road back there?"

"I don't know. I wasn't looking for a road."

Peters walked to the body, pushed it over with his foot in order to examine the puncture wound in the back. There was virtually no bleeding. "All right," he said, "let's assume there is one. If not, we'll find someplace else to dump him. It's a rugged countryside."

"Where are our three watchdogs?" Alexandra asked.

"They're on their way to Peleoro," Peters replied. "Every one of the Germans is gone, so we only have the hotel staff and a few of our own people to worry about. With the exception of the desk clerk, I'll bet most of the staff is sacked out by now."

"Let's get it over with, Rick," Alexandra said tightly.

"Okay. You go downstairs and check out the situation. The workers must have their cars parked somewhere in the back. See if you can get to one. We can take the body down the stairway in the back and out through the delivery entrance. I'll take care of the dumping; you stay here to run interference if anything happens."

Alexandra nodded curtly. "I can always stage one of my sexy drunk acts."

"We'll eyeball this guy's room when I get back."

"I'd like to help," John Finway blurted out.

Alexandra still would not look at her husband. Peters shrugged casually, said, "Sure. You can help me get rid of the body."

John

He felt blurred—a spectral, peripheral presence in some-one else's dream.

A confident, glittery-eyed Alexandra returned to the room twenty minutes later to report that she had found the employees' parking lot in the back. She had crossed the wires in one of the cars and it was waiting for them, run-ning, near the delivery entrance at the rear of the hotel.

They rolled the stiffening corpse up into a blanket. John lifted the shoulders and Peters the feet. With Alexandra going ahead of them to make sure the way was clear, the men carried the body down a narrow service stairway at the rear of the hotel and out through the delivery entrance. Alexandra opened the back door of an ancient 1956 Chev-rolet and the men slid the body across the rear seat. Alex-andra retrieved the blanket, checked to make certain there were no bloodstains on it, then headed back into the hotel. Peters got into the car behind the wheel and John slid into the seat on the passenger's side. Peters eased the clutch out and steered the car down a narrow, dirt auxiliary drive used by delivery trucks and hotel employees.

Why, there was nothing at all to this spy business, John thought; hell, all you did after stabbing and strangling a man to death was to dump him in a stolen car, drop him off a cliff, and then go back and act as if nothing had hap-pened. All in a day's work for a dragon. Don't worry about being caught; don't worry about a worker coming off duty and reporting that his car is gone; don't worry about conditions in Sierran prisons. Caution: dragons at work. But then, everyone knew that dragons didn't exist.

John swallowed the laughter bubbling in his throat, afraid that once released it would not stop.

He'd been led astray by mythological beasts, John thought. That's what he'd tell the Sierran authorities.

The dream feeling persisted. He was aware that his body was efficiently performing certain actions, but in his mind he wasn't making connections between action, reason, and morality; he was simply hiding somewhere in the dream and letting his body do the work.

But his memory worked all too well.

He could remember the fight; he recalled his paralyzing feelings of ambiguity and terrible vacillation in vivid contrast to Alexandra's instant decisiveness the moment she'd entered the room; he could remember her speed in going to the aid of her comrade.

He could remember the contempt he'd glimpsed in his wife's eyes when she'd looked at him.

Alexandra and Peters were dragons, all right, John thought. But they breathed ice, not fire.

He'd become aware of the fact that the man and woman shared a camaraderie he could never share. Now that he had seen the dragons in action, John fully appreciated just how ludicrous and presumptuous it had been for him to think that he should stay in San Sierra because Alexandra might need his protection. He now realized that Alexandra —this strange woman who was his wife and whom he now felt he had never really known—had never needed his protection. Indeed, he thought, if it hadn't been for this beautiful stranger who'd borne him three children, he'd probably be dead, the victim of an equally strange, chameleon-like man who had given him back his life but who would certainly have snatched it away if Peters had not intervened.

He'd been sucked into an alternate universe, John thought. When he had boarded the plane for San Sierra he had fallen through a crack someplace in space and time, and now the seam had closed behind him. This place—this surreal, self-contained arena of easy lies and quick, violent death—was the dragon's natural milieu. He did not belong in this place; he simply could not function in the manner needed to survive. Here he was good only for disposing of corpses.

He continued to loathe the man sitting next to him. But Rick Peters was the man Alexandra openly admired, John thought. Peters was now the man she was closest to. And John had begun to suspect that Peters was the man his wife would end up with when the trip was over. Still, as much as he despised the man, John's pride demanded he offer what he felt was a due measure of courtesy to the dragon, the warrior who had saved his life.

He now understood perfectly why Alexandra had never told him about her life as a dragon. Before San Sierra, there was nothing she could have told him that he would have understood, no way for her to explain how she and Peters could operate smoothly, even cheerfully, in a lunar landscape of the mind and spirit where he could barely breathe.

Now he was terribly sorry that he knew, and he deeply regretted coming to San Sierra. He knew that his presence on the tour, his witnessing of the kinds of acts dragons could perform without hesitation, had changed him, perhaps forever. For the first time in his life he was tormented by feelings of insecurity, helplessness, and self-contempt, and he sensed that an apparently insurmountable barrier had formed between himself and Alexandra.

Once he'd thought that a woman named Selma was a problem. Now he could not remember what Selma looked like, much less why he'd ever been attracted to her in the first place. It was as if that memory, like everything else in his life before Saturday, had been broken under the feet of dragons.

Nor did he believe that his life would necessarily come back into focus when he returned to Pomona, even if Alexandra decided to stay with him. Once through the crack, he thought, it was not so easy to find your way home again. Things like the pieces of your soul were not where you thought you'd left them. He was not sure he would ever be able to live normally again; he would always be scarred by the memory of the way Alexandra had looked at him.

Peters drove east a mile on the highway, then cut south

and circled back. He found a narrow, pitted dirt road that led almost to the perimeter of the lake, drove up it, and parked the car behind a thick stand of trees. Together, they carried the body to the top of the cliff, then set it down. For a moment John thought that Peters was going to pause for a few seconds in some kind of bizarre memorial rite for a fallen colleague; he ended feeling merely ridiculous when Peters planted his foot against the ribs of the corpse and unceremoniously pushed the body off the cliff to be smashed on an outcropping of jagged rocks below.

John looked down over the edge of the cliff and was vaguely surprised to find that, in this strange new dream world, he did not even feel nauseous at the sight of Swarzwalder's bloody and twisted body. In the company of dragons, the broken lump of flesh somehow seemed a natural part of the landscape.

Alexandra emerged from the hotel's delivery entrance as Peters drove up the dirt auxiliary driveway. She nodded to them, indicating that everything was all right. Then, with the two dragons functioning as smoothly as an Olympic relay team, Alexandra and Peters switched places: Peters got out and Alexandra slid behind the wheel in order to return the car to the parking space where she had found it.

John quickly stepped out of the car. He did not want to be alone with his wife.

"You all right, Finway?"

For a moment John felt confused and panicky when he saw that Peters was not going back through the delivery entrance; the blond-haired man had thrust his hands into his pockets and was walking casually around the side of the hotel, heading toward the front. Then John realized that they were finished with their job; Swarzwalder's body had been disposed of, and they had returned without being caught. They were out of danger. Once again they could appear to be nothing more than members of the tour group enjoying a carefree stroll around the hotel grounds.

"No," John said abruptly. "I'm not all right."

"Then you'd better stay out of sight until you get your act together," Peters said absently. He paused and looked back over his shoulder to make sure that Alexandra was out of the car and following them. "See you later."

Alexandra

She had done it. She had acted without fear or hesitation when it had counted.

"*. . . good thing you popped in when you did.*"

Her reflexes, speed, and strength were as good as they had ever been.

"*Christ, you're beautiful when you're like that.*"

She was as good as she had ever been. The years, the bearing of three children, had cost her virtually nothing.

"*. . . my beautiful, sexy panther.*"

She was an artist, and artists always pay a price for what they do best.

"*. . . some set of steel claws . . .*"

She was an artist deprived of materials; she had thrown away her own paints and canvas.

"*Alexandra!*"

"Huh?"

She was suddenly aware that Peters was in front of her, blocking her path. He put his hands on her arms, then leaned forward and kissed her gently, lingeringly, on the lips. Alexandra stood passively, eyes closed, accepting the kiss and moving her own lips slightly. She had the vague realization that she was not acting; Rick Peters' kiss suddenly seemed the most natural thing in the world, warm and caring flesh that formed a bridge to a past she was beginning to think she had never understood. The man with his lips on hers understood, and she was sorry when he withdrew.

"Where are you?" Peters asked softly.

Alexandra blinked several times, trying to focus her thoughts. The hot, white Sierran sun reflected brilliantly, painfully, off the blue water of the pool to her right into her eyes, and she turned away.

"Trying to figure out where I've been."

"I understand."

"Do you, Rick?"

"Yes. From the moment I saw you through the snow in that parking lot, I knew you'd been living as the stranger in town for fifteen years. You pay a lot of rent for that kind of living."

"I paid a lot of rent to be a dragon."

"Only because you never came to terms with what you were; how great you were, and are."

"Rick, how have you handled being away all these years?"

Peters shrugged. "I'm a hell of a realtor. I've made a lot of money."

"You didn't miss . . . this kind of thing?"

"Not really. Remember, I never felt guilty about being damn good at a job that had to be done, or about my personal needs. Also, I left the dragons on my own terms. You left on John's terms, although, of course, he wasn't aware of it. You talk about lies, but you've been living a lie by trying to be a person that you thought John wanted you to be."

"Rick, I feel so . . . very strange. God, I hope I don't screw this thing up."

Peters laughed easily. "You've got to be kidding. In fact, I think the layoff may have done you good. You've never been better."

"Thank you for saying that."

"I want to say something else," Peters replied evenly. "I love you, Alexandra. I've never stopped loving you. We're the same. We could live together and be happy because there are no lies or false expectations between us. The Company might damn well want us on staff after this, but that isn't the point. Even if we're never involved in the business again, we could love and be at peace because we know what we are, how good we are, and we'd take pride in it. Maybe now, after fifteen years, you realize that you need me as much as I need you."

Not trusting herself to speak, Alexandra said nothing. She turned and started walking. When Peters came up beside her, she reached out and put her hand in his.

John

John felt light-headed and disoriented. He went quickly to his room, where he stripped, leaving his clothes in a pile on the floor, and took a hot shower. When he had finished and toweled off, his limbs felt leaden. He turned off the air conditioner, slipped on a pair of shorts, then sat down heavily on the side of his bed and stared blankly at the empty bed across the room.

He should get dressed, John thought. He should stop thinking about Swarzwalder. But he did not feel like getting dressed, and he could not stop thinking about Swarzwalder. He did not feel like doing anything, and he decided he would simply sit and wait for dinner.

John sat for many hours; the scheduled dinner hour came and went, and still he sat. Finally he toppled over on the bed and slept fitfully until seven-thirty in the morning, when they came for him.

Thursday, January 24; 11:15 A.M.

Raul

He wouldn't be in this position if they'd built the hotel with a bugging capacity, Raul thought angrily. People who were not planning to commit crimes should not object to having their conversations overheard.

Raul was very conscious of the microphones in the desk and the presence of the two Sierran intelligence agents in the anteroom behind him. If the DMI had been monitoring the conversations of these people during the week, Raul thought, they would already have their answers and he wouldn't have to do this job.

Raul glanced at his watch. The three Americans had been kept waiting in a locked room for more than three hours, and Raul was certain they'd seen or heard the buses leaving earlier. He was satisfied they would be feeling increasing pressure, if they were guilty of anything.

It was the alternate possibility that disturbed him; if the Americans were not guilty, Raul thought, they would be feeling an ever-increasing sense of outrage, and Raul had no doubt whatsoever whose head was going to roll if Sierran intelligence had made a mistake. He would undoubtedly be thanked privately for doing his patriotic duty, perhaps even secretly honored by the Party. But he strongly doubted that he would finally be admitted to Party membership, and he would almost certainly be publicly criticized and humiliated, all so that the Americans would continue to come with their dollars and their stupid ideas. The DMI would shrug its massive bureaucratic shoulders and go back to its other business, and he would end up having to work ten hours a day in a factory or on a farm. He deeply resented the fact that he was being set up as a token sacrifice

172

in the event other people were wrong, but he knew there was nothing he could do about it.

He could only hope that the suspicions of the DMI men were correct. His job, his future, depended on how skillfully he could interrogate the Americans. He had to prove the intelligence people correct. It had been arranged that way; San Sierra could not afford to have American tourists frightened away.

Raul's stomach growled audibly as he sat down behind the desk in the manager's office. Gas, he thought. His stomach always rumbled when he was upset, and it had been rumbling virtually nonstop all though the morning.

He knew that, as a Sierratour guide, he had a coveted job. It was an assignment he had earned as a result of his dedication to revolutionary ideals, work with his neighborhood *Komiteh,* and six months of fighting in Africa, where he had almost died of fright. He had been rewarded for his loyalty to the Revolution with one of the most prestigious and easiest jobs his country had to offer. He rode around the countryside in air-conditioned buses the year round, enjoyed the best food at the finest resorts. And all he had to do was be nice to the Americans.

The problem, Raul thought, was that he was not good at his job. There were too many things he could not forget.

He could not forget a childhood in a poor, dust-cloaked, and disease-ridden village. All that had changed, of course, since the Revolution. His parents were still alive, thanks to Manuel's redistribution of food and medical facilities. And all the while the Americans had supported Sabrito. The Beach of Fire had demonstrated to him that most Americans would, if they had the power, change things in San Sierra back to the way they had been. Raul simply could not understand why such rich, fat people would want the Sierrans to be poor and sick. He hated Americans.

He especially hated the Americans who came as tourists. He had found the vast majority of them arrogant and condescending, full of stupid questions and snide remarks; they were constantly clucking their tongues at the "quaint" way of life in San Sierra; they commented on the "poverty" they saw when they knew nothing at all about real poverty and when they themselves, by virtue of their country's policy of economic boycott, were responsible for the crude way of life they did see.

Try as hard as he might to mask them, Raul knew that his feelings showed. There had been complaints in the past; the Sierratour officials would not tell him how many, but Raul suspected that the number was considerable. He had become expendable, and he knew that was another reason why he had been given this particular job.

But then, he thought, the situation might change if he did a good job. If the Americans confessed.

The door behind him opened, and Raul swiveled in his chair to look up into the cold eyes of the tall, brown-skinned man with slicked-back hair who had given him his initial instructions.

"We're sending them in," the DMI agent said evenly. "You've studied the dossier?"

Raul patted the thin manila folder in front of him. "Yes, sir," he replied, not daring to add that he had been up all night and that it was hard to concentrate under such conditions; he did not want to be reported as uncooperative. "Uh, are you sure it wouldn't be better for you people to question them separately?"

"No, Raul," the man said wearily. "We want to observe the interaction between the three of them. We'll be monitoring the conversation and watching through the peepholes. You don't mind doing this for us, do you?"

"No, sir," Raul said quickly.

"Good. We want you to follow the line of questioning we've outlined as closely as possible. You can read the questions, if you feel the need, but we'd prefer that you try to make the interrogation sound spontaneous."

"I understand, sir."

"Very well," the tall man said, stepping into the anteroom and closing the door.

The door facing the main corridor opened. Raul drew himself up in his chair and glowered in what he hoped was an appropriate manner as the woman and two men entered the office. His gaze swept over the faces of the Americans as he searched for some indication of their guilt or innocence.

He noted that Peters and the woman were gripping each other's hand tightly. The woman looked nervous and annoyed, while Rick Peters simply looked angry; the pale eyes of the man glared balefully back at Raul. Theirs was, Raul thought, perhaps a natural reaction of innocent people suddenly detained without explanation in a foreign country while their tour group had gone on without them. His stomach growled loudly, and he cleared his throat to cover the sound.

John Finway was much more difficult to read. The lawyer's face was drawn and pale, and his gray eyes seemed dull and sunken in their sockets. Raul looked for fear in the haggard face, but could find only disinterest. Raul found that odd, but he reminded himself that the American had been acting strange throughout the trip.

"Now look, Raul—"

"Be quiet, Mr. Peters!" Raul snapped, pleased with the ring of authority he had managed to summon up in his tone. He had been practicing lowering the pitch of his voice all through the early morning hours. "Sit down, please! All of you sit down!"

Raul observed that Finway moved like an automaton. The lawyer walked slowly, stiffly, across the office and seated himself in one of the three wooden chairs that had been set up in front of the desk. Peters and the woman hesitated and glanced uncertainly at one another, but then they too came across the room and sat down.

Raul swallowed. He was beginning to experience stage fright. His mouth was dry; he suddenly felt panicked, and he had to resist the impulse to open the folder on the desk and look at the questions—his lines—the DMI agents had written out for him. He knew that it would be a mistake to display signs of nervousness, but he felt tense and terribly insecure. Perhaps, he thought, it was not yet too late to get up, walk into the anteroom and tell the men he could not do this. The Americans were sure to see his fear, sense his vulnerability.

He was grateful when the phone rang. He picked up the receiver and listened as one of the men in the other room provided him with the information that they had just confirmed and that he had been anxiously awaiting. Suddenly Raul felt his anxiety fall away from him; he knew exactly how he would proceed. His stomach had stopped growling.

There would be no farm or factory work for him, Raul

thought as he slowly replaced the receiver in its cradle. There would be honors in a public ceremony when it was noted how he had broken these people down. Maybe, at last, he would even be given a Party membership. Catching spies was serious business.

He stared up at the ceiling for a few moments, as if he could see all his dreams projected there. Then he suddenly shifted his gaze to John Finway and spoke in his new, deeper voice. "Did you know that the man who called himself David Swarzwalder is dead?"

Finway slowly moved his attention from the wall to Raul's face. "No," he said quietly, frowning. "I didn't know, and I'm very sorry to hear it. David seemed like a very nice man. What happened, Raul?"

"It is my place to ask questions, Mr. Finway."

"Come on, Raul, that line was old before the revolution," Peters interjected, half rising out of his chair. "Miss Scott and I knew; we saw the ambulance taking him away. I heard the body was found by some couple looking for a place to screw. So what? What the hell does that have to do with us?"

"You *will* sit down, Mr. Peters," Raul said without taking his eyes from John Finway's face. He found that he was actually beginning to enjoy himself. There was a tingling sensation in his lower belly and groin that was almost sexual. It occurred to him that, for the first time in his life, he had real power. He could say virtually anything to these people, and they would have to sit and listen; he could order them around, and they would have to obey. "If you can't remain silent, I will have you taken away and I'll question you at a later date. A much later date."

The woman pulled at Peters' sleeve and the blond-haired man sat down, as Raul had known he would. He'd *had* to sit down, Raul thought. Yes, power felt very good.

"When did you last see this man, Mr. Finway?"

"What man?"

Raul frowned. "Are you trying to make a joke with me?"

"No," the lawyer said in a flat voice. "God forbid I should try to get funny with you, Raul."

"I am referring to the man who called himself David Swarzwalder. When did you last see him?"

The lawyer shifted his gaze back to the wall. "Yesterday morning, just before he left for Peleoro."

"You did not know that David Swarzwalder did not go to Peleoro?"

"I saw him get on the bus."

"Did you know this man before this week?"

"No."

"You had never met?"

"No."

"Did you know that he approached one of our people on the plane and asked if Sierratour would book the two of you into the same room?"

"Yes. He asked me if I'd share a room with him. He told me he wanted to save the extra money he'd have to pay for a single room. I told him I preferred to be alone."

"Why do you suppose he came to you?"

"Swarzwalder said he and I were the only singles on the trip."

"Please look at me, Mr. Finway."

Raul saw color rise in Finway's neck. It was the first sign of animation he'd seen in the other man. The gray eyes shifted toward him and glinted with anger.

"Anything you say, Raul," the lawyer replied sharply, arching his eyebrows slightly. "How's this? Would you like to see me cross my eyes? Wiggle my ears?"

He'd made a mistake, Raul thought. Finway was, after all, a strange and powerful man with many connections; he was not to be pushed too far. He could see the anger in the other man, and it frightened him. Given his freedom, Raul thought, John Finway could be very dangerous.

"Now, Mr. Finway—"

"Let me tell you something, my Sierran *amigo:* you and Sierratour had better have a goddamn good reason for laying this crap on this other couple and me, because I'm going to raise a stink they'll smell all the way to the Russian bases at the South Pole. Now, I want to talk to someone who carries a hell of a lot more weight than you do."

Raul hesitated for just a moment as his stomach started to growl. Then he felt his own anger rising. "We'll see what kind of a stink you raise, Mr. Finway. I think there is a stink *here!*"

"Someone with authority, Raul."

"In time. It so happens there are three other singles on this tour. This man lied to you. Why do you suppose he did that?"

"Your voice sounds terrible, Raul. Do you have a cold?"

"Answer my question!"

"I haven't got the slightest idea why he lied. Maybe he liked my looks, for Christ's sake. Look, I'm sorry Swarzwalder is dead, but I don't see what it has to do with these people and myself. If you won't let us see someone with authority, how about getting to the point?"

Raul wished he smoked. He had once seen an American movie where the investigator lit a cigar and blew a large, perfect smoke ring just before he destroyed a suspect with a single piece of information. He would like to pause and blow a smoke ring now, but he settled for drumming his fingers rhythmically on the desk top as he stared hard at each individual in turn, snapping his head around in tiny, birdlike jerks.

"This man indeed got on the bus for Peleoro," Raul said at last. "But he got off almost immediately. He seemed to be in considerable pain, and he complained of having an ulcer attack. Yet his body was found at the base of a cliff down by the lake. Don't you think it strange that a man in such terrible pain would decide to take a strenuous hike?"

Raul grinned triumphantly as he leaned back in his chair and folded his hands across his stomach.

Nothing happened. The eyes of Peters and the woman were riveted to his face, while Finway continued to stare absently at the wall to his left. Raul's smile slowly faded.

"Mr. Finway?"

"Oh, you were asking me?"

"Yes, I was asking you! Don't you find it strange that a sick man would want to walk around a lake and hike up a cliff?!"

"I don't know, Raul. I've never had an ulcer attack."

"Well, I am telling you that it is strange!" Raul shouted, hopping to his feet. "You *know* it's strange!"

Raul paused, sucked in a deep breath, and bit his lower lip. He regretted his outburst and the fact that he'd jumped out of his chair. Mistakes. However, now that he was standing up, he decided to remain on his feet. He walked quickly around the desk, stopped in front of Peters and the woman. "There was a disturbance in your room yesterday morning," he continued in a clipped voice. "Please tell me what happened."

Peters and the woman looked at each other. Peters shrugged, and it was the woman who answered. Raul noted with satisfaction that there was a slight tremor in her voice.

"Raul, I explained it all to the desk clerk when he called. Rick and I just felt like loosening up a little. We started drinking and . . . I guess we got drunk and a little rowdy. We're sorry about that, but I don't see how—"

"Ah? Then you and your friend were having a party, Miss Scott?" Raul started to glance at John Finway, then looked back at Peters when the blond-haired man's voice cut though the silence.

"And it isn't all that easy getting drunk on Sierran booze, Raul. Christ, your rum is terrible. That said, I think you'd better let us the hell out of here and take us back to our group. We've all had enough of this chickenshit."

Raul smiled thinly, vaguely surprised to discover that Peters' anger and open contempt did not bother him at all. Power put you above and beyond so many things. "Chickenshit, Mr. Peters? Are you and Miss Scott lovers?"

Peters made a sound of disgust in his throat. "Of course we're lovers, for Christ's sake. And don't tell me Sierratour thought we were brother and sister when they gave us our visas. You were happy to take our money, Raul, so don't start getting puritanical on me. We fought for the revolution, too."

"I'm aware of that. Miss Scott, how long have you known Mr. Peters?"

"My God, Raul; Rick and I have known each other for years. We met in college. We found we had the same political instincts, and we've been together ever since." She frowned, hurt in her eyes. "You say you know our background, Raul. Then you must know that Rick and I believe in the same things you believe in. We fought too. Why are you treating us like this? We haven't done anything wrong."

Raul turned, slowly walked to the one window in the office, and stared out. He could feel the muscles in his chest and stomach begin to tighten, but it was an erotic, pleasant sensation. He imagined it was how a hunter felt when, after much difficult stalking, he at last had an elusive prey in his gunsight.

"It seems odd to me that you and Mr. Peters never married, Miss Scott."

He listened carefully to the woman's voice. It was soft, slightly tremulous.

"Rick and I have always felt that marriage is so bourgeois, Raul. We just like our relationship the way it is. We look on our living together as a way of maintaining our revolutionary consciousness. We've always felt as one with your people. This kind of treatment hurts us, Raul. Please tell us what you think we've done."

Raul lifted his hand and slowly traced a design on the windowpane with his fingernail. "Miss Scott? How long have you known Mr. Finway?"

Raul waited, listening in the silence. The woman's pause was too long, he thought; far too long. But then, he'd known it would be. He abruptly wheeled and caught fear prowling like an animal across her face, clouding her eyes and shadowing her features. Peters' large, whitish eyes remained cold, but Raul could see that mottled white patches had appeared high on his cheekbones. Only Finway appeared totally unconcerned as he continued to stare at the wall.

"Miss Scott?"

"I . . . I'm not sure I understand your question, Raul. John Finway's a very famous lawyer. Obviously, I know *who* he is. He defended us in court years ago when the cops tried to put Rick and me in prison. Naturally, we both recognized him right away. You remember; he was sick at the airport, and we helped him. Rick and I had hoped to resume our friendship with Mr. Finway, but he seemed very upset and distracted. We've respected his privacy."

"That's an interesting response, Miss Scott," Raul said, his voice rising with excitement. Again he felt a tingling sensation in his groin, and he realized that he had an erection. These people were finished, he thought. He was so choked with excitement that his next words were thick and rushed, tumbling over one another. "I might even say it's a very, very strange response in light of the fact that John Finway is your husband."

Raul grinned malevolently as he watched Rick Peters and Alexandra Finway brace in their chairs and grow pale. For just a moment Raul thought that Peters was going to leap out of the chair and attack him, but even that prospect didn't bother him. He did not want to be hurt, but he was confident that the DMI agents in the next room would quickly intervene if it appeared that he was going to be injured. In fact, he assumed that a physical attack on his person by a suspect he had been questioning would look good on his record, even heroic.

Raul watched with mixed emotions as the woman's hand flicked out and gripped Peters' wrist. The blond man slowly settled back in his chair, but his flesh retained its pasty, parchment hue.

"We simply didn't believe that a man in such great pain would choose to go for a strenuous walk," Raul continued. He had himself under control now, and his tone was that of a man relaxed and magnanimous in victory. "We immediately had our people in the United States begin to check all visa applications and make inquiries. One of the first things we discovered was that Mr. Swarzwalder was not who he'd said he was. The physical description of the David Swarzwalder who'd made the visa application bore no resemblance to the man who fell off a cliff. The man who died was carrying a false passport. We do not yet know who this man was, but we will certainly find out. We—"

Raul suddenly stopped speaking, distracted by the sight of John Finway, who had abruptly slumped forward in his chair and covered his face with his hands.

Raul looked away, torn between feelings of triumph and a depth of sympathy for the Americans that took him completely by surprise. "As a security measure, we began checking everyone on the tour," he continued uncertainly. His most fervent desire had been to break these people down; actually seeing John Finway crumble made him nervous. His hatred had disappeared, along with his erection. There was no question in his mind that these people would be imprisoned, and that caused him vague discomfort which he could not understand. He was a tour guide, Raul thought, not a prosecutor. Power could hurt. He found he actually felt protective toward the woman, and that bothered him. Still, this job had been forced on him, and he knew that his future depended on how well he did it.

"That's when we found out, Mrs. Finway, that you haven't used your maiden name since the mid nineteen sixties, when you married your husband. The passport you're traveling on was issued only a few weeks before the trip." He paused, took a deep breath and exhaled it slowly. "Now I would like the three of you to explain why Mr. Peters is traveling with Mrs. Finway, and why you have been behaving as if Mr. Finway were a stranger."

"It's all my fault," Finway said in a hoarse voice. When he took his hands from his face and looked up his eyes were red-rimmed, his face wet with tears. "Oh God, Raul, now I can see why you're so suspicious. You don't understand." He laughed bitterly as he turned toward the woman. "I guess I've really put us all into a jam, haven't I? I suppose it was stupid of me to try to hang onto you."

"Stupid is your middle name, John!" Alexandra Finway snapped savagely. "That's why I left you. Why I ever . . . Just tell Raul the truth so we can all get the hell out of here!"

Raul's stomach began to rumble ominously. He didn't realize he was backing away until he was stopped by the edge of the desk.

"My wife left me a month ago," the lawyer said, once again lowering his head to stare at the floor. "Our marriage had been . . . falling apart anyway. I knew she had a lover, but I didn't know who it was. I found out Alexandra was going to San Sierra, and I had the crazy notion that I could win her back if I followed her. Alexandra didn't know until we landed here that I was following her, and I hadn't known she was traveling with . . . him. I confronted them here at the airport. You saw what happened to me, Raul. I looked into my wife's eyes and . . . I guess I truly realized for the first time that she didn't love me anymore. I knew then that I wasn't going to get her back. I just . . . fell apart."

"Hell, we didn't want to make a scene at the airport," Peters said easily. "John goes out of his head sometimes, but he's a decent guy. Losing Alexandra kind of got to him. Getting into that kind of scene at the airport wasn't going to do his reputation any good. Also, buddy, we didn't

want to embarrass you people. As you saw, we got John
on the bus at the airport and managed to calm him down.
The three of us agreed that it was best to act as if we just
didn't know each other; otherwise, John would have been
the laughingstock of the group all week. That would have
ruined the trip for everybody. You can understand that,
can't you, Raul?"

Raul felt the blood rushing to his face, but he was powerless to stop it. "You've been sleeping with this man's wife
right under his nose?"

"Please, Raul," John Finway rasped. "I don't want to
talk about this anymore."

"John's been my husband in name only for a very long
time," Alexandra Finway said stiffly. "We're in the process
of getting a divorce. He's known for months that I was
in love with someone else. He had no business coming
along to spy on me, and I wasn't about to let him ruin a
vacation I'd been looking forward to just because of his
jealousy and childishness."

Raul opened his mouth to speak, but he could think of
nothing to say and no sound would come out. He closed
his mouth and half turned in the direction of the door behind him, as though looking for help.

"Oh, shit, man," Peters said. "You thought *we* might
be—?" He threw back his head and laughed loudly. The
laughter finally trailed off; Peters looked at Raul and
opened his eyes wide, mockingly, as he thrust his head
forward. "Hey, Raul, maybe we're spies."

"Raul?" Finway said softly. "I've made enough of a
fool of myself. I know I'm . . . not well. I think . . . I know
I'd very much like to go home now, if you can arrange it."

"Just a minute," Raul said tightly. "Uh, the three of
you wait right here."

"Don't be too long, Raul!" the Sierran heard Peters
call after him as he slipped through the door into the
adjoining room. "We paid for this chickenshit vacation,
and you're wasting our time!"

The two agents had unplugged their tape recorder and
were packing up their other equipment. Raul stood just inside the door, breathing heavily. The tall, brown-skinned
man motioned for him to come closer, and Raul walked
across the room on legs that felt wooden and unsteady.

"We'll bring you two cars," the man said. "Have Constantina take Peters and the woman on to Angeles Blanca. She'll smooth things over with them. You—"

"What if they're lying, sir? Who was this Swarzwalder, and what was he doing here?"

"Keep your voice down, Raul," the man said coolly, his dark eyes flashing a warning. "We'll trace the dead man. We don't think these three had anything to do with him. Finway's a lawyer, not an actor, and he did get his visa at the last moment. In any case, this matter is no longer your concern; running this tour smoothly is. You know the importance Manuel attaches to tourism. Take Finway directly to the airport and send him home as he asks. Put him on the first plane that will take him back. Sierratour will pick up any additional expense."

Raul cleared his throat noisily, fighting back a growing sense of panic as he watched the two men preparing to leave by the rear exit. "Uh, sir? Sir, I'm afraid I'm going to get into trouble as a result of this. I'm sure there'll be a formal complaint." He coughed drily. "Sir, I'm afraid I'll lose my job."

The tall man paused and glanced back over his shoulder. "Don't worry about it, Raul," the man said not unkindly. "We'll make sure you're not dismissed; you make sure Finway is on this way home as quickly as possible. Be nice to him, be courteous, but get him on a plane. Under no circumstances allow him back with the others. If he's going to have a breakdown, we don't want him to have it in San Sierra. Let them work out their personal problems in their own country." The tall man paused again, looked at his partner and smiled thinly. "San Sierra doesn't need any unfavorable articles in the travel section of the *New York Times*."

The second man grunted, then spoke for the first time. "Or in the *National Enquirer*."

"Yes, sir," Raul said. "Thank you, sir." But the two men were already gone.

He took a series of deep breaths in a futile effort to relax himself, then returned to the other room. Peters and Alexandra Finway were on their feet now. They were talking excitedly with one another, their voices taut with outrage. Finway was still slumped in his chair, his face covered with his hands.

"Excuse me, please," Raul said, putting a hand over his mouth and coughing loudly. He felt like an animal at bay. He hated the thought of being in thrall to the Americans, but he hated the thought of losing his job even more. He had been told to be courteous.

Peters and the woman stopped talking and looked at him with open hostility on their faces.

"Please accept my apologies," Raul continued thickly, addressing himself to the standing man and woman. "There was a misunderstanding, but now it has been cleared up. It was a matter of security." He paused and smiled tentatively. "The rest of the trip will be wonderful for you. You will see. You will have a wonderful time in Angeles Blanca."

Peters slowly and deliberately looked at his watch, then placed his hands on his hips and leaned forward slightly. "You've got to be kidding, Raul. You hang us up here for hours, insult and yell at us, then tell us we're going to have a wonderful time?"

"Constantina will drive you to Angeles Blanca," Raul said quickly. "The trip is much faster by car. Mr. Finway, I will personally drive you to the airport as soon as you've packed."

"I want to talk to my wife."

"Excuse me?"

"Oh, John!" Alexandra Finway said, throwing her head back and clenching her fists in exasperation. "What is there left to say?"

John Finway slowly took his hands away from his face and looked up at his wife. When he spoke, Raul thought the man's tone was subtly different, more controlled. "I would like to talk to you before I leave, Alexandra. Perhaps you can give me that. I'll try not to embarrass you."

The woman glanced at Peters and sighed wearily. "Whatever will make you happy, John."

Finway rose unsteadily to his feet and blew his nose. "Are we free to go, Raul?"

"Of course you are free to go," Raul said nervously. "Why don't we all plan to meet at the front of the hotel in, uh, half an hour? Call the desk clerk when you're ready and he'll send someone to bring your bags down."

"Thank you, Raul," Alexandra Finway said sweetly. "I'm sure everything's going to be fine now."

John Finway turned and walked out of the office without another word. The other two followed. Raul cursed under his breath, then strode quickly across the room and slammed the door shut.

John

"Jesus H. Christ," Peters breathed as they walked away from the hotel, following John toward a small, wooded knoll a hundred yards from the entrance.

"John," Alexandra said quietly, "you were magnificent."

John said nothing, nor did he look at the other two people until he had reached a shaded area protected by two large trees. When he did turn around he could see Constantina pacing nervously, head down and arms crossed over her chest, in the driveway at the front of the hotel.

"That was some number you did on our Sierran *amigo* back there," Peters said evenly. "You saved our big fat collective ass. Nice job, John."

"Okay," John replied curtly. "Maybe that makes us even. Now I'd like to talk to my wife. Privately."

Peters' cold, pale eyes stared at the taller man. "I don't know if that's a good idea, John," he said softly after a long pause. "We're out of it. Why take a chance on screwing up now? For Christ's sake, Constantina's right over there, and you know that red-faced runt is going to be watching us out of the window."

"Get the hell out of here," John said evenly to Peters.

Peters stayed where he was, staring hard at John.

"Go, Rick," Alexandra said, lightly touching the blond-haired man's arm.

John looked into Alexandra's eyes as Peters abruptly wheeled and walked back in the direction of the hotel. He sensed that Alexandra was waiting for him to speak, but he simply continued to stare at her. He was searching for a glimpse of his wife somewhere in the liquid depths of the dark brown eyes, but she wasn't there. The memory of the scorn he had seen in her eyes the day before still seared and shamed him. The contempt was gone now, but it had merely been replaced by a hot excitement that John knew had nothing to do with him.

"You *were* magnificent, John," Alexandra said at last.

"Not really," John replied evenly. "It wasn't a big deal. It was the kind of situation where I operate best. Raul isn't exactly Mr. District Attorney, and any rookie lawyer would have recognized that scene as a fishing expedition. How much could they have found out overnight? As soon as they rounded us up and put us in that room, I knew that Sierran intelligence had found out about Swarzwalder and us, but the moment I saw Raul I knew they weren't sure what to make of it. They were looking for us to show them the connection, if there was one. If they hadn't been fishing, we'd have been interrogated by someone a hell of a lot tougher than Raul. He was just trotted out to test our reactions. They're worried about adverse publicity."

Alexandra nodded thoughtfully. "Of course you're right. I should have figured that out. I was just too frightened."

"He was milking that buildup to our marriage hard enough to rupture a herd of cows. I kept hoping you'd short-circuit him by stepping on his punch line." John smiled wryly, without humor. "You're the actor in the family."

"Laurence Olivier couldn't have played that scene better than you did, John. Your face; your tears."

"I'm a nickel-and-dime method actor; any lawyer has to be. If you think *I'm* good, you should see some of my clients." The suggestion of a smile disappeared. "I knew I had to make it look convincing. I managed the tears by imagining Kara and Kristen trying to explain to Michael why it would be a very long time before he saw his parents again. I visualized him living with our relatives, calling some other couple Mommy and Daddy."

"God, John," Alexandra said in a hushed voice, a veil of hurt momentarily clouding her eyes. "It's hard enough for me without you saying something like that."

"Don't 'God, John' me, Alexandra! There are people back in the real world who need you. I need you. If I knew how to make it harder for you, I would. For just a second, when I mentioned our children, I saw my wife standing in front of me. Now she's run off someplace again."

Alexandra glanced around her nervously. John followed the direction of her gaze and saw that Peters was talking to Constantina.

"She isn't gone, John," Alexandra said quietly. "She's working. Now I have to go. I'm glad you're going home. I'll be there Sunday."

"Will you, Alexandra?"

"I don't know what you mean," Alexandra said. But she would not meet his gaze.

"You're going through a lot of changes here. It's not just the pressure. You like the pressure, the excitement; I can see that, even if no one else can. You're still flying high, and it isn't from fear or out of concern for me or the kids. You remind me now of what you were like when I first met you: hyper and hidden, with big, empty spaces inside you. Now I understand. This business sucks something good out of you; it's twisting you out of shape, Alexandra. I'm not sure if you're ever going to get right again—or even if you *want* to get right." John paused. When Alexandra didn't reply, he continued, "Can you look at me and tell me for sure that you'll be coming home when this is over?"

He could see the muscles in her neck quiver, as if she were struggling against some great weight pressing against the back of her skull. Slowly her head came up. Her mouth was set in a thin, tense line, and her face was ashen. "This is a hell of a time to ask me something like that, John."

"That's Exhibit A," John said tightly. "I have to leave San Sierra now whether I want to or not. The fact is that I want to. Come home with me, Alexandra. Right now. I still don't believe the CIA would mount an operation like this. There's something wrong with the feel of this thing; very, very wrong. Let's pack our bags and get the hell out of here while we can, together."

"You know I can't do that."

"I know nothing of the kind. The man you were after is dead."

"There could be a second man. Rick explained that to you."

"Maybe there is, maybe there isn't. One thing for certain
is that their top gun is out of the way."

"John, that isn't certain at all. Swarzwalder, or whoever
he was, may not have been the principal assassin. He may
have simply been an errand boy. He was searching rooms,
remember?"

"So what? Peters can handle the baby-sitting chores tomorrow night by himself. Don't forget that Salva will be
surrounded by his own security men. Even if there is another assassin, he's going to be off his feed after what happened to his partner. If he's as smart as the two of you
seem to think he is, he'll call the operation off and come
back another day. Let Peters mop up. You've done your
job. Let's have an instant reconciliation and get out of
here."

"Not yet, John," Alexandra said firmly. "It's just not fin-
ished. I can't leave Rick here to handle things by himself.
This kind of operation requires two people to do it right.
I just can't walk away from this."

"That's what worries me most, Alexandra. This business
stinks; you know there's something wrong with it, and yet
you can't walk away. So I give you Exhibit B: neither of
us is in the clear on this marriage question."

"Well, it's not helping that we're standing here so long,"
Alexandra said with annoyance. "I don't feel like putting on
a performance now, John. I don't want to have to start
yelling to make it look good. Please go home and let me
do my job."

"Let me finish. You must realize that Raul was just the
point man, a stalking horse, back there. There had to be
pros listening in, behind the other door."

"Of course. But they told Raul to let us go."

"For now. You don't know what they're thinking; they
can reverse that decision any time they want. Remember,
they had just one night to vet us. Everyone's open for
normal business today. You know I did a lot of ad-libbing
back there, and that story isn't going to hold up if they
really start to look at it. If they find out we lied, you and
Peters are going to prison. If you're questioned again, it
won't be by Raul and it won't be in a resort hotel. You
may not make it to this evening, what's more to Sunday.
It seems to me that Peters is safer by himself; it'll take the

pressure off him if you come back with me now. This is a case where one head, Peters', is definitely better than two." He held out his hand. "Mrs. Finway? I think the kids will be very happy to see the two of us back together."

"I can't, John," Alexandra said quietly, taking a step backward.

John dropped his hand to his side. "You won't."

"I've got a job to do."

John stood still, watching Alexandra walk toward the hotel entrance where Peters and Constantina waited. Peters was staring at him. From where John was standing, the short, blond man's eyes looked even larger than usual, burning with pale fire, triumphant, malevolent, and mocking.

"Good-bye, Alexandra," John whispered.

LANGLEY, VIRGINIA; CIA HEADQUARTERS

Thursday, January 24; 12:15 P.M.

Harley Shue

Harley Shue finished typing the letter ten minutes before his scheduled appointment with the Director of the CIA. He noted three mistakes, considered correcting them in pen, then decided not to bother. Few people would see the letter anyway, he thought. If things worked out as he hoped, the letter would be destroyed.

He took a handful of his prized Cuban cigars from a desk drawer and stuffed them into the inside breast pocket of his gray suit jacket. In the event that he had to leave the intelligence service he loved so much, he'd decided that the cigars would be the only things he would take with him. There would be no mementoes. The cigars would go up in smoke, like his past and the record of his victories and defeats. Perhaps, he thought, like the CIA itself.

He allowed himself one last glance around his office, then hurried into the corridor to begin the seven-minute elevator ride and walk that would take him to the CIA Director's office.

He was absolutely convinced that America's future as a superpower would hinge on the results of his upcoming meeting with Geoffrey M. Whistle. He knew that it would not be so if he had handled the San Sierra matter in a different way, but he did not regret the maneuvers he had made. He'd believed at the time, and he still believed, that it had been in the best interests of the country and the CIA to deny Manuel Salva options, to play for time and information by using Alexandra Finway as a stalking horse in Rick Peters' assassination plot. At the time, Harley Shue thought, he had been in a position to manipulate the

191

decision-making process; his present situation was much more difficult.

If he lost this last great battle, Shue thought, he would immediately go into retirement. At seventy-four, he considered it arguable whether he would live to see the precipitous decline, the accelerated meltdown, of the nation, a condition he considered inevitable if the United States did not make one crushing, irresistible move to reconsolidate its power and check the Soviets. But he knew that decision was the President's. The only thing he could do now was to bear witness to his convictions and try to convince his superior of the necessity for taking the first step, quickly. It was a burden from which the CIA Director would not be able to walk away.

He would do his best, Shue thought, and he would privately dedicate that effort to a fine, courageous young man he had looked upon as a son and who had died in the service of his country.

Harley Shue thought of himself as an exceptionally toughminded man, and so he was faintly surprised to find memory, not plans, playing in the theater of his mind as he walked through the empty corridors of the labyrinthine CIA complex.

Born in Belgium to American parents in the diplomatic service, he'd shown an enormous facility for languages at an early age, and had picked up one language after another throughout his childhood. By the time he had finished his training as a dentist, he had spoken eleven languages fluently.

He'd enlisted in the U.S. Army at the outbreak of World War II and been assigned to a medical unit. He'd been with the unit for slightly more than a week when a general with an impacted tooth discovered his talent for languages; the next day Harley Shue had reported for duty in a rusted, leaky Quonset hut that was then the headquarters for the embryonic American intelligence service.

He had played a key role in the postwar organization of the Central Intelligence Agency, and he had moved up rapidly, all the while maneuvering for the post of Director of Operations, an office he had helped to design and that he knew was best suited to his penchant for secrecy and hidden, real power.

He'd had a full life, Harley Shue thought. He knew there had been times during the past four decades when he had been one of the ten or fifteen most powerful men on the face of the planet. Yet perhaps less than a busload of people knew who he was, and even less knew exactly what he did. His picture was never published, his biography never released. Now, at the end of his life and career, he knew he faced his most difficult battle, one that had to be fought with words and nuances, by proxy. But then, he considered that only fitting; except for his time in the army, Harley Shue had never carried a gun.

As was the custom when they met in the CIA Director's office, all clerical personnel, with the exception of a lone secretary cloistered down the hall, had been sent away. The suite of offices had been electronically swept a half hour before.

General Geoffrey M. Whistle was sitting behind his massive, oak desk looking very uncomfortable as Harley Shue walked in. He was a man who had quickly learned that an emergency meeting called by his Director of Operations was never for the purpose of bringing him good news.

"Good afternoon, Harley," Whistle said tersely, rising and extending his hand.

Shue gripped the other man's hand firmly. "Good afternoon, sir."

"Shall I have some lunch sent in?"

"Not for me, Geoffrey. Thank you. I'm hoping this matter won't take up much of your time."

Whistle laughed without humor. "You're making me nervous, Harley. I take it something important has come up since our regular meeting this morning?"

To say the least, Shue thought. He took the letter out of his pocket and placed it on the desk in front of the CIA Director. "I'm afraid so, sir. The dragon situation has changed. This is my letter of resignation, in which I take full responsibility for what's happened. You'll need it when you see the President."

Geoffrey Whistle stared down at the paper on his desk as though it were an onerous piece of foreign matter that had suddenly, inexplicably, materialized before his eyes. "I don't understand what you're talking about, Harley. What's happened?"

"A half hour ago I received word from one of our men in DMI that Harry Beeler has been killed." He paused to allow his superior time to absorb the information and its implications, but also to consider whether or not he should tell the other man about John Finway's unexplained presence in the tour group. He decided to keep the information about Finway to himself, at least for the time being. That curious development was irrelevant to the immediate crisis.

"Jesus," Whistle said in a flat, dry voice. "How did that happen?"

"I don't know, Geoffrey. I hope to have more details later, but I thought I should come to you with this at once. Agent Beeler's death is confirmed. It means, of course, that Peters has a free run at Manuel Salva. The President will have to be told, and I assume he'll want to warn Salva immediately."

Whistle shook his head, then poured himself a glass of water from a silver pitcher. His hand trembled slightly. "I may as well prepare my own resignation."

"Not necessarily, sir. I believe mine will be sufficient."

Geoffrey Whistle stiffened, and the timbre of his voice changed slightly, vibrating with annoyance and indignation. "I don't want to hear that shit, Harley. I can take heat. Whatever you did, you acted on my authority, or should have. Frankly, I'd rather resign or get fired than wind up looking like an asshole who doesn't know a subordinate is cooking up a potential major confrontation right under his nose. Besides, there's a hell of a lot more at stake here than our careers. With what Alexandra Finway knows, or thinks she knows, our organization is going to be blown out of the water. *Shit!* The Russians are buttoned up and on the move, and the CIA could end up gutted."

It was the reaction Harley Shue had been hoping to see: the leader and man of character behind the equivocator; the seasoned, hard warrior beneath the soft, plastic carapace of the politician. And Geoffrey Whistle's words were what Shue had wanted to hear. It was time for his first, small maneuver.

"I'm afraid you may be right, Geoffrey," Shue said evenly. "It's always possible that Salva will give us a little room on this dragon thing out of gratitude for saving his life. Maybe he'll just send Peters and the Finway woman back to us."

"The fuck he will," Whistle said, pounding a fist on his desk. "I have to assume the DMI will eventually make Beeler, and then Salva will know we've been gambling with his life. He'll have the CIA by the balls, and we both know he'll twist them right off."

"Yes," Harley Shue said mildly. "That's probably exactly what he'll do."

Whistle crumpled up Shue's letter of resignation and hurled it across the office. "I don't want your resignation, Harley. I want options. Are there any?"

Harley Shue felt a gentle, warm swell of satisfaction rise from his stomach into his chest. "May I smoke?"

"Of course you can smoke," Whistle replied impatiently.

Shue removed one of the cigars from his inside breast pocket, lit it. He drew himself up very straight, put one hand behind his back, and used the cigar in his other hand to check off points on an imaginary board in front of him.

"First, sir, let us review the world situation vis-à-vis the Russians. We know, as you so aptly put it, that they're 'buttoned up' and ready to move through their part of the world like a battleship at any time. The Russians care nothing for world opinion. They've put their own house in order, and they could be getting ready to put on some additions. They have never given up their dream of world domination, and my guess is that they've made firm plans to push harder and harder throughout the rest of this century. With good reason. Our house is in disarray. The actions of our allies are limited to words because they no longer have confidence in us. It's up to the United States to check the Russians, and to check them hard and deliberately now to force their long-range planners back to their drawing boards. The questions is, where?"

"San Sierra," Geoffrey Whistle said tightly. He paused for a few seconds, as though listening to the words echo inside his mind, then softly repeated them: "San Sierra."

"Yes, sir," Shue said, squinting as he waved away a wisp of blue-black smoke that had curled up into his eyes. "At the moment, we're in a no-win situation. If we warn Salva, he picks up Peters and Alexandra Finway and we're lost.

He'll stage a circus with them, and Congress will go out of its mind. The CIA could well be emasculated precisely at a time when an efficient covert capacity is most desperately needed.

"If we do nothing, Salva will almost certainly be assassinated and it will be blamed on us anyway. The Russians, considering the present mood of their leadership, could seek to punish us by making countermoves, perhaps even in Western Europe. They'll probably move combat troops into San Sierra and dare us to do something about it; they're still smarting over their defeat in the missile crisis. The point is that the CIA will be blamed in either event, and we could be permanently damaged. We'll absolutely lose whatever credibility we gained in the Third World after the Russian invasion of Afghanistan and events in Poland. It will be extremely difficult for us to maneuver, either diplomatically or militarily, after the fact. I don't feel it's an exaggeration, sir, to state that the defensive posture of this nation, the pride of our citizens and, perhaps most important, how we are perceived by the rest of the world for the remainder of this century may be dependent upon what the United States does in the next few hours.

"The third option is the one I believe we must exercise. After all, we didn't plan to kill Salva. Quite the contrary. But if he is going to be killed, as seems likely, then we should begin to make contingency plans immediately. The heart of those plans, in my opinion, should be to seize San Sierra when and if Salva is assassinated. Then there will be a number of factors working in our favor. The Russians will certainly be bellicose, but they'll most definitely be impressed by this single, bold stroke; action and decisiveness are things they understand. In my opinion, they will decide that they have enough things to keep them busy in their own sphere of influence. State counters accusations against us by releasing its notes on the secret negotiations with Salva, and we claim Salva was assassinated by Russian agents because the Soviet Union had found out about his dealings with us. Naturally, there'll be flak, but we'll be in a much better position to deflect it. Indeed, the flak will be irrelevant. The important thing is that we'll have San Sierra back. We'll have reestablished the Monroe Doctrine, and our sphere of influence will be intact once again. We'll claim we were forced to invade in order to keep the Russians from taking over, and we'll use what happened in Afghanistan as a case in point.

"Finally, although this point is insignificant compared with the others, it should be noted that no one need ever know about the agency's involvement with the dragons, past or present. As far as the President, State, and the National Security Council are concerned, we've only just now received the information we're asking them to act upon. Hughes-Ryan makes it impossible for us to act effectively by tomorrow night. A Presidential Directive, based on national emergency, is required."

"Christ, Harley. We're staring down the barrel of World War Three."

"Yes, sir. However, I believe, firmly, that we've been looking in that direction since long before this Salva business came up. I believe it's imperative that we finally stop blinking. I strongly recommend the third course of action."

General Geoffrey M. Whistle tapped his index finger three times on the surface of his desk, then reached into a drawer and took out a dark blue telephone that had no dial. He stared at Harley Shue for a few moments, then picked up the receiver with a quick, decisive motion. He waited a few seconds, then braced slightly as he spoke.

"Good afternoon, Mr. President. We have a potential Condition Red here, sir. I would like to meet with you at once, and I request that you convene the National Security Council."

Harley Shue knew that the words of the Director of the Central Intelligence Agency, delivered over the direct line linking Langley with the Oval Office, would be sufficient cause for the President of the United States to immediately cancel all other business and summon the members of the National Security Council. Shue had not expected to hear any extended conversation over the telephone, and there wasn't any. After less than a minute, Geoffrey Whistle replaced the receiver in its cradle. His eyes were cold, his mouth set in a firm line.

"I agree with you, Harley. Now let's see if I can convince the only man whose opinion counts."

"We'll need a gunner, sir."

"I don't want to talk tactics now, Harley," Whistle

snapped impatiently. "I'm on my way to try to convince the President of the United States that we should organize a strike force for the purpose of invading another country within thirty-six hours."

"Yes, sir," Shue replied evenly. "But we must anticipate that it will take some time for the President to reach a decision. By then, every minute may count. I'd like your permission to arrange for a gunner to be part of the ABC television crew that will be going there. It's going to be difficult, but I think I can make the necessary arrangements, if I have the time. Then, if the President decides to go ahead, we'll be ready."

Whistle thought for a few minutes, finally nodded. "All right, Harley. Proceed as if we have a go-ahead."

Harley Shue nodded curtly. He walked to the door, paused, and said, "I'll be waiting in my office. Good luck, Geoffrey."

Shue waited. When there was no reply from the other man, the CIA's Director of Operations stepped out into the corridor and closed the door quietly behind him.

THE BEACH OF FIRE

Thursday, January 24; 5:37 P.M.

John

"Things here aren't what some people say they are."

John stood on the beach and stared out over the water. There was a wind rising from the northwest and the surface of the bay was choppy. In the distance a three-stack freighter plowed slowly along the line of the horizon, racing an approaching storm, painting ribbons of black smoke into a blood sky.

The real world was out there somewhere beyond the freighter, John thought. The other side of the looking glass.

To his right, a long wooden pier jutted out into the water from its base in a deep field of glass-smooth, pearl-colored stone pebbles. At the end of the dock a lone fisherman sat on a milk crate, resting his back against a wood piling while he tended his three lines.

Why the hell would Swarzwalder have said a thing like that? John thought. It seemed obvious that the man had been play acting all along, establishing a cover, but John could not understand why a professional killer in such a high-pressure situation should not only have gone to the trouble of saving his life, but then so dramatically stepped out of character to issue what now, replayed and examined in the echo chamber of his memory, sounded so clearly like a warning.

Unless, John thought, his mind was playing tricks on him. The electric shock had blotted out pieces of memory from the tapestry of time that had unrolled before the accident, causing shards of thought to bleed together and shift in and out of focus; now it occurred to him that he might not yet be able to focus clearly on events that had happened *after* the accident. Yet he was sure he remembered Swarzwalder's words accurately.

"You have any enemies, John?"

John shook his head in frustration, shoved his hands into the pockets of his light jacket, and walked slowly down the beach.

He'd been through an emotional and physical holocaust, he thought: his brief but transcendent embrace with death as the electricity had coursed through his body; watching Swarzwalder's life being beaten, stabbed, and squeezed out of him; the entire situation with Alexandra. He knew that the deadly, unending pressure had to have taken its toll on him, and perhaps nothing he was thinking could be taken too seriously. Certainly, he must still be in a state of shock.

And yet . . .

And yet something just wasn't right.

John stopped walking and laughed out loud at his thoughts. Something wasn't right? Nothing was right. And what else was new?

Then why the painful and persistent additional misgivings?

Alexandra and Peters had shown themselves to be complete professionals, he thought. He had witnessed a solid demonstration of their considerable skills, and it had been clearly shown that he was simply in their way, a very real danger to them. The dragons' principal target was dead, and it was arguable whether there was a second assassin. If Sierran intelligence left them alone, the rest of the trip should be a milk run. It seemed to him that he should be worrying about rebuilding his marriage after the week was over, but he wasn't even thinking about that. He could not shake the prickling, oppressive feeling that he was the key to Alexandra's survival and that, by leaving San Sierra, he was sentencing the woman he loved to death.

John laughed again. He'd had that feeling before, he thought, and he'd been proven an idiot. Espionage and counterterrorism weren't even remotely within his range of skills, and he normally didn't need more than a light tap on the shoulder to absorb a lesson. This time he'd been poleaxed, yet, inexplicably, he was still tempted to loiter at the schoolhouse door.

"Mr. Finway! Mr. Finway!"

John turned in time to see Raul come running down the cement concourse that connected the beach to a small shopping arcade, parking lot, and highway beyond. Raul jumped off the end of the ramp onto the beach, then waded laboriously on his short, stubby legs through the deep, clinging sand toward John. By the time he had closed the distance his face was crimson and he was out of breath. He panted for almost a minute, then sat down hard on the sand.

"Well," John said easily, trying not to smile. "Hello, Raul. You trying out for the Olympics?"

"You . . . you . . ." The words would not come yet. Raul panted a few more moments, wiped a glistening sheet of perspiration from his face, then finally caught his breath. "You should have stayed in the town."

"You ran all the way from there?"

"You should not have left!"

John shrugged. "Why? Am I under arrest?"

Raul shook his head angrily at John's extended hand, then struggled to his feet. He swayed unsteadily for a few seconds, but managed to remain standing. "No," he replied at last. "But I was concerned about you. Uh, have you talked to anyone?"

John narrowed his eyes. "What do you mean, 'have I talked to anyone'?"

Raul glanced around nervously. "Have you *talked* to anybody?"

Puzzled, John also looked around. They were alone on the beach. "Just to the mechanic at the garage," he said, turning his attention back to Raul. "He said it would be hours before the car was fixed, and he mentioned that the Beach of Fire was just a couple of kilometers down the road. I wanted to see it, so here I am. What's the big deal, Raul?"

"No big deal," the Sierran said quickly, shaking his head. "No big deal."

John gestured at the beach around them. "There's only one little sign up on the concourse identifying this as the Beach of Fire. If our situations were reversed and this were the United States, there'd be a twenty-foot granite monument every fifty yards. Granted it doesn't look like much, but then neither do most historical sites."

"We like to look to the future," Raul mumbled, "not the past."

John grunted. "You're not very talkative this evening, Raul. I'd have thought you'd be dying to give me a historical lecture. This *is* the Beach of Fire, isn't it?"

"Yes. It is the Beach of Fire. But we have to go back now."

"You think the car's ready?"

"I don't know," Raul replied in a tone of voice that clearly indicated he didn't believe it was. "But it is time for you to have dinner. I have made arrangements." He tried to smile, but he only managed to crease the skin on his cheekbones. "I apologize for the delay."

"There's no need to apologize. I think it's nothing short of miraculous that you can keep these nineteen fifties' junkers moving at all; every village looks like it's having an antique auto show." He paused, studying the other man's face. "You're really anxious to get rid of me, aren't you?"

"I don't know what you mean, Mr. Finway," Raul answered. But he would not look at John.

"You're some piece of work," John said wearily as he turned and started back up the beach. "Come on, *amigo*," he called over his shoulder. "So much for the Beach of Fire. Let's go eat."

LANGLEY, VIRGINIA; CIA HEADQUARTERS

Thursday, January 24; 9:15 P.M.

Harley Shue

Harley Shue's eyes burned with fatigue, and he had turned off all the lights in the office except for a small, recessed spotlight in the ceiling above his desk. Now he sat quietly, half in and half out of the night, staring into the darkness beyond the sharply circumscribed circle of light.

He had sat, virtually unmoving, in the same position for close to an hour and a half, but his mind had been far from idle. All of the physical preparations he would be responsible for in the event of an affirmative decision by the President had been completed. Now he was thinking about the things that would have to be done in the days, weeks, months, and years following an invasion of San Sierra.

If there was to be an invasion.

There was a soft knock at the door. Harley Shue pushed a button under his desk that activated the lighting in the rest of the room. "Come in, sir," he said, getting to his feet.

The door opened and Geoffrey M. Whistle strode into the room. His normally handsome face was now gaunt with fatigue and tension, but his eyes gleamed with excitement. "It's a go, Harley. We have a directive. If Salva's assassinated, we move into San Sierra. State files on their talks with Salva are a foot thick. That's our propaganda weapon. As you suggested, our rationale for world consumption will be that Salva was most certainly killed by a Russian agent as a prelude to a full-scale Soviet invasion: we'll be forced to act. Goddamn."

"Yes, sir," Shue said mildly. "Goddamn." He had purposely kept himself emotionally distanced during the long, draining hours of waiting and preparation. Now he realized that he had expected this decision all along; it was too right, too logical, too *necessary* to disregard. He did not resume his seat, nor did he suggest that his superior sit. He sensed that that CIA Director preferred to stand, as he did.

"Where are we, Harley?"

"We're in place, Geoffrey. On your order, COMSAT will begin feeding a worldwide update on Russian troop positions and movements on the half hour to wherever the President wants it. Beginning at six-thirty tomorrow evening there'll be a constant readout. As far as the assassination site is concerned, I consider it unsound to rely solely on ABC's broadcast signal, so I've made arrangements for a specially outfitted U-2 to be in the air over San Sierra all during the boxing matches. The plane will be equipped with two high-resolution television cameras and other sensory equipment."

"Very good, Harley. Is everything on the Orange list checked off?"

"Yes, sir. In addition to the U-2, I've added seventeen other items that I thought pertinent to this particular operation."

"I'll look at them later."

Shue drew himself up. "The agency is ready to go, sir."

"You have a gunner?"

"Yes. He'll be threaded into San Sierra by way of the unions. He'll be there as a gaffer with the standby electrical crew that leaves for Angeles Blanca tomorrow morning. He'll be very close to the action."

"Good man?"

"I can't vouch for him personally, Geoffrey, but we've used gunners from this source before and they've always proved reliable. He has very specific instructions and, of course, he's deep-insulated. He has a clear description of each of his targets, and he thinks he's carrying out a Mafia contract. Indeed, he *is* carrying out a Mafia contract."

Whistle ran his fingers through his thick, wavy hair. "It's too bad Alexandra Finway has to be taken out with Peters. Christ, she's a civilian who wouldn't even be there if she didn't think she'd been tasked by us. Harley, is there any way we can let her out of the net?"

"Yes. I can change the gunner's orders any time right up until the moment he leaves in the morning; after that there would be considerable security risks in trying to contact him."

"What do you think, Harley? Can we let her go?"

"The problem is that Alexandra Finway has information that could prove very damaging to our national security. She knows that the CIA was aware weeks ago of a plot to kill Salva. At the moment, there's no reason to suspect that she will not remain reliable; she could carry what she knows with her to the grave. But there is no guarantee. As you know, I believe our action is crucial to the interests of the United States and our allies. We're looking into the next century. As long as Alexandra Finway lives, she'll possess information that could undo much of what we're trying to accomplish. Our propaganda offensive and the deniability of certain facts will continue to be of critical importance for years. As much as I hate recommending this action, I simply do not believe that the nation can afford to be hostage to Alexandra Finway's continuing mental stability or political reliability."

Whistle grimaced as though he had been hit. "Well, Harley, we get paid for making decisions like this, don't we?"

"I believe so, sir, for making sure that other people don't have to make such decisions."

"Shit! You're right, Harley. Alexandra Finway's a loose cannon we can't afford to have rolling around. She has to go."

"By the way, sir," Harley Shue said evenly. "The gunner has instructions to take out one other civilian. John Finway. It's been confirmed that he's in San Sierra with his wife and Peters."

Whistle blinked rapidly, frowned. "John Finway?! What the hell is *he* doing there?!"

"I have no idea, sir. In fact, by now he may be on his way back to New York. The same source who reported Agent Beeler's death says that Finway is leaving the tour."

"John Finway," Whistle said absently as he began to pace. "Why? What the hell has been going on over there?!"

"We have no way of determining that, sir. Finway's a wild card. For obvious reasons, he's more dangerous to our mission than his wife. Perhaps infinitely so. He may know everything his wife knows—which could explain why he's in such a hurry to come home. Given half a chance, Finway will try to destroy the agency."

Whistle abruptly stopped pacing. "Why hasn't he told the Sierrans?"

"I don't know, sir. He may be trying to protect his wife, but that's a guess."

"He definitely has to be taken out."

"If he remains in San Sierra, he's on the gunner's list. I have two men at Kennedy Airport in case he comes home."

"Who's at the airport? Gunners or our men?"

"Our men. I need you to give me some direction on that end."

"Are they good?"

"The best, Geoffrey. Totally reliable."

"Jesus," Whistle said, angrily shaking his head. "We can't have Finway walking around over here; he's sure to go straight to the *Washington Post* or the *New York Times*. Tell your men to pack him safely away, with instructions to take him out only on your order."

"Yes, sir. Those were the preliminary instructions I gave them, subject to your approval, of course."

Whistle stared intently at the other man, respect and admiration clearly reflected in his eyes. "Thank God you're on our side, Harley."

"Thank you for the compliment, Geoffrey. The same could be said for you. But the fact of the matter is that the KGB also has excellent personnel. What happens tomorrow is only a beginning. We're in for a very long struggle."

"Yes," Geoffrey Whistle said distantly.

"I've had rooms prepared for all key agency personnel, sir. The coded list is in your safe. I'm going to my room to rest now. May I suggest that you do the same? You look very tired."

Whistle nodded absently. He seemed to stagger slightly as he turned and walked to the door. He paused, said,

"Harley, do you think there's any way the President, the Joint Chiefs, or the NSC could know about the dragons?"

"I'd say it's impossible, sir."

"Strange," Whistle said, his voice muffled by his close proximity to the door. "The Joint Chiefs have code-named the invasion of San Sierra 'Operation Saint George.' "

ANGELES BLANCA;
AQUA AZUL AIRPORT

Thursday, January 24; 10:42 P.M.

John

"Things here aren't what some people say they are."

"There's no need for you to wait around, Raul," John said, frowning slightly as the memory of Swarzwalder's words continued to distract him. "My bags are checked and I'm perfectly capable of getting on an airplane all by myself. Why don't you go to the hotel and get some sleep?"

Raul, his body sacked by fatigue and tension, was leaning forward in one of the airport lounge's hard, molded-plastic chairs, resting his forearms on his knees. When Raul glanced sideways, John could see that the Sierran's eyes were bloodshot from exhaustion and the strain of driving for many hours; as night had fallen, they'd discovered that their car had only one dim headlight. On at least a half dozen occasions John had been certain they would have an accident. However, Raul had gotten them safely to the airport. The Sierratour guide had booked him on a delayed flight rescheduled to leave at one in the morning for Toronto, where he would connect with a Pan Am flight to New York. He would be home by midmorning.

"I will wait with you," Raul said thickly. "You do not speak Spanish. You may need help if there is a further delay."

"All the airline personnel speak some English. I won't need any help."

"Still, I will wait."

"Suit yourself. I'm going to get some coffee. What about you?"

Raul shook his head sullenly. John rose, purchased a

cup of weak, tepid coffee from a gurgling vending machine, then walked across the deserted lounge to a high, wide bank of windows that looked out over a line of buses and food-vendors' trucks parked on the macadam one story below. Their images reflected in the polished glass, three soldiers leaned against the walls of the lounge, dozing, their spectral shapes floating somewhere out in the night.

"Things here aren't . . ."

John had lost track of the number of times he'd relived the confrontation in the Sierras Negras Hotel, but his memory seemed to be clearing with the passage of time, and he now began to review it all once again.

David Swarzwalder certainly hadn't been what he'd claimed to be, John thought. However, John was no longer convinced that the big man had been what Alexandra and Peters thought him to be, either.

Raul had told him that there were three other singles on the tour besides himself and Swarzwalder, and John continued to ponder the question of why Swarzwalder had lied to him on the plane and told him they were the only two. What had he wanted? Had Swarzwalder already approached the others and been turned down? Not enough time; they'd just boarded the plane. Swarzwalder seemed to have specifically wanted to room with him.

In order to be close to him? Why?

Could Swarzwalder have known about the dragons? Even if he had, John thought, that would not explain Swarzwalder's apparent desire to share a room with the husband of one of them. Quite the contrary; logic would seem to dictate that an assassin keep as low a profile as possible throughout the week, and he would certainly go out of his way not to attract the attention of the two people who were hunting him.

Could it have merely been a coincidence that Swarzwalder had asked to share a room? Again, Swarzwalder had lied to him about the other singles.

Why had Swarzwalder saved his life?

John finished his coffee, returned to the machine, and bought another.

He made an effort to recall the exact sequence of events that had occurred after he had burst into the dragons' room. Before, everything had seemed to race through his consciousness in milky fast-motion. Now he concentrated on slowing things down, separating the entire sequence into its separate components, clearing away the haze and putting the events into sharp focus.

Swarzwalder had been standing over Peters' suitcase, holding one of Alexandra's barrettes in his left hand. Swarzwalder had spun around, hesitated, then dropped the barrette on the bed and attacked him.

The man had been incredibly quick and powerful, John thought. Before he'd had time to think or react, Swarzwalder had knocked him down with a hammer blow to his heart. Then Swarzwalder had leaped on top of him and pressed a knee into his chest; the man's hand had been raised, the knuckle of his middle finger extended in preparation for a killing blow to his throat . . .

But the blow had not come. Remembering back, the image etched clearly in his mind, it seemed to John that Swarzwalder's fist had remained cocked, quivering with pent-up force over his throat, for a very long time. Then the other man's eyes had changed, softened, as death had left them.

For some reason, Swarzwalder had decided not to kill him. Why? What possible alternative had been left to Swarzwalder, the assassin?

"Let them send you home."

An earlier warning after the accident with the shaver— if it had really been an accident.

"You have any enemies, John?"

The wires in the electric razor had not looked frayed when he'd packed it, John thought. Had someone tried to kill him? Certainly not Swarzwalder, for it had been the big man who'd brought him back to life. Had Swarzwalder's words been a warning? Of what? About whom? Had Swarzwalder been sending a warning about *himself?* Why would he do that?

Swarzwalder drowning . . .

Then Peters had arrived in the room, swooping down on Swarzwalder like some white-eyed angel of death wielding a scythe of leather and steel. The loop of leather had dropped around Swarzwalder's neck and the big man had exploded backward in a blur of motion.

John did not remember getting to his feet. His next

recollection was of standing, paralyzed by confusion and indecision, watching as Swarzwalder broke free. At that point, he had expected Swarzwalder to kill Peters and then come back after him. Swarzwalder had done neither. Instead, clutching at his broken throat, the big man had turned away from Peters. Toward him.

And pointed at the bed.

Swarzwalder floundering in the water: Swarzwalder, who didn't usually rise particularly early, drowning in a dawn sea . . .

"*Things here . . .*"

Suddenly Alexandra had burst into the room. The radio had blared; Alexandra had attacked. He had tried to stop them and been knocked unconscious. He had regained consciousness to find Swarzwalder lying dead, his neck broken, a tiny rivulet of blood leaking into his shirt.

John shook his head. Why had Swarzwalder pointed at the bed? Or had he been pointing at the suitcase? Alexandra's barrette? Why?

Barrette.

Alexandra had used her barrette to stab Swarzwalder.

At the time, John had simply assumed that Swarzwalder had searched Alexandra's luggage first and for some reason kept the barrette. But why would the man do that? he wondered. Why pick up such an insignificant item in the first place, what's more hang onto it?

The barrettes were from the past, John thought, and in that past he had never known Alexandra to carry an extra barrette with her. Why should she bring an extra barrette for a one-week trip to San Sierra?

Swarzwalder had been searching Peters' suitcase, John thought, not Alexandra's. *Peters* had been carrying the barrette in *his* suitcase.

There was something about the barrette.

Swarzwalder had been trying to warn him about *Peters,* John thought. Swarzwalder had been following him on that morning; the drowning had been staged. Swarzwalder had been trying all along to protect him from Peters.

"What's the matter, Mr. Finway?"

John, dazed, slowly looked around to find Raul standing beside him. The gnomish Sierran had an anxious expression on his face. "What did you say?" John asked distantly.

"You dropped your coffee."

John absently glanced down to see that the front of his slacks was stained with coffee; he had never even felt the warm liquid spill on him. He heard a rattling sound, his plastic cup rolling away.

"You know, *amigo,* I think I'd like to stay."

"I don't understand," Raul said tightly.

John brushed casually at the stains on his slacks, then smiled broadly at the Sierran. *Control,* he thought. "Something just clicked inside my mind, Raul. What the hell; my marriage is finished, and I just realized that I don't really give a damn. It's a good feeling, let me tell you."

"I'm sure it is, Mr. Finway, but—"

"I feel like celebrating. Come on, *amigo,* I'll buy you a drink."

Raul shook his head. "I'm sorry, Mr. Finway. You can't—"

"Hey Raul!" John said sharply. He struggled to keep smiling, to remain calm. "Why the hell shouldn't I see Angeles Blanca too? I think I'll stay and finish this tour just to show my wife I don't give a damn what she does."

Raul's eyes went wide, and his pudgy hands clenched into fists. "You must get on the plane, Mr. Finway."

"This is important to me, Raul," John said, gripping the other man's arms. "You saw what happened at Sierras Negras. I made an ass out of myself. I was humiliated. You're a man; you can understand why I'd like to salvage a little dignity and self-respect. All I'm asking is that you let me finish the trip with the others. Let me leave San Sierra like a man."

"You are not well, Mr. Finway. You don't know what you want. You must go home and rest. You'll be there in a few hours." He paused, shrugged nervously. "Besides, how can I get your bags back?"

John stared intently at the other man for a long time as he concentrated on keeping his breathing even. "Have my bags sent on to New York," he said at last. "I don't need them."

"You must go. It's been arranged."

"We'll compromise. My wife and Peters will be at the Coconut Club right now with the rest of the group. Zip me over there just long enough for me to tell Alexandra

I don't give a damn anymore. I promise you I'll keep it private and won't make a scene. All I want is five minutes—one minute!—alone with my wife. How about it?"

"No, Mr. Finway. Please sit down and try to relax."

"You sit down and try to relax!" John snapped, abruptly stepping around Raul and heading for one of the three exits. "I paid for this trip, and no one's officially told me that I'm being thrown out of the country. I'm goddamn well going back with the others. If you won't take me, I'll walk or hitch a ride."

"Guard! Guard!"

John stopped walking as he saw the soldiers snap to attention, blocking off the exits.

Think! You've got to get out of here!

He wheeled and strode quickly back to Raul. He wrapped his fingers tightly around the Sierran's upper arms and lifted the other man up on his toes. "Listen to me, you stupid little bastard," John said through clenched teeth. "Rick Peters is planning to kill Manuel Salva and my wife. If you don't let me out of here, he's probably going to get away with it."

Raul's eyes seemed to swell in his head until they appeared like chocolate-brown balloons inflated with shock and panic. "You are a crazy man!" he blubbered. "Get away from me! *Guard!*"

John fought against the panic rising in him, clouding his mind. He could go quietly with the guards and try to get someone in authority to listen to him, but there was no guarantee that he wouldn't be ignored; his story could easily fall through the cracks of a bureaucracy notorious for being filled with people who loathed making decisions or upsetting their superiors.

Think!

Even if the authorities did believe him and decide to go after Peters, it could easily be mishandled and Alexandra could die. If Peters didn't kill her, the Sierrans might—if not by design, by accident. Alexandra would end up a hostage, and saving her life would not be high on the Sierran's list of priorities. The Sierrans might decide that the easiest way to deal with the dragons was to shoot them both.

Once he went with the guards, the matter would be completely out of his hands; he would be totally dependent upon the Sierran authorities to save Alexandra's life.

Suddenly, with absolute clarity, John understood that Alexandra would die if he could not get to her.

He could hear the guards' footsteps directly behind him. There was only one way left to go, and John knew he did not have the time or the courage to consciously debate whether or not he could survive the attempt. The time for thinking was over, and he allowed the volatile fuel of residual panic to flow through him unchecked, launching him into an action his mind would call madness but which his heart, his love for his wife and children, demanded. He slammed his fist into Raul's face, then sprinted toward the bank of windows.

Pieces of rational thought danced in the fire within him; it occurred to him that the glass would be heavily reinforced and that he would break his neck or cut his throat if he tried to go through it headfirst. As he ran he instinctively pulled the collar of his jacket up around his neck and hunched his shoulders. He leaped up on a chair to catapult himself the last few feet, somersaulting in the air at the last second so that his back absorbed the force of his impact with the glass.

It felt as though he were hitting a wall, but then the window exploded around him and he tumbled out into the hot night air amid a shower of glass. His forehead, hands, and right thigh suddenly burned with what felt like bee stings, but he had chosen his spot correctly; he tumbled through the air and landed hard on a metal surface that gave slightly under him as it emitted a loud bass-drum sound. Disoriented and out of breath, John reflexively threw his arms across his face to protect his eyes from the shards of glass raining on him, then rolled to his right. He fell off the top of the truck to the roof of the cab, then slid down the windshield and fender to the ground. He landed on the macadam and immediately started running.

He stumbled and fell, cushioning the shock with hands that were warm and slippery with blood. In an instant he was up and running again, racing directly away from the terminal building toward the field of darkness beyond a network of runways trimmed with tiny, bright lights.

There were sounds behind him like a multitude of

popping champagne corks, and John realized that the guards were shooting at him with their automatic weapons. The macadam around him erupted in small, black puffs. His lungs burned, and he had lost feeling in his legs. He put his head down and pumped his arms as he ran across an alleyway of light. Then he was past the first runway. He tripped and rolled onto a dry, ragged carpet of grass as bullets whined in the night around him.

Friday, January 25; 12:07 A.M.

Alexandra

"Do you believe this chickenshit?" Peters whispered. "This must be what they think Las Vegas is like, without the gambling. Outrageous."

"Oh, I don't know," Alexandra said with an amused, casual shrug. "I think it's all rather quaint."

"Obviously, there are some things the revolution didn't change."

Alexandra's initial reaction to Angeles Blanca's open-air Coconut Club had been one of wry amusement. If it were not so difficult to spend money in San Sierra, and if there were not so few travelers to begin with, she would have thought the club a typical tourist trap.

Upon arrival, their group had been ushered to six of a hundred or so tables that had been set end-to-end to form dozens of arrow-straight, cramped rows radiating from the lip of a vast, multilevel stage that had been constructed between and around the massive trunks of five towering trees. The trees were lit by cleverly hidden spotlights of different colors, creating a startling and not unpleasant contrast to the garish neon illumination in the seating area.

However, contrary to her first impression, Alexandra had soon learned that the nightclub was not primarily set up for tourists. Maria had informed her that an evening at the Coconut Club—like everything else in San Sierra that was classified as sport or entertainment—was offered as a reward to the workers who, like the tourist groups, were brought to the club in buses. Again like the tourists, each worker was given two weak rum-based drinks of his choice.

"You'd think they'd at least have an ample supply of Stolichnaya," Alexandra said, sipping her drink.

216

"They've got it; they're just damn careful how they dole it out. You know the old story about alcoholism in the Workers' Paradises of the world."

Alexandra did not share Peters' contempt for the show in progress on the great, extended stage. While she agreed that the dance acts and thinly veiled political skits were amateurish, hopelessly heavy-handed, and outdated, she found the sinuous, continuous movement on the many tiers of platforms and webs of rope ladders in the trees above the stage spectacular and strangely haunting. Gaudily plumed "bird women" materialized high up in the glowing foliage and danced along swaying rope bridges as male dancers gyrated to an infectious, fist-hard beat laid down by bare-chested drummers on a bewildering array of percussion instruments. Perhaps it was kitsch, Alexandra thought, but it was sincere kitsch. The Sierrans were openly proud of their nightclub, and Alexandra found that she was enjoying herself.

She fingered the four blue and pink swizzle sticks in front of her, slowly forming them into a square. "Get me another drink, would you, Rick?" she asked pleasantly.

Peters grunted with amusement and arched his eyebrows. "Your wish is my command, m'dear. May I count on you getting drunk?"

"That's not likely to happen with this stuff. God, what I'd give for some Scotch."

"One triple Scotch for m'lady as soon as we get back on the plane," Peters said, rising and starting to make his way down the narrow aisle between the tables.

She wasn't even close to being drunk, Alexandra thought. She felt immune to liquor; it was as if the alcohol she had consumed were circulating somewhere in an outer shell, away from her mind. She felt deeply submerged within herself, viewing the people and activity around her as if through a kind of psychic periscope. She found it a very pleasant sensation; like some potent narcotic, it gave her a floating feeling of easy peace and total command, superiority and power.

She had been in this deep place before, she thought, and she recalled—vaguely, distantly, as in a dream—that hard sex could cause her to surface for brief periods. Sex and pain.

It had happened, Alexandra thought matter-of-factly. The familiar metamorphosis of which she had once been terrified was almost complete.

However, now that she was settling back into this dark place in her mind, Alexandra could not remember exactly what there was about its psychic geography of which she had been so afraid. She *was* different from other people, she thought. Like Rick. People who could change into dragons formed an elite. As Rick had reminded her, the two of them were special people with special needs.

It had simply been too much before, Alexandra thought as she lazily traced her index finger around the perimeter of the square formed by the swizzle sticks. She had stayed at it too long; being in constant danger twenty-four hours a day, day in and day out, year after year, would burn out anyone. But she understood now—as she had understood then, but had run away from—that this work was undeniably what she did best. She liked being a member of a small elite, and she knew she was going to be reluctant to leave it again. She would not leave it again. She had three beautiful children whom she loved very much, she thought, but her children, like John and her home, were part of a phase of her life that was finished now. Pomona was no longer enough for her. She was ready for a change. The situation was certainly different now from what it had been when the dragons had been born, and she hoped the CIA would accomodate her with a post. She wanted to be with people who appreciated how very special she was and who could use her very special talents.

She felt Peters' hand gently caress the nape of her neck a moment before he placed her drink in front of her. The sensation of the hand on her flesh was pleasant, and Alexandra arched her neck slightly.

"Your drink, m'lady," Peters said as he slid back into his chair.

"Thank you," Alexandra said huskily. She looked directly into his pale, bottomless eyes as she slowly raised her glass. "Here's to the good guys."

Peters grinned broadly. The blue-white eyes glinted with genuine amusement as he raised his own glass. "To the good guys, wherever they may be," he replied. He laughed and drained his glass.

"Speaking of said good guys," Alexandra murmured, lowering her voice as she moved closer to Peters, "how do you want to handle our business at Tamara Castle?"

Peters inclined his head toward Alexandra until his lips were touching her ear. "I found out from Constantina that there are twelve other people who requested tickets to the matches." His tongue flicked out and touched her earlobe. Alexandra tensed slightly, but she did not move away. "We'll talk about it later. Too close quarters here."

"All—" Suddenly Alexandra was aware of Peters' hand resting on her knee. The feel of his fingers gently kneading, slipping around and exerting pressure on the soft, sensitive flesh behind her knee had an almost paralyzing effect. She realized with only vague surprise that she wanted Peters to make love to her. But not yet.

"Goddamn," Peters whispered hoarsely, his voice breathy and quavering. "It's been a long time."

Alexandra swallowed and slowly ran her tongue over her lips. Rum and desire made her mouth feel dry and cottony.

The hand moved up the inside of her thigh; his stroking was gentle, yet insistent. "I can tell things have changed," he said. "You're not going back to John, are you?"

Alexandra started to move away, but found she couldn't. She didn't want to. It was as if Peters, using no more than the gentle pressure of his fingers and palm, were able to control her mind and body.

"It's true."

"I don't know, Rick. This isn't the time for decisions like that."

Peters' hand was between her legs now. He slipped three fingers beneath the elastic legband of her panties, shifted his body slightly, and tried to thread his middle finger up her sex. Floating in her deep, warm place, Alexandra badly wanted to spread her legs and let the stiff finger slide up and into her. On the evening before the event that would mark the end of their task and the beginning—the resumption—of an exciting career, she found that she wanted to be masturbated as she drank and listened to the music and watched the dancers.

"God, Rick," she sighed, surfacing slightly, focusing her will and shifting her hips away from the insistent, probing finger. "Not here."

"Come on, baby."

"After . . . the boxing matches," Alexandra said in a trembling voice. She pressed a cold, sweating glass against her hot forehead and shuddered as the flesh contracted. *"Maybe* after the matches. I've got enough to think about right now, Rick. Let's both keep our minds on business until we're out of this."

"Let's do it now."

"Excuse me, please! Let me through, please!"

The pressing fingers left her leg. Out of the corner of her eye, Alexandra saw Peters bring his hand from beneath the tablecloth and place it back on top of the table. With Peters, she twisted around to watch a battered-looking Raul squeezing his way down the aisle between the tables. The Sierran's face turned a familiar shade of crimson as the people whose vision he obstructed hissed at him.

"Rick?"

"Shhh!" Peters reached over and gripped Alexandra's forearm. "Take it easy. If it were anything serious, it wouldn't be Raul paying us a visit."

Raul, breathing heavily, finally reached them. He squatted down in the aisle, supporting himself by resting a hand on the back of Alexandra's chair.

"Hello, Raul," Peters said easily. "You look like the Lone Ranger. Who busted your beak?"

Raul flushed even more and self-consciously touched the wide band of adhesive tape holding his broken nose in place. There were huge, ugly blood-bruises around his eyes. "Would you come with me, please? Both of you."

"Oh, come on, Raul!" Peters said angrily. "Haven't we had enough of your fun and games for one day? We're enjoying the show."

"Please." Raul's tone was soft but insistent, with a strong undercurrent of quiet dignity and assertiveness Alexandra had not heard before. He stood, and his muddy eyes reflected the same almost sad dignity. "I am sorry to bother you, but you must come with me."

Alexandra's heart had begun to beat rapidly, painfully. "Let's go, Rick," she said, flashing a quick, nervous smile at the Sierran. "Raul wouldn't be disturbing us if it weren't a serious matter."

They followed Raul up the aisle, then to the sidewalk outside the walls surrounding the seating area. Twenty yards away, on the other side of an arbor of roses, two soldiers armed with automatic rifles appeared to be standing guard.

Alexandra tasted blood and realized with consternation that she had bitten into the soft tissue inside her mouth.

"What's the matter, Raul?" Alexandra asked, managing to smile sweetly. She was a dragon, she reminded herself. A professional. All of her fear had to be pushed aside, completely erased from her face and voice. "Is there a problem?"

"Have you seen your husband, Miss—uh, Mrs. Finway?"

Alexandra frowned, then offered Raul a puzzled smile that was genuine. "John? My God, he must be back in the United States by now. He's probably in bed."

Raul shook his head impatiently. "We had a breakdown on the road. He ran away from the airport, and I must find him."

Alexandra felt the blood drain from her face, sucked from her brain to her heart and stomach like air into a vacuum. Her body began to shake, and she was afraid that she was going to faint. To cover her reaction and steady herself, she quickly reached out and grabbed Raul's right arm with both hands. "Raul? John did this to you?!"

"He is a crazy man," Raul said with a curt, angry nod. "A nut!"

Alexandra saw Peters' eyes narrow. A muscle in his cheek began to twitch.

"Did he tell you why he didn't want to get on the plane?" the blond-haired man asked in an even tone. "Did he say anything?"

"No, no," Raul said quickly. "He didn't say anything that made any sense. Just crazy talk. *Nut* talk. We don't want him talking to anyone else; it would be very embarrassing and disruptive. I just want everyone to relax and have a good time."

Alexandra forced herself to smile. "Raul, is . . . uh, is John all right?"

Raul took a few moments to think about his answer. "Your husband is in a great deal of trouble," he replied at last. "Before he went crazy, he said he wanted to talk to you. I thought he might have made his way here."

Alexandra shook her head. Her lips and tongue felt numb. "We haven't seen him."

Raul sniffed, then winced in pain and touched his nose again. "As I said, I am sorry to bother you, but I must ask you to do something for me. Mr. Finway will be arrested immediately if he comes here, so there may be a small disturbance. Please do not try to go to him, and please do not discuss this matter with anyone else in the group. You understand; we don't want anyone's evening ruined by this unfortunate incident."

"We understand perfectly, Raul," Peters said in a firm, sympathetic tone.

The Sierran nodded absently to the two of them, then turned and walked back toward the soldiers, who were talking and smoking.

"My God," Alexandra said softly, electric tension flashing through her muscles. "What the hell does John think he's doing?"

"Goddamn good question," Peters replied tersely. "Maybe he really has flipped out. That was some rabbit he pulled out of his head back in Sierras Negras; maybe the bunny had bigger teeth than we thought."

Alexandra closed her eyes and shook her head, trying to listen to the winds outside the shell that was threatening to close in her thoughts and feelings. "John isn't crazy," she said at last. "He knows what's at stake; if he broke away, it had to be for a very good reason. Raul said he wanted to talk to me."

"Yeah? Well, let's hope you're the only person he wants to talk to. Raul said he was 'talking crazy.' I'd love to know what that means." Peters sucked in a deep breath through clenched teeth, then shook his head in frustration. "You go back inside and stay loose. I'm going to walk around a bit. John may be waiting for us somewhere out there."

"I should go, Rick. John's my husband, my responsibility."

"No," Peters said, squeezing Alexandra's arm reassuringly. "It's better if I go. You're too conspicuous; the Sierrans might follow you. Let's just hope that I see John before they do. From the look on Raul's face, I think they'll just shoot the dumb son-of-a-bitch on sight."

"Rick, do you suppose John could have found out something about a second assassin?"

But Peters was already walking away.

Peters

Finway knew! Somehow, he knew!

The assassin had no way of determining what it was—some subtle mistake on his part, a bit of information, or simply phantom intuition—that had ruptured belief in the other man's mind, but he had to assume that Finway had guessed the truth. It was the only explanation for the explosive act that was so potentially catastrophic for all of them.

Peters knew that only a sheer stroke of luck could explain the fact that the authorities were after Finway rather than him, and he strongly suspected that he had Raul's curious and abrasive single-mindedness to thank for his good fortune. He'd already had more than his quota of good luck, Peters thought, and he was not fool enough to look for more. He was running on empty, finished. With things the way they were, he knew it would be a considerable feat just to escape the island with his life and freedom.

If it were possible to kill Alexandra and leave San Sierra at once, Peters thought, he would. But it was not possible. He had only one escape route, and that was by speedboat. There would be two fifteen-minute "windows," from eight-forty-five to nine and from ten to ten-fifteen, during the course of the boxing matches. These were the times when Claude Moiret would be prepared to speed into Angeles Blanca's harbor and pluck him from the sea at the base of the cliffs around Tamara Castle. If he missed these windows, he would be on his own—which was to say that he would be dead.

Indeed, Peters was certain that he was a dead man if he could not locate and kill Finway before the authorities found him, or before Finway got to Alexandra. Then he would be the hunted man; if the Sierrans did not summarily execute him, Peters thought, he would certainly die in their prisons.

Wanting to avoid Raul if possible, Peters went back into the amphitheater, walked around to the bar, then out through another exit to the sidewalk ringing the theater. There were soldiers posted at the half-dozen entrances to the amphitheater, but there were a number of other people walking outside, stiff-legged refugees from the cramped seating arrangements, and he was ignored.

Peters casually strolled away, smoking a cigarette, and started around the perimeter of the club. He did not expect Finway to come to him even if the lawyer were there, but he made the circuit on the off chance that he might see or hear a movement in the surrounding wooded area. He did not, and he stopped walking when he was just short of completing a circuit.

He wasted no time in making his next decision.

He recalled that Raul had described Finway as "crazy," and he thought it possible that any accusations leveled by the lawyer just might be dismissed as the senseless ravings of an insanely jealous husband, as long as there was no evidence to back up such a story. If he hoped to get out of San Sierra, he knew that he would have to get rid of the radio and the poison-filled plastique barrette.

He pushed through a row of hedges bordering the sidewalk, then ran low and silently through the surrounding trees until he was outside the park and on the street. He ran a half mile south, then stopped and waited impatiently for the headlights of a car to appear from either direction.

He would have to move very fast, Peters thought, and he could not risk leaving any tracks; he had to make every effort to be back at the club, going back in the way he had come out, before the group left, or risk arousing suspicion and raising questions he might not be able to answer.

To his annoyance, he discovered that in Angeles Blanca cars were few and driven sparingly. However, after a five-minute wait Peters saw headlights approaching from his left, on his side of the highway. He waited on the shoulder until the car was less than thirty yards away, then doubled over and staggered into the road.

Ancient brakes grabbed and finally caught in a banshee

wail of protest. The car fishtailed and screeched to a halt, barely missing Peters, who was crouched in the middle of the road, clutching his stomach and moaning. The driver cursed loudly for a few seconds, but his anger faded quickly. He got out of the car and hurried toward the man whom he assumed to be hurt.

"Que pasa, señor? Yo—"

Peters snapped erect and smashed the side of his right hand into the man's trachea. The man's eyes glazed and he collapsed to his knees. Peters stepped behind him, seized his head, and twisted sharply, snapping the man's neck. He quickly dragged the body off the road into a thick copse of trees, then sprinted back to the car, got in and sped off.

He made it to the hotel in nineteen minutes. Not wanting to risk being stopped in a car for which he had no papers by the soldier who stood at the entrance to the hotel driveway, Peters parked the old Plymouth at the curb down the street, then hurried down the block to the rear of the hotel. After waiting in the shadows a minute or two to make certain he was unobserved, he let himself in through a fire exit. He ran up the stairs to the fourth floor, paused behind a thick glass door long enough to assure himself that the corridor was empty, then walked quickly to his room. He reached for the knob—and froze with his hand in the air.

There was a bloody handprint on the jamb. The door was slightly ajar, and the light wood around the lock was splintered where it had been forced.

Peters tore his belt off, threw open the door and leaped into the room, ready to attack. There was no one in the room. The radio was still in its place on the nightstand, but his suitcase was open on the bed. His clothes were strewn over the floor, and he did not have to look to know that the plastique barrette was missing.

There was a hastily scrawled, bloodstained note inside the suitcase, and Peters picked it up with hands that trembled with frustration and fury.

Peters—
 Your play is finished. Now get lost. Hurt Alexandra and I'll have both the CIA and KGB tracking you. Leave her alone and we can deal.

Peters put his belt back on, then deliberately, savagely, tore the note into small pieces, which he flushed down the toilet. He leaned hard against the wash basin, gagged and was almost sick. When the spell of nausea had passed, he went back into the other room, sat down on the edge of the bed, and dug his fingers into the side of the mattress. He closed his eyes and struggled to bring his breathing and heartbeat back to normal. He cursed himself for not booby-trapping the suitcase with his poison needles; it had seemed unnecessary after the death of the CIA agent.

How?

At Sierras Negras, in order to save time at the next day's check-in, the assigned room numbers for the Angeles Blanca Libre had been passed out on mimeographed sheets. Obviously, Peters thought, Finway had seen the list and remembered this room number. The lawyer had somehow managed to get in and out of the hotel, past the soldiers.

Finway was getting cagy, Peters thought, and he found he was developing a grudging respect for the other man. The lawyer was right not to trust his wife's fate to the Sierrans, whose only concern would be to remove the threat to Manuel Salva. Finway was making the right moves.

Finway knew that the barrette was significant, Peters thought, but it occurred to the assassin that the other man might not know why the item was important; he might not know that the material was in fact an explosive impregnated by a deadly poison, or that the barrette was now armed.

Indeed, it was very possible, Peters thought with a grim smile. Finway obviously had not known, or guessed, that the triggering mechanism was a transmitter inside the portable radio. He was certain that Finway was keeping the barrette to show Alexandra, which meant that the lawyer had pocketed his own death. If so, the assassin knew that he could still escape from San Sierra with at least half his mission accomplished—Alexandra's death. John Finway's death would be a small bonus, some salve for his pride, and compensation for the fact that he would lose the greater part of two million dollars. There would be other contracts, other paydays.

All he had to do was find Finway.

Or get within a hundred and fifty yards of him.

Peters felt calmer now—if not supremely confident, at least once again in control of his emotions and with a workable plan to salvage what he could. He took Alexandra's suitcases from the closet, opened them, and ransacked the clothes inside. He did the same to the clothes in the dresser drawers before picking up his portable radio and leaving the room.

He paused in the stairwell, set the portable's tuning dial at the specific frequency that would activate the shortwave transmitter inside the radio, then pressed a small panel on the back.

There was no explosion. Finway was not hiding in any of the other rooms in the wing.

Then where?

The bloodstains were an indication that Finway was hurt, Peters thought, but he had no way of knowing how serious the other man's injuries were. Finway had to be somewhere close by if he wanted to get to Alexandra. If the lawyer were bleeding, he would need a secure hiding place somewhere near the hotel.

Or on the hotel.

Not knowing the layout of the hotel and painfully aware of the passing time, Peters risked using the elevator to go to the top floor. Within seven minutes he had found a maintenance access stairway leading up to the roof.

In an isolated area the odds shifted radically in his favor, Peters thought with growing excitement. If he could somehow manage to surprise Finway in a place like the hotel roof, the man could be easily killed and the assassination tool recovered.

Everything would turn once again.

Buoyed by the faint but intoxicating possibility that he could still carry out the twin killings of Manuel Salva and Alexandra as he had originally planned, Peters employed all of his considerable stalking skills, quietly and stealthily moving out on the roof, avoiding the patches of bright moonlight and keeping low so as not to be silhouetted against the surrounding sea of lights that was Angeles Blanca.

It took him a half hour to cover the entire area, and he found nothing. He returned to the stairway and, as a final precaution, once again pressed the panel on the back of the radio. As before, there was no explosion.

Where?

Finway could very well be at the Coconut Club at that very moment, Peters thought; the lawyer could be talking to Alexandra, or to Sierran security officials. However, Peters dismissed that concern from his mind; he was simply finished if Finway managed to touch base with Alexandra or the Sierrans. Since there was nothing he could do in the event Finway had made it to the Coconut Club, he refused to waste time and nervous energy worrying about it. There was no turning back. He had to find Finway, or die.

It occurred to him that Finway could be somewhere out in the streets, waiting for the buses to return and hoping to intercept Alexandra on her way into the hotel. However, a bleeding American would certainly attract attention, and he assumed that the police were already searching the area around the hotel. He decided that the surrounding streets were too much territory for him to cover in any case.

By a process of elimination, he could only think of one other place where Finway, looking to intercept Alexandra, might try to hide, and where he had a reasonable chance of finding him. It was a very long shot at best, Peters thought, but it was his last shot, and he had absolutely nothing to lose by firing it. He knew that it was no longer possible for him to make it back to the Coconut Club before the group left. He would have to rely on Alexandra to think of some way to cover for him.

He needed to get lucky one last time.

He left the hotel by the same route he had entered and returned to the dead man's car. He started the engine, made a U-turn, and headed toward the harbor area. Twelve minutes later, he was on the wide concourse in front of Tamara Castle.

He knew that the castle's exterior had been lit during the early evening, but now the massive, rough stone structure was cloaked in darkness relieved only by moonlight and a residual glow from the few weak streetlights on the concourse. The castle loomed against the night sky like some great ancient monolith incongruously sprouting steel barnacles that were radar and radio antennas. Although he could not see it from his position, he knew that the opposite side of the castle rested on the edge of a cliff that dropped precipitously to the sea. That would be his escape route, he thought—if only he could find a way to stop things from unraveling.

Peters parked the Plymouth down by the harbor and walked back up the concourse to the castle. He waited, watching and listening, in the shadows across the street. Despite Manuel Salva's well-known contempt for elaborate security precautions within his own island fiefdom, Peters thought it likely, in view of the next evening's event, that some kind of security had been arranged for the castle. While he waited, he once again went over in his mind what he knew of the stone killing ground that loomed before him in the night.

He had memorized every detail of the layout of the castle and, coincidentally, learned a great deal about the mysterious tidal phenomena constantly occurring in the massive rock formation beneath the structure. He knew that, despite the castle's medieval facade, much of the building's interior was used for military and civil service offices. It was, he thought, certainly not a particularly convenient place to stage a sporting event, especially in view of the fact that the Sierrans had built a huge People's Sports Palace not far away. But he had to agree that the castle was picturesque and symbolic of San Sierra; the site had obviously been chosen to capture the attention and appeal to the collective imagination of an American television audience.

It was a site perfectly suited to his purposes, Peters thought, the cornerstone of his plan. Anxious—for whatever unexplained reason—to impress the Americans, the Sierrans had not only provided him with an opportunity to assassinate their president, but chosen a site that afforded him a fast and relatively easy escape route. It was evident that Salva and the Sierrans were going to enormous trouble and expense, and Peters, although he did not consider it important, could not help but wonder why they were doing it.

Platforms for television cameras had been erected at key positions on the concourse around the building, and Peters knew that in a few hours platoons of ABC and Sierran cameramen and technicians would be swarming over and around the site as they made final preparations for the evening's telecast. According to the information he had obtained months before, many of the offices inside had been gutted. Banks of bleachers with a seating capacity of perhaps fifteen thousand had been erected around the interior courtyard, rising from virtually the lip of the boxing ring to a cantilevered stone balcony that ringed the courtyard. In attendance would be a carefully planned mix of government officials, workers, tourists—and Manuel Salva.

Peters was concerned that the one man who could stop him had arrived early.

Twenty minutes later a black, Russian-built police car pulled around the corner and stopped at the curb in front of the castle. A powerful searchlight mounted on the side of the car threw a sharp cone of light on the main entrance to the castle. The large circle of light moved over the stone, sweeping back and forth over the facade, momentarily erasing the night shadows, which then rushed in to fill its passing wake. The light went out, a door opened, and one of the policeman got out and walked up the steps to the castle. He turned on a flashlight, checked the door, then began playing the light on the windows as he walked around the castle.

Ten minutes later the policeman had completed his circuit of the castle. He got into the car, which moved slowly away.

Doubt began to gnaw at Peters, burning the lining of his stomach like acid. While the security precautions he had witnessed were certainly loose enough to allow someone with the necessary skills to break into the castle without leaving a trace of his passing, Finway did not have such skills.

If Finway was not here, Peters thought, he would have to run—hide somewhere in the city, then try to make it to the harbor area when his first escape window opened. But he could not leave without checking.

Clutching his radio, Peters hurried across the street and up the broad flight of stairs to the outer courtyard in front of the castle's main entrance. To his left was a row of windows looking in on what had been architectural offices.

He walked slowly in that direction, testing each window, then expelled a small, pent-up puff of breath through pursed lips when he found what he had been looking for.

One of the windows slid open; the pieces of the broken lock that had been carefully arranged on the sill to make it appear undamaged clattered to the floor inside. The window had been jimmied.

How and where Finway had obtained a tool to open the window did not concern him; he was certain that the lawyer was inside.

He opened the window and stepped over the low sill into the castle. Then he closed the window and repositioned the pieces of the broken lock on the sill, as he assumed—hoped—Finway had done. There was sufficient moonlight spilling in through the windows for Peters to see that the office he was in had been cleared to make room for television monitors and other electronic equipment. According to the floor plans he had studied, the newly constructed boxing arena would be to his left, at the end of a narrow stone corridor.

With his right hand pressed against a rough-hewn stone wall, Peters groped his way down the passageway until he came to a Y. He followed the dim glow of moonlight in the branch to his left and emerged a few moments later in the arena.

Now actually standing in the Tamara Castle courtyard, Peters was even more impressed by the work the Sierrans had done. He was in the mouth of an entrance tunnel on the north side of the castle, just below the overhang of a section of the balcony. The boxing ring, bathed in moonlight, was directly below him. There was considerably more space in the courtyard than he'd assumed there would be from studying the floor plans. Relatively wide aisles formed grids between banks of freshly painted bright-red bleachers. The whole was now spotted with scattered blotches of cold moonlight that made the alternating areas of shadow seem even blacker.

As far as Peters could tell, the normally ubiquitous posters of Manuel Salva were conspicuously absent from the arena, and the assassin once again speculated on Salva's motives for staging the televised spectacle. Salva, he thought, was certainly not going to earn any points with his shaky Third World coalition for this blatant "pandering to capitalist interests."

He smiled as an amusing thought occurred to him: it was almost as if the fable he had told Alexandra about Salva and the United States negotiating for rapprochement between the two countries were true. The spectacle of the Goodyear Blimp floating over Manuel Salva's San Sierra was most certainly not a sight most Americans had ever thought they would see in their lifetimes.

But Salva's motives were not his concern, Peters thought. All he cared about was arranging for the American television audience to see the killing of the dictator and Alexandra Finway. One man stood in his way, and he was very sure the man was close by.

In the time he had, Peters knew that it would be impossible to find Finway if the man did not want to be found; the castle was simply too big, its corridors too labyrinthine, and now every minute that was slipping away put him in ever greater danger.

He had no choice but to offer himself, Peters thought, and hope that an opportunity to kill him would be sufficient motivation to draw the other man out of the depths of the castle. If he were there.

"Finway," Peters said as he stepped out of the tunnel. He had not spoken loudly, but his voice carried clearly in the thick night filling the empty arena. He walked down to the floor of the arena and stood in a patch of moonlight next to the apron of the boxing ring. "Where the hell are you, you chickenshit bastard?"

There was no response.

Peters had not really thought there would be; even if Finway were in earshot, there was no reason why the other man should respond. It had been only a faint hope. Peters had learned that the seasoned lawyer was far too thick-skinned to be goaded by personal insult. Still, Peters thought, if Finway did have any button that could be pushed, he was going to have to discover it soon.

He slowly circled the raised ring, absently slapping his palm against the padded canvas above his head, then climbed halfway up a steeply banked aisle on the north side. He stopped and slowly turned, trying to see into the shadows.

There was no movement, no sound.

"You said we could deal if I didn't hurt your wife."

He thought he heard something behind him. He spun and crouched, aware that Finway could have some kind of weapon in his possession, but the sound had only been the faint echo of his own voice. He sucked in a deep breath and held it, listening for nervous breathing, a scrape—any sign that he was not alone in the castle.

Then he saw a movement out of the corner of his eye; but it was a shadow, not a man. Far to his left, an elongated stick of shadow spun lazily across a luminescent screen of moonlight on a stone wall.

He cried out and ducked as an iron bar flew a half inch over his head, brushing against his hair. The bar bounced off the padded canvas of the ring with a muffled thud, skittered across the stone floor, and crashed into the first row of ringside seats.

"Peters, you just keep on popping up like a bad penny. Someone should take you out of circulation."

Close, Peters thought as a cold film of sweat broke out on his body. But Finway was in the castle, which was all that mattered. Also, the man had courage and pride—which could prove to be his liabilities.

"All right, Finway," Peters said, still crouching in the aisle. "Come on down and we'll talk."

There was a long pause, and then the voice came again. Peters tried to fix its direction, but the echoes in the large space made that impossible; Finway's soft voice seemed to come from everywhere.

"Fuck you, Peters. Let's play hide and seek. The sun'll be up in a couple of hours, and then we'll have a lot of company. Maybe you'll even get to wave to your mother on television."

He was right, Peters thought. Finway had time on his side, and the lawyer knew it. It was impossible to find the other man in the darkness, and the assassin made the decision not to waste another minute.

Peters suddenly leaped to his feet and brought the radio close to his chest. "Here's a tune for you, Finway," he said, and pressed the panel on the back of the radio.

John

He lay panting in the grass for almost a minute, desperately trying to suck air into his lungs. He was still out of breath and his back hurt, but he knew he could not stay there; soldiers and police would be pouring out of the terminal at any moment, swarming over the field, searching for him.

He assumed the first place they would look for him would be in the surrounding countryside or on the access roads leading to and from the airport. He decided that his only chance to escape was to do the unexpected; he had to head back in the direction of the terminal building.

He could feel the blood on his forehead, hands, and right thigh, but could not tell in the darkness how severe the cuts actually were. He knew he did not have time to concern himself with his injuries. He rose to his feet and began trotting to his left, describing a wide arc around the glowing nimbus of the terminal building on his right. Each time he came to one of the lighted runways he got down on his stomach and wriggled across the macadam, then got up and started running again when he was on the other side.

He had made three quarters of a circuit around the terminal when he saw a small, brightly lit parking lot at what appeared to be the rear of the building. Now he paused, knelt down on the grass and watched an ancient, clanking Pontiac wheeze into the lot and stop in a line with four other cars in the lot. The lights went out, the engine chattered, clanked, and died. A bald man in a green maintenance man's uniform got out, casually slammed the door shut behind him and went into the building.

John rose and, keeping low, ran to the lot.

He waited for a few moments on the blacktop just outside the perimeter of light; when he saw no one, he lowered his head and walked briskly to the Pontiac. The door was unlocked and the keys were in the ignition. In the back seat was a long tool box and a crumpled, grease-stained uniform identical to the one the man had been wearing.

John quickly opened the door and got in behind the wheel. It took him almost a full, nerve-racking minute of grinding the starter before the engine finally turned over. With a kind of cold, eerie calm born of his training, his battles, and his knowledge that all his bridges were burned, he put the car into gear, then headed out of the parking lot, following the airport signs indicating the direction to Angeles Blanca.

He knew it was dangerous to stop, but blood was continuing to flow freely down his wrists and through his fingers, making it difficult to grip the steering wheel. He realized that he would have to take time to inspect his wounds and apply tourniquets if it appeared that any veins had been severed. He pulled off to the side of the road, but left the engine running as he stripped down to his shorts.

He looked in the rearview mirror and saw that the cuts on his forehead were minor and had already stopped bleeding. He found he had suffered a series of slashes on the backs of his wrists and forearms, and one long slice on his right thigh. These wounds were still bleeding, but as far as he could tell they were relatively superficial. However, the bleeding had to be stopped.

He tore his shirt and undershirt into strips, then wrapped the improvised bandages tightly about his thigh and hands, leaving his fingers free to grasp the steering wheel. He dressed in the workman's dirty uniform, then put the car back into gear and continued toward Angeles Blanca.

He did not dare to stop and ask directions, and it took him some time to find the Angeles Blanca Libre. However, he was relieved to see that there were no guards posted at the hotel's entrance, and he speculated that the authorities were still concentrating their search for him in the area around the airport. If so, he thought, he just might be able to get to Peters' and Alexandra's room. He did not speak Spanish, and he knew there was always the danger that he could be stopped and questioned. However, he felt that he had no choice but to make an effort to get the unexplained extra barrette from Peters' luggage. He was almost certain that he knew what it was, but he would need it in his possession if he hoped to get Alexandra to listen to him; if he were right about its composition, the barrette was proof of who and what Peters really was, and what he planned to do.

He parked the car on the street across from the hotel,

reached over the seat and picked up the tool box from the back. He pulled the worker's shapeless cap down low over his forehead, then got out of the car and walked quickly across the street, angling away from the main entrance; with his bandaged hands and dirty uniform, he knew he could not risk going in the front door. He walked slowly around the block, looking for another way to get in. There was a double door on the hotel's east side, but it was locked from the inside.

He waited. Five minutes later a couple dressed in formal evening clothes entered the small vestibule just inside the door, and came out. John quickly walked forward and just managed to catch the door before it closed and locked again. He immediately turned to his left and headed up a stairway. There was no one else on the stairs, and he made it to the fourth floor unchallenged.

He hurried down the corridor, checking the room num-against the door. The wood cracked on the first try, then gripped the knob and without hesitation threw his weight splintered and gave around the lock on the second. John bers. When he found Peters' and Alexandra's room, he stepped into the room, quickly closed the door behind him, then leaned against the wall to catch his breath and wait for his heart to stop pounding. He could hear no sounds outside, no indication that anyone had heard him breaking in the door.

He heaved Peters' leather suitcase off a luggage rack and onto the closest bed. He jimmied the small locks with a screwdriver from the tool box, then opened the case and rummaged through the clothes inside, throwing them on the floor. He finally found the ivory-colored barrette in a cloth bag taped to the bottom of a side pouch. He put the barrette in his pocket, started to leave, then hesitated as it occurred to him that Peters might well kill Alexandra when he discovered that the barrette was gone.

He could wait in the room and try to ambush Peters, John thought, but soldiers or police might well come to search the hotel before the tour group returned; he was probably running on borrowed time already. If he were caught now, he would almost certainly be beaten, and probably locked away in solitary confinement. It could be a long time before he was able to get anyone to listen to him. By then, Alexandra could be dead.

He decided to leave a note, which he wrote using one of Alexandra's eyebrow pencils and hotel stationery he found in a desk drawer. He placed the note inside Peters' suitcase, reasoning that even if Alexandra and Peters saw the note at the same time, his wife had shown more than an adequate capacity to defend herself.

He knew he needed to take time to wash the sticky, caked blood off his fingers and change the bandages on his hands. The sheets on the bed were old and of poor quality. He chose the most threadbare and easily tore it into wide strips. Then he removed the blood-soaked bandages, washed his hands, and rebandaged them. He considered rebandaging his thigh, but decided he could not risk staying in the room any longer. He picked up the tool chest and left the hotel the same way he had come in.

John knew that he had no way of determining what Peters would do when he found the barrette gone. The only thing of which he was certain was that he had to remain free if he hoped to be able to exert any kind of control over the situation. He needed some form of sanctuary that would also give him a chance to contact Alexandrda, however briefly; all things considered, Tamara Castle seemed to him the best place to wait, assuming he could find a way to get in without being caught. Even without the barrette, John thought, Peters would almost certainly be forced to come to the castle; if he wanted to maintain his credibility with Alexandra, Peters would be hard pressed to come up with a reason not to attend the boxing matches in order to "protect" Salva.

If they did not come, John thought, he would then contact the authorities.

He drove to the harbor area, left the car two blocks away, and, keeping to the night shadows, walked the rest of the way to the castle. He waited for a time, watching. Then, satisfied that the castle was not regularly patrolled, at least on the outside, he went up the stone steps at the front. He found it surprisingly easy to break in, using a crowbar from the tool chest to pry open one of the windows. After he had entered, he closed the window and replaced the pieces of the broken lock on the sill, then squatted in the darkness, listening, for almost ten minutes. When he heard no one moving inside the castle, he used a book of matches from the tool chest to light his way through a maze of corridors until he finally found his way into the boxing arena.

Wanting to get as far away from the front entrance as possible, he went down to the ring area and climbed a bank of bleachers on the opposite side to a row just below the stone balcony.

He went to the moonlit area, sat down on the edge of a wooden bleacher, and took the barrette from his pocket. From his years of experience defending radicals and terrorists during the Sixties, John was familiar with various types of explosives. He assumed that the barrette was plastique inside some kind of laminated shell. From what he had read, and learned from prosecutors, John suspected that the material was C-5; if it were C-5, or some even more advanced compound, he estimated that the heavy barrette would have almost the explosive force of a stick of dynamite. It was not a lot of firepower, John thought, but it was enough to do the job if Peters could somehow maneuver Alexandra through a net of security agents to within a few yards of Salva. Or there could be more to the weapon, some deadly wrinkle that would give it an even greater range.

In any event, John thought grimly, even if the barrette were just plastique, it was more than enough to do a job on Alexandra.

Then again, John thought with a faint smile, the object in his hand might be just one of Alexandra's barrettes. He could have it all wrong, which would make him the hands-down favorite for Dangerous Dunce of the Year.

He knew that plastic explosives required some kind of triggering device, and his fear that he could be suffering paranoid delusions was dispelled a few moments later when he pressed hard against the base of the steel hasp anchoring the needle to the laminate. The small steel panel slid back to reveal a tiny electronic module embedded in the material.

John shuddered as he thought of what the explosive would have done to Alexandra. Rage stiffened his muscles, and for the first time in his life he knew what it felt like to desperately want to kill a man, no matter what the cost. Perhaps he would yet, he thought; if Peters hurt Alexandra, he would definitely kill the man, or die trying.

He removed the electronic component from the barrette, placed the barrette and module in separate pockets.

He knew he could not afford to allow his mind to be clouded by hate; it was absolutely necessary that he remain clearheaded and calm. Without his small bomb, Peters was going to have to do some quick improvising; John wanted to see how fast the other man could think on his feet.

He moved out of the moonlight and lay down on a bleacher, balling his shirt and using it as a pillow. He dozed for a few minutes, then was startled wide awake by the sound of Peters' soft but resonant voice knifing through the stillness.

"Finway. Where the hell are you, you chickenshit bastard?"

Resisting the impulse to spring to his feet, John carefully turned his head and looked around the arena. He spotted Peters and watched as Peters descended from the opposite side, slowly circled the ring, then came halfway up the aisle toward him. John used the faintly echoing sound of the other man's footsteps to mask the click produced when he lifted the lid of the tool chest. He took out a hammer and the crowbar, then eased himself up into a sitting position.

"You said we could deal if I didn't hurt your wife."

John judged Peters to be perhaps twenty yards away when the other man stopped and slowly turned in a complete circle. John gripped the crowbar at the straight end, cocked his arm, and let the steel bar fly. For one jubilant moment he was certain that the heavy tool would smash into Peters' head, but the man ducked at the last moment and the bar clattered harmlessly into the darkness.

John removed his shoes and set them aside. He rose silently, stepped onto the balcony, and moved off a few yards from his original position. It was now a matter of getting close enough to the other man to use the hammer.

"Peters," John said softly, "you just keep on popping up like a bad penny. Someone should take you out of circulation."

"All right, Finway." The tone of voice was seductively reassuring, soothing. "Come on down and we'll talk."

John moved a few steps to his left. "Fuck you, Peters. Let's play hide and seek. The sun'll be up in a couple of hours, and then we'll have a lot of company. Maybe you'll even get to wave to your mother on television."

John waited, watching the area where Peters had ducked down in the aisle. Suddenly the other man leaped up. In the moonlight John could see a crazed, ragged wave of rage and triumph sweep across the other man's face as he clutched his radio to his chest.

"Here's a tune for you, Finway," Peters said in a cracking voice that rose at the end and broke off just short of a hysterical laugh.

For a few moments John was mystified by the man's behavior: Peters grimaced, flung his free arm over his head, and fell face down in the aisle, disappearing from sight below the line of bleachers. Nine or ten long seconds passed. Then Peters poked his head up and looked around slowly, a baffled expression on his face.

The significance of the other man's actions suddenly came to John: he would have been blown into bloody pieces if he had not removed the triggering mechanism from the plastique barrette.

John experienced a wave of nausea that almost caused him to vomit; something cold circled his heart and squeezed. However, the sick, icy giddiness was rapidly supplanted by wry amusement, and he decided that everything he had gone through was almost worth the opportunity to see the look of puzzlement, frustration, and outrage on Rick Peters' features.

John took the electronic module out of his pocket and threw it toward Peters, tossing it in a high arc up into the air in order to disguise the direction from which it was coming. "Here," John said. "Why don't you stick this up your ass and see what happens?"

The component fell at Peters' feet and broke with a small popping sound. Peters jumped, startled. He recovered and abruptly whipped off his belt. His face was set in a rigid mask of murderous, uncontrolled rage as he tore off the leather shield and charged up the aisle, swinging the buckle around his head in a deadly, whistling arc. John watched the other man disappear into the darkness of the bleacher section where he had been a few minutes before, and for a time John could track the man only by the sound of the singing steel. Then there was nothing but silence.

John crouched down behind the balcony railing, gripping the hammer as best he could with his bandaged right hand. He dared not move while Peters remained still and listening, and he knew he would be in trouble if Peters decided to circle the balcony. However, a few minutes later Peters emerged from the bleacher section and slowly made his way down the aisle through a rippling chiaroscuro of moonlight and night. It seemed to John that the other man's rage was now spent; Peters' movements and demeanor appeared calculated, thoughtful.

Alexandra had told him that Peters was dangerous, John thought. The description seemed to him now a remarkable understatement. The man was not big, but in the few minutes that Peters' outburst had lasted John had experienced the illusion that he was being stalked by some jungle beast—an enraged, sinewy, and powerful panther crashing through the brush, capable of rending everything in its path with fangs of leather and honed metal.

But now the panther was at bay, John thought, and it was his job to keep it off balance.

John watched, his breathing rapid and shallow, as the slight, blond-haired man leaped nimbly up on the apron of the ring, stepped between the ropes and stood erect in a corner of the moonlight-bathed square of canvas. He set the radio down, then leaned casually against one of the thick, elastic ring ropes and peered up into the darkness.

"You did say we could deal," Peters said at last. The hysteria was gone from his voice and manner, and John was astonished to realize that the tone was almost petulant, as though he had wronged Peters by not allowing himself to be blown up or not stepping into the path of the whirling belt buckle.

He was, John thought, dealing with a madman, a clever paranoic beyond reason or mercy.

John walked silently and stealthily twenty-five yards to his left before he answered. "You've got it. The deal is that you walk out of here right now. And you keep walking away from Alexandra and the rest of the tour group. Don't even go back to the hotel. I want you to get lost somewhere in the countryside; crawl back under some rock. Make up some story to tell the Sierrans and let them put you on another plane. Or swim back to Miami; the exercise will do you good, help you to get rid of some of your excess energy. I think you tend to get a little overexcited."

"Maybe I'll go back to the hotel and kill your wife, Finway."

"Will you? She may be laying for you by the time you get back. I don't have to tell you that Alexandra's not stupid. You tricked her pretty good, but the mirrors you used may be getting a little foggy by now. How are you going to explain being out all night? Did you tell her you were going out for a glass of coconut milk? Besides, I'll bet I can find a telephone in here before you can get back there."

There was a prolonged silence. John knew that his hammer, wielded in a clumsily bandaged hand, was no match for Peters' belt, and he wondered if he should move again. He decided not to, inasmuch as Peters showed no signs that he intended to come after him again.

"I can get out of San Sierra any time I want," Peters said at last. In the bright moonlight, the man's blond hair seemed to glow with a ghostly penumbra, like some demonic halo. "I don't need the Sierrans."

"Then go."

"I have a problem with that, Finway. Both you and Alexandra have good contacts with some very heavy people who are potentially nasty. If I leave now, I'll be spending the rest of a short life looking over my shoulder. You *could* probably have both the KGB and CIA tracking me. And they'd find me. I'm just not in the mood to commit suicide."

"Just take off, Peters. That's all I care about. Alexandra and I won't say a word, won't do anything."

"Things aren't that simple. That was a CIA agent whose body you helped me get rid of."

The words blew through John's heart with the force of a cold, numbing wind, and he cursed himself for not realizing the truth earlier, for not *knowing* that Swarzwalder was not an assassin. If he had thought more clearly from the beginning, if he had paid attention to his emotions and instincts, the big man who had saved his life once, and had spared it in their last encounter, might still be alive. He had sorted things out too late, John thought, and it had cost Swarzwalder his life. He found that his eyes had suddenly filled with tears; he was astonished and terribly saddened to realize how much he missed Swarzwalder. It was almost as if he were responsible for the death of a friend.

"You see the problem, Finway," Peters continued in a conversational tone. "In any case, I just don't believe that you wouldn't try to get me. By now I imagine you're pretty pissed at me, huh?" He paused, laughed, and then his voice turned hard and cold. "But even if I didn't doubt your sincerity, and even if I didn't know the CIA is eventually going to be climbing all over you, it still wouldn't make any difference. You're not going back to the United States for some time; you're headed for a Sierran slammer. The Sierrans are going to want to know what the hell's been going on between the three of us, and they'll just let you sit and rot on a bread-and-water diet until you tell them a story they'll believe. You see my point? You and I are just going to have to put our heads together and come up with another solution."

"Maybe you'd like me to kill myself?"

"I'd appreciate it," Peters replied evenly.

John knew that Peters had no choice but to try and kill him, but he could not understand what the man was hoping to accomplish by standing in the boxing ring carrying on an inane conversation. John was certain that Peters had to be feeling severe time pressure, regardless of what excuse he planned to offer Alexandra or Raul for his absence. His own watch had been broken in the escape from the airport, but he estimated that it was now three or four in the morning. He could stay there indefinitely, John thought; Peters could not.

If Peters wanted to stand around and chat, John thought, he would certainly oblige him.

"What's the going rate these days for a good killer?" John asked casually.

"Oh, I'm supposed to be paid a great deal of money for killing Salva. You're hurting me in the pocketbook, Finway."

"And Alexandra? What did you do, pull her name out of

an old hat?" John had tried to keep his voice flat and emotionless to match Peters', but now it began to quiver with barely suppressed rage. "Why did you drag her into it, Peters? The plastique barrette is clever, but I don't believe that a smart fellow like you couldn't have come up with a plan for killing Salva that didn't involve blowing an innocent woman's head off."

"Yes," Peters replied easily, "I suppose I could have. But you must admit there's a certain elegance to this plan."

"You cold-blooded bastard: I'm going to enjoy the thought of about a dozen good agents tracking you down."

"Alexandra was mine before she was yours," Peters said, sudden anger lending an even harder edge to his voice. "She was mine by choice and by nature. She shouldn't have left me for you."

John swallowed. His mouth was dry, parched by hatred. "You want to kill a woman because she *left* you fifteen years ago?"

"Yes," Peters replied in a tone that was once again dry and matter-of-fact. "You've got the basic picture."

For a few moments John's rage and hate were superceded by stunned bewilderment. "You're insane," he said at last. "Jesus Christ, don't you realize that?"

Peters suddenly pushed off the rope he had been leaning on. John tensed and prepared to move to another position, but Peters only walked to the center of the ring. The man removed his light green sleeveless sweater, pulling it up over his head and dropping it at his feet.

"You don't have the slightest idea what your wife is all about, Finway," Peters said as he began to unbutton his Oxford shirt. "One thing you don't understand is that there's an unstable center there—a little rumble, if you will—that makes Alexandra something special. All really special people have that rumble; try to damp it down and the person will explode. A woman like Alexandra needs outlets. If you hadn't stumbled along on this trip, you'd still think she was your average happy little housewife. Don't kid yourself, Finway; if Alexandra weren't here in San Sierra this week, she'd eventually have ended up someplace else just like it. For Alexandra, San Sierra's a state of mind. It's that rumble; it won't be denied."

"The only rumble I hear is your mouth," John said,

puzzled and distracted by the bizarre strip act taking place in the moonlit ring directly below him. Peters, now naked to the waist, casually looped his belt around his neck. He kicked off his cowboy boots, then began to remove his slacks.

"She's wasted on you. You don't know shit about what makes her go. I understand her better than she understands herself, and you don't even live in the same world she and I do. Right now she's back the way she used to be. It's the way she is—and it's how I want her when I kill her. With her head the way it is, having it blown off will be like the best fuck she's ever had. She'll really get off on it in that hundredth of a second, Finway, believe me."

Unwilling to trust his voice, John said nothing. He stiffened and prepared to run as Peters suddenly turned his head and stared directly up at the section of the balcony where he was standing. But Peters still made no move to leave the ring. The other man took the belt from around his neck, gripped it by the tongue end, and lazily swung it around his head three times before letting it fly. The belt sailed in a long, high arc through alternate patches of moonlight and darkness and landed with a dull clang on the stone a few yards from where John was standing.

"Let's you and I get it on, Finway," Peters continued in a tense voice. "There's a weapon for you." He paused, carefully folded his slacks, and placed them next to his boots, shirt, and sweater. "That belt's the easiest thing in the world to use; I'm sure even a chickenshit lawyer like you can figure out how it works. The edge of the buckle is sharp as a razor. All you need is one good shot and you can slice me up like a carrot. I'm stripped down so that you can see I'm not armed. A duel; that's the solution to our problem."

The point, John thought: a last, desperate attempt on Peters' part to take him out. Or perhaps it wasn't all that desperate. Even with the belt and hammer, and even if his hands were not bandaged, John knew there was no reason for him to go up against a professional killer; in fact, it would be a sucker play for him to do it. He remembered the finger jabbing into his solar plexus, the speed and moves Peters had demonstrated in his battle with Swarzwalder. Peters' body was his weapon, John thought; the man was highly trained and conditioned, and lightning fast. Killing was Peters' business. No matter how well armed he was, he would probably have only one chance at Peters before the other man commenced taking him apart with his hands and feet. If he were forced to fight physically for Alexandra's life, he certainly would, but he did not see that he had to, or that he should. Time was still in his favor, and it was Peters who was out in the cold and desperate.

He had talked enough, John thought, and he would say no more. He remained motionless, and for long minutes there was no sound in the arena.

"Let's talk about your kids, you chickenshit coward," Peters said at last, his voice rising in anger and frustration. "If you don't come down and fight me now, I walk right out of here and use an escape route to get out of San Sierra. The first thing I do when I get back to the States is kill your kids. That would be Michael, Kara, and Kristen, right? If I'm going to be hunted, at least I'm going to have the satisfaction of leaving your kids' corpses behind for you to remember me by. That's it, Finway. If you won't fight me for your wife, how about fighting me for the lives of your kids? Don't you doubt for a second, Daddy, that I won't do what I say I will."

John had no doubt, and he knew there was a real possibility that his children could die as a result of what he did or did not do at that moment. Peters' threat was viable, and it would have to be taken into consideration, weighed.

If Peters could get out of San Sierra immediately, John thought, it would be a race between the assassin's ability to find the children at his sister's house and his own ability to get the Sierrans to listen to him, believe him, and then request appropriate action from the FBI and New York City police.

If he went down to fight, he just might be able to kill Peters. The nightmare would be over . . .

Or his children could end up orphans. If he were killed, there would be no one left to stop Peters from killing Alexandra along with Salva . . .

If he did not go down to fight, Peters would hunt his children . . .

His willingness to risk his and Alexandra's life in a duel,

against the possibility that Peters could track down and kill his children if he chose not to.

John slowly turned his head and looked toward the area of the balcony where Peters' belt lay in the darkness. A hammer and a belt with a razor-sharp buckle against an unarmed man, John thought. It appeared that he had all the advantages, including superior height and weight. He was in good condition too. Why, then, did he hesitate? Was he a coward?

No. The man waiting for him in the ring was a professional who had already offered ample proof that he knew his business well. Peters had not been able to mask his confidence and a kind of electric anticipation in his voice. It was obvious, John thought, that Peters had no doubt about the outcome of such a duel. The other man badly wanted him to come down—and nothing that Peters wanted him to do could possibly be in his or his family's interest.

John remained silent.

Peters waited almost five minutes, but he did not speak again. Finally he abruptly snatched up his clothes, climbed down out of the ring, and walked quickly back the way he had come, disappearing into the darkness.

John remained very still, considering the dimensions of his new dilemma as he stared into the sector of night where Peters had gone. If the man were doubling back, or even just waiting and listening, John did not want to betray his position or movements with any sound. On the other hand, Peters could be hurrying back to the hotel to kill Alexandra before escaping from San Sierra, and John knew that he had to find a telephone inside the castle so that he could call the hotel and warn his wife.

He slowly counted to one hundred, then moved as quietly as he could to the spot where Peters' belt had landed. He picked up the belt, then held his breath and strained to hear any sound in the darkness. There was nothing. There were probably a dozen telephones within a hundred yards of where he was standing, John thought, if only he knew where they were. If he could find a telephone, he should have no difficulty making the operator understand that he wanted the Angeles Blanca Libre.

The problem was that even at that moment Peters could be close by, stalking him. Still, John knew that he could wait no longer. He had to assume that Peters was going for Alexandra, which meant that he had to move.

Of necessity, John tried to dismiss from his mind the ominous threat of Peters remaining in the castle to hunt him. He began to walk at a fairly rapid pace around the balcony, looking for some kind of office. There was none, and he began to feel panic rising in him; if Peters were on his way back to the hotel in a car, John thought, he would almost be there by now.

He decided to risk heading back toward the main entrance to the castle. However, not wanting to cross the potential killing ground of the open arena itself, he began to search for a stairway leading down to the ground level.

Groping his way along the wall, John felt a stone entrance way. There was a sign on a heavy chain strung across the opening, but John could not read the Spanish. He ducked under the chain, descended a few steps, then abruptly stopped when his face was brushed by cobwebs. He lit a match from the book in his pocket. The stairwell was all pitted, cobwebbed stone, apparently a part of the original structure; the passageway was very narrow and winding, and obviously unused. John doubted it led anywhere. He started to turn, and in the flickering light from the match caught a movement of stocking feet out of the corner of his eye.

He ducked just as the crowbar, swung like a club, whistled over his head and slammed into the stone wall with a loud crack.

Deep in a primitive part of himself, John was exultant. He *wanted* to fight. He had wanted to fight before, but he had realized that his and Alexandra's best chance for survival lay in his using his intelligence. But now he had no choice, and the terrible yearning of his rage and hatred was unleashed. He wanted to kill the other man, and that savage part of him was grateful that Peters had waited and found him.

He flattened himself against the rough, curved wall, flipped the belt buckle back behind him, then yanked hard on the tongue, bringing the sharp metal at the end of the leather singing through the air over his head. He clenched his teeth in joyful anticipation of the tug of the metal biting into flesh, the sound of the other man's screams. Instead, the buckle smacked against stone, firing off sparks. John fell on his belly as the notched crowbar once again sailed through the air over his head, hit the wall and showered sharp chips of stone over the left side of his face.

He rolled on his left side, cocked his arm and flung the hammer into the night above him. This time there was the dull thud of heavy metal striking flesh, then a sharp cry of pain and surprise.

John again snaked the belt buckle behind him, then lunged forward, extending his body and whipping the sharp metal piece back over his head. This time the buckle did not strike flesh, nor did it smash into stone. There was a sudden, sharp tug, and John realized that Peters had managed to snag the belt with the crowbar. John tried to twist away to his right, but he was too slow; Peters' heel smashed into the center of his forehead.

He was going to die, John thought as he tumbled backward down the spiral staircase and came up hard against a wooden barrier that might have been a door but felt soft and rotten. He had to get up, but he couldn't make his muscles work. Instead of darkness there was light, but John knew that it was a false light smoldering somewhere behind his eyes and in his mind, a sick phosphorescence sparked from nerve endings that screamed in pain, robbing him of strength and consciousness.

He did not pass out completely. As if from a great distance, he heard Peters coming toward him down the stairs. Time and consciousness seemed to flicker like candles in a candelabra of eternity; then the other man was kneeling over him; searching his pockets; lighting a match; taking the barrette.

Don't do that!

He would beg, John thought.

Don't kill Alexandra! Please please please don't kill Alexandra!

But then he realized that his words were trapped in his mind, with no more focus or force than his fragmented thoughts. He could not speak any more than he could move.

The match flickered out; there was a blue-green flash of light as another was lit.

Floating in a nether world of semiconsciousness, totally

unable to defend himself, John found that he suddenly felt nothing but mild curiosity as to how Peters would choose to kill him. The edge of the belt buckle across his throat or the back of his neck? A sharp blow? He was vaguely surprised when nothing happened.

A third match was lit, and he heard the door behind him creak open.

Peters seemed to be talking to him, but John could not tell what the other man was saying; he could hear hatred in the voice, but he could not understand the words. He wanted to talk back, fight, kill. But he was too tired and hurt.

He felt Peters grab his wrist, and the next moment he was being dragged along a cold, flat stone surface. He wanted to sleep, just for a few seconds. He was so tired. He wanted the false lights behind his eyes to go out so that he could rest for a few moments, then get up and fight.

Perhaps he had fallen asleep, John thought. Or passed out for a few seconds. The next thing he experienced was a sensation of plummeting through space.

This was not in his mind, John thought; he was falling.

He instinctively rolled his body up into a ball, clutching his knees to his chest. He winced as he anticipated a final, searing flash of pain at the moment he was crushed on stone or earth.

7:30 A.M.

Alexandra

Where are they?! John? Rick?

Alexandra sat stiffly on the edge of the bed, both feet flat on the floor and hands folded tightly in her lap, feeling very small and confused. Her thigh and vagina burned where Rick Peters had stroked her, as though his fingers had left behind an ineradicable film of acid on her flesh.

She should not have allowed him to touch her like that, Alexandra thought. If she had immediately pushed his hand away, she would not now be lacerated by guilt and uncertainty; she would be able to handle her present situation better. As it was, all she could do was sit and concentrate on keeping her features rigid. It was permissible to show concern, but not fear. Never fear.

She felt the need to move. She rose and began to undo her hair, removing the barrette and leaving it on the nightstand beside her bed. The she picked up a brush and began to work it over and through her shoulder-length hair.

"Would you like me to leave now so that you can sleep, Mrs. Finway?"

For God's sake, yes! Alexandra thought. But she knew that she could not afford to appear too anxious.

She turned around to face Raul, who was slumped wearily in a chair by the window. The Sierran's eyes were red-rimmed, and he kept nervously running the fingers of both hands over the stubble on his face and through hair that had grown greasy and matted.

"I won't be able to sleep until I find out what's happened to Rick. But you should go now, Raul. You're exhausted, and you've got the rest of the group to worry about. I can always sleep, but you've got a big day and night ahead of you."

Raul stood up and shook his head stubbornly. "No. It is my job to find out what has happened. There is so much trouble on this trip; more trouble than I have ever had before. First there is this business of your husband and his craziness; now Mr. Peters has disappeared, and your room has been broken into. There are clothes with blood on them. So much trouble. If you don't mind, I will wait a little longer."

Alexandra waited two beats, then said carefully, "Well, now that you mention it, I think I would like to lie down for—"

"We do not have crime in San Sierra," Raul said angrily. "Manuel does not allow it. This is a Communist society; there is no need to steal. I do not understand this burglary!"

"Raul—"

"What did you say was stolen, Mrs. Finway?"

"A camera and some cheap costume jewelry," Alexandra replied with a shrug. "It's not important, Raul. These things happen. Rick and I didn't have anything of real value to steal."

"What kind of camera was it, Mrs. Finway?"

"I don't know," Alexandra said impatiently. "A Minolta, I think."

Raul's eyes narrowed. "I don't remember seeing either you or Mr. Peters carrying a camera."

"Come off it, Raul!" Alexandra snapped, deciding that it was an appropriate time to display a touch of anger. "We're both tired, and there's no sense in arguing! Do you think I'm lying to you? Rick and I were more interested in seeing your country and talking to people than in taking pictures. I don't give a damn about the camera, and the jewelry wasn't worth anything. I'm concerned about Rick—and John, even though John's a stupid ass. So forget this break-in, okay?"

"I am sorry," Raul said stiffly. "You are right, of course. It's not your fault that your room was broken into, and we should not have sharp words." He shook his head. "Much, much trouble on this trip. It makes me very nervous and unhappy."

Alexandra stretched, yawned loudly. "Would you leave

me alone now, Raul? I really would like to lie down for a little while."

Raul nervously glanced at his watch. "Perhaps if I wait just another twenty minutes. I cannot understand what has happened to Mr. Peters."

Alexandra was about to protest when she was startled by the sudden, raucous blare of Latin music cutting through the morning stillness. The music grew even louder in volume, building in an approaching crescendo that reached a pounding, clamorous peak just outside the door. There was a rattling sound as someone fumbled with the knob. A few seconds later the door crashed open and a drunk Rick Peters staggered into the room.

"Hey, hey, folks," Peters mumbled thickly, his eyes rolling in his head. His voice was a dull, slurred mumble barely audible above and between the clangor of cymbals and snapping beats of a conga drum. "Raul, you ol' rascal, what're you doin' here with my lady?"

"Rick?" Alexandra walked quickly across the room to Peters but she was too late to catch him. The blond-haired man staggered backward until he came up hard against the wall, then slowly slid down the plaster to end up sitting splay-legged on the floor. Alexandra bent down and turned off the radio.

"Whatsa' matter with the fuckin' door? Somebody busted the fuckin' door, Raul. I want the bastard who did it hung and shot. Godit, kid? There's some fuckin' capitalist, imperialist, Zionist burglar loosh in this Communist wonderland!"

Peters fumbled with the radio dial as he tried to turn it back on. Alexandra reached down and pushed the radio away, then gripped Peters under the right arm and tried to pull him to his feet. She got him halfway up the wall before he slipped out of her grasp and crumpled back down to the floor.

Alexandra was suddenly conscious of Raul standing behind her, and she turned to face him. "My God, he's drunk," she said with a sigh, shaking her head in disgust. "Raul, I'm so sorry you had to stay up all night just because this idiot felt like getting drunk."

"Where have you been, Mr. Peters?" Raul asked tightly, his own voice blurred by exhaustion.

"Havin' a nip or ten of your rum, Raul, ol' buddy. Man, you gotta' drink an awful lot of that stuff to get a buzz on. Do you know how much I—"

"Why did you leave the group?"

Peters, glassy-eyed, stared drunkenly back at Raul, then suddenly reached out and gripped Alexandra's wrist. "I love you, Alexandra," he moaned, his voice cracking. "Sh'not fair, John comin' around and meshin' with us." His head bobbed, lolled forward on his chest, but he managed to turn his attention to the Sierran. "I love her, Raul."

"Yes, Mr. Peters," Raul said stiffly, "but—"

"You love me, Alexandra?"

"I love you, Rick," Alexandra said wearily, watching Raul out of the corner of her eye. The Sierran seemed angry and confused.

"Sh'not fair, baby," Peters whined. "Why'd he have to come here and try to make you love him again? Sh'not fair."

"It didn't work, Rick. It doesn't matter what John does or doesn't do. I love you."

"Thank you, baby."

"Where have you been, darling?! I've been going out of my mind worrying that something had happened to you, and poor Raul's been up all night waiting with me."

"Got . . . upsh—upset when Raul came and said John was lookin' for you. Made me mad! I wanted to beat him up. I went out lookin' for him, kept drinkin'. I got drunk and fell down out there in the woods sh-someplace. Couldn't get up." Peters hiccupped, then threw back his head and laughed shrilly. After a few moments the laughter trickled off, punctuated by another sharp hiccup. "By the time I woke up, the buses had gone without me. Pissed me off. I show 'em. I took a coupla' bottles from the bar and *walked* back here. Show 'em. Whaddya' think of that, huh?"

Alexandra glanced quickly, furtively at Raul. The Sierran-tour guide had backed up a few paces and was shaking his head in annoyance; his lips moved as he mumbled a silent litany of anger.

"Rick," Alexandra said, feigning breathless astonishment, "that's miles!"

Peters again laughed drunkenly. "Good exercise. And I had my bottles to keep me company. Took 'em from the bar, but I left some money." He rolled his bloodshot eyes toward Raul, slowly blinked. "You gonna' 'rest me, ol buddy?"

Raul grunted with disgust, then marched woodenly, his back stiff with anger, out of the room, trying unsuccessfully to slam the broken door behind him.

Alexandra waited, unconsciously holding her breath as she listened to the sound of Raul's receding footsteps. She slowly exhaled as she heard the elevator doors down the corridor sigh open, then close.

"God, Rick, you really are drunk," she said quietly, grabbing Peters' outstretched hand and helping him to his feet.

Peters grunted, nodded sluggishly. "It was the only ex-cuse I could think of for mish-missing the bus. When did they s-start to miss me?"

"Not until we got back here. The police have been searching for you, you know. I hope Raul believes your story about getting lost."

"He believes it."

Alexandra swallowed drily, put a hand to her throat. "Did you find John?" she asked in a low, hoarse voice.

"Yeah. He's okay. I've got him stashed away in a safe place."

"Well, tell me what happened!"

"First things first," Peters murmured, stumbling toward the bathroom.

"Rick, what's the matter with your side?"

"I'll tell you all about it later," Peters said. "I'd appreciate it if you'd call the desk and try to rustle up a roll of adhesive tape." He went into the bathroom and closed the door behind him.

Peters

He braced himself with his left hand on the wash basin and poked the index finger of his right down his throat. His stomach violently purged itself of the rum he had drunk out of a bottle stolen from the hotel bar an hour and a half earlier. The stomach contractions wrenched his body, and he gritted his teeth against the grinding pain in his side. He judged that his ribs were cracked, but not broken. He could live with the pain, he thought; he had suffered far worse.

Finally the last of the rum was out of him. He dry-heaved for a minute or two, and then the spasms stopped. He washed down the sink, stripped off his clothes, and stepped into a stinging cold shower that slapped his nerves with the force of an electric shock. His body shuddered in protest and he groaned in agony, but he stayed under the flaying, needle-sharp spray, fighting the cold with his will, enjoying the challenge.

After a few minutes he adjusted the water to body temperature, then crouched down in the tub and let the warm, soothing curtain of water cascade over his body, relaxing his muscles. He tried gingerly lifting his left arm over his head, but the pain in his left side was too great; he quickly lowered the arm and cradled his cracked ribs. It would be all over that night, he thought, and the pain was a small price to pay for his impending triumph.

It helped to know that at that very moment his own suffering was being repaid a thousandfold in the currency of agony and terror, if Finway were not already dead. Peters hoped he was not.

The end of that hunt had been sweet, he thought, and for a few minutes he used the anesthetic of memory to dull the pain in his side.

He remembered the jolt of surprise and anticipation he'd experienced when, stalking Finway in the darkness shrouding Tamara Castle, he'd heard the rattle of a heavy chain and then footsteps descending stone steps. According to the floor plans he'd seen and the research he had done on the castle, there was only one stone stairway leading off the balcony; Finway had chosen the best of all places to trap himself. The narrow, spiral staircase had been closed off inasmuch as it led to nothing more than an unusable arte-sian well sunk when the castle was built in a futile attempt to tap the freshwater table in the stone formation on which the castle sat. In less than ten years the lower walls of the well had collapsed, victim to the inexorable force of the corrosive sea water that swelled and ebbed in mysterious, not always synchronous, tidal flows through the labyrinth of caves that veined the limestone. The pit at the end of the stairway was a natural tomb. Anyone falling down it would be lost forever, flushed back and forth by the tides in the endless matrix of caverns, perhaps one day to be expelled in white calcium pieces into the harbor sea. By then, Peters thought, it would long ago have ceased to matter. Even the sharks would not be interested in Finway's bones.

He hadn't expected Finway to have a second weapon; the lack of anticipation had been a lapse that could have killed him. But it hadn't; it had been Finway who had ended up unconscious at the foot of the stairway. He'd considered killing the lawyer immediately, but had decided not to. The fall down the well would probably kill Finway anyway, he'd reasoned, and if it didn't it pleased him to think of the other man trapped in caverns filling with water, helplessly waiting in total darkness to drown.

He'd dragged Finway fifteen yards to the slightly raised mouth of the well and unceremoniously dumped the body over the edge. He'd waited to hear the distant splash, then hurried back up the stairs to retrieve his boots. Within seven minutes he'd been back in the stolen car, heading for the hotel.

It had remained for him to think of an excuse to cover his absence, and that had come to him soon after he'd abandoned the car three blocks from the hotel. He had not seen any bars in Angeles Blanca except for those in hotels or official entertainment centers, and consequently he'd gone directly to the Angeles Blanca Libre. He'd let himself in through a rear service entrance and walked up a flight of stairs to the mezzanine. He'd found it deserted, as he'd expected, and he had quickly picked the lock on the sliding glass door leading to the pool and bar area.

He'd sat down behind the bar and drunk three-quarters of a bottle of rum. He'd taken his time, consuming the liquor over a period of an hour and a half in order to avoid alcohol poisoning, knowing that the length of his absence no longer made any difference, while the quality of his performance and his appearance would. He could not risk trying to fake it. When he'd felt suitably drunk, he'd splashed some rum on his clothes, then gone up to the fourth floor and snapped on the radio.

He'd fully expected to find Raul waiting for him.

Now it was almost finished, he thought. There was one more small detail to take care of, but then he could almost coast through the evening. The rest was technique and precision timing.

There were no more unknowns.

He turned off the shower and stood in the tub for a few moments, lazily blinking away water while he assessed his mental condition. He decided that he was still very drunk, but he knew what he was doing; he could control his movements, and he could think clearly enough to take care of the business at hand. That was important, he thought; although the next detail was small, it was crucial.

"Rick?" Alexandra called anxiously. "They brought the tape. Are you okay? You want some help?"

"I'm all right. Be out in a minute."

He toweled himself off, then slipped into a terrycloth robe. He'd rearmed the recovered plastique barrette with a spare detonator from inside the radio, and now he put the barrette into one of the robe's large pockets, took a deep breath to steady himself, then went back into the other room.

"Christ," he sighed wearily, "that feels better."

Alexandra was standing across the room, staring out the window. The bright morning sunlight pouring in through the clear glass glowed in the thick crown of her hair, highlighting the strands of gray. She turned quickly at the sound of his voice.

"Rick, you took so long in there! Tell me what happened! Where's John?"

"I knew I had to find him before the Sierrans did," Peters said easily. He strolled casually around a bed and stopped in front of the nightstand where Alexandra had placed a wide roll of adhesive tape next to her barrette. "I had to find out what was on his mind and what the hell he thought he was doing pulling a stunt like that with the boxing matches coming up." He laughed tightly. "Also— just in passing, of course—I didn't want the silly bastard shot."

"How did you find him?!" Alexandra asked impatiently.

"First, I checked out the grounds around the Coconut Club," he said, turning his back and beginning to toy absently with the barrette on the stand in front of him. "When I couldn't find him there, I figured he might be waiting somewhere around the hotel."

"You came here?"

"I stole a car." Peters twisted his body slightly to the right, picked up Alexandra's barrette and dropped it into his left pocket, then shifted the other way and put the plastique barrette down on the wooden surface. "I knew it was a big risk, but I figured I had to take it," he continued after a pause that had lasted no more than two or three seconds. "Your husband could have blown everything."

Now he slowly turned back to face Alexandra. Her features were very tense, but Peters could tell that her concern was for her husband. She gave no indication that his slight swaying motion had aroused any curiosity at all; if it had, she'd apparently attributed the movement to his drunkenness.

It was done, Peters thought as a languorous calm settled over him like a warm, weightless cloak. Everything was in place. A decade and a half of resentment and hatred had meshed with more than two years of planning to bring him to this moment. A thousand hurdles, tangible and intangible, had been overcome. That evening fate and fortune would fuse and explode in one final, blissful instant of destruction.

As soon as Alexandra put her hair up, his weapon would be triggered. It would remain only to maneuver Alexandra, his delivery system, into position.

"I just kept walking the streets around the hotel," Peters continued. "I finally found him—or, rather, he found me. He was waiting for the buses to come back."

Alexandra shook her head nervously. "Why did he run away from Raul at the airport?"

Peters shrugged. He went to his dresser, opened the top drawer, and made a show of searching through the disheveled clothing until he finally came up with a bottle of aspirin. "He simply panicked. He started thinking about you, worrying about tonight, and he just flipped out. He was afraid he'd never see you again. Your husband's devotion to you is rather touching."

Alexandra stared out the window for a few more moments, then turned and walked slowly across the room.

She sat down on the edge of her bed, then glanced up at Peters. "I can't understand it," she said absently, her eyes reflecting her confusion. "It's like you're describing a stranger. John knows what's at stake, and how critical it is for us not to attract any more attention. If he were so worried about me, why do something that would put me in even more danger? It doesn't make any sense."

"What can I tell you?" Peters replied sharply, tossing the aspirin bottle in his hand as he walked past Alexandra, and paused in the bathroom door. "He did do it, Alexandra. And after fucking around with the stupid son-of-a-bitch all night, I don't feel like standing here trying to psychoanalyze him with you. If that rotgut I had to drink eats a hole in my stomach, I'm going to take it out of your husband's hide when we get back to New York."

He stepped into the bathroom, out of Alexandra's line of sight, and turned on the cold water in the wash basin full force. He put three aspirin tablets in his mouth, then took a plastic cup from a holder over the sink and put it under the open tap. He glanced behind him to make sure Alexandra was not in the doorway, then took Alexandra's barrette from his pocket, squatted down, and shoved it into a space where the molding had cracked and the plasterboard had separated slightly from the tile floor. He pushed the molding back into place, rose, and swallowed the aspirin. He turned off the water and went back into the other room. Less than thirty seconds had passed.

Alexandra was still sitting stiffly on the edge of the bed. She looked up and stared at him. Peters stared back, thinking that it might have been better if he had come up with another story. But he wanted her to believe that her husband was safe; he wanted her mind at peace so that she would be thinking of nothing but what he wanted her to do.

"He intended to go to the Sierrans," Peters said at last, casually tossing the bottle of aspirin onto his bed. "Thank God he wanted to see you first so that he could tell you he was going to do it. It took me most of the night to talk him down, and another hour after that to get myself properly drunk so I'd have some story to tell Raul. Anyway, the important thing is that I convinced him that the best way to get you home safely is to go through with things the way we planned. If we're lucky, there's no assassin left to worry about."

Alexandra frowned and passed a hand over her eyes. "Where's John now?" she asked quietly.

"Taking a very long, lazy walk around the Plaza de Revolucion. The place is always full of Third World and Russian tourists, so nobody is going to bother him there. He's going to stay lost until tomorrow morning. He's coming to the hotel around eleven, and then we're all going to have a gloriously emotional reunion. He's going to make up with the Sierrans, and we'll all leave together on Sunday."

"If the Sierrans let him go," Alexandra said tightly.

Peters snorted contemptuously. "They'll let him go. Raul will be at the airport watching us leave and cheering himself hoarse."

Alexandra smiled thinly. "That I can believe."

Peters picked up the roll of adhesive tape from the night stand and handed it to Alexandra. Alexandra watched, puzzled, as Peters shrugged off the top of the terrycloth robe and tentatively lifted his arm to reveal a very large, ugly, purple and black bruise.

"Patch-up time," Peters said wryly, allowing himself to grimace with pain. "I think I can use some tape on these ribs."

"For God's sake, Rick!" Alexandra said, rising, taking his right arm and gently maneuvering him onto the bed. "What happened to you?!"

"Your husband got a little excited when he first saw me. As a matter of fact, he pushed me into a concrete railing. I think I've got a couple of cracked ribs, but I'll survive with a little tender loving care."

"Damn. I'm sorry, Rick."

Peters raised his right arm above his head, and his left arm as far as it would go. Alexandra knelt on the floor in front of him and began to slowly and gently wrap the tape around his rib cage.

"I think it's time we talked about tonight," Peters said carefully, watching Alexandra's face.

"All right," Alexandra said distantly. She paused, shook her head slightly, then resumed speaking in a stronger voice. "How do you think we should handle it?"

"Let's play it loose and easy," Peters said through clenched teeth, wincing. "After all, we won't know what kind of a set-up they've got until we get there."

"But we do know the other people from our group who are going."

"Right. There aren't many, and we shouldn't have much trouble keeping an eye on all of them. Let's use a funnel zone. When Salva shows up, you position yourself in front of him as close as possible. Salva likes good-looking women; you'll be able to get closer to him than I will, and that will cut down the angles. I'll get as high up as I can and try to keep moving; you've got the point, and I'll sweep the rest of the funnel. We'll try to keep watch on everyone in our group, and also maintain eye contact with each other. If either of us sees anyone acting strange, we'll signal. Hell, it may be enough just to call attention to the target. Salva will be surrounded by security men, and they may as well earn their paychecks."

"You know it may not go down that way, Rick. An assassin will certainly have taken security into account in his planning. It may come down to you and me. Salva's security personnel will have the whole arena to watch; we only have a dozen people."

"Right. We move if we have to. Whoever's closest takes the man out and gets the damn thing over with. We can always claim we saw a person acting suspiciously, reacted instinctively, and got lucky. I doubt whether the Sierrans are going to be thinking too much about anything but the fact that one of us saved their glorious leader's life."

Alexandra shook her head. "If you want my opinion, I don't think there is anybody else."

Peters nodded, watching her face. "Let's hope you're right. We still have to go through the motions."

"I know."

Peters sighed. "When these boxing matches are over, I'm going to get very drunk all over again."

"And I'll keep you company, drink for drink. We'll let the Sierrans carry us both back to the hotel." Alexandra finished taping Peters' rib cage, then patted him gently on the shoulder. "All done. How does it feel?"

Peters cautiously lifted his left arm, grunted. "Almost as

good as new. But if there's any really heavy action tonight, I'm afraid you're going to have to take care of it."

"I can handle it, Rick," Alexandra said evenly. "You know I can."

Peters smiled. "That's for sure." He leaned forward and kissed her on the forehead. "Thank you. I'm going to get some sleep. Talk to you later."

Peters lay back on the bed, pulled the covers up over his chest, and closed his eyes. He fell asleep almost immediately.

John

John absorbed the greatest part of the force of impact on his left hip and thigh. With his knees pulled up to his chest, the shock was dissipated throughout his body and no bones were broken. However, the wind was knocked out of him and there was a sharp, electric, stinging pain along his left side as he plunged down through the black, cold water like a stone snapped from a slingshot.

With the air exploded from his lungs, knowing that he was in imminent danger of drowning, John immediately uncoiled his body in order to halt his downward motion. With lungs that felt crushed and with hot lights flashing behind his eyes, he clawed and kicked his way to the surface. Just as he thought he would pass out, his head broke the surface and he desperately sucked air into his outraged lungs.

The left side of his body still throbbed with pain from the impact, but he immediately recalled the fight with Peters and felt a rush of exhilaration at the realization that, incredibly, he was still alive.

"Not yet, you little fucker," he gasped aloud, and then released a wheezy, aspirated whoop of joy. His voice echoed loudly in the darkness around him.

He was alive, yes, John thought, but for how long? The darkness around him was absolute, and aside from the all too obvious fact that he was in water, he was completely disoriented.

He allowed himself to sink below the surface, peeled off his socks, and let them drop. He surfaced and used a lazy breaststroke to ease his body forward until his fingertips collided painfully with rough, slimy rock. Treading water, he worked his way to his left and discovered that he was inside a cylinder of rock perhaps eight or nine feet in diameter. He knew he was fortunate not to have smashed his skull against the walls on his way down.

He could not remember what had happened after Peters kicked him in the head, but he assumed that the assassin had dropped him into a well inside the castle. However, he could not understand what kind of well would be filled with salt water. Also, thick, splashing streams of water were cascading down the rock wall from at least two different sources somewhere in the darkness above his head.

John shouted in sudden blind terror as something very large and long with grit-rough skin lazily scraped across his belly, spinning him completely around in the water.

Shark! his mind screamed as he lunged for the wall, clawing at the rock face in a frantic, panicked search for a hand grip. The thick, waterlogged bandages around his palms made it difficult to hold onto the slippery stone, but he finally found a crevice above his head into which he could jam his fingers. He hauled himself partly out of the water, scrabbling at the rock below him with his feet, pushing with his toes, finding another small coign that would accept his fingers with their broken nails, pulling with all his strength. He finally managed to lift his body out of the water, and clung desperately to the rock face. The muscles in his chest and belly spasmodically twitched and writhed in autonomic cellular reponse to the need to fasten to the wall. Minutes that seemed like hours passed. His mind howled with primal terror as his fingers and toes went numb under the torture of his body weight, began to ache, then flamed with the strain of holding his body on the wall.

There was absolutely no doubt in his mind that the rough-skinned, leathery fish that had brushed against him in the water had been a good-sized shark. The question of what a shark was doing in a manmade well that was inexplicably filled with sea water was superceded by the bewildering, crushing certainty that he would be attacked a few seconds after his fingers and toes lost their grip on the wall. He was going to be dismembered, disemboweled, chewed on. He assumed that his bloody hands and thigh had attracted the shark—or sharks. It, or they, would be circling just below the surface, waiting to literally tear him to pieces. He had been brought back from the dead only to be eaten.

His fingers and toes would not hold him up any longer. With a silent scream of terror and rage, John dropped into the water.

He recalled reading somewhere that sharks were surface feeders, and for no other reason than an instinctive desire to cling to a few more precious seconds of life, John stiffened his body and knifed down into the depths. As his feet touched a bottom of silt and rock, he cringed and tucked his body into a ball.

Nothing happened. There was no great, rough weight slamming into him, no rending teeth. Still he waited, exhaling a bit of air to achieve negative buoyancy and swallowing to ease the pain in his ears.

As his initial terror receded he slowly became aware of a strong pressure on his face and torso actually pushing him backward. He allowed himself to drift with the flow for a few moments, then realized with a fresh stab of panic that he had been carried a number of feet beyond what would be the boundary of the well wall.

He raised his hands over his head and scraped his raw knuckles against stone.

Panic would only make his heart beat faster and suck oxygen from his tissues, John thought. He concentrated on remaining calm as he turned around and rolled on his back. He stuck his fingers up into the rock crevices over his head and pulled hard, hand over hand, against the increasingly powerful current. A few seconds later he reached up and touched nothing but water. He pulled himself out of the mouth of the tunnel, planted his feet on the bottom and shot back to the surface.

This time he did not waste energy trying to climb out of the well; that appeared to be impossible. Instead, attempting to deal with the most immediate danger, he gripped a section of the wall with his bandaged hands and hauled his right leg out of the water. He groped with his bare foot until he found a toehold, then pulled himself up a few inches. He rested in that position, his bleeding hands and thigh out of the water, letting the salt water support the rest of his weight.

So much for the shark and any of its friends, John thought with a shudder. Obviously, the well was connected to the sea by at least one underground cave. He assumed he was many feet below sea level, for the water pouring into the well from somewhere above his head would indicate the presence of other caves snaking to the sea like stone umbilical cords. The current would be due to tidal surge.

He suddenly realized that his chest had moved a few inches closer to the fixed position of his hands and right leg. The water in the well was rising. With absolutely nothing better to do, he thought, he would just hang around and see how far up the water took him.

He smiled wryly and almost laughed aloud, thinking that it would be funny as hell if the rising water carried him all the way to the top of Peters' carefully considered torture chamber and death trap.

Peters would not be amused, he thought, and his smile vanished. He would make damn well certain that Peters was not amused. He would kill the man at the first opportunity, in any way he could. Then he would go to the Sierrans.

The thought of Rick Peters bloated him with rage, and he threw back his head and shouted to release the terrible, black pressure in his soul. He kept shouting until he was hoarse, then stopped and cursed himself for wasting his breath and strength. He doubted he could be heard so far underground, and even if his shouts were audible, there was probably no one yet in the castle to hear him. He decided he would try shouting again later.

He closed his eyes, floating with his hands and right leg out of the water and trying not to think of what could happen if the shark that had brushed him and turned up its prehistoric nose did not have good hunting elsewhere.

10:43 A.M.

A Gunner

"Hey, man, where the hell's the fuckin' coffee?"

The gunner snapped shut the lid of the equipment trunk on the floor in front of him, then looked up at the man who had stepped into the room. "I don't know," he said evenly.

The other man angrily pounded his fist against the door jamb. "The fuckin' network was supposed to make sure we had plenty of coffee here!"

"Why don't you look for Cosell? He's probably got all the coffee."

"Hey, you tryin' to be funny?"

"No," the gunner said mildly. "Just making a suggestion."

The man was silent for a few moments, sucking his teeth. He looked as if he were trying to decide if he should be offended. "I don't understand what's goin' on," the man said at last. "What, they gonna' depend on the fuckin' Commies to bring coffee to an American crew? We're union, goddamn it!"

"Maybe they've got some coffee outside."

"Nah. I checked." The man looked hard at the gunner, frowned. "What the hell do you do?"

"Gaffer."

"I ain't never seen you before."

"I work out of the Queens local. One of your men got sick last night, and I was the only guy they could find to come on such short notice."

The other man snorted with disgust. "It don't make no difference who's here and who isn't. We're gonna' be sittin' on our asses most of the time, anyway. Damn, I

267

hate the thought of those fuckin' Commies usin' our equipment."

"The Sierrans look like they know what they're doing," the gunner said easily. "If you didn't like the job, why didn't you stay home?"

"Yeah? Well, fuck you too, Commie-lover." The man again slammed the door jamb, turned, and walked out.

"Hope you find some coffee," the gunner said quietly, his lips pulling back into a faint smile.

When the man's footsteps had died away, the gunner opened the equipment trunk and resumed the task of assembling the specially constructed revolver and silencer that had been rebored to fire the relatively heavy 6.7 millimeter Russian-made bullets the Sierrans used in their automatic rifles. As he had anticipated, the disassembled weapon, packed in with two hundred and fifty pounds of electrical equipment, had easily passed through Customs.

The hybrid revolver was a nice piece of work, the gunner thought, and he wondered who had built it. He had received it only a few hours before leaving, and he would normally have demanded a few days to practice with a new weapon. However, he had been assured that the weapon had been thoroughly tested and all necessary adjustments made. The shootings would be at close range, and he was not concerned.

He vaguely wondered where his employers had acquired such an odd weapon, one so perfectly tailored to the job at hand. However, the gunner never asked questions about matters that were not his concern. All he ever required were instructions, and his instructions for this job were precise: the odds were very high that Manuel Salva would be assassinated that evening; immediately following Salva's death, the gunner was to kill Rick Peters and John and Alexandra Finway if they were present in the arena. He had studied their descriptions and available photographs; he would have the best possible sight angles. The gunner did not anticipate having any trouble in spotting them.

The gunner wondered who had been given the contract to kill Salva and how much the assassin was being paid.

He finished assembling the revolver and transferred it to a padded, hidden pocket inside a small equipment bag that he could strap around his waist and carry without arousing suspicion. Then he leaned back against the wall and lit a cigarette.

He knew there might be some difficulty executing the kills if the targets were widely spaced in the large arena, but he was being paid a large fee to deal with such exigencies. There would be enough chaos inside the arena to cover a dozen killings. The hybrid revolver would be thrown over the castle's ramparts into the sea, and he would leave the country the same way he had come in, with the ABC television crews. Even if he were questioned, he thought, there would be no problem. He was, in fact, a card-carrying member of the electricians' union he had mentioned.

The larger operation, of which he had been told nothing, intrigued him, despite his basically non-curious nature.

His skills in his chosen profession were considerable, but the gunner was not an educated man, and his knowledge of other matters was rather limited. His first reaction upon learning that Salva was going to be killed had been that the Mafia was maneuvering to recapture the control over San Sierra they had enjoyed under Sabrito. Then he had given the matter more thought and come to the conclusion that even the Mafia was no match for the Russians; it would not be enough just to kill Salva. Yet, although he had not been told so, there was no doubt in his mind that the assassination was a Mafia operation. Since he worked for the capos, the gunner found it reasonable to assume that the Mafia was acting as a contractor for another interest, perhaps one of the Sierran terrorist organizations, or even a government. The Mafia, in his opinion, had simply subcontracted a portion of the work to him.

He had never heard of Rick Peters or Alexandra Finway, but he certainly knew something about John Finway. He didn't like Finway. The gunner normally took a professionally detached attitude toward all his contracts, but he had to admit to himself that he hoped Finway would be in the arena that night; he would take personal satisfaction in killing the man. The gunner thought of himself as a patriot, and he considered the activist lawyer a Communist and a threat to the security of the United States.

Finally, the gunner could not help but wonder about the connection between his three targets and Manuel Salva.

However, he had never thought to ask, because he did not want to know; such knowledge could be decidedly dangerous. The gunner had begun his career at the age of fifteen as a "soldier" in New York's Little Italy. He was now sixty-three, and he knew he had managed to live so long because he did exactly what he was hired to do, and no more; he was reliable, but in no way inquisitive.

The gunner crushed out his cigarette on the floor. He put the carrying bag with the revolver back into the equipment trunk, then left the room and followed a thick, black electrical cable to the arena where the Sierrans and the various American crews were setting up for the evening's telecast.

John

The rising water was not going to take him to the top of the well, John thought. He had never really believed that it would; it had been no more than a dull gleam of hope in a nether world of rock and water that seemed to offer no other.

At the time when the water had stopped rising, John had found himself at the level of the two caves that had been pouring water into the well. He had explored their mouths with his hands and found they were barely large enough to accommodate his head and shoulders. Realizing that the tunnels could snake through the rock for hundreds of yards without ever growing larger, he had decided not to attempt to go that way; once in, he could easily become stuck and then drown when the water rose again.

The water had begun receding rapidly as the tide reversed itself. The two small caves formed a kind of natural stethoscope enabling John to hear into the heart of the rock; there was a throbbing, hissing rumble as tons of water surged through the veins and arteries of the stone channels, fleeing back to the sea under the inexorable pressure of gravity.

Still in utter darkness, John couldn't determine how close to the top of the well he had been carried by the rising water. He estimated that hours had passed since Peters had thrown him into the well. It would be midmorning; there should be people in the castle above him.

He began to shout again, using low hooting sounds rather than words in an attempt to save his voice. He proceeded systematically, sustaining a shout for as long as he could and then listening for some sign that he had attracted attention. Aside from lingering, rumbling echoes, there was no response but resounding silence. He concluded that he was too far underground to be heard.

He tried climbing again, but only made it five or six feet before he slipped from the rock face and fell back into the water. He moved around the circumference of the well, trying different routes to the top. The result each time was the same.

Finally he tried stretching his body across the diameter of the well. He was barely able to bridge the distance, but the gap was far too wide to enable him to inch his way up; he had virtually no leverage, and the strain on his arms, legs, and back was too great. He slipped back into the water, then clung to the wall and tried to clear his mind of the despair and panic that constantly threatened to overwhelm him.

The good news, he thought, was that the shark had not returned—yet. He had removed the bandages from his hands, and as far as he could determine, he was no longer bleeding; the salt water and the passing hours had served to close his cuts.

The bad news was that he was rapidly succumbing to fatigue, losing strength, body heat, and concentration. He was not going to die of old age rising and falling in the well, he thought grimly. He was a strong swimmer and could probably hang on for many more hours, possibly even a few days; he might still be alive long after Alexandra's head had disappeared in a bloody mist. But eventually he had to fall asleep, or pass out from cold and exposure. He would slip down into the black water and drown.

"Damn it!" John yelled in frustration. Adrenalin began to flow back into his muscles, and he shouted louder, "God-damnit!"

The water level was continuing to fall rapidly, and John was just able to reach up and grab the lip of one of the small caves. He kicked hard and managed to pull himself up into the opening. He started to hunch forward, then stopped when the tunnel narrowed even further and it became impossible to crawl. He wriggled back, dropped down into the water.

He strained to reach the lip of the second cave, but could not get his fingers over the edge. With his muscles fueled by rage and panic, he started to claw at the rocks in an attempt to climb to the second cave; then he thought better of it, stopped and took deep, measured breaths in an effort to calm himself and slow his heartbeat. He could not be sure that he would have any better luck with the second cave than he'd had with the first, and he knew he could not afford to waste any more of his rapidly diminishing strength.

The problem, he thought, was that, even allowing for the bizarre hydrostatic effect that the water in the maze of caves might exert, almost an entire day would be lost before there was another tidal surge. By the time he rose up again to the level of the second cave, Alexandra's death might be only minutes away.

The possibility that the rim of the well might be only a few feet above him, just a few lucky hand- and toeholds away, tormented him. He started to search for a new handhold, then sighed with despair and sank back into the water. He had fallen a long way.

He knew he could not climb to the top.

Another idea came to him. The thought was terrifying, causing his stomach and throat muscles to contract, making it difficult to breathe. But the action had to be considered, he thought, and it had to be considered at once; in a short time it would be too late.

John took a deep breath, pointed his toes and stiffened his body, then pushed hard against the rock wall. His body knifed downward. Almost immediately he felt the current grab him and pull, bringing him quickly to the bottom. He thrust his hands over his head just in time to grab a lip of rock as the surging vortex sucked the lower half of his body into the mouth of the underwater cave.

It was as if he were in a huge bathtub, he thought. Earlier, he had felt the pressure of the water coming in; now it was draining back to the sea.

He pulled himself back up the rock face until his head broke the surface of the water. He clung to the wall, breathing hard, resting his head against the backs of his hands as his heart pounded.

Don't think. Just do it and be damned. You're going to die anyway.

Trembling with fear and cold, John used his left hand to remove his undershirt. He shrugged it off, then felt it sucked under when he held it out in the center of the well; the whirlpool in the middle of the well was growing in power. Next he removed his slacks and shorts, let them go. He was naked.

Stop thinking about it; there's nothing to think about. You're a strong swimmer. If you die this way, at least it won't be a passive death. It's the only chance Alexandra has. Do it! Do it while you still have some strength left.

John hyperventilated for a few seconds to void his lungs of carbon dioxide, then sucked in a deep breath. He turned in the water, rolled forward, and pushed hard with his feet against the rock at the same time as he pulled with his arms. He shot down into the depths at the center of the well, executing one last powerful kick and pull and extending his body as he shot into the mouth of the underwater cave.

He knew that he had to concentrate on relaxing and minimizing water resistance if he were to go a maximum distance underwater; fear, a voracious consumer of oxygen, was his greatest enemy. He closed his eyes and tried to imagine that he was doing nothing more strenuous or dangerous than swimming lazily under a dock in some shallow lake; air and burning sun were only a few yards away.

As he slowed, he put his arms out to his sides and discovered that the tunnel was wide enough for him to take short strokes. He pulled with his arms at the same time as he used a narrow scissors kick to propel himself along with the current. When his lungs started to ache he opened his eyes, desperately hoping that he would see some glimmer of light. The water remained a stygian, hope-crushing black.

He was going to die, John thought. His stomach muscles

had already begun to twitch spasmodically, contracting and expanding as part of his body's outraged, drumbeat demand that he open his mouth and breathe.

Ah well, what the hell . . .

The realization that he could face death with a certain measure of equanimity was strangely comforting to him; it relaxed him and strengthened his resolve to go on a little farther.

What this situation needs is some light at the end of the tunnel.

Oxygen deprivation was making him feel silly, John thought.

Maybe I'll die laughing. What the hell's so funny?

He decided that he would start counting to a hundred, and try to at least make it to the end of the count. After that, he would simply breathe in a lungful of water and be done with it.

One.

He kicked hard, at the same time pulling his arms down sharply to his sides and straightening his body in order to lessen the drag of the water. He followed each kick with a slight undulating motion of his lower body generated by his hips and knees.

. . .

Thirteen.

Mary had a little lamb, little lamb, little lamb . . .

. . .

Twenty-two.

His head, chest, and stomach felt ready to explode, and John decided he would settle for counting to fifty. He estimated that he had already been under water for at least two minutes.

Fifty and screw it, folks. Enough is enough.

Sing, sing a song . . .

. . .

Thirty.

He began to hear bells, great, clanging gongs that seemed to reverberate through every bone in his body.

The inside of his brain was lighting up. Electric blue neon.

Who says you can't kill yourself by holding your breath?

Three minutes? Four? I wonder what the Guinness record is? Who'll know? Ah well, what the hell.

...

Forty-two.

He could go no farther. Involuntary reflex action caused him to make his final surge upward. His head broke the surface of the water. His pent-up breath burst from his lungs and he sucked in . . . air.

Gasping hoarsely, John thrashed in the water. He threw his arms out, and the fingers of his left hand cracked painfully against what felt like a ledge. He lunged for the rock, fighting against the raging current that clutched at his body. With the last of his strength, John pulled himself out of the water onto the ledge a moment before he passed out.

11:43 A.M.

Raul

Raul lay in bed with the sheet pulled up to his chin, staring wide-eyed at the ceiling of his small hotel room. He lived in Angeles Blanca and could have gone home for a few hours if he'd wanted to. But he had not wanted to; he had too many things on his mind.

He had to get some sleep, Raul thought. He had shaved, taken a warm bath, then closed the blinds in the room and stretched out between the worn but clean sheets. He had been up all night, he was exhausted, and he had fully expected to fall asleep immediately. He wanted to sleep. Why, then, couldn't he?

Finway had told him that Rick Peters planned to kill Manuel.

Raul deeply, bitterly, resented the fact that the lawyer had said such a thing; it had been an absolutely crazy statement, the wild accusation of an insanely jealous man who would do or say absolutely anything to discredit his wife's lover and, out of spite, disrupt the tour. Raul was sure that there was nothing at all to the accusation, but the angry, desperate words were causing him all kinds of problems; they were robbing him of much-needed sleep.

It had to be nonsense, Raul thought, but he could not forget that Finway had spoken the words, and he did not know what to do about it. He would like to erase, had desperately tried to erase, the words from his memory, but they would not go.

If he told the DMI men, Raul thought, they would probably laugh at him. They would laugh and accuse him of trying to cover up or excuse his own incompetence in letting John Finway get away. Then they would remind him that

276

he had been ordered to be courteous to Peters, not to make outrageous accusations.

Or, Manuel would be advised to stay away from the boxing matches. The authorities would investigate Peters and conclude that Finway's accusations against him were groundless. Then Manuel would want to know who was responsible for causing him to miss such an imporant event. Manuel would be told that a Sierratour guide had made the accusations in a clumsy attempt to cover his own incompetence.

At the very least, Raul thought, he would lose his job. He could go to prison. He might even be executed. He'd heard that Manuel still ordered summary executions when he was especially displeased with someone.

Or, Finway could be telling the truth. An investigation would reveal that Rick Peters was an assassin. Then, Raul thought, he would be asked why he had waited so long to tell the authorities what John Finway had said.

He would lose his job. He could go to prison. He could be executed.

But if Finway had been telling the truth and he said nothing, the man who was the savior of the Sierran people would be assassinated.

Tormented by the agony of his dilemma, Raul moaned aloud. Finally he rolled over, drew his knees up under his stomach, and jammed the pillow down on his head. He tried counting sheep, but that didn't help either.

John

He awoke with a start, at first disoriented and afraid that he had been blinded but then exhilarated as he remembered the nightmare swim through the underwater cave. He had survived.

His next feeling was a sense of crushing despair; he could not know how much time had passed. Alexandra might already be dead.

A great chill wracked his naked body and he shuddered violently. He rolled up into a ball and wrapped his arms around himself, but that only increased his discomfort; the wet stone felt so cold that it burned his flesh like a gelid branding iron cooled in the bowels of some ice planet. He was freezing, John thought. He couldn't remain still. In a few minutes, whatever reserves of adrenalin that had been pumped into his system in response to his initial relief would be absorbed and he would quickly succumb to exhaustion. Somehow he had to keep moving, or die.

He got up on his knees and groped around him in the darkness until he felt the surface of the water. The underground stream was still now, in stasis between the incoming and outgoing tides, or whatever combination of forces powered the great, watery engine.

He couldn't have passed out for more than a few hours at most, John thought. It had to be the same day. There was still time to save Alexandra. If only he could find a way out.

He slowly crawled forward on the ledge, trailing his right hand beside him in the placid water. He had gone only a few feet when his head collided painfully against a wall of rock. He rubbed the swelling knot on his head, then explored the rock face with his hands; it extended over and came down to the surface of the water like a final curtain of stone falling on whatever hope he'd had that he would be able to crawl along the stream to freedom. If he wanted to continue in that direction he would again have to swim under water.

He would not go back in the water, John thought. He *couldn't* go back in the water. He simply didn't have the courage for that. He had died in that stream, as surely, if in a different way, as he had died as a result of the electric shock. He had lost a large chunk of his soul somewhere in the watery darkness, and he knew there was no way he could ever again will himself to suffer that kind of mental and physical agony. Perhaps, he thought, there were other, above-water caves radiating off the rock shelf on which he was kneeling. There *had* to be.

He backed away from the edge of the stream, then slowly straightened up, raising his hands over his head to protect himself. He found that he was able to stand inside the space. Slowly, carefully, he groped his way in the darkness, exploring the rippling, coigned surfaces around him.

He discovered five tunnels radiating from the chamber.

But only two seemed large enough for him to crawl in, and only one of these led in what he assumed from the previous flow of the stream was a seaward direction.

John could not be sure that it wasn't some phantom of hope generated in his imagination, but he thought he could detect a faint draft blowing in his face from the mouth of the seaward tunnel. He got down on his hands and knees and began to crawl.

He had gone about ten yards when he stopped, bowed his head, and uttered a deep sigh. He was afraid: afraid of the water, but also afraid of the rock prison he was entering.

While he could not conceive of ever again being able to force himself into the underwater cave, he knew he had to face the fact that the stream seemed to be the only sure way out—even if all it spewed out in the end were his bloated corpse.

It occurred to him that he could as easily wait for death sprawled in the darkness at the edge of the stream as lost in an endless maze of tunnels, crawling and, he assumed, finally howling like a dog on his hands and knees.

Go, you cowardly son-of-a-bitch! You're not dead yet! Stop feeling sorry for yourself!

He searched with his hands and scraped together a pile of pebbles. He scooped up a handful of the stones and began dropping the largest between his knees as he wearily crawled on.

He was aware of a new enemy strongly vying for his attention: thirst.

Harley Shue

"Harley, we're having some problems with resolution on the U-2 signal."

Shue swung around in his swivel chair to face Geoffrey Whistle, who had just entered the Central Communications Control room. "Yes, sir, we're aware of the problem. There's some technical difficulty here on the ground."

The CIA Director strode across the room to stand next to his Director of Operations. Both men studied the bank of television monitors flickering before them.

Shue shook his head angrily as the picture transmitted from the U-2 continued to roll and break up. He was not unappreciative of the complex technology involved in keeping what was essentially a glider circling in the stratosphere over San Sierra for close to twelve hours while at the same time sending back television pictures from cameras with lenses that could resolve the clear image of a man standing on the ground.

But it was not the time to marvel over technology, Shue thought; it was time for the technology to be working, and it wasn't.

Geoffrey M. Whistle impatiently drummed his fingers on top of the set that was monitoring the ABC signal from San Sierra; it showed a standard color test pattern. "When's ABC supposed to start transmitting pictures?"

"Five o'clock."

"Saint George can't be dependent on ABC, Harley. This operation is keyed to the assassination of Salva, and timing is everything. We have to launch our troops before the Sierrans or Russians have time to react, and after the assault we must have constant information on enemy troop movements throughout the island. We could lose ABC at any time. The President won't let Saint George go in half blind. The cameras on that plane have to be working, or the President will abort the mission."

As if on cue, the black-and-white images on two of the television screens suddenly cleared, showing a perfectly focused picture of Tamara Castle and the dozens of men in and around it.

"That's it, Geoffrey," Shue said, allowing himself a thin smile of satisfaction. "The signal's being relayed directly through our facilities at Guantanamo."

Whistle frowned. "Isn't that risky?"

"I don't think so, sir. Even if the Russians are monitoring that band—and we have reason to believe they aren't—it will take them more than a day to break that particular telemetric code. By then, of course, it won't make any difference."

"One way or another, it should all be over by this time tomorrow," Whistle said in a distant tone. "At least the initial fighting phase will be over."

"Precisely, sir."

The green phone set up on a metal stand beside the monitors rang. Whistle picked up the receiver, listened for a few seconds, then hung up.

"Home Plate's brushed off and ready for play, Harley," the CIA Director said quietly. "You're off. There's a plane waiting to take you to Miami. Do you need anything?"

Shue rose too quickly and had to grip the back of the swivel chair to steady himself. Adrenalin was pumping into his system, causing his heartbeat to race precipitously. *Relax*, he told himself. "No, Geoffrey," he said evenly. "Everything I need has been loaded."

"Home Plate is a brilliant idea, Harley. But you don't have to be the one to go out on the point like that."

"Oh, I want to." Harley Shue pulled himself up very straight. When he resumed speaking, there was the slightest trace of a tremor in his voice. "I believe we're present at the dawn of a new age of American prestige and power, sir. Let's hope we've learned enough since nineteen forty-five to be able to hang on to it this time."

"Godspeed, Harley."

ANGELES BLANCA

Friday, January 25; 4:45 P.M.

John

Now this is what I call a real pain in the ass.

He tried to speak, but he could only manage a ragged croak. He had literally shouted his voice away, John thought, and now his throat was raw and sore.

He had reached the end of the tunnel some time before. Bellowing with near-hysterical joy and excitement, he had scrambled on bloody hands and knees toward a faint glow of light. He had ended in a hemispherical chamber perhaps four feet high in the center and five feet in diameter. Warm sunlight that was both blessing and cruel taunt seeped in through cracks in the rock. John could tell that he was very close to the sea; there was a green salt smell on the thick air wafting in through the cracks. However, the crevices were barely wide enough to admit his arm; the last barrier of rock separating him from the sea and freedom was at least six feet thick.

The tunnel was a dead end.

He screamed as loud as he could, at first in the hope that he would be heard and later out of rage and frustration. He screamed until he was no longer able to force sound from his swollen throat. The only response had been the soft, sibilant soughing of the sea on the far side of the rock.

It was a siren song of death; John could tell by the sound of the lapping waves that the sea outside his prison was rising.

He had been able to slake his thirst from a spring of fresh water that leaked from the rocks inside the chamber, but that was scant comfort to him. He suspected, from the increasingly insistent gurgling of the sea beyond the wall, that the chamber would be filled with water within an hour or two.

Once again he exploded in a paroxysm of fury, pounding and clawing at the rock face. Exhausted, he finally collapsed to the stone floor. Blood ran in tiny, crimson rivulets down his wrists and pooled between his fingers. Then he wept.

Finally he did what he had known all along he must do. He only hoped it wasn't already too late to escape the water that was certain to be coursing through the small tunnel in a very short time.

John turned his back on the fading, false promise of sunlight and resignedly sank down on his hands and knees once again. Using his hands to grope in the center of the tunnel for the large pebbles that would guide him back to the large chamber by the underground stream, he crawled back into the terrible, eternal night of the caves.

6:20 P.M.

Alexandra

The early evening light was copper-colored, suffusing the far corner of the room with a warm glow. To Alexandra the light seemed otherworldly and funereal, an omen signaling the end of much more than just another day. She knew she should get up and dress, but she felt drained of strength and will, filled with foreboding. She pulled her bathrobe more tightly around her but remained on the bed, continuing to stare at the ceiling.

Peters suddenly appeared in her field of vision. He was wearing a pale yellow shirt under a blue sleeveless sweater, tan corduroy slacks, cowboy boots. In the dim, golden light, his pale eyes seemed unnaturally bright, without pupils.

"I thought you were still sleeping," Peters said quietly. "You want me to turn on the light?"

"Not yet, Rick. Please."

There was a short pause, then, "You should be getting dressed and putting your hair up. The bus leaves in an hour."

Peters had spoken in the same soft tone, but Alexandra had the odd, unsettling impression that there was something new in her companion's voice, a quality she could not define but that brought to mind some amorphous beast—tension, perhaps—straining on a leash, barely under control. The closeness and desire she had felt at Sierras Negras, and again last night, was completely gone.

She was startled to see the glow of Peters' eyes go out, then come on again. Then she realized that he had only blinked.

"I'll be ready."

"What's wrong, Alexandra?"

284

"I don't know."

"Are you sick?" Again, the curious tension in his voice that he seemed to be trying to veil.

Alexandra looked directly at Peters. The man's eyes were staring down at her, revealing nothing. "I don't know, Rick."

"This isn't like you, baby. The Alexandra I used to know would have been dressed and ready to go three hours ago. By now you'd be doing calisthenics to stay loose."

"I'm not the Alexandra you used to know, Rick."

"You certainly were at Sierras Negras. And you almost were last night."

"It was an illusion, Rick, a trick my mind has been playing on itself. For a while I thought I was that person, but I'm not."

Peters smiled thinly. "I see. You're just a happy house-wife and mother?"

"No," Alexandra replied faintly, ignoring his sarcasm. "I'm not that either. I'm not a dragon, but I'm not an ex-dragon either. I don't know what I am any longer."

Peters sat down on the edge of the bed, reached out and gently stroked Alexandra's hair. "Hang on just a few more hours, sweetheart. Then it'll be over. You're the toughest woman I've ever known. I know you can handle it."

"Don't patronize me, Rick."

"All right, I won't!" Peters snapped, abruptly pulling his hand away from Alexandra's hair and stiffening. "I don't know what the hell this sudden identity-crisis nonsense is all about, but I'll talk to the Alexandra I know. I don't understand this chickenshit prima donna act you're trying to lay on me. The boxing matches start in an hour and a half, and we have to be there. That's the reason we're here, baby. For Christ's sake, you're a professional. You're the *best*, which is why you were approached in the first place. Now, all of a sudden—"

"I don't believe that, Rick."

There was a long pause. When Peters finally spoke again, Alexandra thought she heard an unnatural thickness in his voice. Fear? she thought. Of what?

"You don't believe what?"

"I don't believe we're the best, much less the only, people

the CIA had available to task for a mission as important as this one."

"You think I lied to you?" Peters asked tightly. "You received a second confirmation, the same as I did."

Alexandra propped herself up on one elbow and turned on the lamp beside her bed. Peters shied almost imperceptibly, as though afraid of the light. His features appeared stiff, and there was a slight tic in his left eyelid.

"What if the CIA lied to both of us, Rick? Think about it: the Company has a complex that spreads over a hundred and forty acres, God knows how many personnel, and a budget that probably goes well over a billion dollars a year. Why should they round up two ex-dragons and task them for an operation so sensitive that a miscalculation could trigger a world war?"

"We've been through this. I told you. After—"

Alexandra impatiently shook her head. "I don't care about Watergate, Company purges, blown networks, or what's left of Hughes-Ryan. You know what those agency people are like. I just don't believe they'd let Congress gut them to the extent they'd need us for a job like this. Do you really believe it, Rick?"

"You know I do. It's why I'm here risking my life. I believe everything they told me precisely because it is so tricky. That's why they had to use us. You believed it a week ago. What's happened to change your mind?"

Alexandra, unwilling to look into the pale eyes any longer, turned her head away. It seemed so simple to him, she thought. Rick Peters was one of the toughest and most cynical men she had ever known, yet he seemed to accept without question what he had been told by the CIA. Why, she wondered, couldn't she?

"Tell me again what John said."

"You're kidding," Peters said irritably. "You want the whole conversation word for word? We do have one other little item of business to take care of tonight, you know."

"You should have arranged for John to talk to me."

"Sure, and you could have brought Raul along to keep us all company. Raul would have been overjoyed to see John." Peters grunted angrily. "What's the matter, Alexandra? I told you John's brains ran out his ears when he started worrying about you. Now he's thinking clearly again.

At eleven o'clock tomorrow morning the two of you can talk all you want."

"I don't understand how John could panic like that."

"You said that before. Was it like him to tag along after you when you came here? Whatever excuse you gave him didn't take. You've got yourself a jealous husband."

"No. You don't understand."

"Then explain it to me."

Alexandra wasn't sure whether she wanted to go into it. She didn't seem to be able to organize her thoughts. "John's been in trouble," she said at last.

She turned her head in time to see Peters' eyebrows arch slightly. "What kind of trouble?" he asked.

Woman trouble, she thought, and said, "It's not important. He followed me to San Sierra because it was important to him to show me that he loves me. If you know that, maybe you can understand the pain he must have felt when he saw us together, and what he's been feeling all week."

"That's interesting, Alexandra, but irrelevant. We both agreed that tonight will probably be a milk run. We finish up this evening, and tomorrow you meet John. You've got the rest of your lives to work this other thing out."

Alexandra barely heard him. "The point is that my marriage was at a flash point when you came to see me, Rick. I think I decided to accept this task partly, maybe mostly, because I was hurt and angry. In a way, maybe I was trying to hurt back."

"This is a hell of a time to bring up something like this!"

"I'm sorry. You're right, of course, but I haven't been . . . thinking too clearly. I'd forgotten how really dirty this business can be, and what it does to my head. Coming to San Sierra was a kind of escape from my problems. I realize now that if I hadn't been so confused at the time about the rest of my life, I probably wouldn't have accepted. And I'd probably have advised you not to accept. John said that it just didn't feel right. Now I know exactly what he meant."

"You're upset, which is understandable. We're both under a lot of pressure. I'd have accepted the task, no matter what you said. I told you: I believe the Company's story. I thought then, and I think now, that I owe it to my country to help in any way I can. This is what I was asked to do." He shook his head and nervously ran his fingers through his hair. "Why the hell would the CIA want to manipulate us? For what purpose?"

"I don't know, Rick," Alexandra sighed. "I just have this feeling that something terrible is going to happen to—well *may* happen if you don't get your beautiful ass out night."

Peters laughed without humor. "Something terrible damn well *may* happen if you don't get your beautiful ass out of bed so we can go to the boxing matches. Salva could be killed. *I* could be killed, which is even worse. You say the Company may have lied to us, but you're forgetting one little detail: Swarzwalder. There sure as hell was at least one bad guy on this trip, and he wanted to kill us as a warm-up to killing Salva."

"But how could he have known about us, Rick?"

"I don't know, Alexandra. And this isn't the time to talk about it. Let's discuss it later, after we know Salva is home and safely tucked into bed."

"Rick, I—"

Peters abruptly reached over and turned out the light. The next thing Alexandra knew, Peters' hand was inside her robe and squeezing her breasts, kneading her nipples, pushing her back down on the bed. Then his head was on her chest. His mouth moved over her flesh, frantically licking her belly, kissing her breasts, and sucking her nipples.

The strange, abandoned foray against her body had come so fast and unexpectedly that Alexandra barely had time to react. She pushed against Peters' shoulders, but her arms felt totally drained of strength.

"*Don't!*"

"*Please*, Alexandra," Peters murmured, his voice muffled by her soft flesh. His right hand passed down her belly, slipped into her panties and began to press urgently against her vagina. He pushed her thighs apart and slid two fingers up into her body. "I'm afraid, too. I know you don't need my body, but I need yours. Help me. Please let me have you."

Alexandra felt paralyzed. There was no desire in her, only a terrible devil's wind of confusion swirling in the empty place that had been her will. She was powerless to resist as Peters tugged her panties down and off her legs.

Then he was suddenly on top of her, in her and rutting, holding her legs up and apart with his hands. Alexandra wanted to cry out, to beg him to leave her alone, but no sound would come out of her mouth. The face above her was no longer boyish: Peters looked much older now, like a bizarre reflection in some carnival mirror. His eyes were closed, his features contorted with lust. Sweat ran off his forehead and lips, spraying over Alexandra's face and breasts.

She wasn't giving herself to him, Alexandra thought absently. She was just unable to stop him from taking her. It meant absolutely nothing; he might as well be masturbating.

Yet, despite the fact that Peters was not physically hurting her, his brutish, somehow-pathetic lovemaking was producing in her the fiercest torment she had ever experienced. This pain transcended her flesh and was beyond tears. As Peters pounded, panted and poked, all Alexandra could do was lie passively beneath him with her mouth open, her eyes wide in horror, submerged in abyssal depths of despair and anguish so hot and caustic that they seemed to be melting her soul.

Peters ejaculated with a kind of strangled whimper. He collapsed on her and lay breathing heavily. He stayed there for long minutes, until his breathing became regular. Then he wearily pulled out of her, sat up on the edge of the bed, and wiped himself with a corner of the sheet.

Alexandra, still stunned by her profound sense of fragmentation, simply stared at Peters as he pulled on his pants, straightened his sweater, and combed his hair. He looked at her strangely for a few seconds, then turned and walked across the room to his bed. He picked up his radio from the nightstand and went to the door, where he stood cloaked in shadow. Alexandra could not see his eyes in the gloom, and his body was no more than a dim outline.

When Peters spoke, his voice sounded strained and rasping. "I'm going to wait in the lobby, Alexandra. There's not a whole hell of a lot I can do about it if you don't want to come with me. There probably won't be anything going down anyway, and if something does I'll just have to try to handle it myself the best way I can."

There was a long pause during which Alexandra could hear Peters breathing; then the voice came again, this time taut with anger. "I just want you to know I resent the fact that first you agreed to be my partner in this, but now you're folding up on me just as we're about to cross the finish line. I love you, baby, but frankly I thought you were better than this. We both accepted a task, and *I'm* going to keep my part of the bargain. If I don't, and if anything happens, I'm afraid I won't think much of myself."

Alexandra cleared her throat. She wanted to speak, to reassure him, but she still could not seem to dredge words from the soup of bewilderment boiling in her mind.

Peters pushed the door open, started to leave the room, then slumped in the doorway. "Forgive me, Alexandra," he continued very quietly. "Forgive me for the stupid thing I did a few minutes ago. I didn't mean to humiliate you; I just had a . . . terrible need. And please forgive me for talking to you like that. The pressure's getting to me too. The fact of the matter is that I'm very much afraid there may be another man. I need you with me, baby. I can't cover the entire arena by myself, and I know I'm likely to get myself killed if I try and there is a second assassin. In a couple of hours it will be finished. Please come and help me."

"I'll be down in a few minutes," Alexandra said in a voice she hardly recognized as her own.

"Thank you, baby," the disembodied voice said softly. "I'm taking the radio along so I can tune in the broadcast from Miami. Maybe we can get some advance word on Salva's plans."

Alexandra said nothing. Peters stepped out into the hallway, then closed the door quietly behind him.

Alexandra lay still for almost five minutes, staring at the ceiling but not seeing it; she was looking at, absorbed in, the walls of her mind. Finally she sat up and slowly pulled on her panties. It had never occurred to her not to go; it was the cold emptiness inside her chest, the terrifying sensation of splitting up into little pieces of disembodied personality, that had stalled her and temporarily paralyzed her will.

John had put her together once, she thought. He might be able to do it again, but somehow she doubted it. Now John knew what she had been, what she was. Judging from what Peters had told her, things in John had broken too.

So there was nothing left to consider or worry about, Alexandra thought. Not any more. There was only this last piece of the task she had agreed to do; after that she would passively wait in the center of her emptiness and see what happened.

Alexandra turned on the light. She picked up the barrette from the table beside her bed and began to put up her hair.

John

In mindless terror he scrambled the last black thirty yards with water coursing around his arms and legs, foaming over his buttocks and back, thrusting him forward. He fell into the large chamber, slipped and went under water, was twirled around and smashed by the force of the water against the opposite wall. He finally managed to get his feet under him and stood up, reeling, spitting water, coughing and gasping for air.

He pressed back against the rock and put his hands over his face, stunned by and in awe of the magnitude of the roaring forces unleashed about him in the utter darkness. Not only was water swirling and rushing about his knees, it also seemed to be hissing from the very pores of the rock surrounding him. The phenomenon involved much more than tidal movements, John thought, wryly amused to find that he could think of anything other than the fact that he was going to die in a very short time if the water didn't stop rising. It occurred to him that the entire cliff on which Tamara Castle stood was like a huge sponge. Or a bucket: the water, set in motion by the pressure of tides eons ago, was still sloshing around, back and forth, up and down.

Rivers of water were cascading down on his head, snatching air from his lungs. When he tried to move to his left, his feet were swept out from under him. Rather than struggle, John let his muscles go limp and went with the water, allowing himself to be carried like a great fleshy leaf bobbing and floating in a lazy, undulating circle around the perimeter of his stone prison as the chamber continued to fill.

He crossed his arms over his head to protect his skull

from the rocks and tried to lose himself in the not unpleasant sensation of weightlessness. There was, he thought, simply nothing else to do but wait for the cold, deadly touch of stone on his face that would signal the end of his struggle.

He found he was no longer afraid of dying. He had tried everything, and it was almost a relief to have nothing left to do but float in the water and let natural forces decide his fate. He was simply too exhausted to care any longer.

8:41 P.M.

A Gunner

The gunner squatted beside a pile of coiled electrical cables and watched the action in the corner of the ring just above him. Two youthful lightweights were fighting in the second bout of the night. The American had backed the Sierran up against the ropes and was peppering him with jabs that to the gunner looked more stylish than effective. The Sierran counterpunched with a right uppercut that snapped back the American's head and splashed heavy globules of sweat over the gunner's face and clothes. The gunner moved back and knelt down in an aisle.

From this position the gunner had a clear view of the brilliantly lit arena, except for the blocks of seats directly opposite the elevated ring. To his right, high up in a tier of bleachers just below the cantilevered balcony, a section of perhaps a hundred seats had been roped off; the gunner knew that would be where Manuel Salva would sit with his entourage when he arrived.

The gunner could see Alexandra Finway sitting in an aisle seat adjacent to the reserved section. She was, the gunner thought, big, beautiful, and very easy to pick out. She seemed to be following the action in the ring closely, cheering for both the Sierran and American fighters. Occasionally she exchanged good-natured smiles and nods with the Sierrans sitting around her.

Alexandra Finway had the appearance of someone who was thoroughly enjoying herself, but the gunner knew better; he could tell that the woman was distracted by something. The gunner knew how to look at people in order to see past their surface behavior, and he knew that Alexandra Finway was acting. She was very nervous; she was holding her body too stiffly, and her smiles and applause were forced.

All of which the gunner noticed, and then dismissed. The gunner's only concern was in knowing exactly where she was at all times.

Rick Peters posed a far more difficult problem, the gunner thought. The short man was slippery, elusive.

Peters had been constantly in motion since the start of the bouts, generally staying high up near the balcony, casually wandering around with a large portable radio propped on his shoulder and held close to his ear. At the moment the gunner had lost sight of the blond-haired man, but he was fairly certain that Peters was somewhere on the balcony just behind him and above his head. He would not worry about it, the gunner thought, until Salva came in. Then he would act quickly to pinpoint Peters' position.

The gunner, ostensibly checking equipment, had been around the perimeter of the arena three times, and planned to make yet another circuit in fifteen minutes. Up to that point he was satisfied that John Finway was not in the arena. In which case, the gunner thought, Finway was not his concern. His instructions were to kill any of the three people who were in the castle, but only after Manuel Salva had been assassinated. He reminded himself that he was not being paid to hunt, but only to kill under specific circumstances.

The gunner stood and stretched as he looked up at the night sky over the open arena. The Goodyear blimp moved slowly across the full moon, its bright running lights making it appear like some strange, sightless beast tracking currents in the depths of an ocean of night. The gunner moved his hands as though to rub his back and lightly touched the hard shape of the revolver to make sure it was properly seated in his belt next to his spine, covered by the loose, oversized nylon windbreaker he wore.

The gunner stretched again, yawned. He would, he thought, be paid the same fee even if Salva, for some reason, stayed away, or came and was not killed. However, the gunner found himself hoping that the dictator would come to the arena, as everyone supposed he would. He wanted to see Salva in person, and if Salva were assassinated the gunner would be an eyewitness to an important historical event.

He was sure his grandchildren would be impressed.

John

He stood in the rapidly receding water breathing deeply and trying to calm himself. His heart was beating so fast that he feared, in his exhausted state, that he would have a heart attack. He did not intend to die that way, nor from exposure or madness; there was still one option left, and he had decided to exercise it. He would go back into the maelstrom of the underground stream and hope that it flushed him out of the rock before he drowned.

The decision had been simple, he thought, pulling his lips back in a thin, humorless smile that was close to a grimace; the problem lay in finding the courage to actually implement the decision. He had already wasted precious minutes, paralyzed with fear and doubt, as the water had continued to rush out of the chamber.

Once again, as he had done twice before, John clung to the wall and inched to his right, probing beneath the surface of the frothy, hissing water with his right foot for the edge of the rock shelf on which he was standing. He found it, flexed his knees slightly, and felt the force of the current pushing on the instep, ankle, calf.

Memory, the vivid recall of what it felt like to be trapped underwater with lungs and brain bursting in a narrow tube of rock, had brutally gutted his two previous attempts. Now he concentrated on what would happen if he did not go in.

What would happen was—nothing. He would remain trapped forever inside the black chamber. The stream was the only way out.

He knew he would probably survive the next flooding of the chamber, and that he might work up the courage to go then. But that event was many hours away; if it were not already too late to save Alexandra, he knew it would certainly be too late then, even if he did get out alive.

He thought about freezing and thirst and how he would feel about himself at the moment of death if he did not go back into the stream.

Three times and out, John thought. He would not back off again. He hyperventilated, sucked in a last deep breath, and plunged into the water.

8:47 P.M.

Claude Moiret

Moiret glanced at the luminous face of his digital watch and smiled with satisfaction. He had timed his first pass perfectly, he thought. Everything was on track. The sea was calm, and the hundred-mile crossing from Key West had been uneventful. With the extra fuel tank built into the hull and the two fifty-gallon drums of gasoline lashed on board, Moiret calculated that he had fuel to spare for extensive evasive maneuvers, if they became necessary, as well as for the return trip.

The full moon was both a benefit and a handicap. He had been able to make the entire crossing without running lights, but he felt exposed now that he was drifting near the cliff face beneath Tamara Castle; he had thirteen more minutes to wait in this escape window.

He would certainly know if Peters had succeeded, Moiret thought; Peters had told him that he would hear an explosion. Peters would escape by diving from the castle ramparts into the sea. He would pick up the assassin, and they would be on their way. Two million dollars richer.

The currents were bringing him dangerously close to the cliff, now only ten or fifteen yards away. Moiret engaged the clutch on the engine and tapped the throttle lightly with the heel of his hand. The powerful, double-muffled motor purred a bit louder, and Moiret steered the boat away from the cliff. When he had retreated fifteen or twenty yards, Moiret let the engine idle back and again allowed the boat to drift. He was not worried about being heard; he knew that the roar of water cascading from channels high up on the cliff face was more than sufficient to cover the sound of his engine.

Again he glanced at his watch. It was eight-fifty-two.

When Moiret looked up, he was astonished to see a man's splay-limbed, naked body hurtling through the air. It landed with a loud splash at the base of the cliff, no more than twenty yards from the boat.

Moiret had heard no explosion and he had seen no movement on the castle's ramparts. It was, he thought, almost as if the body had been spewed from one of the caves in the side of the cliff, yet he could not conceive of the man being anyone other than Rick Peters. He immediately eased the boat forward toward the ripple marks at the spot where the man had gone under.

A head broke the surface of the water. Moiret tossed a small black life preserver overboard in the direction of the dazed, struggling swimmer. The man grabbed it, and Moiret pulled him to the side of the boat. He reached down to grasp the man's hand, then recoiled in shock when he saw that the swimmer was not Rick Peters.

The man in the water had dark, burning eyes and gray hair marked with a wide swath of silver. His features were drawn and haunted.

"What the—"

"My name's John Finway," the man gasped hoarsely. "Time . . . no time. Help me, please. Salva and my wife . . . inside the castle. Going to be killed. Have . . . to hurry."

Moiret punched at the man's head, missed, and almost fell over the side. The man had ducked away, but he still clung to the life preserver. Moiret recovered his balance, than yanked hard on the attached rope with one hand while he reached with the other for the pistol in the pocket of his windbreaker. He brought out the gun and pointed it at the swimmer's head. The man released his grip on the life preserver and disappeared under the dark water.

He didn't dare fire the gun without a silencer, Moiret thought. The sharp crack of a gunshot could pierce the torrent of sound around him, echo across the water, and be heard by security personnel inside the castle. But he knew that he had to kill this man who, somehow, knew what was about to happen.

He gripped the pistol by its barrel and walked slowly around the perimeter of the boat, peering down into the

water. He spun around at the sound of splashing behind
him and saw the man in the water ten yards away, between
the boat and a spit of land perhaps two hundred yards
away. The swimmer stared back at him for a few seconds,
then rolled over and weakly struck out for the shore.

"*Merde!*" Moiret shouted as he leaped to the boat's helm
and got the gun's silencer from a cabinet behind the steering wheel. He quickly screwed the silencer onto the pistol,
took careful aim at the fish-white, ghostly body floundering
in the water ahead of him, and squeezed off three shots.
Shimmering, silver plumes of water spiked just ahead and
to either side of the man's head a moment before he
jackknifed forward and dove from sight.

The Frenchman cursed again, then froze for a moment
in indecision. Good sense, he knew, would dictate that he
abort and head back to Key West. He should abandon
Peters and save himself. But pride, mingled with greed and
fear, would not let him do that: Peters was his client. And
there was a great deal of money involved. Also, Peters, if
he managed to get away on his own, would find and kill
him.

Moiret gunned the engine into life.

He steered the boat in an arc until he knew he had to be
between the swimmer and the shore, then eased back on the
throttle and waited, bracing himself against the gunwale as
the boat wallowed in the wake it had created. The man
surfaced to Moiret's right, gasped for air, then dove under
again as Moiret fired.

This time Moiret thought he might have hit the man. He
leaned out over the gunwale, gun poised, staring at the
surface of the water. Almost a minute passed, and then he
heard a faint splashing sound out in the direction of the
open sea. Moiret looked, but could see nothing. The splashing stopped.

Moiret's body was filmed with sweat despite a cool
breeze blowing in from the sea. The Frenchman reloaded
the gun, then stood in the middle of the boat and slowly
turned, his eyes straining to see movement on the glittering
surface of the sea. He heard a splash behind him, wheeled
and squeezed off three more shots in rapid succession. But
there was nothing there.

Then there was the unmistakable sound of a man struggling hard for shore. Moiret lunged for the controls and shoved open the throttle. He heeled the boat around in a tight, scudding half-circle and headed directly toward the spot where he had heard the sound. He went twenty-five yards, executed another hard turn and cut back the throttle. He braced his knees against the starboard gunwale of the pitching boat and used both hands to hold the gun stiffly out in front of him, swinging the weapon back and forth in a broad arc.

He suddenly became aware of another sound rising above the soft, whirring purr of his engine and the constant hissing of the water cascading from the cliffs.

The swimmer's head surfaced no more than ten feet to his left. Moiret braced to fire, but was startled by an incandescent glare that suddenly bathed him and the surrounding area with a blinding white light. Moiret wheeled and looked up, then instinctively threw his right arm across his eyes to shield them from the burning glare that seemed to be right above his head, bearing down on him.

Moiret groped blindly for the controls, found them, opened the throttle.

Harley Shue

Harley Shue sat stiffly erect in an anchored chair on the starboard side of the blimp's spacious gondola, alternating his attention between the mercury-light glow of Tamara Castle far below and the clear color pictures on the six ABC monitors suspended from the gondola's ceiling. Beside him, the blimp's cameraman was idly smoking as he awaited instructions for his next shot.

Shue, watching the monitors, could see that one of the cameras inside the castle was fixed constantly on a section of empty bleacher seats. Between rounds, the show's director would occasionally cut to that picture for transmission while Howard Cosell alternately speculated on what might be delaying Salva and commented on the fact that there were many bouts yet to be fought and that there was still an excellent chance that Manuel Salva would appear.

If Salva didn't show up, the Director of Operations thought, neither would Saint George. He would have lost one night's sleep in exchange for a rather pleasant ride in the Goodyear blimp.

Shue himself had pointed out that the blimp—Home Plate—would make an ideal observation and communications post from which to monitor activity on the island in the event Salva was assassinated and an invasion launched. Geoffrey Whistle had agreed, and the CIA Director had personally made arrangements with a senior member of the Goodyear Board of Directors to have Shue ride in the blimp as an "observer."

The Director of Operations knew that as far as the flight crew and cameraman were concerned, he was merely a friend of someone in the parent corporation who had pulled some strings to get a ride in a blimp. The other men on board had been coolly polite, but for the most part had ignored him. That was exactly the way Shue wanted it; only if Operation Saint George were launched would he reveal his credentials and exercise his authority.

The captain and the co-pilot of the blimp, Jack Barnes and Terry Factor, were both retired Air Force officers, and Shue was confident they would follow his orders when they saw what was at stake. If the need arose, Harley Shue had authority to place a call to the President of the United States, by means of the special communications equipment that had been secretly loaded on board the blimp earlier in the day.

Now, he thought, there was nothing to do but wait and see what happened.

The television director's voice, piped into the blimp through twin loudspeakers, suddenly filled the gondola. *"We're going to segue in from the next commercial on a long shot, gentlemen. Approximately two minutes. I'll give you a count from ten. Please get ready. Let's make it a pretty one."*

"Hey, Jack," the co-pilot said as he looked down from his side window. "I've got the controls. Come over and take a look at this."

Captain Jack Barnes removed his headset, stood up, and leaned over his co-pilot. Shue turned in his seat and looked down. Below, a boat without running lights was clearly visible in the moonlight as it carved a wide arc in the water, heeled sharply, then abruptly stopped.

"I don't see what—"

"Just watch, Jack," Terry Factor said abruptly. "There's a man in the water. He'll come up in a minute."

Shue felt the cameraman move up behind him at the same time that he saw a man's head break the surface of the water below. The man ducked under almost immediately as water erupted in sharp spikes around him; he could be seen swimming underwater in a direction lateral to the boat, his arms and legs straining, his body skimming just below the surface like some great pale fish.

"One minute, gentlemen. Gentlemen? Anyone home up there?"

"Do you believe this, Jack? The guy in the boat's shooting at the guy in the water!"

"Twenty seconds. Hey! Give me some confirmation up there!"

Jack Barnes returned to his seat and flipped a switch on the blimp's control panel. "You'll have to run by us on this one, Molly. We've got something going on here."

"What the hell are you talking about, Jack? What are you guys doing up there?"

"Be quiet and listen," Jack Barnes said, his voice calm but hard with authority. "Just cut to something else. Let Cosell talk. In the meantime, get the Sierran authorities on the horn and tell them they've got a problem, an emergency, in the water on the seaward side of the castle. There's a guy in trouble down there, and they should bring a boat around as quickly as possible."

"Hey, Jack, I've got a television show to—!"

The director's voice was abruptly cut off as Barnes peremptorily flicked two switches on the control panel. "Terry, see if you can raise the Sierran Coast Guard, or anyone who has a boat."

"Will do," the co-pilot said, quickly donning a headset and tapping the earphones. He made a tense, sucking sound with his teeth. "I don't think they're going to get there in time."

Shue saw Barnes nod curtly. "I'm going down there and see if I can't scare that guy off," Barnes said in a clipped voice. "I don't think he realizes he has company upstairs." He turned around and spoke to Shue. "Strap yourself in there, mister, and lean away from the window. We're taking a little side trip."

"Perhaps this is a matter the Sierran authorities should handle," Shue said carefully. "They may not appreciate our involving ourselves."

The captain, if he had heard Shue, paid no attention. Almost immediately the blimp began to drop with what was to Shue surprising speed for such a large, unwieldy craft.

Ignoring the captain's suggestion, Shue stood up, then moved aside as the cameraman rudely shoved his camera into the space beside him and aimed it at the water below. For a few moments the boat and the gunman's back were clearly visible. Then the captain executed a quarter turn to come in directly behind the gunman, and the scene slipped out of sight.

"Damn it!" the cameraman said to himself, irritably slapping the top of his equipment. "This could get me a fucking Emmy."

The blimp turned slightly to allow for stronger air currents near the surface, and the boat came into view. The gunman still seemed oblivious to their approach as he aimed his gun out over the water. Ignoring the cameraman's impassioned pleas to move out of the way, Shue saw a flash of white appear in the water a moment before a head surfaced very close to the boat.

"Oh, Jesus," the co-pilot said tensely, wincing and reflexively pressing back in his seat. "That's it. The guy must not have seen the boat. If he doesn't get back under quick, he's going to catch a bullet between the eyes."

"He's out of breath! Hit them with the searchlight, Terry! Fast!"

The co-pilot lunged forward and moved a chrome lever. Instantly the water below them was flooded with harsh, white light. The captain executed a sharp starboard turn to avoid the sheer cliff rising from the sea, and Shue could clearly see the gunman throw an arm across his face. Temporarily blinded, the man groped for the controls. He found the throttle and gunned the engine. The boat's prow lifted out of the water and the craft shot forward along the cliff, heading away from the castle. Suddenly it made a quarter turn to port and headed directly toward the rock.

The co-pilot jerked forward in his seat. "Hey, Jack, the guy can't see—"

The gunman in the boat finally saw the direction in which he was heading. He clawed desperately at the steering wheel, but it was too late. The boat heeled sharply to starboard and shot parallel to the cliff face, millimeters away from destruction. In the blimp they could hear the faint but unmistakable screech of metal scraping against rock a few moments before the boat hit a jutting promontory. There was a rending crash, a scream of wood and steel, then an oddly muffled whooshing sound as the boat and the man in it exploded in a ball of flame. Fiery pieces of metal and wood arced through the night air, a few passing just below the blimp.

"Jesus," Terry Factor said in a low, stunned voice. "The guy must have been carrying half a gas station with him."

"He's gone," Jack Barnes said tensely. "What about the guy in the water?"

"He's right down here," the co-pilot replied quickly. "Nine o'clock, Jack."

The captain turned in his seat and impatiently waved Shue to one side. "Frank," he said sharply to the cameraman, "open the starboard bay door and throw him one of the tether ropes. You, mister, you'll find some blankets in that green trunk back there under the medical kit. How about getting them out?"

"Right away, captain," Shue said evenly.

Shue went to the rear of the gondola, opened the locker trunk and removed two heavy gray blankets. He came back, spread one blanket out over the floor in the center of the gondola, held on to the other.

"Hey!" the cameraman shouted as he braced his right foot against the jamb of the bay door and strained at the rope. "Somebody give me a hand here. I've got him, but he's too weak to climb. We're going to have to pull him up."

Shue and the co-pilot grabbed hold of the rope and, with the cameraman, began laboriously pulling it in hand over hand. A few seconds later, the man—whom a startled Shue instantly recognized as John Finway—was hauled into the gondola.

How—?

Finway's presence in the blimp changed everything, Shue thought, his calm facade belying the turmoil inside him as he wrapped one blanket around the violently shivering man and helped the co-pilot ease him down on the other. He pulled the top blanket up to Finway's chin as Terry Factor massaged Finway's arms and legs. Then Harley Shue rose and walked to the rear of the gondola. He needed time to think and evaluate this new situation.

The captain adjusted the controls. As the blimp began to ascend, he leaned forward and flipped on the two radio switches. "Okay, Molly," he said drily. "Now, where were we?"

"Hey! Kiss Frank for me! We've got that explosion and fire on tape; we'll show it as soon as we find out what happened. And you want Sierrans, we've got Sierrans! They're all over the place down here, and you've got a boatload coming around the bend. What the hell happened?"

Shue frowned as he watched Finway wrestle an arm free from the blanket, reach up and grab the front of the co-pilot's shirt. He pulled the man's head down and whispered in his ear. The co-pilot listened intently, then tensed and turned toward the coockpit.

"Jack? This guy's saying something about his wife and Salva getting killed tonight."

"Hey! What's that?! Terry, what did you say?"

"T-turn off the radio," John Finway stammered, his lips still blue and quivering from cold and exhaustion. "Important. People going to d-die."

"Jack, I know this guy," Factor said, staring hard at the man lying on the floor beneath him. "It's John Finway. The lawyer."

Shue watched as Finway once again clutched feebly at the co-pilot's shirt. Terry Factor got down on one knee and leaned forward, putting his ear close to the other man's mouth.

No matter what now happened inside the castle, Shue thought, Operation Saint George could not be launched as long as John Finway was alive. Shue had no idea how the lawyer had ended in the water or who the gunman had been, but he had to assume that Finway knew much more than he should and that the lawyer would tell what he knew. There would be no way to control him—especially if his wife were killed.

"Hey! Damn it, what's happening up there?"

Shue knew that the time for consideration and debate was over; he had to act immediately if he hoped to have any control over future events. He crossed the length of the gondola in quick strides, reached over the pilot's shoulder into the cockpit and turned off the radio switches.

"My name is Peter White," Shue announced to the startled captain and co-pilot. The two men were staring at him as though he had gone mad. He took the credentials wallet from the breast pocket of his suit jacket, flipped it open and held it at arm's length for the two men to examine. "I'm here on the direct authority of the President of the United States," he continued in the same steady tone. "I can arrange for you to speak to him personally, but we'll save time—very valuable time—if you'll just accept my authority for now."

There was a long silence while the captain studied Shue's credentials. "You're in charge, Mr. White," Jack Barnes said at last. "Just tell us what you want us to do."

"Thank you, Captain. Can you rig your communications gear so that we can maintain an open channel without anyone on the ground being able to hear what we say?"

The captain removed a headset with an attached microphone from a metal peg beside him. He put on the set, plugged a cable into a jack hole on the control console, and snapped on one of the two radio switches. "Okay," he said. "I can cover the mike with my hand when you're talking, but you'll still have to keep your voices down."

Shue tensed slightly at the tortured, gasping sound of John Finway's voice.

"White, you son-of-a-bitch; you're one of the people responsible for my wife being in that castle down there, aren't you?"

Harley Shue turned to face the other man, who had somehow managed to struggle to his feet. Finway was swaying and trembling as he held the blanket tightly around him, but his eyes were brimming with hate, bright and hot as glowing coals in a face the color of ashes. The man had come to the open sea out of hell, Shue thought.

"That's not true, Mr. Finway," Shue said mildly. "The

government only recently received intelligence reports that something unusual might happen tonight. That's why I'm here. I don't know anything about you or your wife, and I certainly would if the United States government were involved in any way. I want to hear what you have to say, but I think it should wait until we get things straightened out with the people on the ground. Otherwise, we're likely to have a jet fighter or two for company. Agreed?"

Shue paused. When Finway turned away, the CIA's Director of Operations spoke to the cameraman. "Did you get any clear shots of Mr. Finway?"

"No," the cameraman replied in a surly tone. "You were in the way. Who the hell did you say you were?"

"He's the man giving orders here, Frank," Barnes said flatly. "Just do as he asks."

Shue inclined his head toward the captain. "So they don't know we've picked up a passenger. Let's keep it that way. Stall them any way you can."

"I have to get down there!" Finway shouted.

"Wait a moment, Mr. Finway. Be quiet, please. Captain?"

"Molly?" Barnes said casually into the microphone. "You there?"

"Am I here? I'm here! Where the hell are you?"

"A couple of minor problems here, Molly," Barnes said in a calm, soothing tone. "We went down to see if anyone survived that explosion. Negative. But I think we may have been hit by some debris. I don't think there's any serious damage, but we'll need some time to check it out. You can get by without us for a while, huh?"

"Sure. You're coming back into sight now. You want me to call in some help?"

"Negative. At least not yet. We'll check things out ourselves first. Over and out, Molly."

"Roger, Captain Jack. Take care."

Shue waited for the captain to shut off the transmission switch, then turned to John Finway. Incredibly, the lawyer, his muscles apparently fueled by the same terrible need and hurt Shue saw burning in his eyes, was pacing impatiently back and forth across the narrow width of the gondola. Shue could see that the other man was not shivering as violently as before, and some color had returned to his face.

"Now, Mr. Finway, would you care to tell us what happened down there?"

"I don't have time to talk to you about it! I told you I have to get down on the ground!"

"There's no way we can get you there, Mr. Finway," Terry Factor interjected. "We have permission to fly over Tamara Castle, not land on top of it." The co-pilot shrugged, continued. "And you can't just set a blimp down in Angeles Blanca, even if the Sierrans did give us permission to land."

Finway clenched his fists, pounded the side of the gondola.

Shue held up his hand in a pacifying gesture. "Why is it so important that you get down there, Mr. Finway?"

"Is Salva in the castle?"

"No. At least he wasn't when we went down for you. Now there seems to be some question as to whether he's coming at all."

Shue could see that John Finway was barely managing to keep his emotions under control. The man's eyes, as well as the sharp tone of his voice and the tight lines around his mouth, revealed the intensity of his inner struggle. His entire body sagged with exhaustion, yet his voice when he spoke seemed to grow increasingly stronger, as if reflecting some energy source at his core that only death could stamp out.

"You have to get the Sierrans to keep him away," Finway said, speaking slowly and carefully emphasizing each word. "He's going to be killed if he goes into that castle. A man by the name of Rick Peters has planted plastic explosives on my wife. She doesn't have the slightest idea what's going down, and her job is probably to get as close to Salva as she can. If Salva shows, Peters will blow them both up."

"Jesus Christ," Terry Factor said.

Shue stepped up behind Jack Barnes. The captain was sitting stiffly erect, his hand hovering near the transmission switch. "Did you hear that, Captain?" Shue asked softly. When Barnes nodded curtly, the Director of Operations continued, "We have to locate this man's wife, which means some specific pictures up here. Can you set up closed two-way communications with your director?"

"Tough," Barnes said tightly. "The telecast is a cooperative deal. We're supposed to be training the Sierrans, and they're doing a lot of the technical work down there."

"Never mind," Finway said in a soft, haunted voice. "There she is."

Shue glanced up at the monitors. The set on the far right displayed a shot of empty bleacher seats: Alexandra Finway could be clearly seen at the edge of the picture, seated on the aisle.

"My wife is the tall woman with the dark hair," Finway continued in the same hollow voice. "You can't see it from this angle, but she has a barrette in her hair that's made out of plastique. Peters is somewhere in there. He's carrying a radio that can transmit a signal that will fire off the explosives."

"I'll have to explain the situation to the Sierrans," Barnes said flatly. "They can get the woman out of there and nail this Peters joker."

"No!" the lawyer said sharply, his voice breaking, changing from a command to a plea in the single syllable. "I told you; Alexandra has no idea what's really happening. She thinks she's there to protect Salva, so she'll be on guard. She can't be approached by anyone but me. If she even begins to suspect that something's wrong, she'll signal Peters. Peters knows he's a dead man if the Sierrans catch him, and he'll probably blow away Alexandra out of spite. I have to be the one who goes in there."

Shue studied the other man, decided that the lawyer was probably right: Finway alone had the best, if not the only, chance to save his wife. Rick Peters was paranoid, volatile, and totally unpredictable. Operation Saint George was off if Salva didn't appear, and there was no sense in having a fine woman die needlessly.

On the other hand, Shue thought, having Finway inside the castle would make the lawyer their gunner's responsibility. Then, if Salva did appear and were assassinated, John Finway would be eliminated, as originally planned.

In either event, it was best to let Finway go.

"You're very weak," Shue said carefully. "You don't have any clothes; even if you did, you'd be recognized."

"My physical condition isn't your concern!" Finway snapped. "If this man will lend me his clothes, the cap will cover my hair."

The cameraman nodded. "You've got anything of mine you want, buddy," he said, quickly removing his long-billed cap and starting to unbutton his shirt. "There's a pair of coveralls and boots in the back I can wear." He shrugged off his shirt, handed it to the lawyer. "There's a credentials badge in the pocket. It's a lousy photograph, and you might get past them with it; I didn't need it working up here, but you'll have to have it pinned on if you expect to get into the castle."

"Captain," Shue said, "you did tell your director that we have a crippled ship. Will the Sierrans cooperate if you tell them you have to bring it down?"

"Let's find out," Barnes said tightly, flipping on the transmission switch and tapping the microphone on the headset. "Molly, can you talk?"

"I've got you, Jack. How're you doing up there?"

"Not good. I've lost hydraulic pressure in my right aileron. I've got to bring her down, and fast. The square in front of the castle looks wide enough. The problem is that I don't have permission to land, and I don't have time for interrogation by their air controllers. Take care of my chatter for me, will you? I don't want them to think that the Goodyear blimp is leading some kind of invasion."

"Will do. It's an emergency. What can they say?"

"They can say anything they want as long as they don't shoot. The Sierrans will have to clear the area, and I'll need some men to hold the tethers."

"Jack, what the hell can you do to a blimp parked in the middle of the street?"

"I won't know that until I can get out from behind the controls and eyeball things," Barnes said testily. "But landing in the street sure as hell beats ditching in the ocean. Do what you can for me, will you, Molly? My wife won't like it if I come home with an assful of bullets."

"I'll notify the Sierrans, and they can handle it any way they want. Don't worry about this end, Jack. You just get everybody down here in one piece. Got it?"

"Roger. Thanks, Molly. Over and out."

Barnes once again switched off the radio, then eased the

controls forward. "Here we go, folks," he said tersely. "This could be hairy, you know. The Sierrans may go apeshit when they see this big son-of-a-bitch floating down on top of them."

"We have to take the risk," Shue said evenly.

His own risk was the greatest of all, he thought, at least in terms of national security, global politics, and war. The Sierrans and the Russians would dearly love to capture on Sierran soil the man who had been the CIA Director of Operations for close to three and a half decades. However, clearing the way for Saint George necessitated the gamble.

"I can't set this thing down on the ground, you know," Barnes said. "It would take half the night to set up a proper mooring. Mr. Finway's going to have to use the rope ladder." He paused, added thoughtfully, "He's going to have to climb down right into the arms of the Sierrans."

"I'll make it into the castle," Finway said, his tone flat and distant. It sounded to Shue as if the man were talking to himself. Finway was already standing by the bay door, dressed in the cameraman's clothes. "I have to."

Shue looked at the monitors. The action in the ring had stopped and everyone inside the arena was looking up at the sky. He turned, glanced out the side window. The ground was coming up fast; the plaza had been cleared, and barricades erected at both ends. There were perhaps two dozen men below them, all craning their necks to look up at the descending blimp. At least ten of the men were uniformed soldiers armed with Kalashnikov assault rifles.

"You understand that we'll have to deal with the Sierrans if they stop you," Shue said evenly to the man waiting anxiously at the bay door. "They'll have to be told what's going on."

"I understand. And I appreciate being given this chance. I know all of you are sticking your necks out."

Both Barnes and his co-pilot responded with a thumbs-up sign. "Hey, buddy," the captain said with feeling. "I haven't got the slightest idea what this is all about, but you go get your wife out of there safely."

"And don't get your ass shot off," Terry Factor added.

"All bets are off if Salva shows up, Mr. Finway," Harley Shue said, raising his voice slightly and glancing in the direction of the two men in the cockpit to make sure they had heard him. "Of course we can't gamble with Salva's life."

John Finway said nothing. A number of the men on the ground were waving, their faces anxious but friendly. Shue smiled broadly and waved back at them.

The airship floated down. Barnes halted its descent when the bottom of the gondola was nine or ten feet from the ground. Finway and the cameraman flung the bay doors open and tossed out four heavy tether ropes, two on each side. The ropes were quickly seized by eight men, two to a rope, and pulled taut to steady the blimp.

Shue was relieved to see that none of the men appeared to be suspicious. One soldier was speaking into a walkie-talkie, but there was nothing in his expression that caused Shue to feel alarm; most of the soldiers had apparently come over merely to watch or help.

If there were DMI men in the crowd, and Shue was certain there were, they had seen no need to make their presence known. Barnes and Factor immediately got out of their seats and made a show of frenetically checking controls and equipment. On the monitors, the bouts had been resumed at the urging of the referee. Shue noted approvingly that Finway did not rush. The tall, gaunt man waited a minute or two, then walked over and leaned casually against the frame of the open doorway. He glanced down at the ground, then called loudly, but not too loudly, over his shoulder, "We're busted for this trip. There's nothing for me to do here. I'm going in to watch the fights."

Barnes, without pausing in his frantic activity, merely waved him away. Finway tossed a rope ladder with aluminum rungs out the door, turned around and, with what seemed to Shue surprising strength for a man who had been struggling in the sea only minutes before, agilely descended to the ground. Shue tensed slightly when he saw the lawyer challenged by two nervous soldiers, but Finway handled it correctly. The lawyer flashed his credentials badge in the soldiers' faces, then gestured angrily at the blimp and shrugged. Without a trace of anxiety or hesitation, he pushed the cap back on his head—but only to the hairline. Almost immediately he turned his head to the side sharply, as if in disgust with the broken blimp. It worked. The soldiers conferred for a minute or two, but they did not give the murky photograph more than a cursory glance. Both men nodded and smiled at Finway. The soldier with the walkie-talkie conferred with someone inside the castle, read the number off Finway's badge. He received an answer, then nodded an affirmation to his companions. Finway was clapped on the back and good-naturedly shoved toward the entrance to the castle. Shue grunted, slowly exhaled.

"Will you look at that?" Terry Factor said distantly, as though he could hardly believe what he was seeing. "Marches right into the castle just as cool as snakeshit. The guy's got guts."

It was true, Harley Shue thought. John Finway appeared to have rare courage—like his wife. Harry Beeler had possessed that kind of courage. It would be his duty and challenge, Shue thought, to make certain these people's deaths were not squandered.

And yet . . .

Harley Shue was vaguely surprised to find himself hoping that Salva found whatever he was doing at the moment more attractive than the boxing matches.

"Finway's too late," the cameraman said, his voice thick with disgust, exasperation, and fear. "Salva just walked in. They must have brought him in through the back."

Shue shook himself as a fever-chill swept through his body. At the same time he felt beads of sweat break out on his forehead. Mouth slightly open, he spun around and fixed his gaze on the monitors above his head. The action in the ring had again been halted between rounds. The tall, unmistakable figure of Manuel Salva, dressed in combat fatigues and surrounded by his entourage of security men and friends, was on his feet, waving his freshly starched cap and acknowledging the frenzied cheers of the crowd. Alexandra Finway could be seen to the far right of the screen. The woman was on her feet, cheering with the others.

"Mr. White?"

"What?" For a moment, Harley Shue had forgotten his cover name. He looked around to find Jack Barnes staring at him intently. The captain's hand was on the radio transmission switch.

"I assume it's time we talked to Sierran security," Barne said tightly.

"No."

Barnes frowned. "I don't understand, White. You said—'

"We'll give Finway fifteen minutes. His wife's life is or the line. At this point he has just as much chance of stopping this thing as the Sierrans have. Maybe better."

Saint George's entrance was going to mean his own permanent exit, Harley Shue thought. He was now going to have to kill Jack Barnes and Terry Factor, and the only convincing way of doing that was to arrange for the mid-air destruction of the blimp—after the craft had served its purpose.

Unless Finway could prevent the assassination, which to Harley Shue seemed highly unlikely; he expected to witness the deadly explosion at any second.

Barnes continued to stare hard at Shue, and his hand remained on the transmission switch. "I don't know, White The woman's no more than twenty feet away from Salva. It seems to me that we're assuming one hell of a big responsibility."

"The responsibility is mine, Captain," Shue said in a clipped, forceful voice as he turned his back on the two men and strode quickly to the rear of the gondola. "I speak for the President. You agreed to follow my orders. Please do so. You've found the trouble with the blimp and fixed it. Now let's get this ship back into the air."

Alexandra

Alexandra had the persistent feeling that she was slowly smothering in some thick-aired world where light and sound were subtly distorted. Her stomach burned; it had burned all through this strange afternoon and evening.

Yet she could not identify the cause of her discomfort. Thus far she had experienced no difficulty in keeping track of the others in the tour group who had come with them. Not counting Rick Peters and herself, all but two members of the group were sitting together on the opposite side of the oval arena. The other two had chosen—like herself, but for different reasons—to sit with Sierrans, and it was to these Americans that Alexandra had paid the closest attention. However, neither of the men had moved from his seat since the matches had begun, and they were a comfortable distance away from the rows of empty bleacher seats across the aisle from her.

Of course, she thought, anyone in the group could make a move at any time in an attempt to improve his position and firing angle. She knew that it was very possible some kind of weapon had been secreted somewhere in the arena, perhaps taped beneath one of the bleacher seats.

However, there had been no movement among members of the tour group, and none of them was acting the least bit suspicious. This fact, combined with Salva's conspicuous absence, should make her feel more at ease, Alexandra thought. Instead she felt high-strung and skittish, as if the acid in her stomach had eaten through to her nerves. Things were somehow different in this slow-motion, prismatic world. She could not shake the conviction that important events were happening around her in the dark periphery of the brilliantly lit arena inside the castle.

Yet, as in a nightmare, she seemed to be the only one who sensed anything unusual.

She had been constantly sweeping her gaze around the arena, trying to fix every detail in her mind, searching for the tiny circumstance that seemed out of place—a quick movement, an anxious expression on someone's face. While she had been looking toward the seaward side of the arena she had seen the Goodyear blimp suddenly and inexplicably begin a rapid, steep descent and then disappear from sight below the castle's ramparts. A minute or two later she'd thought she had heard a muffled explosion, although it was difficult to be certain with the deafening crowd noise inside the relatively small arena.

No one else had seemed to take any notice; everyone's attention had remained riveted on the action inside the boxing ring below.

Alexandra tried to put the incident from her mind, reminding herself that her sole responsibility was to watch the crowd in the arena, and, specifically, members of her own tour group. However, she found herself constantly glancing in the direction of the seaward wall. Then, a few minutes later, the blimp reappeared, floating in the air like an oblong, luminous bubble escaped from the depths of the night sea. It stayed aloft for a few minutes and then, to Alexandra's consternation, once again began to descend almost straight down, a direction she judged would place it directly in front of the castle.

Now a murmur rose from the crowd; arms were extended, fingers pointed. People across the way turned in their seats and craned their necks as the huge blimp floated down, filling the sky. For a moment the blimp created the illusion that it would touch the castle walls, but then it passed from sight below the ramparts.

At the height of the confusion the referee had stepped between the boxers, suspending the fight. Now an official appeared at the apron of the ring and spoke with the referee, who nodded and in turn spoke to the fighters, who then went to their corners. An announcement in Spanish was made over the loudspeakers. The people sat down, and the fight was resumed.

From the woman next to her, Alexandra learned, through a combination of sign language and a few English words, that the blimp had been forced to descend for repairs. Alexandra wondered. The blimp's strange movements made her nervous. She wanted to discuss the situation with Rick Peters, but she knew that she could lose her seat if she left; that was a risk she dared not take.

A few seconds later, her concern about the movements of the blimp were abruptly pushed from her mind. The bell at ringside signaled the end of the round, and suddenly the people in the seats directly across from her began to wildly clap and cheer, rising from their seats in brightly colored waves. The undulating swell of rising people swept in opposite directions from its epicenter around the arena toward her.

Alexandra stood up and turned in time to see Manuel Salva stride down the aisle, leading a group of thirty or forty men and women.

Suddenly Alexandra experienced an unreasoning terror, and she found she was panting. She swallowed hard and licked her lips, forcing herself to remain standing on trembling legs, applauding. She clapped with steadily increasing intensity until the palms of her hands burned almost as much as her stomach. Still she felt terror, all the more horrible because she could not understand it.

She forced herself to toss back her head and grin as she watched the tall, heavy-set man doff his fatigue cap and acknowledge the cheers of the crowd.

Salva *was* magnetic, Alexandra thought, and for the first time she began to understand how he could keep massive crowds spellbound for five or six hours with no more than his voice and presence. She felt that presence now as an almost palpable force filling the arena.

Many famous men Alexandra had seen in person had disappointed her with their physical presence, or lack of it. Manuel Salva had quite the opposite effect on her, and Alexandra recognized the appeal as sexual; it was certainly not political. Perhaps, she thought, it was his courage. Alexandra knew of no other world leader, dictator or democrat, who traveled about his country and among his people so freely, contemptuous of the danger to which he was exposing himself, as he was doing that evening.

Alexandra was startled when the Sierran leader suddenly looked directly at her. His gaze remained on her face for a few moments, swept past, then returned to her. Alexandra smiled, and nodded her head slightly.

She saw Salva lean to his left and whisper something to the uniformed man standing beside him. He finished, then gestured broadly around the arena to indicate that the crowd should sit down. The people continued to cheer until Salva and his entourage sat, then the cheering subsided as the crowd belatedly followed its leader's example. The bell at ringside sounded, and the match that had been in progress was resumed.

The amorphous, shimmering terror in Alexandra had eased somewhat, but she continued to sit stiffly erect at the edge of the hard, wooden bleacher seat with her legs coiled under her. She made another quick visual survey of the arena; everything appeared to be the same. No one from the tour group was missing or had changed position.

She should try to relax, Alexandra thought. The danger was focused now: Salva was in the arena, and she was in the neck of the funnel designed to protect him. It was counterproductive to be hypertense; the nervous state would exhaust her quickly, and she knew she still had a long night ahead of her. She could not afford to lose her concentration for a single second.

Her thoughts returned to the blimp; it had suddenly reappeared in the night sky, and that concerned her more than if the ship had simply remained out of sight and grounded. She wished her partner would come around so that she could discuss it with him, but she knew that he would not; he should not. And she could not leave her position.

"*Señora? Por favor, Señora.*"

Alexandra started and almost cried out when she felt a hand touch her shoulder. She turned to her right and was surprised to find that the man whom Salva had spoken to was kneeling in the aisle and addressing her. She glanced over the man's shoulder and could see Salva, an unlit cigar held up to his chest and a faint smile on his lips, staring directly at her.

"I am sorry to disturb you, *Señora*," the man said in passable English delivered with a heavy accent. "I did not mean to startle you. *Por favor.* Manuel has asked me to tell you, with all respect, that he would like you to sit with him. You would go? I will take your seat."

Alexandra smiled and pretended to be searching for her purse while she tried to think. She knew that actually sitting next to Salva was definitely not the best position for her to be in; he would want to talk, and she could not carry on a conversation with Salva and still watch the arena and her partner, as she must.

On the other hand, she thought, Rick Peters was constantly moving around the arena; her partner was an all-important extra set of eyes and, regardless of the circumstances, she should be able to maintain visual contact with him. Sitting next to Salva would immeasurably improve her coverage of attack angles. The critical balcony area directly behind her would simply remain Rick Peters' responsibility.

"*Señora?*"

"Yes," Alexandra said, glancing across the aisle toward Salva and smiling again. "I'd like that very much."

Alexandra rose, and Salva's entire entourage rose with her. She stepped across the aisle and walked to where Salva was waiting. There was a murmur of excitement from the watching crowd, but it was diverted to the ring when the boxers, skilled middleweights, launched a final-round toe-to-toe battle.

She reached Salva, shook the hand he extended toward her. His grip was gentle enough to acknowledge the fact that she was a woman, firm enough to be sensual.

"Welcome to San Sierra," Manuel Salva said, leaning close to Alexandra in order to be heard over the crowd noise. "Miss—?"

Alexandra introduced herself, then sat when he did. The rest of the entourage sat.

"Thank you for joining me, Alexandra."

"Thank *you*, sir," Alexandra replied. "I—"

"Sir?" Salva's eyes glinted with amusement. "I call you Alexandra, but you call me 'sir'?"

Alexandra's smile felt forced, stiff. She was very conscious of the fact that, for the first time since she had entered the castle, she was unaware of what was going on around her. She had the eerie sensation that at any moment the familiar face in front of her would register shock, then crack in pain; she would see the eyes roll back in his head just before Manuel Salva crumpled to the floor. Yet she knew she had to keep looking at him; to suddenly glance around her would seem a suspicious act, and she knew that dozens of security men had to be watching her closely; she could easily end up an unwilling but fatally effective decoy.

"I'm sorry, sir. I'm afraid I don't know what to call you. Mr. President?"

"My people call me Manuel," Salva said. His eyes glowed with good-natured, teasing laughter. "If you think you might like me, you should call me Manuel."

Alexandra smiled coyly even as a new, fierce wave of acid heat washed the lining of her stomach. "I think I like you, but I can't feel comfortable calling you Manuel."

Salva laughed. It was a hearty, booming sound, and a few heads turned in their direction. The dictator frowned, and the heads quickly turned away. "Then perhaps you should call me Mr. Manuel."

It was Alexandra's turn to laugh. "All right, *Manuel*. I give up. Besides, all of a sudden I feel comfortable calling you that. Thank you very much for inviting me to sit with you. I'm honored."

The Sierran President clenched his unlit cigar between his teeth, spoke around it. "Do you think I asked you to join me because you are a beautiful woman?"

"Yes, Manuel," Alexandra said evenly. "As a matter of fact, I do. Your reputation precedes you."

The booming laugh came again, but this time Salva quickly turned serious. "It is true, Alexandra. But there is another reason I asked you to come over. You are an American, of course. You came with the tour group?"

"Yes."

Salva nodded almost imperceptibly in the direction of the Americans sitting directly across the arena from them. "They are Ameicans, too, but they prefer to stay to themselves. Americans are almost as bad as the Russians; most Russians and Americans are contemptuous of everyone but their countrymen. You chose to sit with my people. Why?"

Alexandra shrugged. "I came to San Sierra to see the

country and meet Sierrans. In the past week I've found that I like Sierrans very much."

Salva narrowed his eyes. "And no one follows you around, right? No KGB here. You can go where you want, talk to anyone you want?"

"As far as I could tell in a week, yes."

Salva nodded approvingly. "I know you are a sincere person; I could tell that by looking at you. That is one reason I asked you to sit with me. Politics is one thing; politics is very important. But human beings should not always think and talk of politics. I want my people and your people to see that Sierrans and Americans can be friends."

Salva gestured with his cigar toward the arena floor where a television camera, its red signal light glowing like a live coal, was pointed up at them. "The television cameras will be on us all evening," he continued. "You will be a celebrity when you return home. This evening you and I will talk. The Americans will see that not all Sierrans want to leave here, and you will be able to tell the Americans that I am not a monster. It is good public relations. You see? I am willing to gamble that you will like me."

"You're very candid, Manuel. You've just told me that you're using me."

Salva glanced sideways at Alexandra and smiled around his cigar. Lights danced in his eyes. "Ah, but I can afford to be candid with you because we both know that the most important reason you are here *is* because you are a beautiful woman. Beautiful women are even more important than public relations or politics." He chuckled in appreciation of his words, then turned his attention back to the ring below them. "We will watch the fights now, talk later."

Alexandra felt her muscles relax slightly as she was finally able to take her eyes from Manuel Salva's face and surreptitiously glance around her. The first person who caught her attention was Rick Peters.

The man was leaning on the wide stone railing of the balcony, directly across from and slightly above her. Despite the considerable distance separating them, his pale eyes seemed unnaturally large and bright, boring into her. Alexandra was startled to see that his features were twisted into a grotesque, hate-filled mask.

Alexandra recoiled in astonishment and revulsion from the frightening expression and averted her gaze. But perhaps it had only been her imagination, she thought, for when she looked at Rick Peters again a half second later his expression was benign. He smiled slightly, nodded and winked in what seemed a gesture of approval. Alexandra saw him lift his large portable radio with his left hand and rest it on the balcony railing. Then his right hand came up and rested on the back of the radio.

Alexandra nodded and winked back, then tensed and almost rose out of her seat when she recognized the familiar, red-faced figure of Raul pushing his way toward Rick Peters through the crush of people crowded onto the balcony.

Peters

Peters' heart pounded and his stiff penis throbbed as he leaned on the balcony railing and savored the sight of Alexandra and Manuel Salva sitting together across from him. It was all so perfect and final, he thought, transcending even his fantasies. Alexandra was practically sitting in Salva's lap, and the explosion alone would be enough to kill them both.

It was a just and fitting end to it, Peters thought, a suitable reward of propitious circumstance for his courage, intelligence, and skill.

He felt a twinge of sadness and self-pity when he realized that, in all probability, there would never again be a time in his life as satisfying as the moment when he pressed the panel on the back of the radio and watched the woman who had maimed his soul and humiliated him disappear, along with the man whose death would make him rich, in a misty cloud of smoke, blood, and tissue.

He'd even possessed Alexandra—not in the manner he'd hoped and planned for, but it was enough that the act had occurred. He was her last lover, the last man to have enjoyed her body before her death, and it was all he could do to keep from shuffling his feet in a little jig of joy.

But he knew he still had to be careful. Alexandra's face had dramatically changed when she'd glanced up at him, and he'd realized with alarm that she was reacting to the expression on his own face. He'd quickly smiled, forcing the intoxicating mix of exultation and hatred back down deep inside himself, away from Alexandra's probing eyes.

He rested the radio on the balcony railing, then brought his right hand up and placed his fingers on the rear panel.

He glanced at his watch: it was ten o'clock. The window was open.

He had fifteen minutes, Peters thought. Salva and Alexandra were not going anywhere, and there was no need for him to rush things; Claude Moiret would be waiting in a fast boat on the seaward side of the castle from ten to ten-fifteen.

He decided that he would press the panel at seven minutes after ten, in the center of the window. In another minute he would begin slowly making his way along the fifty feet of balcony that would lead him to the waist-high retaining wall overlooking the sea. Once there, he would push the panel on the back of the radio and then dive over the wall into the sea. He considered it possible that in the din and confusion no one would even notice him, but even if he were observed, Peters thought, it wouldn't matter: Moiret would have him out to sea before any pursuit could be organized.

He knew that the dive was going to be very painful. The strain on his cracked ribs as he stretched through his dive and especially the moment of impact with the water, would be agonizing. Also, he knew that he had to enter the water at precisely the right angle, for a rib could snap and puncture his lungs. However, he knew he could tolerate the pain, and he was not worried about executing the dive. He was convinced he would make the dive successfully, and the satisfaction he would feel when he pressed the panel would be worth any pain.

His watch read one minute after ten. It was time to start walking.

As he stepped back from the railing, he felt a hand grip his arm.

"Mr. Peters! I must talk to you!"

Peters wheeled around and was startled to find himself looking into Raul's face. Peters knew he had trouble. The Sierratour guide's bloodless lower lip was quivering with tension; his eyes were hard, determined.

"How are you doing, Raul?" Peters asked casually. "Great fights, huh?"

"Mrs. Finway is sitting with Manuel!"

"Yeah, I noticed. Impressive, isn't it? It's going to make

her an instant celebrity. She'll have a lot to talk about when she gets home."

"Why is she not with you?"

"The woman and I aren't glued to each other, Raul," Peters said irritably. He turned and started to walk toward the seaward rampart. "Talk to you later, pal."

"Wait, you!" Raul's voice, although high-pitched and quavering, was nevertheless commanding. A moment later Peters once again felt the Sierran's fingers grip his upper arm. "You must come with me!"

Peters stopped, took a deep breath, then slowly turned back to face the Sierran. He was very conscious of time passing, and was already considering the difficult problem of how to kill the man in the midst of the crowd.

"Get lost, Raul. For Christ's sake, I'm trying to watch the fights. If you don't get the fuck away from me right now, I'm going to make sure Sierratour nails your ass to a pineapple tree."

"You can't threaten me, Mr. Peters!" Raul said, spreading his legs slightly and thrusting out his chin. His fingers continued to grip Peters' upper arm. "I have a right to question you! I do not like the fact that your girl friend is sitting with Manuel!"

"Tough shit, Raul. What do you expect me to do about it? I didn't know you were queer for your great leader."

"John Finway told me you are planning to kill Manuel! I want you to explain to the authorities why he should say such a thing!"

He was going to have to kill the Sierran right away, Peters thought. "Oh, that," he said casually. He looked down at his feet and shrugged. "It just so happens that I do know what he meant."

"You do?" Raul said, obviously confused and taken aback. His fingers slipped from Peters' arm. "What?"

"Come on," Peters said, quickly stepping around the Sierran and heading for the nearest corridor leading off the balcony. "I want to show you something."

"Hey, you! Wait!"

Peters deftly slapped Raul's hand away as the Sierran grabbed for him. He hurried along, pushing people out of the way, then turned left into a crowded corridor that led to toilets. He could sense Raul following in his wake, felt him clutching at his shirt, heard him shouting. It was exactly what Peters wanted.

The assassin shoved ahead another ten paces, then abruptly stopped and spun around. Raul collided with him. The wide-eyed Sierran opened his mouth to speak, but no sound came out. Peters' stiff right thumb rammed up into Raul's solar plexus, just under the rib cage, with enough force to explode the Sierran's heart. Raul died on his feet, and by the time his body had crumpled to the stone floor Peters was already shoving his way back toward the balcony.

A Gunner

The gunner watched with mounting concern as Alexandra Finway moved across the aisle, sidled past six men, and sat down beside Manuel Salva. The gunner knew that the close proximity of the woman, who was his responsibility, to the principal assassination target meant an increased burden for him. If Salva were killed, Alexandra Finway would be swallowed up in the crush of people who would rush to Salva's aid, making it difficult and dangerous for the gunner to get close to her.

The gunner's instincts, fine-tuned by nearly fifty years of experience, told him that something was about to happen. He quickly moved out from his position at the mouth of a tunnel and looked up at the balcony section behind him. He was relieved to find that Rick Peters was still standing where the gunner had seen him last.

If and when the assassination took place, the gunner thought, he would take out Peters first, and he could then wait in what was certain to be chaos and look for his best opportunity to move on Alexandra Finway; the police, army, and DMI, if they managed to get organized at all, would be looking for a gunman trying to get out of the castle, not one moving to its center.

The gunner lowered his gaze, turned to his left and started walking toward an aisle that would take him to the balcony. He almost bumped into a tall man wearing a green ABC windbreaker and a long-billed cap. The man's face was tortured and gaunt with gray-hued flesh, but his

:harcoal eyes blazed with a desperate, haunted frenzy as
they scanned the arena. The man's cap was pulled down
ow over his forehead, concealing his hair, but the gunner
vas certain he recognized the face.

The gunner felt his stomach knot with tension and he
nstinctively reached out and grabbed the man's shirt in
order to hold him for a few more seconds; he had to know
for certain if the man was John Finway.

It was.

"Get the hell out of my way," the man growled through
clenched teeth, shoving the gunner's hand away and step-
oing around him. The gunner watched the man walk
around the ring apron and approach the section of seats
where Manuel Salva and Alexandra Finway were sitting
together.

What the hell's going on?

The gunner glanced up to confirm that Rick Peters was
still in the balcony.

Peters was gone.

Feeling confused and harried, the gunner spun around
n order to watch Finway. As the lawyer reached one of
the two aisles leading up to Salva's bleacher section, two
ourly Sierrans rose, blocking Finway's way and grabbing
his arms.

John

"I have to get up to the balcony," John said gruffly, glancing back and forth at the two security men, then raising
his gaze like a prayer toward Alexandra.

Look at me, Alexandra! For God's sake, Look at me!

The man on John's left shook his head curtly. A thick,
greasy curl fell down over his forehead and he quickly
brushed the lock aside with his free hand. "No one may go
into this section who was not here when Manuel came in."

"I'm working," John said loudly. "You see my badge."
He craned his neck and rocked from side to side, trying to
catch Alexandra's attention, but his voice would not carry
above the noise of the crowd, and Alexandra was looking
at the section across the way. "ABC. I have to get up there
to check some cables."

"Go around."

"The cable's up there!"

"You can't come up this way." The voice was cold, stolid, implacable.

John struggled against panic as he tried to think of a way to get to Alexandra. He tensed as he saw the second security guard studying his badge, then his face. John's mouth suddenly went dry.

He had acted too quickly, John thought; he had made the wrong move. He should have anticipated the presence of a large security force in the section where Salva was sitting, and guessed that they would be controlling traffic tightly. Even if he did get up the aisle, he would not be able to speak with Alexandra or attract her attention without attracting Peters' attention, which was the one thing he had to avoid at all costs. He realized now that if Alexandra did see him she would almost certainly react, and that reaction could kill her.

Peters had all the advantages, John thought bitterly. All Peters had to do was touch the panel on the back of his radio. Indeed, John could not understand why the man had not already carried out his plan for the double murder; the circumstances were perfect. John knew he could not have much time left, and he was endangering Alexandra's life by his mere presence near the section where she and the Sierran leader were sitting.

He had to find Peters, John thought. Somehow, he had to disable Peters before the man could transmit the signal that would kill Alexandra.

The second Sierran, who apparently didn't speak English, was continuing to study John's identification badge.

He was finished if either man asked him to remove his cap, John thought. The cameraman's red hair showed clearly in the color photograph, and John assumed that all of the security personnel in the area had been briefed on his own description. Without the cap, John knew that he would be immediately recognized and arrested; Peters, seeing what was happening, would instantly kill Alexandra and Salva.

The second man was raising his hand, reaching for John's cap.

"All right, for Christ's sake!" John rasped, backing away

slightly and looking directly at the second man. "I'll go around the other way. Hell, I'm just trying to do my job."

The thick hand paused in midair; a stubby index finger was extended and pressed against John's chest.

"*Va!*"

"Do your job somewhere else," the first guard said. He nodded to his partner. The hands came away from John's arms, and he was free.

John turned his back on the two men just as a hot fever sweat flushed out of his forehead and ran in thick, milky rivulets down his cheeks to drip off his chin. He quickly wiped his face with his forearm. His legs felt rubbery, about to collapse under him.

Don't fold now! Not now! Hang on just a little longer! Find the bastard!

John squatted down below the ring apron and leaned his head forward. He closed his eyes and took a series of deep breaths. His head slowly cleared and feeling came back into his legs. When he opened his eyes and glanced up at the balcony section at the opposite end of the arena, he saw the flash of a blue sweater and a thatch of blond hair moving like threads through the thick tapestry of people crowded on the balcony.

Peters!

Then the man was gone. However, John had seen that Peters was moving down the arena in his direction; when John looked up behind him, toward the seaward side of the castle, his breath caught in his throat and a fresh wash of sweat squeezed out of his pores. Suddenly he understood why the unlighted boat had been waiting in the sea, and why its pilot had tried to kill him.

Peters doesn't know! The son-of-a-bitch thinks the boat's still down there! He's going to do it now!

John straightened up and began walking rapidly to his left, toward another aisle that led up to the balcony.

Too slow! He'll get there before you do! He's going to blow them up and dive into the sea!

To his right, in the ring above him, men pounded each other with leather gloves; out of the corner of his eye he could see the spectators in the seats on his left staring at him curiously.

John broke into a run. The floor area surrounding the

ring was clear except for a television cameraman and a gaffer, and John was at the foot of the aisle in a matter of seconds. The people standing in the aisle reacted, squeezing to either side as he came bounding up toward them.

John glanced to his right; the people in that area of the balcony were still crowded tightly together and were milling about. He could not see Peters, and he turned his attention back to the aisle. The people in front of him had moved back as far as they could, and now John had to burrow and squeeze the rest of the way to the stone balcony. He immediately turned right, and ran into an even more tightly packed wall of people.

Peters could be anywhere, John thought—a few inches, a few feet, a few yards away. Peters would also be pushing forward, trying to get to the wall overlooking the sea.

Perhaps not; Peters might consider the swirl of movement to be an advantage. At that very moment the assassin could be pressing his fingers against the panel at the back of the radio . . .

John was forced back against the six-inch-wide stone railing overlooking the arena. Desperate now, afraid that Peters would pass by him on the other side, John put his hands on top of the railing, braced, and leaped up on the narrow ledge. For a moment his head spun and he tottered precariously, but then he put his arms out to his sides and regained his balance. Crouching low, scanning the faces of the people on the balcony, he moved along the tightrope of stone.

A sudden hush spread over the arena, eerily punctuated only by the sound of leather colliding with flesh. John sensed the people below him turning in their seats to stare up at him with astonishment and alarm. He could hear isolated shouts of anger. People on the balcony shied back as a man they obviously considered mad made his perilous, swaying way toward them.

Then John saw Peters crouched near the balcony railing; his features reflected confusion as people moved away, leaving him isolated. Then he saw John. His right hand began to reach across his body toward the radio he held in his left.

"*ALEXANDRA!*" John screamed as he dove through the air toward the hand holding the radio.

He hit the arm an instant before Peters' right hand could touch the radio. He locked the fingers of his right hand around Peters' left wrist and, as he fell to the floor, wrapped his left arm around the radio and cradled it tightly in the pit of his stomach like a fullback protecting a football. His cap flew off as he twisted to his left, pulling Peters to the floor with him.

They hit the floor together, hard, but Peters' fingers maintained their grip on the radio's plastic carrying handle. John scrambled to his feet and yanked, trying to pull the radio free. But Peters had also risen to his feet, and the assassin was now positioned behind John, pressing him up against the stone railing at the same time as he tried to reach around John's body with his free hand in order to push the panel on the radio.

Leaning forward with his breastbone pressed painfully against the edge of the stone railing, John found himself looking down into a blurred watercolor wash of movement and startled faces.

The entire crowd seemed to be on its feet, staring up at him.

The fighters in the ring were standing still, hands at their sides, staring up like the others.

Heavy-set security men struggled to make their way up the packed aisles.

Soldiers had climbed up onto the ring apron; shouldered rifles were aimed in his direction.

Bu there were no shots fired, and John assumed that the soldiers were afraid of hitting the men and women milling all about Peters and himself.

John glanced down the length of the arena, and his gaze locked with Alexandra's. Her mouth hung open, and her eyes were wide with stunned bewilderment.

"*The barrette!*" John shouted, his strained voice cracking. "*Throw the barrette away! It's a bomb!*"

The hand that had been groping around his right side suddenly withdrew, and a moment later John felt a fist smash into his back, just above his right kidney. His knees started to buckle and his vision blurred as sick pain arced like lightning through his body, making his stomach turn, forcing green-tasting bile up into his throat. Still, he somehow managed to maintain his grip on Peters' wrist and the radio. He shook his head, clenched his teeth, and his vision cleared. He caught a swirl of movement out of the corner of his eye and once again looked down the length of the arena.

He could see Alexandra's thick, free-flowing crown of black and silver hair bobbing back and forth as she ran up the aisle.

"Throw the barrette away, Alexandra! Get rid of it!"

John cried out in pain and surprise as Peters' teeth bit through his shirt and flesh and buried themselves in the muscle and tendons of his right arm, just below the elbow. The fingers of his right hand reflexively popped open, releasing Peters' wrist. A fist again slammed into the same area of his back over his kidney, and John knew he was going to lose control of the radio.

He set his feet firmly under him and whipped around to his left, his fist held rigidly in the air. He had been trying to hit the side of Peters' head, but the pain in his back caused his arm to drop; his fist flew under Peters' extended left arm and smashed into the man's ribs.

To John's astonishment, Peters' eyes bulged and he screamed in pain. The assassin clutched at his left side and staggered sideways through a narrow corridor of stunned Sierrans across the width of the balcony to the retaining wall overlooking the sea.

Trying to ignore the pain stabbing through his own body, John leaped after Peters. He thrust his hands under the man's arms and pressed outward while he kicked Peters' ankles. He hammered at the back of Peters' skull with his forehead, then tried to sink his teeth into Peters' neck. John struggled desperately, horrified at the thought that at any moment he might hear the explosion signaling his wife's destruction.

It wasn't going to work, John thought, tasting panic. Peters had the all-important advantage of leverage; it was easier for the other man to bring his arms together than it was for John to hold them apart.

Peters was winning the battle, inexorably bringing his free hand closer and closer to the hand that held the radio.

John abruptly pulled his hands free, then grabbed Peters' left arm with both hands and yanked with all his remaining strength.

Peters was spun around. The radio popped free from his grasp, sailed over the stone retaining wall and fell into the darkness.

John released his grip on Peters, turned and staggered back to the inner railing of the balcony. Further struggle was meaningless; the plastique would explode when the radio hit the water.

Strong hands gripped his arms as he collapsed over the edge of the railing. He glanced toward the far end of the arena and moaned aloud.

Oh God, no! No, Alexandra! You can't make it! Throw it away and save yourself!

Alexandra had run into a knot of people near the top of the aisle. She was holding the barrette over her head, waving it back and forth as she struggled to squeeze through the panicked onlookers.

An eerie silence had descended over the castle, and John could hear Alexandra's voice clearly.

"Explosives!" Alexandra shouted. "Get out of my way! It's going to blow up!"

A narrow space gradually cleared in the aisle before her as people wrestled and clawed in a desperate effort to move back out of her way.

Alexandra reached the top of the aisle, turned left on the balcony.

She was not even going to try and make it to the seaward wall, John thought, despair reaching deep into him and squeezing his heart. It was just too far away. Instead, it appeared that she was trying to make it to the narrow, closed-off stairwell where he and Peters had fought.

It's too late, Alexandra! I love you! I don't want you to die! Save yourself! Throw it away!

"THROW IT AWAY, ALEXANDRA!"

Alexandra tripped or fell or leaped as she approached the stairwell. The mane of black hair plunged from sight.

An instant later there was a flash of bright light, followed almost instantaneously by a dull, thudding explosion that sent a shock wave through the stone of the castle; John could feel the blast in his feet, a repulsive, shuddering ripple of death. Then the walls around the mouth of the stairwell crashed down on the balcony in a malignant, sere fog of dust and smoke.

At first the only sound in the castle was the rumbling echo of the collapsing stone. Then people began to scream. John heard the sounds, but they seemed to be coming from a great distance; they were meaningless vibrations from another world that no longer had anything to do with him. Everything, all thought and sensation, was peripheral to the central, devastating fact that Alexandra was dead.

John wanted to cry, to howl, to scream with the others, but he could not. All feeling and protest was clogged inside him, and he could only stand and tremble under the crushing weight of an invisible cloak of horror and emptiness that clenched him in its folds like some great snake.

He twisted his head around and looked behind him. Peters had vanished.

He knew where Peters had gone. The icy cloak surrounding John suddenly twitched and contracted, squeezing him even harder in a vise of mindless sorrow and rage, causing him at last to cry out. He clenched his fists, threw back his head and howled like an animal impaled on stakes of pain, despair, and terrible, all-consuming hatred.

Adrenalin surged through his body, and he twisted free from the hands holding him. He was across the width of the balcony in three great strides. He jumped up on the retaining wall and leaped far out into the darkness.

Suddenly it was as though all sound had been cut off except for the high-pitched whistle of wind in John's ears. It seemed to him that he fell for a long time, but he was not afraid. Now he could think only of killing Rick Peters.

He tensed his muscles and stretched out as the shimmering, moonlit surface rushed up at him, and he knifed cleanly into the water. He relaxed immediately, spreading his arms and legs to slow his descent. He felt a piercing pain in his ears, and he swallowed to equalize the pressure. Finally he slowed to a halt. He kicked off his shoes and began to pull for the surface.

He looked up to see the water above him begin to glow; a few seconds later he surfaced into a pool of brilliant, blinding light cast by searchlights mounted on the castle walls.

An automatic rifle coughed once. A bullet whined past his right ear and splutted into the water.

John ignored the danger from the guns as he turned

lowly in the water, squinting and searching in the white
glare for Peters. He refused to be distracted from his sole
purpose; like everything else not related to the task of
killing Rick Peters, the riflemen on the walls were not important to him. He felt strangely invulnerable.

A voice shouted something in Spanish, and there were
no more shots. John heard the stuttering, hollow roar of a
large boat starting up somewhere on the other side of the
distant spit of land separating the harbor from the open
sea.

"Finway."

The tortured voice was faint, but close by. Behind him.
John scissor-kicked and turned in a semicircle, searching.
The brilliant arc lights continued to glide in crisscross pat-
erns over the surface of the water. A cone of light swept
over Peters' head, then darted back and held steady on the
other man.

John flinched at what he saw.

Peters was floating at an odd, twisted angle; the man was
apparently only barely able to keep his head above the
water. Blood, shiny as red vinyl, flowed from his mouth
and nostrils. Naked pain filmed the pale eyes like a cloudy
membrane.

"I've got a rib through my lungs," Peters gasped. "Help
me, Finway. Please. I don't want to die."

John's tongue and gums felt dry and gritty. He rinsed
his mouth with sea water, spat it out. It was insane, he
thought, but he realized that he felt pity for the other
man. "I've died at least twice this week," he said at last. "I
want to see you try it once."

The large boat was coming closer, its roar becoming a
whine increasing in pitch and volume.

"Can't . . . stay up. Please. I can't stand the pain. Just
hold me up . . . until the boat gets here."

John felt a curious mixture of amazement and self-
loathing when he realized that he did not have it in him
to let a helpless Rick Peters drown.

He straightened out in the water and whipped his legs
back in a frog kick, propelling himself toward the other
man with a powerful but controlled breaststroke. He had
approached within a yard of Peters' head and was about
to reverse his direction in order to grasp the man's chin

when something changed in Peters' eyes; the pain wa
abruptly supplanted by hate. Peters' features twisted and
he hissed with fury as he lunged at John.

The assassin's right hand burst from beneath the surface
of the sea trailing water like tongues of argent flame. The
metal of the sharpened belt buckle flashed in the brillian
light, and then the glinting metal began to descend in a
whipping blur toward John's head.

Peters had timed the attack perfectly. John knew he
could not move back quickly enough to avoid the razor
sharp edge. He tried to duck under the surface, at the same
time lunging to his right and sweeping his arms up unde
the water. The belt buckle deflected slightly when it hit the
surface and sliced into John's left shoulder, driving him
even deeper under water.

Pain ripped through John's left arm and up into his nec
muscles. He rolled forward, pulled with his good arm, and
kicked with all his strength. He shot forward beneath the
surface and collided with Peters' lower body. John imme
diately drew his legs up to his chest and executed a quarter
turn to his left, bringing him into position on Peters' lef
side. He ducked under Peters' flailing left arm and pressed
his head against the man's rib cage, at the same tim
reaching out and wrapping his right arm securely around
Peters' waist. He simultaneously pulled and kicked, driving
his forehead like a battering ram hard into Peters' broke
ribs.

Peters' entire body twitched and convulsed like some
lump of laboratory muscle stimulated by electric shock
Then they were going down. John heard a strange sound he
at first identified as the bray of the boat's engine carrying
under water. Then he realized that the sound was Ric
Peters' screams.

John maintained his hold around Peters' waist and con
tinued to press his forehead into the fractured ribs. The
liquid, bubbling scream sustained itself for what seeme
a very long time, measured in cruel units of crushing wate
pressure and cold. Peters' body became a deadweight a
the air streamed out of his lungs, and they both shot dow
into the increasingly frigid depths.

Then the eerie, undulating sound stopped. There was a
gurgling sound like a baby's cry, a hiccupping, bubblin

ough, and another faint gurgle. Then, with the bone of is skull acting as a solid conductor and amplifier, John eard the sibilant whisper of water rushing into the man's ungs.

Peters' body convulsed twice, then went limp. John re-ased his grip and pushed the corpse away from him. When e looked up, the floodlit surface of the water seemed an mpossible distance away. Billowing clouds moved lazily cross his field of vision, and John vaguely realized, as if a dream, that the clouds were composed of his and eters' blood.

His lungs burned and his vision was blurred. His left rm had gone numb and floated uselessly at his side. He ulled weakly toward the surface, expecting to be hit by a hark at any moment and not really caring. John now iewed his survival with only passing interest, and he was urprised and vaguely amused when his head broke the urface. He gasped for air, swallowed water that tasted of lood. Hands grabbed for him, and then he passed out.

Wednesday, February 20; 3:15 P.M.

Constantina

Constantina paused at the entrance to the embassy garden
and studied the figure of the man sitting on a marble bench
inside. She wondered what he thought about besides his
wife—if, indeed, he ever thought of anything else.

She had been present at a number of his interrogations
and he'd always told the identical story in the same low,
patient, dispassionate voice. Constantina had confirmed
those details of his story that she had witnessed.

She hated some of the things her people were doing to
this man, did not see the need for the drugs or the terrible
lie, but she knew that it was not her place to question. She
did what she was told, and John Finway seemed totally unconcerned with what was done to him. As far as she knew,
no pain had been inflicted.

At least, Constantina thought, they had apparently accepted his story, as indicated by the fact that they had
moved him from a prison cell to the unused former American Embassy. However, in the week and a half that he had
been here, he had given no indication that he cared any
more about his surroundings than he had the drugs or the
interminable interrogation sessions. Whatever his thoughts
about being the sole inhabitant of a huge mansion guarded
around the clock by teams of security men, he kept them
to himself.

He was, she thought, three-quarters dead, like a man
who had been lobotomized by loss.

Constantina had come to like John Finway very much.
She thought he bore his immeasurable sorrow and captivity
with a quiet dignity, leavened by what Constantina could
only describe as a general disinterest in everything but his

orrespondence with his children. He ate, exercised, kept
imself clean and well groomed, but gave no glimpses into
imself.

She cleared her throat, then walked into the garden. She
topped in front of him and, when he looked up, smiled
varmly.

"Hello, John."

"Hello."

"You were hard to find this afternoon. It's a big house."

"Yes, it is," he replied flatly. "I can't imagine a roomier
rison. But it's still a prison, isn't it?"

Constantina was vaguely surprised; it was the first time
he had heard the man express anything approaching a
omplaint. She decided it was a good sign, and she was
leased. "How's your shoulder?"

"It's coming along."

"I'm glad," Constantina said quietly.

He glanced up at her, and Constantina saw an uncharac-
eristic flash of curiosity glint momentarily in his sad,
harcoal-gray eyes.

"You're Catholic?"

Constantina touched the gray smudge on her forehead.
Yes. It's Ash Wednesday. Are you Catholic?"

"No." He dropped his gaze. "I was just curious. I didn't
now you were allowed to practice openly."

"Here's your mail," she said, holding out three envelopes.

He took the envelopes, placed them beside him on the
tone bench. "Thank you."

"Is your son better?" When he glanced up and arched
is eyebrows, Constantina added quickly, "You know we
ave to read your mail. I read the letter Kristen wrote tell-
ng you that Michael had the flu. I'd just like to know if
e's better."

For a few moments she did not think he would answer,
ut finally he nodded and said, "Yes. Michael's all right."
He smiled thinly, touched the envelopes beside him. "You
vant to read these?"

Constantina shook her head, surprised that the man
ad the power to hurt her deeply. "No. They've already
een censored by someone else. It was my job, John. I
idn't mean to pry."

"Then you won't mind if I read these in private."

"I know you're anxious to read them, John, but
have to ask you to go back to your room."

"Why? Is the local Committee for the Defense of th
Revolution accusing you of coddling criminals?"

"I'm not supposed . . . I don't have permission . . .
Constantina swallowed as tears of joy suddenly welled i
her eyes and flowed freely down her cheeks. She choke
back a sob, then bent over and wrapped her arms aroun
the surprised man. "Go to your room, John," she whispere
in her ear. "Your wife is waiting for you there. God bles
you both."

John

John was trembling violently as he opened the door to th
vast, first-floor library that served as his living quarters
When he saw the figure sitting across the room on the edg
of the bed, he let out a choked cry of joy and then bega
to weep.

Dressed in ill-fitting Russian-made slacks and a loos
woolen peasant blouse, Alexandra sat for long momen
staring back at him. Then she rose unsteadily, supportin
herself with a three-legged aluminum cane that she grippe
with her right hand. Her hair had been cut short an
ragged, and there were scabby patches of bare scalp wher
hair was just beginning to grow back in. The left side of he
face was swathed in bandages held in place by wide band
of adhesive tape wound around her head. John could se
the movement of her upper left arm under the sleeve of th
blouse, but the cuff of the sleeve hung limply in the spac
where her hand had been.

John's body continued to shake as he released his gri
on the door handle. Alexandra tentatively set the cane asid
and hobbled toward him. John rushed forward and caugh
her in his arms as she fell. They held each other gently
wept cheek to cheek, then, without relaxing their grips o
one another, tilted their heads back and looked into eac
other's eyes.

Alexandra hiccupped and smiled crookedly, then kisse
John's tear-stained face. "I guess I'm still trying to get m
sea legs," she managed to say through jaws that had bee

wired shut. "I don't suppose you brought a hook with you? Any hook will do for now, but I have my heart set on eventually picking up some chic designer's number."

John slowly shook his head in dazed wonder. "They told me you were . . . I thought you were dead."

"And I was told you died killing Rick. I only found out you were alive a half hour ago, just before they brought me here. I suppose they figured they could get more information out of us if we each thought the other was dead."

"Out of you, maybe," John said, rage burning in him anew like poison in an infected wound that would not heal. "I started telling them everything I knew from minute one. When I think what our people—" His voice broke, and his anger was temporarily washed away by the joy of holding his wife in his arms. "I can't believe you're here. You didn't throw the barrette away. The explosion—"

"I didn't want anyone else killed because of my stupidity. I made it to the empty stairwell where I wanted to throw it. I dove the last few feet and managed to get my hand down there; I just couldn't get it back out in time. The walls were at least four feet thick, so all the explosion itself did was tear off my arm at the elbow. Actually, losing my arm saved my life. Dear Rick didn't miss a trick. The barrette was like a fragmentation grenade filled with liquid nerve gas; they found traces of it in the missing pieces of me."

John shook his head and tried to speak, but he couldn't.

"Most of the blast's force was channeled up and down the stairwell," Alexandra continued. "I really got busted up when those damn stones fell on me." She laughed, winced, and touched her wired jaw. "If you think I talk funny and look bad on the outside, you should hear my insides rattle. I feel like something that came off a Detroit assembly line on a Friday afternoon."

"Alexandra, you've never looked more beautiful to me," John finally managed to say in a hoarse whisper. "Your eye?"

Alexandra shrugged. "The jury's still out. Incidentally, if I look like I'm suffering from jet lag in addition to everything else, it's because I've been to Moscow and back this week. They have a good eye institute there. Everybody's been giving me tender, loving care, and I've been talking

my head off. When I thought you were dead, I . . . I ju
told them everything I knew, or could guess."

"I assume you know you were set up twice, first b
Peters and then by the CIA."

Alexandra closed her eyes and sighed deeply. "I know
But it won't do any good to—"

"They fucked us both over pretty good, Alexandra,
John said, his voice once again taut with rage. "If we eve
get back home, I'm going to kill some people. It may tak
time to find the people responsible, but I will. I swear
will."

Alexandra slowly shook her head. A single, fresh tea
appeared in her unbandaged eye, rolled down her cheel
"It may be years before we can go home, John. Understan
that."

"Why? You saved the bastard's life!"

"We both saved his life. That probably explains wh
we're together now in this place instead of in prison, but
won't get us home. Remember Francis Gary Powers? We'r
too valuable to Salva for him to let us go until he's receive
a great deal in return. He'll use us. And I can't really sa
I blame him."

"Maybe, maybe not. We both told them what we knew
because it was the truth. I won't cooperate with him be
yond that. But if he lets us go, he'll love the job I'm goin
to do on the CIA when I get home. With the story we hav
to tell, I'll keep Congressional committees busy for year
The Sierrans told me that your father used to be with th
agency. When Robert sees what his old buddies have don
to you, he'll help me find the men I want."

"No, he won't. He'll grieve for me, and he'll suffer hi
own rage, but he'll do it in silence. He'll never even adm
to you that he was with the agency. John, my darling, i
we do ever get home, all we can hope for is to be left i
peace. The price we'll have to pay for that peace is silence
There's nothing to be done. If you try to make troubl
they'll . . . bother us." She squeezed John hard with he
right arm, shuddered. "I don't want to talk about that an
more."

"No."

"The children?"

"The Sierrans let us write to each other. They're stil

ith my sister, and they're okay. Michael had the flu, but
e's over it now."

"Do they think I'm dead?"

"Yes. They were all watching the broadcast that night."

"Oh, God."

They held each other in silence for a few minutes.
inally, John murmured, "Alexandra, I love you so very,
ery much."

"Even with pieces of me missing?"

"It looks to me like all the important pieces are still
here."

"I love *you* so much," Alexandra sighed, pressing her
heek against John's. "I guess we've both got other wounds
side us, don't we?"

"I don't know what you're talking about."

"Yes, you do. We have a way to go before we get home
gain; I mean our real homes, in each other's hearts. There's
great deal I have to tell you, but it will take some time
get it all out."

"We have a long time to work on it."

"I don't ever want anything hidden between us again."

"No."

"John, I want you to make love to me."

John smiled. "You do, huh? I thought you were all
usted up."

She looked into his face, smiled back. "I am," she re-
lied seriously. "But we have to make sure all those im-
ortant pieces are working properly, right? All I've been
inking about since I was able to think again is you. And
mean sexually; your body and mine. Since I thought you
ere dead, you can imagine the problems that created for
e." She kissed him on the mouth, winced with pain from
e movement, then ran her fingers over his lips. "As long
you don't rattle me around too much, I'd like to see what
e can manage to do. How about it?"

John grunted, kissed Alexandra gently on the forehead,
en led her slowly to the bed.

7:45 P.M.

Manuel

He got out of the car and waved the driver on. He glance
to his left and right to make certain the guards aroun
the embassy had retreated to a discreet distance, then too
out a cigar and lit it.

Perhaps he was mellowing, he thought, as a number o
his advisors had hinted. It was possible, but he did no
think so.

He always knew where the Sierras Negras range lay, an
he turned now in that direction. He could still recall ever
sound and sensation from his days in those mountains, re
member every bullet he'd fired in every battle, every com
mand given. Every comrade killed.

So many of his people had forgotten, he thought. Thos
people who had left were better off in the United State
and San Sierra was certainly better off without them. Thos
people would be at home there; the United States was
nation where short memory had become an institutior
virtually a prerequisite for office.

He had personally killed many men; he had ordered mas
executions; he had killed or imprisoned men who had onc
been his friends and comrades in battle. None of thes
actions had bothered him at the time, and they did no
bother him now. Severe measures had been necessar
then, and still were on occasion. As far as he was concerne
the disease of economic slavery as represented by mora
perverts like Sabrito always sank deep into the soil of rape
and abused nations. The latent germs could never be reall
destroyed, but only kept at bay by sustaining fire in th
souls of men who led revolutions. Such cleansing fir
could go out if not tended carefully.

The Chinese at least understood that, if they understood tle else.

The Russians? He was not sure what the Russians understood. Like himself, the Soviets were brutal and passionate.

However, he thought, the Soviets' passions, unlike his own, extended only to Mother Russia; for the rest of the world under their domination, it was only control and brutality. As far as he was concerned, the Sierran revolution was far purer than the Russians'.

His revolution could be sustained, he thought, but certain adjustments were now going to have to be made.

He had never liked the Russians. He was, he thought, going to thoroughly enjoy getting rid of the Russians before they got rid of him. The Americans had tried to get rid of him on a number of occasions and had failed; a man rarely survived a single such attempt by the Soviets.

No, he thought, he had not grown soft. Nor would he. The fire still burned in him. He would die a revolutionary, caring about and fighting for the wounded peoples of the world.

Realigning San Sierra with the United States was going to require some banking and redirection of the fire inside him, but the flames would not go out. The Americans would soon realize that, if they did not already. He would remain the leader of San Sierra until he died, and he would make certain that those who followed him possessed sufficient revolutionary ardor; their memories must be good. However, the economic and, to some extent, the political future of San Sierra was now with the Americans; he would not leave San Sierra to be gnawed at and perhaps swallowed by the Russians when he died.

In the end the Americans, for all their confounding arrogance and stupidity, held out the best hope for his land.

Which was why he believed he was choosing the correct option in regard to disposing of John and Alexandra Finway. It would give him personal pleasure to go in this direction because Alexandra Finway had risked her life and broken her body to save his life and the lives of many Sierrans. Both she and her husband possessed rare courage, and he would certainly be dead if it were not for John Finway. But these considerations in themselves would not have been enough to tip the balance in their favor, he thought. Many men, women, and children had died in the revolution, and it was his ongoing responsibility to use whatever means were available to defend the fruits of that revolution and do what was in the best interests of his people.

If it were in San Sierra's interest to rig a trial, imprison or even execute the Finways, he would not hesitate to do so. Hard, cruel deeds were often necessary, he thought, for San Sierra's enemies were often hard and cruel, and he could not afford to be less so.

But the dragons were no longer a threat to him; one dragon was dead, and the dragon's fire in the other extinguished forever. While it might serve some propaganda purposes to keep the Finways imprisoned in San Sierra, he had decided that sending them home to the United States could serve a number of more useful purposes, especially now that he had a clear picture of what had happened.

And what had almost happened.

The Americans had lofted a bomb at him; more precisely, the CIA had permitted it to be thrown, and the agency's masters had then hovered like vultures over San Sierra, waiting for the bomb to explode.

First, he would use the Finways to make certain that the CIA suffered far more than mere lingering disappointment. He was going to throw the broken but still dangerous fragments of their bomb back at them and let it land in the State Department; it would amuse him to see how well they managed to juggle these pieces, and he would try to assure that the juggling act lasted for years.

His own agents were busy filling in the spaces, he thought, but he already had enough evidence to prove that the CIA, by default, if not by original design, had conspired to assassinate him and, perhaps, even invade San Sierra. He had hours of film and videotape recordings of the Finways' interrogations, and he now knew all about the dragons; the man who had been killed at Sierras Negras had been identified, and he had Harry Beeler's body as evidence of CIA knowledge of and complicity in the plot against his life; he had an aged gunman in custody, a man who, despite his obvious ignorance of everything but his assignment, had been sent to eliminate the problem the Finways now reprented, the dilemma the Finways were now in fact going to esent for the CIA.

The Finways did not know about the gunman, but he was out to tell them.

From John Finway's description of the man in the imp, he knew, although he could not prove, that Harley ue himself had been on the scene, probably to coordinate 1 invasion if the assassination attempt had succeeded. He anted the Finways to know that, too.

There was a great deal he wanted to tell the Finways efore he set them free.

He puffed on his cigar and exhaled slowly. He smiled rimly as he reflected on the fact that about the only thing e did not know was the identity of the group or individual ho had hired Rick Peters in the first place. But he considered that piece of information irrelevant; there would lways be somebody trying to kill him.

This attempt, he thought, had been the most serious; it vas the closest he had come to death since the early days f fighting in the mountains. But now, as then, he had ained a considerable advantage and reward: then a country, and now a powerful weapon to make things better for is people. Thanks to Rick Peters, the Finways and the CIA, the economic boycott against San Sierra was about o end. It would be America's first act of restitution, the irst price he would exact for not sharing his considerable knowledge with the rest of the world, including the American public.

Having made this decision, he thought, there was now ime and room for kindness.

Alexandra Finway's body needed more time to heal, and he wanted her fit as possible before he let her go. Also, judging from what he had learned from the interrogations, the two of them would need time alone together to heal their considerable psychological wounds, to come together again as man and wife. He would see that they had the necessary time and space, perhaps two or three months. During that time they would be his guests, and they would experience his country as no tourist ever had or could. In a few weeks, perhaps, he would make arrangements to bring their children down to join them.

Then would come his next scheduled secret meeting with the United States' Secretary of State. He would bring the Finways with him to present to the Secretary as a special "present"—along with copies of the interrogation video tapes. He had no doubt that the Finways were a gift that would insure long-term fidelity on the part of the Americans in the upcoming marriage of common interests.

He ground out his cigar and walked quickly into the embassy.